DREAMSCAPE

Tenille Berezay

For 'The Girls',
May you always recognize your worth.

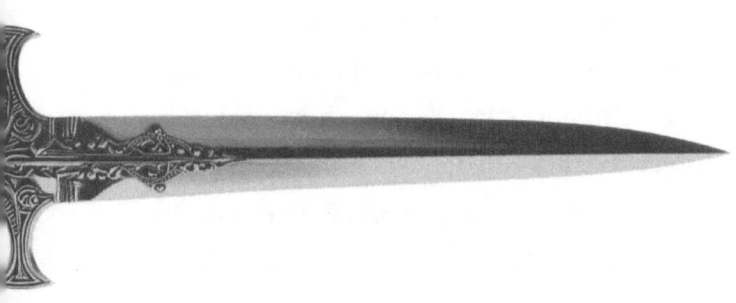

CHAPTER ONE

The fumbled knife spins wildly, its hilt tripping across two knuckles before clattering onto the cave floor.

"You're leaving?!"

My screech chases the sound of the discarded weapon, tattering my threadbare nerves. There's too much chaos, too much noise. There's only one sound I want to hear. The sound of Betah, my favorite half-orc, reassuring me she'll stay. Instead, Betah ignores the chaos left by her pronouncement and—with clear dismissal—climbs from our refuge and disappears into the icy plain.

Snapping my gaping jaw shut, I scoop up my abused throwing knife, secure it beside its companions, and scramble toward the cave opening. Behind me, the three other members of my crew continue their celebration of our most recently completed job. They're so absorbed in recounting the raid, basking in the glory of another success, and arguing prize distribution that Xandra, Asha, and Reilynn don't notice Betah's exit and my rushed pursuit.

I flip my cloak behind my shoulders to climb the small rock wall and squeeze through the slit-like entrance. Ducking under the jagged lip of the obsidian rock, I exit the snow cave. The driving wind flings icy shards into my unprotected face, hitting me as hard as Betah's sudden abandonment. I shield my eyes from the stinging, blinding whiteness. The stark paleness of the landscape stretches before me. A place for lost things.

Our cave and rendezvous point lies on the border of this extreme and civilization. Clenching the handles of the scimitars strapped to my hips, I peek behind me toward the edge of the plain, sighting the nearest road. But, of course, Betah isn't heading that way.

Turning, I spot the half-orc plowing directly into the heart of the consuming cold.

Like Betah, The White Plains are unpredictable—petal-soft snowfall turning to rock-hard hail, blinding bright sun fading into impenetrable darkness, crystal clear breezes morphing into ice flinging tempests. From one breath to another, the land transforms from a lively beauty to an ugly death.

I lunge through the drifts of knee-deep snow, hurrying to my companion, hoping I can change her mind. But Betah says she's leaving, and Betah doesn't do threats. She doesn't do warnings. Heck, she barely does words. She's action, all action.

And, right now, she's walking away. The moment is heavy with significance. I can't explain how, but I know this is different from her typical disappearances. This time, she won't be returning in a couple of days with secrets and souvenir scars. No, this time she's done.

I grab at her wrist. Having no chance of spanning her massive arm, my fingers curl around the edge of her protective bracer. "Betah, don't go," I plead, pulling on the worn leather.

As she slowly turns her head toward mine, I release my hold, all too aware of her impulsive nature.

Betah is made of extremes. Standing at about seven feet, her body is more orc-like than human. A slightly greenish color, she's covered in a mix of metal and leather armor. Her greaves, bracers, and breastplate are leather inset with metal spirals. The metal armor covering her hips and lower torso connects to flutes, which lie like scales and encircle her whole body, reaching down past her thighs. Across her hips rests a leather pouch filled with ingredients for Betah's one true love: explosives.

Two large battle axes are magnetically attached to the armor at her back, their handles protruding past the overlarge metal pauldrons rising from Betah's shoulders. Half of her hair is buzzed with spirals shaved into the side, while the other half is a short wave of purple and pink stripes skimming her ear and falling over her barely-there forehead. With her jutting jaw, slightly bulbous nose, and overly large purple eyes, she isn't necessarily attractive. But she's a unique, talented mix. Too interesting to ignore or do without.

Hearing a flurry of movement behind me, I look to see the rest of my crew exiting the cave. Returning my focus to Betah, I say, "Just because we didn't need you for this job, doesn't mean we don't need you, Betah. We do." Raising my voice so everyone can hear my plea, I continue, "We want you to stay."

I glance toward the others for backup, but they stop several paces away, watching our interaction in silence. Of course, the *one* time their chatter might be helpful is the only time they're quiet.

Exasperated, I turn back to the towering figure beside me, her face is a mix of sympathy and determination. It's almost more than I can take, that look. It's pity. Like she pities me for just not getting it. I want to shake her because she's the ignorant one. She's the one stomping into the deadly plains, the one leaving without any excuse, without any explanation. But shaking any orc is a bad idea, and shaking one burdened with enough explosives to decimate The White Plains is a downright idiotic one. As if sensing the threat, the icy wind dies down, becoming a faint whistle at our feet.

Needing an outlet for my agitation, I free a small throwing knife. The metal blade glints as I pass it from one fidgeting hand to the other. Stepping beside the half-orc in a pseudo-block, I point the tip at the rest of the crew. "Betah, it's always been us." Memories of battles fought and won side by side wash over me. I stare unseeing at the gleaming metal, my mind on victories—on the success and notoriety we could have never achieved without each member of our squad and their specific skills.

"Five," I mumble. "It's always been us five. The perfect combination. So, just…don't leave."

Shaking her head, Betah slaps my shoulder, her meaty hand driving me backward. "No."

Regaining my balance, I advance on her. "Who will blow things up for us? Who will be the great distraction? You *have* to stay."

"No."

Her simple refusals grate on my nerves. "That's it? No? This has got to be a joke. Who put you up to this? Xandra?" I turn to glare at the spry fighter, but her captivated expression tells me she was expecting this as much as I. I spin back to Betah. "You're not going to say anything else?"

"No," Betah responds before securing her black fur cape to her breastplate, hoisting her pack further up on her shoulder, and striding past me.

I sputter against the finality of her departure. Moving to follow, I'm stopped by a light hand falling on my wrist. "She *will* come back," a soft, lyrical voice says.

Asha.

Her white-blonde hair blows between us as I draw on her hope. The elf is the peaceful element in our group. She plans for us, keeps us focused, and is unfailingly optimistic. Her tactical advice is always spot on, and she can shoot a bow like you'd expect an elf to—with unnerving perfection.

The wind picks back up, pushing and shoving as the snow begins to fall. In silence, we watch the fog thicken and snow flurry until Betah is out of sight. As she disappears, I exhale shakily and sheathe my blade. Shivering, I pull my leather hood over my head and secure the cape across my shoulders. Ten minutes ago, the cape was overly warm, but now it isn't cutting the bleak cold.

"Blinding blizzards, I wasn't expecting that."

Offering one of her many creative exclamations, Reilynn steps to my vacant side. Built and armored like a knight, she blocks the bite of the wind. Reilynn is bold, strong, and capable. Her determination ensures success, and she expects a certain level of conduct from herself and the rest of us, which leads to a lot of disagreements with the last member of our crew.

Xandra joins us, flitting to Asha's side. A tiny sprite of a person, the biggest thing about Xandra is her curly black hair—if you discount her personality and the giant shield strapped to her back. Next to the ornate shield, Xandra carries a ball-and-chain flail. The unique weapon has two chains and two spiked balls instead of the usual one. But Xandra embraces excess. "Of course, she'll come back," she says. "Not many places Betah fits—both literally and figuratively."

She laughs at our collective glare, twisting the chains of her massive weapon around her fingers. "What? It's true!"

"Wow," Reilynn says. "Just when I thought you couldn't get more insensitive."

"I have sensitive areas." Xandra points to a wound slashing across one thick, dark eyebrow. "Proof right here." Flipping her unruly, thick braid aside, she shifts her sleek metal armor to show another slice near her throat. "Here's another one… See? Sensitive. And who knew the duke had such well-trained guards? Surprised? I was."

Reilynn stamps her spear down into the snow but doesn't lean against the staff. Reilynn always stands at attention—a soldier ready for battle, whether physical or verbal. A smile playing at her lips, she says, "Surprised? Surprised that despite your massive shield and incredible proficiency in verbal sparring you were still injured? No. No, I wasn't surprised at all."

"Reilynn," Asha scolds, but her quiet voice is quickly overridden by Xandra.

"I saved your heavily armored hide. Without me, the duke would be eating you for lunch. Or—considering the toughness of your skin—serving you to his hellhounds."

"Bullocks! I'm the one who kept you from killing the man and ruining the whole mission! Without me, you…"

Still reeling from Betah's desertion, I turn from the group and tune out this new version of the same old argument. Ignoring the buffeting wind, I head back to the entrance of the cave. I ease through the narrow opening backwards and drop to the floor with an ungraceful thump. In an absentminded move, I pull a different blade from my sleeve—a heavier dagger—and toss it from hand to hand, gathering myself.

Betah is gone, but I still have a squad to manage. Hearing Asha's light landing behind me, I move forward to peruse our newest acquisitions. Taking Betah's share of the gold, I divide it into the other four piles. Then, reconsidering, I take four pieces from my pile and add them to Asha's.

Before she can argue, I say, "It was your plan that got us in and out so easily. I think the king will be happy to know his duke is again in line and unwilling to cheat him out of his fair share of taxes. But you deserve the bonus."

"It was my plan that pushed Betah away," Asha says in a voice so quiet I have to inch forward to catch the words. "Maybe I should have—"

"No. Asha, your plan was great. We both know that even if we could have kept Betah from blowing the manor apart, she still would have chopped the place to pieces with those two battle axes. We needed finesse and well, you know…Betah."

"You are right," Asha says, a small smile curling her lips. "Besides, she will be back."

"Sure," I answer, wishing I had her faith.

"But I will not take the money." Asha holds the gold out to me.

I ignore her outstretched hand. "Sure you will. You need to be reoutfitted. I saw what happened at the duke's."

Asha's hand goes to her practically new cloak, fingering a tear along one detailed edge where a hellhound got a little too close before I was able to drop it with a throwing knife. At least the death of one of his dear 'babies' got the duke to stop attacking and listen to reason. "It is a shame," she says, sorrowfully letting the damaged fabric slip through her nimble fingers. "Do you think we can travel to Cashia? They have the finest outfitters," she says, her eyes lighting up.

"Absolutely." I smirk. I knew new clothes would convince her.

Quickly, I shove my share of the spoils into a worn pack. I'm eager to be on our way, to leave this cave that suddenly feels far too dark and dank behind. "I'm thinking warmer weather. Why not head to the ocean until—"

"Nix!" Xandra's call cuts me off. Her head appears in the cave opening, her dark mane spilling over the edge. "Greymore is here and he's looking a little more *gray* than usual." She snickers at her poor play on words.

There's a scuffle and Xandra's grinning face disappears. "Sweet swords, Xandra! Just get out of the way so I can get down," Reilynn says. "For such a tiny thing, you're a huge pain in my armor."

"I was going first!" Xandra yelps.

Two sets of legs appear in the opening, followed by torsos and flailing arms before the two women fall, somehow landing on their feet. Instantly, the fight resumes. "Reilynn, you know if there's pain in your armor, there's a problem. Need a new hauberk?" Xandra asks, mocking, but—after a quick shove—Reilynn turns thoughtful.

"I might," she admits.

"Yeah? I think I know a guy you'd like. Great, comfortable chainmail."

"Really?" Armor. The great neutralizer.

I step around the two. "Gather your stuff. We'll leave as soon as I'm finished meeting with Greymore."

"Do not rush your meeting for us," Asha says with a meaningful smile.

Climbing from the shelter, I roll my eyes. I'm not surprised at Asha's insinuation or that Greymore found us here. We haven't yet found a place hidden from him, not that we ever really try. I want him to find us and not for any of the reasons my crew has imagined.

Greymore isn't anything but my go-between with the king. There's nothing between us but exchanges. He passes along jobs and payment from the king, and I pass off all acquisitions.

I find him on the far side of the obsidian rock, facing north, staring out across the vastness of The White Plains. I get the impression he's focused more on a direction than a place, because there's little to see out there. Not even snow cats inhabit this region.

As always, his leather hood is in place. Greymore is a mystery in more ways than one. I don't know how he communicates with the king. I don't know how he always finds us, but—as soon as we finish a job—he's there. Actually, anytime we need him, he's there.

Without turning, he holds his hand out. I pull two large bags from the pouch at my hip and drop them into his outstretched palm. "I already took our cut. Fifteen percent as agreed upon."

After hefting it once, he tucks it away beneath his cloak.

Tossing my cape back, I close my palms over my matching scimitar's handles, actively keeping my hands still and forcing myself not to pull a dagger. Reilynn tells me fidgeting with the blades is unprofessional and unchivalrous. "Duke Windmere says he'll do all he must to ensure we don't have to make a return visit…like pay the king his taxes and send support for his army," I say.

"Good," Greymore says, still focused on the blank landscape before us.

I don't even attempt to catch Greymore's eye. It's pointless. I've never seen his face. Probably never will. No matter the lighting, the angle, or the degree of coverage, Greymore's face stays in shadow. Occasionally, I think I catch a glimpse of his features, a flash of a smile, a gleam in his eye, but it fades like a dream slipping away in the light of dawn. The harder I look, the darker the shadows become, covering him in blackness from one moment to the next.

He's the mystery. An honorary member of my strange crew.

Greymore the Enigma.

Xandra the Protector.

Asha the Believer.

Reilynn the Powerhouse.

Betah the Incomparable.

And Nix the Ringleader.

The fabulous 5.5. At least it used to be five…

The wind pushing at my back, I gaze to the east. Kicking at the snow, I wish we had appeased the half-orc with a little destruction. "Betah left," I admit, again feeling as if there's something I'm missing, a way I could have convinced her to stay.

"So it would seem." From another person, the response would be clipped, rude. But four words from Greymore are practically an epic tale. He takes the strong silent type to new extremes. But sometimes, like now, I think I can *feel* his emotions. I tune into the sensation…

Concern. Right now, he's concerned and not just about Betah. His foot shifts next to mine in the crystallized snow. Instantly, I'm on high alert. Because if Greymore is making an actual subconscious, uncontrolled movement? Well, something really *is* wrong.

"What is it?" I practically growl.

"New job."

I wait, but he doesn't expound. A frustrated sigh escapes me. "I know you can't go over your word quota for the day or something, but I just don't have the energy for twenty questions today. Just tell me the job, Greymore."

"Suspicious activity in the north. People disappearing. Animal attacks." He adjusts the leather holding his crossbow. The weapon is strapped to his wrist and forearm, keeping his hands free to reload or use his other, more deadly weapon. His hand drops, and his fingers slowly curl and uncurl at his side.

With each of Greymore's nervous movements, my muscles tighten until they're quivering with energy, ready for battle. The nipping and biting of the wind, the aches from last night's attack on the duke, and my concern for Betah fade, overtaken by a growing anxiety. "Where?" I demand.

"Your homeland, Nix." His words fall over me, awakening a foreboding storm of emotion. "Avalei."

CHAPTER TWO

"Nix!" My fumbled pencil spins wildly, its barrel tripping across two knuckles before clattering onto my sketch pad.

"Jillian!" I clasp my now free hand to my overexcited heart. "You—"

"I scared you. Yeah, yeah." My best friend plops onto the bench opposite me, eyeing me accusingly as she jerks a sandwich from her bag.

Knowing the reason for her stare, I turn my attention back to my sketch. I shade in Betah's shadow on the page with light, swift strokes. In case I never dream her again, I want to capture this figment of my imagination.

And, as amazing as this day has been, thoughts of my dream world keep flitting through my mind like scenes from a series after a long binge. I can't remember when my dreams took on this strange life of their own. It happened bit by bit, night by night, until I woke up one morning and realized my dreams had become a never-ending story. Each night, I fall asleep and back into the world I left the night before. The cast of characters remains the same, any pain or hurt experienced in the dream world returns, and everything feels absolutely, amazingly authentic.

I'm aware it's a dream, but—more often than not—my wild imagination overpowers my logic. And it seems real. So real.

"When were you going to tell me?" Jillian's overly calm question brings me back to the reality I'm avoiding.

"Dillon told you, huh?" I wince.

Jillian nods before tipping her chin to a stubborn angle I know all too well. She won't move or talk until I answer her question. It's her sneaky way of getting all kinds of confessions out of me.

I shake my head and nervously tap the pencil against the tabletop. Of course, my brother would tell Jillian I wasn't going to play basketball this year, knowing it would cause drama. It isn't like I *wasn't* going to tell her. The whole thing just got…overshadowed.

By Trent.

My *boyfriend*.

Trent. Boyfriend. I hold back a dreamy sigh as the words boyfriend and Trent create an enthusiastic, repetitive loop in my head. It's exciting and amazing and…distracting.

Refocusing my attention on my friend, I study her determined amber eyes. "I'm sorry, Jill. It's just this whole thing with Trent is new, and I wanted more time with him, and I've always been more of a bench warmer than a key player. You know?"

Her piercing dark eyes narrow. "I know I planned on us being on the team together. Like always."

"And we'll have next year!" I exclaim, a little too much excitement coloring my tone. I drop my voice. "Come on, Jilly, you know you guys don't need me, and I'll even go to the basketball torture camp with you next summer."

"Two camps," she bargains, throwing the last bite of her sandwich down. She tries to hide it, but her eyes snap with success as if this was her plan all along. She's always been optimistically resilient.

"Fine, two camps," I say. Though I would prefer a runner's camp, at least they'll keep me in shape and keep Jillian okay with me skipping a season.

Win and kinda-win.

Jillian brushes crumbs from her hands and glances at my drawing before focusing on me. After a lengthy, intense stare, she asks, "Are you sure, Claire?" Her use of my real name surprises me. She only calls me that when she's feeling particularly serious—which isn't often. Usually, I go by Nix. Short for my last name, Nickelsen.

I stop to really reconsider, reviewing all my reasons. I would never see Trent if I played—girls' home games are always during the boys' away games and vice versa. I also really do want to spend more time with my art and running. I know Jillian won't agree, and I will miss her. Avoiding her attempt to sway me, I say, "You know, as amazing as you are, you guys don't need me."

"Well, we might not need you...," she offers me a devious grin, her pearly whites flashing, "but we want you." She's teasing, but the pinch between her brows tells me she still isn't totally on board with my decision. But she'll be supportive even if it is begrudgingly. "Where is your Trent?" she says almost accusingly as she throws a strand of thick, dark hair over her shoulder.

"He'll probably be here soon. He's buying me lunch," I respond, ignoring her tone as my empty stomach rolls with a potent mix of hunger and nerves.

My boyfriend buying me lunch. *Trent* buying me lunch.

It's surreal.

Trent is *that* guy. The guy boys want to be, girls want to kiss, and parents want to have over for dinner. And now, he's kissing me and calling me his girlfriend.

Of course, I always knew of Trent. He's my brother's age, and they've played football together for years. It was actually that connection that brought us together.

Last week, Trent hosted an end-of-the-year football party at his amazing I-have-an-indoor-pool-and-hot-tub-in-my-Mcmansion house. Jillian and I had been enjoying a November swim when she left to 'get a drink' aka flirt. I stayed at the pool's edge, my feet dangling in the water, until a voice behind me drew my attention.

"You're Dillon's sister, Claire. Right?"

"Yep," I said, peering over my shoulder at the guy standing there. He was cute. Tall with dark hair, an oval face, and soft eyes.

"I'm Adam," he said.

"Right, you're the running back. Good game today," I said, getting to my feet, not having noticed Adam's outstretched hand until I was already standing.

With a slightly jerky motion, Adam's hand dropped. "That's me," he said, smiling a bit sheepishly, making him even cuter.

"And I'm Trent." A hand rested lightly on my bare shoulder, drawing my attention to the newcomer. The second my eyes met his, I was rendered speechless—like not enough air to breathe, much less speak, speechless. I had seen Trent from a distance, but always assumed up close he wouldn't be as amazingly attractive because…he just couldn't be. And he wasn't.

He was hotter.

Light brown curls framed his sharp jaw and stunning green eyes. Unlike Adam, he wasn't wearing a shirt, and I could see the rumors about his strict diet and workout routine weren't a lie.

"H..hi," I stammered, a bit taken aback by not only his looks but the warmth of his hand. The hand he hadn't dropped from my shoulder, the hand touching my skin, the hand linking me to him.

"Claire, right?" he said. "I've been hoping to meet you."

And that was it—the beginning of our relationship. We're now Trix. Or maybe Nent.

Unable to hide my cheesy smile at the thought of horrid couple names, I tuck my chin and refocus on the drawing in front of me. Seeming oblivious to my daydreaming, Jillian taps away at her phone, throwing out random comments and occasional huffs of disgust as I sketch.

The late fall sun keeps the school's courtyard comfortably warm, reinforcing my belief that this is the best time of year in Arizona.

I'm adding my initials and an iris to the bottom corner of my drawing—my version of a signature—when suddenly I'm tipped backward. The pencil falls from my flailing hand as Trent plants a fast, fierce kiss on me before setting me upright.

Across the bench, Jillian's wide eyes meet mine. "Well, that's staking a claim," she mumbles.

When there's no response but Adam's muffled chuckle, she adds, "Well, I'm going to get going. They're doing that lunch meeting for basketball today." She eases from the bench, offering me one more imploring look. I give her an apologetic shake of my head and a small smile. With pursed lips and a disappointed gait, she walks away.

"See you around," Adam says, dropping into Jillian's vacated seat.

Not seeming to notice Jillian at all, Trent asks, "How are you, babe?" His glimmering jade eyes lock on mine as he slides onto the bench beside me.

"Better now," I say, reaching to close my pad. I haven't shown Trent my drawings yet, and they really aren't for everyone.

Trent stops my hand, folding it into his own. "What are you working on?" He flicks my sketch pad closer to him with his free hand and opens it. "Hmm," he says, pushing it back my way.

"Hmm? What does that mean?" I ask in a teasing tone, releasing my hand to reach for my dropped pencil.

"Hmm, weird subject, but good execution?" Trent responds, flashing his humble, humor-me smile. I feel a defensive flash for Betah. Weird? She's unique, not weird. Before I can decide how to respond, Trent tosses the sketch toward Adam. "What do you think?"

Righting the pad, Adam twists the drawing his way. Leaning over, he studies my drawing, the edges of his lips curving. "I like it. Especially the battle axes."

"Yeah, there's that." Trent agrees before reaching for our lunch, which I realize is all health food. Catching me eyeing his hamburger, Adam flips my pad closed and hands it to me with a soft smile. I tuck it into my bag, relieved to have it away from Trent's scrutiny.

"You're going to die young," Trent says, grimacing at Adam's burger before chugging a V-8.

"But happy," Adam says, taking an even bigger bite of his burger before nudging his tray of fries my way. I turn away from the greasy temptation. Trent bought me lunch, so the least I can do is eat it without complaining. Besides, eating healthy is good for me. I mean, look at what it's done for Trent. Opening the salad, I pick at the lettuce as the two friends chat.

They are so different and yet so much the same.

Trent's jaw is chiseled and his chin a perfectly rounded edge, while Adam's face is more oval-shaped, his chin narrower. Trent wears his dark hair gelled and spiked, where Adam's is feathered and productless. Trent's eyes are a piercing, arresting green, and Adam's are smaller and light brown. Trent is a couple of inches taller, but both are well-muscled. In fact, I'm surprised Adam doesn't have a girlfriend. He's not as stunning as Trent, but still good-looking—the quintessential wingman.

I push the salad around the container, trying to make it look smaller and imagine the expression on Trent's face versus Adam's if I reached across the table and shoved a handful of those fries in my mouth.

"Babe," Trent interrupts my food dream. "I think you should draw me a landscape to hang in my room."

"I don't really do landscapes much. My character stuff is better. Maybe you could find one—"

"No, I think landscape. I have faith in you." He kisses my temple, and for a split second, I want to move away. The kiss feels so... casually expectant. Like that brief show of affection decides everything, cementing Trent's decision and leaving me without an argument.

But, honestly, what argument do I have? He isn't *not* supporting my art. He's pushing me to try new things, to be better. I shake away my defense, smiling up at him. "I'll work on it."

"Awesome." He links his fingers with mine. "Are you all ready for tonight?"

My smile falls into more ready, natural lines. "Yep, I'll be ready. You're picking me up at 7?"

"Yeah, and I'll give you a ride home today," Trent says as the five-minute bell rings. "Meet me at my locker." I nod as he drops a quick kiss on my mouth and is gone.

I'm gathering up our garbage—including a whole wasted salad—when Adam drops a package of cookies on the table in front of me.

"Salvation," I say, snatching up his offering and tearing the bag open. "Thank you."

"No problem." He shrugs with a light laugh. "If you'll let me see more of your art, we'll call it even." Surprised, I choke on the huge bite of cookie in my mouth.

"Sure," I manage to cough out. "Are you going to be there tonight?"

"To Trent's Dad's work party? No, that's a girlfriend's responsibility. But maybe we'll see you after. Trent usually doesn't stay too long at those things."

"Oh, okay," I say, wondering why Trent made a big deal about the whole thing if we aren't even going to be staying long. Holding up the cookies, I thank Adam again and head to class, unsatisfied. I shake the feeling off, unwilling to let a salad ruin my bliss.

* * * *

Bored, I toss my pack on my bed and absentmindedly scan the room. Painted in greys with white trim and accented with purple décor, my room is perhaps a little juvenile. The scattered stuffed animals, the bright colors, and the fairy lights are all nostalgic leftovers from my childhood.

I straighten my favorite decoration: a rectangular wall hanging made of painted wood and bold, swooping letters. Before they passed, my grandparents had helped me make this piece, Papa routing and sanding the edges of the wood for me, and Grandma instructing me in my carefully painted calligraphy. *With God All Things Are Possible,* it states. I smile at the words, comforted by the reminder.

I consider curling up in the window seat to draw or planting myself in front of my art desk, but my huge dresser covered in memories distracts me. I hesitate in front of last year's team picture, my eyes lingering on the girl next to me. My lip curls at the mass of hair spilling from her ponytail. Where my hair is light, thin, and straight, Jillian's is dark, thick, and coiled.

On an impulse, I grab my mini basketball from under the bed. The hoop set was a gift from Jillian. A gift I joke she bought for herself to keep at my house. She was unrepentant, claiming she needed something to occupy her time when I'm off in 'art zone'. I can't say I blame her.

Not feeling artsy now, I fire a shot off. It bounces from the little backboard, taunting me by rolling to the opposite side of the room. Determined, I start again. I shoot over and over, killing time. I don't have any homework, Trent and

Jillian are both at their first day of basketball tryouts, and I have hours before I need to get ready for the party.

Too many missed shots later, my brother interrupts.

"Dinner—" Spying me, he pauses. "Whatcha you doing, Claire-bear?" His overlong hair flops forward, and he drags a hand back, pushing it from his eyes. "I thought you were too busy with Trent and eyelash fluttering for sports."

"I am," I mumble before tossing the ball aside. "I was just making a couple of baskets."

"No." Dillon points at the rim. "You obviously weren't." Smirking, he turns away.

Following him downstairs, I yell, "It was one missed shot!"

"Missing shots already," my dad says as I enter the room. "This is going to be a rough season."

Mom slides a tray of…something my way. She used to make amazing dinners, but now that she's in nursing school, we get microwaveable gunk…unless I cook. But—since my cooking often resembles frozen mush—we all happily settle for the more edible nuked meal. Mom rushes to toss an apple down next to her offering, saying, "She isn't playing this season."

"What!" Dad exclaims.

I turn to Mom, relieved that I talked my decision over with her last night and got her support. "Let's pray first," she says. "Then Claire can explain."

She offers a simple blessing, then turns to give me a soft nod.

"Okay," I start, not sure how Dad will handle me taking a season off. "You see…I'm a little burnt out from soccer, and my grades could use some help, and I want to be ready for track because I was so close to state last year, and I'd like to see if I could paint and sell a couple more pieces and…"

"…and Trent," Dillon finishes for me.

"You can't play ball because you have a boyfriend?" my dad asks. "I think you should break up. Dating is overrated."

He dodges as my mom reaches to smack his arm. "Claire does not have to play a sport every season. If she wants a season off, she can take one."

I give her a grateful smile and begin shoveling my subpar dinner down.

"And Trent," Dillon says again.

"At least I can commit," I say.

Dillon's a proud, unapologetic serial dater.

"Exactly!" He swings his arm my way as if I've just made his point. "No girl has ever messed with my season."

"That's not…" I glare at Dillon's smirking face. "Oh, never mind! Someone just tell me what our countdown is at."

"What countdown?" Dillon says around a mouthful of slop.

I stare dreamily at the ceiling, tapping my lip with my fork. "The countdown to the most wonderful, glorious day this house will ever experience. A day I look forward to like no other…" I lean closer to him but stage-whisper, "…the day you leave for college."

"Sub 200," Dad responds with a smirk. Dillon fakes offense. Mom shakes her head at us. And I start a new countdown.

The countdown to my date tonight.

* * * *

"You look amazing. I love that dress." Trent's words breeze past my ear, sending a shiver down my spine.

Leaning back in his arms, I brush my hand over his tie. It matches the crimson rose of my dress. The red dress that Trent encouraged me to wear. It is, after all, a Christmas party, and judging by Trent's expression when he first saw me in it, it's working for me. Trent called me stunning, but the way I felt slightly gobsmacked when I first saw him proves he is literally the stunning one. I have never seen him in a shirt and tie, and I'm kind of thinking that look was made specifically for him.

"You're pretty hot yourself, Mr. Evans." I blush but still slide my arms around Trent's neck as we dance. "This is a really, really good look for you."

He raises his eyebrow in that cocky expression I love, saying, "What isn't?"

I grin despite myself. "Point, Trent."

Trent's hand presses against my lower back as he inches closer. "A point, huh? What am I winning?"

"Ice cream?" I say and giggle when his nose curls in disgust. He pulls me closer as we dance between an older couple. This party isn't exactly filled with kids our age, and I can see why Adam didn't want to come.

But Jillian is here, working. Her dad owns a catering business, and she's serving tonight. I missed her while I was getting ready. We've always dressed up for dances and things like this together. But after her basketball tryouts, she was busy helping her dad prep.

I search the dimly lit room for her, remembering she told me she'd be wearing her stylish black and white server's outfit. Scanning the perimeter, I finally spot Jillian in a far corner refilling a tray of bite-sized pastries. Seeing her stooped stance, my friendship sensor tells me something's off. Since I talked to her less than an hour ago and she was fine, I'm assuming it's the usual—her parents fighting.

"Checking out other options?" Trent teases, his hand squeezing my side.

"No," I laugh. "I'm looking at Jillian." The song ends, and our movement slows to a stop. "I'm going to go say hi to her. Meet me at the food?"

"I'll just go with you." He guides me through the crowds. "Can't let you wander around looking available dressed like that."

His proprietary tone makes me blush. "Trent, it's all old people here."

"I know," he whispers in my ear. "Disgusting old grabby men."

I burst out laughing, earning some indulgent looks. Distracted by Trent and his breath on my neck, I bump into a girl at my side. "Sorry," I say as she turns. Opening her mouth, she begins to apologize, but then her eyes dart to

Trent and her mouth snaps shut. Mumbling something incoherently, she stumbles away.

I stare after her in confusion. "Is that...?"

"Gabriella, my ex," Trent clarifies as I recall seeing her with him. I admit I noticed him a lot more than her, but she seemed nice enough. His phone dings, and he slips it from his suit pocket. "Let's go," he says, pulling me toward the door.

"But we just got here and Jillian—" I resist, looking for her in the crowded room. I spot her, noting again her tight smile and the extra tension in her shoulders as she exits through the back door.

"Adam and the guys are starting a movie, and we've made our appearance. Even a movie on Adam's wimpy screen will be ten times better than this party." When I still hesitate, he drops an arm over my shoulder. "I don't want to miss the beginning, and you can text her, right?"

"Yeah, I can text her." With a final glance at the far door, I give in, force away a pang of worry, and let Trent pull me outside.

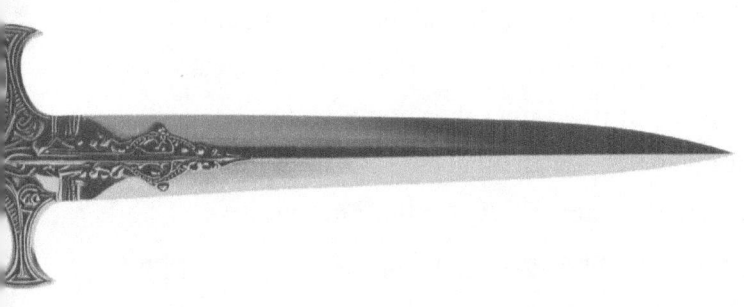

CHAPTER THREE

"Food or outfitter first?" Reilynn asks as we enter Fenton, the first real settlement we've seen in weeks. Our journey to Avalei has been slow and marked with…boredom.

We could have had more excitement taking the shorter route through the White Plains and over the Razor, but—wanting to survive the journey—we chose the longer route to the seaside. Now that we're here, we'll head up the coastline until we reach our destination.

Peering between the thatched roofs and mass of bodies filling the square, I catch a glimpse of sails and blue waters.

"Outfitter then ocean," Asha responds, somewhat dreamily. I guess if an elf has new clothes and gorgeous turquoise waters, they don't need sustenance.

"Food," Xandra says decisively and, like a small sheep dog, herds us through the market toward the tempting smell of baked comfort. Skirting under the shoulder of a well-armored, glaring guard, she chatters about her plans for what she calls civilization reentry. "...I also need to purchase some more herbs and medicine. I used up most of my supply on Reilynn's shoulder wound last month."

Reilynn rolls her shoulder, armor clanking. "My sense of self-preservation thanks you. A knight without her ability to wield a weapon is nothing." Too distracted by the nearby food, Xandra doesn't respond to the wide opening Reilynn inadvertently offers, instead darting through the crowd to the baker's stall.

"Pub," Greymore's voice rumbles in my ear before he slips into the crowd. I watch his hooded head disappear in the direction of a larger and more lively building near the docks.

Once he's out of earshot, Reilynn spins to me, the plume on her helmet swaying at the abrupt movement. She's fully fitted for battle, refusing to take off her armor even in a peaceful setting like Fenton. "Tell me again why he's journeying with us? Will he be needed in Avalei?"

I shrug, watching Xandra's arching hand movements as she negotiates with the baker. "I don't know. Maybe?"

"Well, he's very...stoic," Reilynn replies, which is saying something coming from the most proper and demanding member of my crew.

"He does not waste emotion," Asha explains.

She's always had a soft spot for the king's man, but Asha is all grace and softness—unless you give her a weapon and a reason to wield it.

"Correction." Xandra darts into the middle of our group, her massive shield bumping against Reilynn as she lunges into our conversation. "He has no emotion. None." Spinning in our midst, she distributes a warm loaf of bread to each of us. "That being said, I like having him around. He's handy with that crossbow. With his hunting, we've been eating well."

Finally pulling off her helmet, Reilynn takes a massive bite. "No, this," she points at her steaming baked good, "this is eating well."

I seal my agreement by downing my loaf in a handful of bites. No stingy, healthy diets for me in dreamworld. Brushing the crumbs from my fingers, I stare at the pub down the lane and muse, "Honestly, I don't know why Greymore is determined to go with us. Avalei may be my hometown, but this seems like a pretty standard job otherwise." I slide a dagger from my hip, tapping the flat of the blade against my thigh. "But he's here and he's definitely not emotionless. Don't you guys...can't you sometimes..." I struggle to form my thoughts into words that don't sound crazy. "Doesn't it seem like sometimes that you can *feel* his emotions?"

"What?" My three companions offer me a baffled look. I shake my head, realizing it's just me and more dream weirdness.

"Nothing, let's just split up and meet back here at dusk."
I point to the inn we passed on our way into town. "We'll
stay at the Shady Boar tonight."

The three are quick to leave, Xandra and Reilynn arguing
over what to eat next, and Asha gliding through the crowd
toward the outfitter.

I wander the stalls, mindlessly making purchases. Feeling
listless, I eventually part from the crowd and wander to a
large yet empty gathering area. A well sits in the middle, and
the town's message board is across from it.

Leisurely, I peruse the messages. In the center is a fairly
accurate drawing of a snow cat with the caption: *Lost pet.
Please return to Hades.* Clever. Even my dreamworld has
memes.

I turn my attention to the area map and trace my finger
up the coast. Avalei is still a few weeks journey away. At this
rate, it may take me months to dream myself there.

Exhausted, I make my way to the well and drop onto its
rocky ledge. Though I'm physically sleeping at this very
moment, mentally it seems I never rest. In the past, my
dreams were made up of small missions finished in a night's
sleep. I got closure, woke up, went throughout my day, and
fought another battle in the next dream. But this trip to
Avalei…it's consuming.

For weeks, I've been dreaming of a journey that's starting
to feel more like a quest. An endless quest.

The worst part is knowing I'm doing this to myself. I
tried thinking of arriving in Avalei as I fell asleep, but still

woke up on our journey. Not only is my subconscious wildly creative, but completely unhinged.

I guess I could just go get a room at the Shady Boar and sleep away my time in dream world, but my crew would worry and wake me and ply me with all sorts of nasty concoctions if they thought I was the least bit unwell.

So, I play my part. If I'm being honest, there's a sense of urgency in this world I can't ignore. I'm compelled to act in this place, to protect my crew. To fight with and fear for them.

People would pay a fortune to access the kind of virtual reality I keep finding myself in. The least I can do is embrace it.

Rising, I snatch two daggers from the belt at my waist and begin to juggle them. I spin the blades behind my back, over my shoulder, and under my leg. Then, holding the hilt of one, I use the blade to flip the other higher and higher, catching it on the second dagger and tossing it again and again. Finally, with one last high throw, I sheathe the first dagger, snatch the second with the same hand, and hide it neatly away in my sleeve.

Grinning in self-satisfaction, I flip my long braid over my shoulder.

Dream me *is* rather epic.

"Nix," Greymore interrupts my narcissistic moment.

"Yes, dear?" I respond. I'm not sure why I've come to enjoy baiting the man, but it's fun, and the journey has been boring. Also, he frustrates me with all his secrets. Again, something I'm doing to myself, creating a character whose mysteries drive me insane.

I really am a mental masochist.

"Information," he says, stepping aside to reveal an elderly gentleman.

In a stained tunic and loose hose, he's not the most well-off informant I've ever seen. He grins, displaying an extremely limited number of teeth. "Man says you wanna know 'bout Avalei," he says, puffing out his skinny chest.

I step to Greymore's side and pat his shoulder. "I'm surprised the big guy strung enough words together to ask, but he's right. I do want to know about Avalei."

I keep my eyes on the elderly man, refusing to acknowledge the exasperation rolling off the hidden face beside me.

"Well…" The man scratches behind his ear before studying the filth his itching dislodges. I cringe, but this is what happens when you get information from characters drowning in ale. His words and his scratching continue, "Rumors say it's bein' attacked. Not by men, but animals." Dropping his hand, he steps closer, his rank scent washing over me. "See, little missy. The place is cursed. Doomed to belong to the wild. Death is all you'll find there."

The walking virus is trying to scare me. "Is that all you got?" I free the dagger from my sleeve and tap it against my chin.

"Is…that…," the man sputters, backing away from me. "I was promised pay!"

Greymore tosses him a coin as I say, "Avalei is a refuge. The king's safe hold and under my protection."

Clutching the coin in his filthy palm, he says, "Well, you ain't doing much protecting from here. Is you?!"

Eyes locked on the critical mess of a man, I turn my body from him, catch the blade between my thumb and finger, and expertly fire. With a resounding thump, it embeds itself in the message board ten paces away. "If Avalei needs my protection, it has it." I step toward the now quivering man, perhaps enjoying his fear a bit too much, and continue, "A person would be very, very foolish to call it cursed and dying." Another dagger in hand, I tap the flat of my palm.

Suddenly, much more sober, the man inches away. "Yes, ma'am. I'll make sure to pass the word right 'long." With a jerky bow, he lurches away, mumbling something about needing another drink.

I stride to the board, pulling the knife from the heart of the drawn snow cat. "Animals, huh? That doesn't sound so bad, does it, Greymore? Clear out a few kitties, maybe kill some snakes. With Avalei's wall, the village is easily defended." I tap the blade to my chin. "Why is everyone so fired up about this?"

Beside me, Greymore studies the map, tracing the jagged peaks surrounding the city. His concern washes over me. In our weeks of traveling together, I *think* I've gotten better at reading him. Greymore may not utter many words, but expresses his feelings rather well by releasing waves of emotions—like pheromones seeping from his skin.

But, apparently, I'm the only one of my crew who senses them. I don't really like this new discovery. I also think the hooded guy can close off the emotions he doesn't want me to feel, which really isn't fair at all. On the other hand, he doesn't seem phased by my emotions at all, so I'm pretty sure the connection doesn't go both ways.

I rap the map with my knuckles, turning my thoughts from the mystery beside me to the mystery of Avalei. "It just doesn't seem like the threat is overwhelming, but I suppose we'll know soon enough." Looking away from the map, I spot a partially hidden poster whose dollar sign draws my attention.

Flicking the notices covering it aside, I grin in triumph. "Look what I found, my little *Arrow* impersonator! The perfect side job to kill the monotony of this trip." I trail the end of my knife down until it points at the listed reward. "How do you think the girls will feel about a good old-fashioned pirate round-up?"

* * * *

"I don't like this," Reilynn murmurs, wavering on unsteady feet. Our borrowed vessel—a small cog—rocks in the large waves as moonlight reflects off the water, guiding our path. A league to our left lies the barely visible shadow of the beach. Jutting from the dark water in front of us is a small rock island, and—if pub intelligence can be trusted—we'll find our pirates anchored on the far side.

Xandra stands on the quarterdeck controlling the rudder, the ocean breeze tossing her hair as moonlight glints off the shield strapped to her back. "I don't like this either..." she says, "I love it!"

In response, Reilynn jerks her helmet off and retches over the side.

Xandra chortles. "I told you to take the herbs!"

Regal as a ship's figurehead, Asha glides over to comfort Reilynn. The elf's new outfit shimmers in the muted moonlight. Instead of your typical chainmail or tunic, she's wearing a blue dress/cape made from some type of ultralight fabric-like metal. The capped sleeves and bust are gathered, bunching becomingly over her upper body. At her torso, the dress disappears into a long leather corset. Leather also covers her hips and upper thighs like a medieval pair of bicycle shorts. From under her belt to her ankles, the dress/cape falls in a V with the bottom six inches gathered and tied off with tiny, silver bows. Leather gloves reach to her biceps, and high-heeled boots rise past her knees. A quiver of arrows is strapped on her thigh, and a bow over her shoulder. With her stick-straight blonde hair pulled into a high ponytail to show off her heart-shaped face, fine features, and elfin ears, Asha's the picture of deadly grace.

Slumping against the elf—and looking entirely *un*graceful—Reilynn wipes a shaky hand over her mouth. "Puking Pirates," she murmurs, her short, bright red hair standing on end. "I hate pirates."

"Here, here, my weak-stomached one!" Xandra heartily agrees. "And why prisoners? Why can't we just wipe them all out?" Punctuating her speech with her hands, Xandra accidentally jerks the rudder. The vessel tips dangerously to the side, and Reilynn returns to her vomiting.

"The king believes in reform," Greymore says. A five word sentence. Today's new record.

"Well, if a pirate rushes at me, I will happily *re-form* them myself." Xandra whirls her ball and chain above her head, leaving the cog to its own devices.

Dodging the swinging weapon, I regain control of the ship.

Reilynn comes up gasping for air, before again drooping over the side. I offer a sympathetic grimace to the knight before turning to Xandra. "We make nothing off of this if we have to buy a new boat," I scold. "Now, quiet down, we're getting closer to the island."

Dropping into an exaggerated sneak stance, Xandra slips the handle of her weapon back into its hook at her side. She only carries the one weapon and her great shield. But honestly, the shield can be just as terrifying and deadly as any blade.

Leaving the driving to her and my sick knight to Asha, I join Greymore on the bow. His anxiety creeps over me. "Stop doing that!" I whisper. "I'd rather have Xandra's chatter than your emotional pelting."

His assent drifts on the salty air as he says, "The plan's no good."

"Asha is a brilliant mind." I turn to watch her rub small circles on Reilynn's back—not that the knight can feel them through her armor. "Her ability to see the future is more premonition than planning. Trust her, Greymore. She's saved my life more than once."

"We can't save you when we're split up." Eight words, a record breaker.

"We need cover fire, and you two have the long-range weapons. Xandra, Reilynn, and I will be fine. Besides, I have two new daggers to break in." I grin at him, lifting my eyebrows. My reassurance is ruined by Reilynn staggering to my side, her helmet askew.

"Is it time to abandon ship yet?" she whispers before burping loudly.

I gag on the smell while Greymore inches away. "Why don't you just sit for a minute until we get closer to the rocks and can drop anchor?" With a swift nod, she somehow quietly drops into an armored heap. "Oh, and you can't swim in that, Reilynn." I toss a canvas bag her way. "Get this leather stuff on."

With a sneer, she pulls the lighter armor from the pack and sets it aside. "I'll take my chances with chain-mail."

"And sink like a rock!" Xandra whisper-yells.

Shrugging, I begin to furl the sail and mentally review the attack plans.

Once the boat is secure, Greymore and Asha move to take their position on the highest point of the island, looking down at the pirate's vessel while Reilynn, Xandra, and I ease into the water.

Thankfully, Reilynn seems to be over her bout of seasickness and able to swim despite the weight of her hauberk. More dream magic, I'm sure. Using Xandra's shield as a flotation device, the three of us glide through the tropical water.

We round the island, the noise of the pirates reaching us before the visual. The ale seems to be flowing and spirits soaring. Typical pirates.

Dodging the light cast by their lanterns, we make our way to the far side of the ship. Ropes dangle down the side, skimming the water.

"Look, ladies." I point to the makeshift ladders. "Invitations."

We make quick work of the climb and as one duck behind some convenient barrels. Xandra's shield digs into my knee while Reilynn's spear jams into my side. Contorting my body, I pull a mirror from my hip pouch and give the signal.

Xandra clicks her tongue in a tick-tock sound, rocking her head back and forth as she counts down. A drunken pirate passes in front of our hiding place, stumbling against the barrels and dumping ale over us. I inhale an exclamation, as Xandra hisses something about him being first, and Reilynn flicks the liquid from her spear. Clapping a fellow shipmate on the back and beginning to sing a rowdy song, the offender lurches away.

"Dirty debauch," Reilynn mutters.

"Debauch isn't a word," Xandra hisses.

"Yeah, short for debauchery," Reilynn argues. "Makes perfect sense."

"No, it—"

The first arrow whistles through the night, finding a target. Growling, the pirates leap to arms, rushing as one tipsy mass to the far side of the deck—away from us.

I spring upright behind the barrel, pulling daggers and lining them up in tidy rows. "I have the left side, you two take the right. We meet in the middle. And no killing!" I remind the girls as they creep from their hiding place.

Brandishing shield and spear, they sneak until they are within striking distance.

The cursing of the pirates escalates as more and more of Asha and Greymore's arrows find their mark.

With a nod to the two on the ship, I begin throwing daggers. After my first target falls, taking a hilt to the head, I quit tracking the flight of my attacks. Snatching one dagger after another, I take down the unsuspecting pirates in rapid-fire succession as Xandra brains multiple opponents with each swing of her shield and Reilynn knocks rows out with the blunt end of her spear.

Things get a little exciting when the pirates catch on, but by then, there are only a handful left—including the captain. Pulling a wicked-looking blade from his belt, he rushes at me from across the ship with impressive gusto and an even more impressive war cry.

Flipping over the barrel, I pull my scimitars and land with my blades at the ready. A touch of fear reaches his eyes, but the captain doesn't slow in his forward assault. So much for intimidation.

Out of daggers and unwilling to slice him up, I toss my weapons aside and launch myself at the captain. His blade zings overhead as I fly toward his feet, wrap up his ankles, and take him to the ground. The impact jars my collarbone, and it takes me longer than I'd like to pull the dagger from the captain's belt and press it to his throat.

"Surrender," I pant, hoping he won't test his own blade. And the smart man doesn't.

In no time, our pirates are trussed up and ready for transportation back to Fenton. Asha and Greymore join me on the pirate ship as Xandra and Reilynn follow in the borrowed cog.

"Perfect planning—"

"—and excellent execution." Asha finishes one of our favorite sayings, a pseudo motto that, unfortunately, we can't use as often as I'd like. But today, we can.

Grinning, I turn and meet the pirate captain's eyes. Tied and gagged, he leans against the wood planking, looking up at me with a sort of maniacal gleam. I lean down to his eye level. "What's so humorous, Captain? That it was a group of girls..." Greymore grunts, "and a single man who bested your entire crew?" I pat his head and inch closer. "I find that a little funny myself." The twinkling in his eye dims, but there's still a knowing there.

Curiosity getting the best of me, I pull the gag from his mouth and gesture for him to have his say.

"You may have bested me and my men, but no one beats the beast."

I lean back, propping a hand on the hilt of one scimitar. "Which beast? Sea serpents? Overly confident pirate captains? Really, I'm not too concerned."

But Greymore is.

His hood shows he's looking away from me, studying the sky. "The Cephador," he murmurs.

"Aye, mate," the captain says. With his messy blonde hair falling from its leather tie, dark brown eyes, and smirk, he looks an awful lot like my brother. He drops his voice into the same mocking tone Dillon uses to taunt me. "She'll take your wee vessel first, then move on to this ship. But with Lola's speed, I could save us."

He holds his bound hands out in front of him. "All you have to do is cut me loose."

I shove the gag back into his mouth. With a gesture to Greymore, we move out of earshot.

"What's the Cephador?" I ask, feeling…twitchy.

"Giant squid," Greymore says, searching the sky, our distance from the shore, and the sky again.

I stare at the clouds hanging over us and notice the slight lightening of the sky. "This thing isn't going to drop from above, is it?"

"No," Greymore responds, but his focus remains on the air above, not the waters below.

"Dawn," Asha says, joining us. "The Cephador feeds at dawn."

My gaze darts to the east, behind us. Xandra and Reilynn are fighting over the control of the vessel, oblivious to the approaching danger. As the sun peaks over the horizon, the water churns behind them, something moving in its depths.

"Land!" I scream, "Get us to shore!" I sprint to the back of the pirate's ship and, without hesitation, dive into the sea.

I surface to Asha's piercing cry and Greymore's angry curse. Ignoring them, I cut through the water to the cog. Reilynn rushes to the side to pull me up, "What is—"

A tentacle reaches from the water, wrapping around my ankle and pulling me from the knight's grip. I go under. Dagger in hand, I slice at the beast.

Free, I explode to the surface. This time, Reilynn is ready—in one hand she clutches her broadsword, and with the other she grasps the stays of my jerkin and curls me upward onto the boat.

I drop to the deck, yanking the severed tentacle from my leg. It loosens with a loud pop. Tossing it at Reilynn, I say, "That's what."

Xandra's eyes bulge. "Get us broadside the ship!" I yell, snapping her free from her shocked stupor. Then, with scimitars drawn, I take up position on one side of the boat. Without a word, Reilynn moves to the other.

A split second of breath is all we get before the attack arrives. Tentacles are everywhere. They reach to grasp me, curl around the tiny vessel, and block my vision. I hack through the onslaught, cutting at the creature until my arms quiver in fatigue.

And still the tentacles come.

It's disturbing.

To my right, Reilynn begins to tire, and Xandra gives up on steering and swings her ball and chain overhead. The boat groans beneath us as the creature stops reaching for us and wraps itself around the cog. The boards crack like matchsticks, deadly splinters flying through the air.

I'm about to yell for us to abandon the boat when—through the gore and flying tentacles—I spy a large object rushing toward our helpless vessel. A very large, very pirate-like object.

No, he wouldn't…but as the pirate ship slams into our vessel, it's clear Greymore would and is ramming the pirate ship's prow into the center of our cog, linking the two vessels together and giving us a means of escape.

From nowhere, Asha drops down and begins spinning around, a war fan in her hand. Twisting the deadly weapon like a debutante, she severs tentacles left and right. "Go!" she shouts, waving me away.

On the opposite side of the battered cog, Greymore rolls to a crouch next to Reilynn and Xandra. Unwilling to leave my crew, I plant my feet and slice at a tentacle threatening to encircle Asha's throat.

"Believe…in…the…plan," she says, her words punctuated by her spinning moves, her deadly dance.

Trust. I have to trust her. With a growl, I sheathe one scimitar and charge for the relative safety of the pirate ship. Xandra and Reilynn are already scrambling over the railing. Surprisingly, Asha is right behind me, lunging and twirling and destroying while in retreat.

Onboard the larger ship, I turn, expecting Greymore to follow, but he's placed himself in the center of the vessel and is unfurling his chain and blade.

"Yes!" Xandra hisses at my side.

"Mother have mercy," Reilynn breathes.

"To land, Captain," Asha requests, tucking her fan away. It's only then that I realize the pirate captain and a handful of his men are free, rushing around the ship with fevered, focused intensity.

Leaving them to man their ship, my crew teeters over the railing, watching Greymore on the demolished cog below.

Greymore wields the chain and blade like a whip, first flicking the weapon sideways and severing several tentacles. Then, as the deadly blade snaps back toward him, he crouches, allowing it to soar over his head and again make contact with the Cephador.

On the deck of the pirate ship, my crew stares in momentary rapture at the display of a magnificent, lethal weapon in the hand of a master. The spinning and snapping strikes continue as Greymore attacks the creature with deadly precision.

Shaking myself, I leap to the quarter deck and step to the captain's side. We're heading toward land, and moving fast, pushing the fishing vessel in front of us like a plow. Water crashes over the cog, dousing Greymore. "Is there a way to kill it?" I ask as the beast begins another assault.

The captain's lean, tanned arms flex on the wooden spokes. "Pierce the eye."

Which means we need a visual of the whole body. And to get that, we'll need shallow waters. I stare at the approaching beach, willing it closer.

Suddenly, a loud crack rents the air. The beast has turned its focus from Greymore's blade back to the cog.

This time, tentacles wrap around the entire vessel, covering almost every surface. The ship snaps in two as Greymore rushes forward, springing from tentacle to tentacle in an effort to reach our ship. He's almost made it when a lone tentacle slaps his leg, stealing his balance as the boat sinks beneath him. He'll either be crushed by the larger ship, drowned, or taken by the Cephador.

"He's not going to make it," the captain casually announces, not sounding the slightest bit upset by Greymore's imminent death.

"Just get us to land," I demand before leaping from the quarter deck, darting past my gaping crew, cutting a piece of the rigging free, and hopping on top of the rail. I loop the rope around my wrist and, with a deep breath, lunge from the ship.

Swinging outward, I arch around the side of the ship and to the sinking cog at the prow. Seeing me, Greymore leaps on top of a curled tentacle, loads his crossbow, and shoots. The appendage springs free, launching Greymore skyward.

We collide in the air as he grasps at the rope, his arm above mine.

"Nix," he says as if we've just happened upon each other in the village square.

"Greymore," I return. The ship jolts to a grindingly horrific stop, sending us spinning wildly as we hit land.

Looking down through the tilting chaos, I find it. The creature's eye. But we spin away, losing any shot we may have had. "The eye!" I point with my free hand, then reach for Greymore's quiver, pull a bolt free, and reload his crossbow.

"Thanks," he says before leaping from our rope, twisting in the air to get the needed shot, and firing.

Dangling helplessly above, I watch as he falls into the mix of splashing water, churning sand, and flying tentacles. My frantic spinning brings me back over the ship, and I drop to the deck.

Rushing to the side, I peer down, searching.

The silence on deck contrasts with the struggle below as the pirate crew and my squad gather anxiously at the railing, watching the beast flail in the sand. The movement slows until the beast is still. Its large body floats to the surface—an unseeing eye visible, pierced by a crossbow bolt.

Seconds pass as I feverishly search the waters.

Finally, Greymore bursts from the water, gasping and flinging a tentacle from around his neck, hood still securely in place.

Cheers sound from both crews.

Sagging in relief, I make my way to the dazed captain. He strokes the wood rail of his ship, staring at the mess below, eyes suspiciously wet. "Lola. My sweet Lola. I ran her aground."

I pat his shoulder, giddy with relief. "And I thank you. I'll be sure the king knows you're already well on your way to reform." He whimpers, and I continue, "You'll be a great privateer."

CHAPTER FOUR

I wake feeling ridiculously proud. Subduing pirates is the most fun and fulfilling thing I've done in weeks. Which is pretty sad, considering it's a dream.

Rolling over, I grab my phone and check for texts. My lips curve at the expected messages from Trent, but fall when I see there's nothing from Jillian.

My longstanding BFF and I have grown apart over the past few weeks. Where our phones used to be a constant connection between us, now there's silence. Not angry silence, but a building distance. I'm always with Trent, and the more time Jillian and I spend apart, the less there is to say. My fingers hover, trying to think of something to send.

After a few minutes typing and deleting, typing and deleting, I give up and switch back to Trent's thread.

Morning, Babe. Missing you today. Txt when u get this.

I fire off a quick message in return before tossing the phone to the other side of my mattress. The lingering high from my dreamworld slowly recedes, and I find myself reluctant to let the fantasy go.

Compared to the craziness of life—strained friendships, the holiday frenzy, a new boyfriend, and school stress—being a warrior is easy. Right now, my dream world feels safe and uncomplicated. Fun.

I must doze off because the buzzing of my phone wakes me. Gathering myself, I fling my covers back and fumble for the cursed device.

"Hello," I grumble.

"I thought you were awake," Trent says, his voice jarring me into full awareness.

"I was...I am." I fumble my words as I sit up and smooth my hair.

On the other end, he laughs. "Well, I guess with your boyfriend out of town, you have nothing to wake up for. I'll let you go enjoy your sleep. We're heading to go parasailing. I just wanted to hear your voice this morning."

I smile at his words. "Well, then, good morning. Now I'll consider myself heard."

Trent's warm chuckle makes my stomach flutter. "Man, I wish you were here. I—" he pauses, shouting something to someone there with him. "I gotta go, babe. I'll talk more later." The call disconnects before I can respond, so I text.

Wish I was with u.

Yeah, the Caribbean for Christmas break would be nice. As an only child with parents flush with cash, Trent gets the best vacations. While I'm starting my Christmas break here in bed, he's at a high-end resort in the Caribbean. Parasailing. My phone dings.

What r u doing today? Shopping?

I wrinkle my nose at Trent's message. Shopping? I hate shopping. I bought every single person on my list a gift online and plan to spend tomorrow wrapping them. But what am I going to do today? Usually over the break, Jillian and I watch Hallmark Christmas classics and pretend we live someplace it actually snows. I freeze as the realization sinks in. Christmas is in two days, and we still haven't had our traditional binge. How did I forget about it? A month ago, we joked about maybe getting some boyfriends to cuddle with for our annual tradition, but then it really happened, and I forgot.

I forgot.

I tap the phone to my chin, plotting a way to make this up to her. Decided, I flip the phone over and respond to Trent.

Going 2 Jillians. Have fun!

* * * *

Standing in front of Jillian's door, I shift the bag of our favorite movie snacks from one hand to the other. I'm beginning to think no one is home when the door flies open.

"Claire!" At least Jillian's mom is glad to see me. Her smile is genuine, even if it lacks depth. She's usually a

Christmas fanatic, so her superficial grin looks out of place for this time of year.

I readjust my grip on the plastic bag. "Hi, Mrs. J. Is Jillian here?"

A flash of concern creases her brow. "She is, I'll go grab her."

I enter with a pinched smile. I've never had to wait by the door before. I always just head right up to Jillian's room, practically letting myself in.

"Nix!" Jillian's brother spots me at the door. "Where you been?"

My guilt growing, I say, "Just around. How are you, Tyler?"

The cocky preteen casually tosses a ball back and forth between his hands. Like his sister, he's an incredible basketball player. "Good," he says. "I hit five three-pointers and—"

"—Nix." Jillian's appearance in the hallway interrupts our conversation. Her frigid tone and begone sibling glare kills any hope of reviving it, so—with a sympathetic wave—Tyler ducks out of view. I wish I could just follow him, but looking at Jillian's taunt features, I know this is the explanation part.

"I didn't get a text," she says, arms crossed over her chest.

"I wanted to surprise you," I raise the bag in my hands, "and I wanted to actually see you. It feels like it's been forever since we've hung out."

"It *has* been forever, Nix." Her voice is a mix of anger and hurt.

I gesture to the front porch. "Can we talk?"

With a shrug, she brushes by me and out the door. I follow. With her corkscrew hair piled in a messy bun atop her head and loose t-shirt, she looks the same, but this is all so different.

I swallow at the sudden pressure in my throat and pull my jacket tighter across my chest. It isn't exactly cold outside, but the chill between Jillian and me is cool enough on its own.

Now. Now is where I explain…and apologize.

Jillian leans against the railing of the small porch and raises an eyebrow at me. "What?"

"I'm sorry." I jump right in. "Sorry about not being here. About forgetting about the Christmas binge." I push the words all out in one breath and take another deep one before starting again. "I just got so caught up in everything. And I'm sorry." I fight against the urge to justify it, to blame the distance on my new relationship. To say I forgot because we aren't on the same team, she's always gone playing ball, and we just haven't been together enough to plan. Instead, I hold the candy out. "Is today too late to party?"

Jillian's amber eyes narrow as she studies me. "Are those Milk Duds I see in there?" she finally asks, her stance easing into casual and familiar lines.

Relief punches into me, and I nod like a bobble head. "Yes. I brought all the good stuff. Skittles, Dr. Pepper, and even pizza pockets for later," Jillian reaches for the bag. "With Trent gone, I can stay all night."

Jillian's hand snaps back to her side. "Trent's gone?"

"Yeah, on a cruise," I say, dragging out the vowels in cruise with a smile.

But my smile falls at the tightening of Jillian's jaw and the squaring of her shoulders. Eyes darkening, her expression transforms into a look I've only ever seen on the court. The last time I saw that face, she went on to score twenty points…and foul out.

"So that's why you're here," she says, her words snapping with ruthless precision. "You got bored."

I reach my empty hand out. "No, Jillian—"

"No, listen to me, Nix. I won't be a replacement for Trent." She shakes her head before pointing at me. "You've given up everything for that guy. Basketball. Your friends. But that's not even the worst part. He totally controls you. And you've given up yourself. You're not even the same person. The Nix I knew would never forget. She wouldn't bail on me time after time." Enunciating each word, she steps closer. "She actually cared. You want to know why we don't text? Because you stopped caring!" she practically shouts.

Her words pound into me, seeming to echo down the street and back again. Accusing. My fingers flex on the grocery bag, the weight of my offer pulling on me even as I realize the lack of it. Not enough. It isn't enough to fix this. But, after all these years, this can't be unsalvageable.

"You don't—," I start.

"Yes," Jillian interrupts. "Yes, I do mean it. It's been weeks since you cared about anything besides Trent. You didn't care about me enough to do more than send a few text messages. I wanted to give you the benefit of the doubt, new boyfriend and all. But you've changed. You. Don't. Care. And now, neither do I." She shrugs; it's a movement of sad acceptance like my apathy is a hard truth she's been unlucky enough to discover.

"I do care," I whisper, voice low and desolate. "You know the real me, and I've been stupid. But you are important to me, and you *know* it."

"How would I know that?" Her tone is hard, but her eyes are bright, almost teary. "Actions, Nix. That isn't what your actions say."

"Jill," I reach toward her, truly scared. She never cries. Even when I'm bawling at a stupid movie, she never even gets watery eyes. "I'm sorry. I don't know what else to say. I've—"

She shrinks back, her voice dropping, every part of her pulling away. "I know, Nix. You've been with Trent. Every night until curfew and all weekend long. I was just a passing thought, not important enough for more than a *How are you, Jillian? Good to see you, Jillian.*"

Her expression grows tight with suppressed tears. "But I think you knew, Nix. You could see I wasn't okay. But it wasn't worth your time." Inhaling, she covers her emotions with a dark, detached smile. "They're getting a divorce. My parents. I don't know where we're going or anything, but it's happening."

"No." I stumble forward, arms extended, needing to offer comfort, but I'm stopped by the steely look in Jillian's eye.

"No, Nix. Don't even try to be here for me now. It's too late. You're only here today because Trent is gone. I don't need that in my life. I deserve better. You deserve better, too, but you don't see it."

Reaching, she snatches the grocery bag from my limp grip. "I'll take this, but not your pity. See you around, Nix…maybe."

With that, she leaves, shutting the door in my stunned face. "Jillian," her name leaks from me in an anguished whisper. "I'm so, so sorry."

Not for anything I did, but for what I didn't do.

* * * *

I curl my fingers around my still full cup of hot chocolate. The whole chocolate-makes-everything-better is a farce. Instead, sitting in Jillian and I's favorite coffee shop, sipping on the best hot chocolate in the world, I feel horrible.

An hour ago, I didn't think I could feel worse than I did when Jillian slammed that door in my face, cementing the end of a friendship I undervalued, but I do. That hour has given me sixty long minutes to realize and accept that Jillian was right and justified about everything. Even worse, to realize I have no idea how to make this up to her.

Christmas music blasts from the shop's speakers, contradicting my mood. A steady crowd moves in and out of the shop, some frantic, some joyful, but all busy. The coffee shop is located right in the middle of a shopping center, and the foot traffic seems endless.

Listlessly, I watch people move through the space from my table by the window, the chocolate cooling in my hands as I twist my cup.

Distracted, I don't notice the noise until a third rap draws my attention to the glass. On the outside is Adam, Trent's friend, with an older man standing slightly behind him. Adam's welcome smile falls as he sees my expression. I plaster a grin on my face and attempt a reassuring wave, but if they look as stiff and awkward as they feel, I fail miserably.

Saying something to the man, whom I assume is his father, Adam makes his way to the door.

Dropping my chin, I attempt to wipe away any mascara residue. There may or may not have been some ugly crying earlier in my car. And I didn't really care how I looked or who saw me when I first came in here to drown my sorrows. Now, I find myself caring quite a lot and rush to fix the mess of myself. Instead, I poke myself in the eye and dislodge my contact. Really smooth.

"Nix," Adam drops into the booth.

I glance up at him, blinking hard.

"Contact," I say, pushing at the corner of my eye. At least my clumsiness might explain away the redness of my eyes. Feeling the lens slip back in place, I pull my hand away. "Got it." I offer another hollow smile before asking, "How are you?" Hopefully, I can keep the conversation from me and why I'm sitting sad and alone in a coffee shop...and keep him from mentioning it to Trent.

For some reason, I just don't want to get into the whole Jillian thing with my boyfriend, but it is nice to see Adam's friendly face.

With a start, I realize I have easily spent more time with the guy across from me in the last month than I have with Jillian. Due to my parents' dating rules—I can't be alone with Trent at his house—and their friendship, I'm with Adam almost as much as Trent. And out of all of Trent's friends, Adam's the one I've connected with the most. He's just a nice, genuine guy.

"I'm alright, just shopping with my dad," Adam answers, reinforcing his good-guy status. He offers me a slow, soft smile. "What about you? You in a cheating mood today?"

"What?!" I sputter.

"Your drink. Or is that a low-fat latte?" Adam gestures at my cup.

"Oh, cheating on Trent's diet," I clarify.

"What did you think—" Realization stops Adam's response, and his cheeks redden.

"Are you...blushing, Adam?" I laugh at the absurdity of it all.

He joins me with a deep chuckle. "No, never."

I match smiles with him for a second too long. Embarrassed, I turn my attention back to my drink and say, "I'm not really on a diet. I only eat healthy around Trent."

"Really, why?"

I smirk. "He buys."

"Ah, opportunistic." Grabbing the receipt I left lying on the table, Adam folds it into a square. "Here I thought you were one of those girls who eats healthy all day so she can have the midnight ice cream cheat."

"Really, it's the opposite. I eat junk food whenever I can so I can survive the healthy food Trent buys me," I say and take a big gulp of my chocolate.

"Can't argue with that logic." Adam smooths a crease and makes another fold.

I watch him twisting, folding, and flipping the paper, letting silence fall between us. It's not until I tip the cup that I realize I've finished the entire drink as I've watched him. Pushing the empty container aside, I look out the window and watch a couple pass by hand in hand followed by two laughing teenage girls, their arms loaded with shopping bags. I sigh, dropping my face into my hands.

"Nix." Adam draws my attention, and I peer between my fingers at him. With a light laugh, he pushes my hands out of the way. "Is this about Jillian?"

I flatten my hands on the table, my spine straightening. "How did you—"

"I'm with you and Trent all the time. I'd have to be blind not to see how often you text her…or debate about texting her." He picks the paper up again, fiddling with the folds.

Gathering my courage, I say, "Do you think I'm a good person?"

"Sure," Adam responds dismissively.

"I chose Trent over her," I admit in a whisper.

Adam shuffles, clearly in over his head. "Umm… you didn't—"

"I did. She told me, and she's right. I didn't do it on purpose. I never meant… but I did." Needing to do *something*, I grab the empty cup and twist it in my hands. "And I don't know how to fix it," I vent, unable to stop the words now that I've started. "I can't fix it. I can't go back. And I don't know what I could have done differently. Because when you're dating someone, they should come first. Shouldn't they?"

Catching Adam's stricken expression, I shake my head. I release my abused cup and grab a napkin. Wiping at a non-existent speck on the table, I mumble, "Sorry, it's not your problem."

"I—"

"No, Adam. Just forget about it; I'll figure it out." I toss the napkin aside. Picking up my phone, I start flicking aimlessly through the apps.

"Nix, I will admit Trent is…" My hand freezes over the screen, waiting for his description. I need something from him, some explanation for what I'm feeling. "…intense," he says.

And there it is. I sag a little in relief. I'm not the only one who sees it.

"Yeah, he is," I agree. A part of me wants to add to that sentence. He's intense…but in a good way. But he puts everything into all he does. But treats me well.

Instead, I leave it as is, an admittance that I'm overwhelmed by him.

Looking at Adam, I see the same mix of guilt and validation. Hoping to lighten the moment, I say, "So, you're a pretty easy-going guy. How are you two such good friends?"

Adam laughs. Unlike before, it's not a happy sound, but a pained exhalation. "Trent was there for me when my mom died. He didn't leave like all my other friends who didn't know how to handle it. You can't blame them really. What fourteen-year-old wants to hang out with the depressing kid? But it didn't phrase Trent. He treated me like he always had. Because of him, I didn't live in my grief, you know?" He fiddles with the paper in his hand. "He kept me moving." He meets my eyes, his gaze dark and knowing. "So, his intensity can be a good thing. You know?"

"Yeah, I know," I say in a quiet voice.

My phone dings a notification, breaking into our moment. I glance at the text. "My mom is wondering where I am. I'd better go."

"Sure," Adam says, sliding from the table.

Easing past the crowded line, we walk out the door together. The boisterous noise of holiday revelry fades, and a cold breeze rushes in to fill the void. "I'm this way." Adam gestures in the opposite direction of where I'm parked.

"Oh, okay," I say, slinking into the warmth of my jacket, suddenly regretting oversharing...everything. "Hey, uh...thanks for listening."

I turn to go, but Adam calls me back. He fiddles with the paper in his hand and shuffles his feet, fighting some inner struggle.

I wait, letting the bracing air mingle with my interest. Adam has always been quietly confident, but now he seems almost...nervous.

Finally, he exhales and flicks his eyes to mine. "To be clear...I said Trent was a good friend. Not a good boyfriend. You shouldn't have to give up friends or anything else like that, Nix." With a jerky nod and a lingering look, he places something in my palm and walks away.

Struck by his tentative actions, his genuine concern, and—above all—his fervent words, I watch him until he's out of sight. Opening my hand, I find an origami flower.

An iris.

He remembered the flower from my sketchbook signature, my favorite flower. I swallow a jumble of emotions, more confused now than ever, yet filled with a new, comforting realization.

I may have lost one friend today, but I also discovered another in the most unlikely of places.

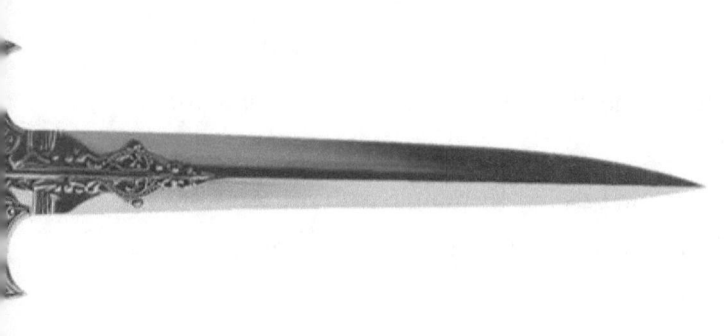

CHAPTER FIVE

A valei.

After weeks, we're finally here. Due to Reilynn's propensity for seasickness, we traveled down the coast by land for the last leg of our journey. A leg that took weeks but could have been days if we had taken our new pirate friend up on his offer of a lift; a fact Xandra won't let us forget.

The tiny nymph pushes between Greymore and me, rushing through the dunes, determined to be the first to see Avalei in all her glory. I step to the side, trying to quell my own growing excitement.

Behind us, a half mile from Avalei, is the dock. As Avalei's main economy is farming and shipping their unique produce overseas, the port is large. Two separate docks stretch over a hundred feet out into the deeper waters. In the center of these, built atop a rocky outcrop, is a tower that serves as both a lighthouse and a lookout. Right now, the area is empty. There must be no ships scheduled for arrival or departure today. We drop down a rise and into the dunes.

Before us, the sand stretches up the coastline as far as the eye can see. To our left, quicksand-like beach meets ocean. To our right, The Razor rises. The mountain range's cliffs tower hundreds of feet above us, bulging out into the dunes and blocking our view of the stronghold.

Xandra sprints through the sand, dodging the rocks that dot the dunes and mark the harder packed earth of the roadway. If she strays too far to the left or right, she'll sink in the sand. I decide against calling out a warning. A little swim in the sand would probably be good for the overly energized fighter.

Today, she's wearing the top half of her hair twisted back in numerous braids held together by a leather tie. Her shield covers her back, dwarfing her with its massive size and making her look more like an oversized beetle than a human being.

Asha follows her, skimming over the sandy path on long, lithe legs. The bottom half of her azure dress streams out behind her, a wave cresting in her wake. The warmer weather seems to agree with the elf, but I can't say the same for my knight.

Reilynn groans at my side. "Blistering beaches, this ocean lifestyle isn't for me." From the corner of my eye, I watch her struggle through the sand, her heavy armor a burden.

"You could pack your armor…" I flick the visor of her helmet closed. "At least pack the helmet."

She shoves the visor upright. "A knight should always be prepared for battle."

"Isn't the sign of a true warrior knowing when to save their strength by showing restraint?" I challenge, a dagger bouncing between my hands and a smile on my face as I stride towards the stronghold.

Reilynn scratches the space between her helm and the plated gorget covering her neck and shoulders, sweat dotting the tiny visible spot of skin. "Your point?" she asks. "Right now, you're wasting energy. Your strength is draining, weakening you with every," I flick my dagger toward the blinding sunlight, "drop of sweat. Plus, I can do this."

Tossing the blade over my shoulder, I catch it behind my back, relishing in the freedom of movement my leather armor offers.

Greymore snorts his agreement, and Reilynn just snorts. However, the knight takes off her helmet, spikey red hair jumping to attention at its newfound freedom.

"Why Avalei?" she asks, shoving her helmet into a pack on her shoulder without breaking stride.

"What do you mean? We're here because the king sent us," I answer hesitantly, her question confusing me. Reilynn has never cared where we go, or what jobs we take—as long as they're sanctioned by the king.

"No," Reilynn replies, running a hand over her mussed hair, which only makes it stick up that much more. With eyes so light brown they are practically clear, she locks her gaze on mine. "Why does it matter?"

"Well, Avalei supplies the kingdom with food, particularly farming produce they can't get anywhere else, specialties like bananas and oranges," I say. "But, more importantly, Avalei is a stronghold. A last resort and place of refuge for the king. If there's a threat or an attack on the capital, the royal family will sail here for protection." I gesture at the cliffs shadowing our path. "You'll see that The Razor's unscalable cliff walls line the whole valley, making it an ideal place for a last defense. The valley is shaped like a giant horseshoe, and The Razor makes it a nice, safe little pocket of land."

Always interested in talk of defense and battlements, Railynn leans toward me, silently asking for more, so I continue, "Adding to the natural defenses, the crown built a massive wall, closing everything inside the valley. It's the safest place in the kingdom..." My voice drifts off, and I pause on the dune as my prideful boasting evaporates, transforming into concern. "At least, it was."

"It sounds amazing," the knight says, a hint of reverence in her voice. "But, why..."

I wait, eyebrows raised in expectation, but Reilynn shakes her head, unable or unwilling to voice her question. Probably because it's personal.

The knight doesn't do well with emotions. Says they're sticky, weakening things.

Greymore huffs in frustration. "Your knight wants to know why you feel the way you do about it, Nix. Why does it matter to *you*?" he says before striding away, leaving us with our mouths hanging open.

"Twenty. Twenty words at once," I murmur in an undertone.

"Wasted wizards, he has a nice voice." I smack Reilynn's arm, my hand suffering the contact with her metal gear. "We should get him to use it more," she continues, unperturbed. "Now, answer the question."

Seeing she's determined to get personal, I sigh. But how do I explain the wave of memories that assaulted me when Greymore uttered this place's name? Memories that flooded me like a dousing shower washing away some kind of mental amnesia and uncovering a lifetime of remembrances. Memories of a childhood in my dreams. Dreams that I don't think I ever had, but feel every bit as real to me as the moment I'm now in. Heartaches, growth, friends, belonging. Avalei.

"I grew up here," I begin. "My parents and I came—"

"You have parents?"

"Yes, Reilynn. Most people do," I snap. "Do you want me to continue?"

The knight waves her hand for me to carry on. Resuming our walk up the final dune before the first glimpse of Avalei, I continue in a much softer tone, "Well, my family was sent to settle the land. My parents died on the boat—"

"—wretched ships—"

"—and I survived. Obviously. I was young, but old enough to work. The people here took me in, allowed me to live and work beside them. I never really took to farming, so I focused on building up the stronghold. For years, I helped build the wall, designed defenses, and trained to protect the people. When that was done…" I pause, reflecting. "I wasn't really needed here anymore. So, I went in search of other people to help and some real adventure. I found our crew and more jobs than can be accomplished in a lifetime. But this place is…"

We crest the rise of the dune and are greeted by the vision of a massive stone wall nestled within the looming jagged mountains of The Razor. The setting sun peeks through the wall's many arched openings, littering the dunes before it with a mosaic of shadows. Happiness spreads over me, lifting my lips. "Home."

"By my blade," Reilynn whispers worshipfully. "That's a defense."

And the wall *is* impressive. Five massive levels tall and almost a thousand feet wide, it's nothing compared to the surrounding mountains, but still a looming proclamation of strength.

Eyes on the wall, we ease forward until we draw even with Greymore. He's unmoving, hood tipped back as he studies the fortification. I try to look at it through his impartial eyes.

Each level is about twenty feet high and has a unique defense built into the structure. On the first, balls of wood with protruding spikes are built into the wall, looking like a mass of gigantic, impaled maces. On the second, ship-like knotted rigging covers the stone. These ropes are embedded with hundreds of glass shards, making them practically impossible to climb. Invisible from this distance, the wall of level three is lined with highly flammable substances. On the inside, torches burn, always at the ready. Once ignited, the fire will spread over and down the wall to the ropes and wooden spheres below. The fourth level is lined with corbels. These massive brackets look decorative from a distance, but they aren't supporting scenic little balconies. No, between each pair of corbels is an opening down to the levels below. Hidden on a platform just behind this opening is a huge pot of tar dangling over a stack of wood. If anyone is lucky enough to make it past levels one, two, and three, they'll be greeted by a hot tar bath from level four, dropped down through the hole between the corbels like a chute.

The top level is lined with battlements and divided by three towers, one in the middle and two spaced between it and the ends of the defense. On the sides where the wall meets the mountain are two thirty-foot-high gates closing The Razor out on either side. Beyond these gates, the fortification is all natural—The Razor's Dual Blades.

Protruding from the ground like gigantic axes, these ridges run right up to the fortification's wall. From their meeting point with the wall, the Blades rise sharply, creating a deadly, steep mountain range.

As formidable as it is, it's also beautiful. Flowering vines creep up and over every floor, covering the defenses and contrasting with the marble-colored rock.

"I likey." Xandra skids to a stop in front of us, bouncing on her toes. "How do I get in?"

I smirk. "That's the best part. You don't." I point to the first level, which is void of any arched windows, doors, drawbridges, or openings of any kind. "They let you in."

Xandra's eyes dart around, cataloging her options. She eyes the arched openings of the second floor. "You think you can toss me that high, Reilynn?" She shoves the knight with her shield. Reilynn doesn't budge. Xandra bumps her with the shield a second time, saying, "Help a damsel in distress and boost me to that window on the second floor. I'll climb in and drop that drawbridge." She tilts her head to the side, studying the massive metal plate tucked behind a portcullis in the second-level wall. "But that doesn't look like it's long enough to reach the ground."

I shake my head. The defense's windows and doors may seem like an easy entry point, but... "Every archway has a hefty metal shutter on the inside that can be barred with a massive block of wood," I point. "You could get on the ledge, but I'm pretty sure you'll be stuck there because the second you attempt to climb that wall—or be tossed up it— they'll lock those shutters down."

"Alright, ruthless leader." Xandra turns to me, hand on her hip, fingers flicking through the chains of her weapon. "You gonna help a girl out...or, in this case, in?"

Grinning, I step back, place my fingers in my mouth, and let out a shrill whistle. Then, I wait, watching the reactions of my crew. Xandra's curiosity is practically imploding from her while Reilynn looks on with a satisfied smirk, and Asha stands with a serene expression on her face. Greymore looks…hooded.

When the ground begins to rumble beneath us, everyone drops into defensive position—weapons drawn—except for Greymore and I. It seems I'm not the only one who's been to Avalei before. Seeing our ease, the squad slowly eases upright, chagrined, but I notice they all keep their weapons in hand.

"There's a whole network of gears and chains running underground. You can't access it from out here. You have to be inside," I say as the scrape of a metal-on-metal sound is heard, and a substantial iron plate begins rising from the ground beside us at a forty-five-degree angle, pointing toward the wall.

In front of us, closer to the wall, a thicker metal block rises straight into the air. The angled plate and block continue to rise until they meet, creating a ramp to a path that sits about ten feet off the ground.

"Now, they'll raise the portcullis and lower the second level's drawbridge." I dart a glance to Xandra, wondering if she'll be patient enough to wait or try to jump for it. Luckily, she's too distracted by the loud clanking and seamless engineering to move. I turn my attention back to the widening opening as the portcullis rises, allowing room for a metal plate to drop inch by inch. Finally, the last piece falls into place, creating a ramp up from the massive block and giving us easy access to the second level.

Shoulder to shoulder, my crew and I step up the ramp, Greymore lagging behind.

As we near the stone wall, a form in a linen shirt and trousers appears under the arched doorway, arms folded across his chest, a smile fighting to overtake the stern expression on his face. Torren Tarklow.

"Nix, you little dagger thrower!" he bellows. "It's about time you found your way back home."

CHAPTER SIX

L ying on my plush rug, I shoot the mini basketball into the hoop and wait for it to bounce its way back within reaching distance. Waiting. That feels like all I've been doing this past week.

Trent is out of town again for New Year's—this time at a ski resort in Denver. It must be storming on the slopes because he's been texting me nonstop this morning. As the ball rolls out of reach, I snatch my buzzing phone, wishing Trent were here in person. I don't feel so bored when he's around, and he distracts me from my guilt over Jillian. I finally told him what happened...at least the short version, and he's adamant I shouldn't feel guilty at all.

I'm not so adamant, but what difference does it make? I've tried texting her, but I'm pretty sure she's blocked me, and I still haven't figured out a way to make the whole thing up to her.

U Me and new MI next week?

I reread the text from Trent a few times, debating, wishing he had asked me before I agreed to go with my family. Trent hates watching movies with someone *second-hand.* His description, not mine. I suppose I could pretend I haven't seen it when we go, but deception really isn't my style. Besides, it feels like a stupid thing to lie about. Fingers flying over the screen, I text him back.

The rents R taking Dillon and I 2night.

Get out of it?

Trent's response is immediate. The truth is, as pathetic as it may sound, I've been looking forward to movies with the fam. After everything with Jillian, I've been on edge. I'm pretty sure I wasn't the most festive person for our celebration this year. And with my mom's schooling and my dad's demanding job at the dealership, we haven't spent much time together recently. It feels like we're in a bit of a family slump.

On the other hand, things with Trent have been great. Maybe it's because I've accepted that he's intense and that's not a bad thing. He makes me feel more intense and driven. And his intensity makes him attentive. So awesomely attentive.

For Christmas, he got me a stunning pair of diamond stud earrings that I wear all the time. It was my second-best gift, coming in behind a new easel and paints from my parents. The two days of break he was around were amazing and magical, but now that he's gone...

I feel less, somehow. Bored, adrift, and alone. I guess that's attachment for you. And because he's the best thing in my life right now, I text him back my agreement.

C what i can do

UR the best, babe

I send a heart-eyed smiley face before plopping down in the window seat to stare out at the unwinterlike scene. My neighbor jogs by in a light jacket, and suddenly I want to be out there, moving. *Doing* something.

Going running. TTYL

I fire the text off to Trent. Then, I find my sweats buried in the back of my closet—so much for prepping for track during my season off. Changed, I gather my shoulder-length hair back in a low ponytail, throw on my dusty shoes, and grab my phone and earbuds.

"I'm going for a run!" I holler, charging down the steps.

"Be back in time for the movie!" Mom calls, but I'm already out the door.

I don't have to run very far to realize just how out of shape I've become. I've lost weight with all my healthy eating, but I've also lost muscle. I gasp. And air, I'm losing a *lot* of air.

Determined to outrun my boredom and overall funk, I push myself onward. Music blasting in my ears, I let my mind wander to dream world—to my highly dangerous safe space.

My feet pound over the pavement, crushing leaves long since fallen. Block after block, I jog, moving my protesting body forward. I don't focus on a direction, just the movement. Going forward, I don't feel so stuck in regrets.

I don't realize where I'm at until I glance to the side and see Jillian's house. There's a *For Sale* sign in the yard. My feet stumble to a stop, and I yank my earbuds free.

She's moving. Maybe even changing schools or states.

With that realization comes another: I always had faith we would figure things out. That I would find some way to fix this. I stare at the place that was like a second home to me in a daze until I realize I must look like some kind of creeper. I make a move toward her walkway, stop, shake my head, spin, and sprint away.

I have nothing to give her but apologies, and she doesn't seem to want them. In fact, my presence will probably just upset her more. She was right. I haven't been a real friend. It seems I can't be one and a good girlfriend at the same time. Adam was right, too. I shouldn't have given up my friends, but what difference does it make now? I can't fight for a friendship that's no longer there.

But I do have a relationship to fight for. Jerking my phone free, I bring up Trent's name.

Count me in!

His response is immediate. *Perfect, babe. Love you.*

I clench the phone in my hand, staring at the screen in disbelief. We've never said those three little words, and this is only two…but it's awfully close.

With lighter steps, I pocket my phone and turn toward home. I may have messed some things up big time, but I'm nailing the whole girlfriend thing. Feeling like I've gained back some control over my life, I jog back home, replacing thoughts of past regrets and Jillian with ones of a perfect future and Trent.

* * * *

"Claire! We're going to be late!" My dad's voice startles me, making me smear paint across the canvas.

I almost had it this time—the landscape I've been trying to paint for Trent. I had hoped to have it done in time for Christmas, had even set aside other projects, paying projects, but I still couldn't seem to get it right. But with my renewed relationship focus and new supplies, I decided to give it another try. And again, it is missing something or *too* something.

Too juvenile, too common, too boring.

And now it's too striped.

Slamming the brush down and mumbling ineligibly, I glance at the clock. The movie. I'd been so consumed by the painting, I forgot about the movie. Probably my subconscious at work, since I don't think my decision to ditch family time is going to go over well. With a quick wash of my paint-splattered hands, I rush downstairs. My mom, dad, and brother are all standing in the foyer, jackets in hand. "Hey, guys," I say.

Dressed in boots, jeans, and a flowery top, my mom eyes my paint-stained outfit. "You're fine going in that?" she asks in that mom voice that isn't exactly critical but still has the power to make you question.

"Geesh, Claire," Dillon says, smelling like a few too many sprays of cologne. "I know your boyfriend is out of town, but you're really letting yourself go."

Smacking Dillon's arm, I say, "I meant to tell you guys earlier, I can't go. I promised Trent I'd go with him."

"You do know that it is physically possible to watch a movie more than once. Right?" my dad quips, looking more dressed up than usual with his hair freshly cut and gelled.

"Dad," I say in a tone usually reserved for the unmagical moments he tells Dad jokes in front of Trent. "You know it isn't the same."

My mom is still giving me the eye, but for a far different reason. "When did you promise him, Claire?"

Seeing where this is heading, I wisely refuse to give a specific answer.

"Earlier."

"How much earlier, Claire?" Her voice is tight, bordering on shrill. "It couldn't have been last night when all of us discussed going together, or I would think you might have mentioned it. So, exactly when?"

Lying is useless; my red face gives me away every time, and even if it didn't, my mom would know.

"This morning," I admit.

Dillon leans his shoulder against the wall—enjoying this far too much—as my mom's grip on her jacket turns into a stranglehold. "Claire Louise Nickelsen! We planned this last night! Now, I like Trent and think he's a nice boy, but I'm tired of you always putting him before your family."

"Mom, it isn't like—"

"Isn't it? What about when you skipped your father's work party to attend his family's get-together? Or when you invited him over to help us decorate the house, then disappeared together to go 'buy more lights'? And what about Christmas Eve, when you missed our traditional nativity recreation because it was one of the few nights Trent would be home this break? Or how you didn't have the time to paint that image Sherly ordered from you months ago because you were drawing something for Trent? And don't forget the time you forgot to pick your brother up from work after you borrowed his car to drive to Trent's game."

"Hey…" Dillon holds his hands up. "Don't drag me into this. That girl I got a ride home with was cuuute."

My mom silences him with a glare before focusing her ire back on me. "What about it, Claire?"

Not sure if the question is rhetorical, or how to respond if it isn't, I keep quiet. Her continued focus makes me feel exposed, like I'm failing and she's just waiting for me to admit to it. To admit I can't get anything right. Glancing from my dad—who looks more sad than angry—to Dillon, who actually looks sympathetic, I finally shrug.

"Claire?" My mom pushes for a real response.

"I'm sorry," I mumble. "It didn't seem like a big deal. I didn't think you would care." But I *knew* Trent would care if I skipped out on all those things. He would have cared a lot.

"Well, sweetie, it is a big deal." My mom tosses me my jacket, and I instinctively catch it. "Now, let's go. If you keep your coat on, no one will see that hideous shirt."

I twist the jacket in my hands as my family turns to the door. They're already all different levels of mad. It isn't even going to be fun. Nothing but a miserable night at a movie I'd rather watch with my boyfriend. Besides, I promised Trent. He'll be upset if I go without him, and then I'll have more people disappointed in me. And he said he loved me today.

"No," I blurt. "I'm not going."

As if in slow motion, everyone spins to me—my mom is livid, my dad stern, and Dillon shocked. I'm a little shocked, too. Generally, I stay out of trouble and rarely disagree with my parents, and I've never, never outright refused to do what they say. In my moment of rebellion, I'm as stunned as any of them.

"Claire."

My dad's voice is a warning, but when Mom says, "What did you say?" it's a threat.

"Mom," I plead. "I promised him."

She chucks her jacket at the hook on the wall, missing. It falls to the floor in a heap. "And you promised me! Why should a promise made to him mean more than a promise to us or anyone else!"

"Because he'll be mad!"

The second the words fly from my mouth, I regret them...they make me look like some cowering pushover. But this is my decision, not Trent's.

My mom flings my words back at me. "He'll be mad! Well, so am I! So where does that put us?"

"I don't know, Mom." I keep my words controlled, my shock and fear and shame fading, leaving an unfamiliar anger to build in me. There's so much frustration I feel but can't express, emotions that have no foundation, no definition, no outlet.

"I think you're getting too close to Trent," my father interjects, and my heart clenches as he challenges the one thing going right in my life. My defenses rising, he continues, "It's things like this and then you moping around here when he's gone—"

"I haven't been moping," I protest, but even I see it's more denial than truth.

"Yes, you have." My dad's voice grows hard, his anger matching my own. "You shouldn't be depressed and—"

"I am not depressed!" I yell, the tight rein on my emotions shattering.

And even though the outburst pounds through my head and floods my heart, it also feels good to just let it all go. "You guys just don't understand. You don't *want* to understand. And maybe you haven't been here for me? You even think of that!? You just want to find everything wrong with me! Well, there's plenty! I've messed up a lot, okay? And I'm sorry I missed the stuff that was important to you. Maybe I'm just a little oblivious. But in reality, I'm also just a regular girl who misses her boyfriend when he's gone and who would rather go to a movie with him than with a family who sees her as nothing but a mopey, depressed child!" A hush falls over the room as I snap the gates of my emotions closed, afraid of what else might come gushing out.

Breathing hard, I say, "I'm going to my room."

"Leave your phone," my mom says, her voice cold, shuttered against all the hurtful things I said.

Jaw clenched, I hold my phone out.

As she reaches for it, her eyes meet mine, searching for something I'm afraid she won't find.

"Thank you," she says, her tone communicating everything but gratitude.

"You're welcome," I snap, spinning to the stairs.

"Oh, Claire?" At my mom's call, I pause on the landing, unwilling to turn around. "You're grounded," she says, choking on the words—I've never been grounded before, never gave her a reason.

With a jerky nod, I launch myself up the last steps and slam the door. Once in my room, I pace for hours. When I stop, I find myself standing in front of my homemade plaque. The words seem to mock me. Everything feels impossible. And God seems far, far away.

I turn from the words, unable to understand what's gotten into me and wondering what it is that left to give it room.

CHAPTER SEVEN

"A man did disappear, but on further inquiry, it was a *disappearance* encouraged by his wife after a gambling mishap. He returned about a fortnight ago, having earned back the money he lost." Torren guffaws at his tale before sobering and continuing in a deep scratchy voice, "The real problem is the mosquitoes." My one-time mentor's worn hands clench his mug of ale. "Unnatural mosquitoes." I study the man before me, feeling the tension build in the air.

Slapping at an imagined bug on her arm, Xandra asks, "What's unnatural about the little blood suckers?"

"There's nothing little about these ones." Torren's brow furrows, deepening the weathered lines of his skin. "The size of swallows and desperate for blood. One got a hold of

Percy, practically sucked him dry." A hush falls over the group as I glance at my companions.

We're all seated at a large wooden table in Avalei's common area. Directly upon entering Avalei, Torren had escorted us here for a little refreshment and a load of gossip. 'Gossip' being disturbing tales of various beasts attacking Avalei. It isn't as bad as the drunken informant made it seem, but it isn't good either. This place of peace isn't overrun with animals, but it is being taken over by fear.

I brush my hand over a deep groove in the tabletop, remembering the knife that created it. Across the table, Asha stares out the window, lips pursed in thought. Beside me, Xandra perches on the edge of the bench, hanging on Torren's every word, desperate to get on with the job. Just down from her, Reilynn sits with her shoulders slumped. The knight seems uncharacteristically tired.

My gaze shifts to Greymore, curious to know his thoughts. He sits at the end of the table, a bit apart from the rest of us. I try to get a read on him, but, as usual, his face is obscured by his hood, and it seems our emotional link is disconnected.

I point out the doorway to a large pile of wood, one of many surrounding the settlement. "Do the bonfires keep them away?"

Torren follows my gaze. "The smoke did. But we haven't seen them in weeks."

I drag a dagger across the worn tabletop before tapping it against my mug. "Do you think they'll come back?"

"Yes," Torren pauses, his hesitation adding weight to his next words. "I'm not sure why they came, but I suspect they'll return for the same reason. If only we knew."

Xandra teeters on the edge of the bench, Asha narrows her focused gaze, Reilynn droops forward, and Greymore thoughtfully tilts his head. I study their varied reactions, looking for an answer, but it seems one isn't forthcoming.

Troubled, Torren taps his fist on the table. "It could—" A scuffle at the wide entryway interrupts his words. Seeing the cause, Torren's lips curve. "Zel."

"Zel?" I spring from the bench, barely gaining my feet in time to catch the girl's body as it collides into mine.

"Nix!" she screeches, squeezing me so tight a muffled grunt leaks from me.

Placing my hands on her shoulders, I push her back. "Let me look at you." Bright brown eyes and a wide smile greet me. Zel's hair falls in soft auburn curls, framing a face that's a charming mix of childish innocence and womanly beauty.

I offer Torren a sympathetic smile. "You're going to be in trouble with this one."

"Going to be?" he asks, humor filling his words. "I've been in trouble since the day she came squawking into this world." He drops an arm over her narrow shoulders. "Thirteen long years."

"Father," Zel says in a long-suffering voice. "You know they've been the best years of your life."

"Longest," Torren quips, before turning to my crew. "Now let me introduce you to Nix's friends."

Seeming to finally notice the other people at the table, particularly Greymore, Zel brushes a hand over her simple brown dress and straightens her hair. As Torren makes introductions, she offers a demure, well-executed curtsy to each member of my crew.

Acquaintances made, Zel says, "Welcome to Avalei. Has Father shown you around?"

"He didn't get the chance," Xandra chimes in. "Nix was too eager to get rumors and food."

"As weapons for hire, we literally live off of both," I respond before pulling Zel from under her father's arm. "But let's show them the place!" Gesturing for the group to follow me, I drop my arm across my young friend's shoulders.

Head bent toward hers, I say in an overloud whisper, "Let me tell you about this wild group. Reilynn trained with knights but couldn't technically become one because—as a woman—she was smarter than them." Zel grins at my feminist dig, and I shrug. "Their loss, our gain. But she is very knight-like, lots of honor and all that."

We exit the building, our feet slowing as we reach the middle of the clearing.

Sensing the crew crowding around us, I continue, "Now, Xandra came from a town near the base of the White Plains. Tough, hardy stock, but for some reason the maker saw fit to put more size in her heart and less in her stature. She left her family of 12 to find a better use for her talents. And to escape comments about her size...which didn't actually work. I mean, look at how tiny she is. I think she must be part fairy, all flitty and petite..." I hear an angry huff behind me and add, "But the way Xandra uses that shield and ball and chain really is magic."

"That's right!" Xandra exclaims, using my shoulders to launch herself above us and peer down at little Zel.

Shaking her off with a smile, I say, "Asha came from across the sea, from the land of dragons. She's everything she appears to be, which is saying something. I would praise her more, but her humble sensibilities would be greatly offended, and you don't ever want to offend an elf."

"What about Greymore?" Zel asks, her long, dark lashes fluttering.

"Greymore?" I raise my voice to be sure he'll hear my assessment. "He doesn't have much to say. I think he's embarrassed by his girlish voice."

"Untrue," Greymore says, his voice rumbling and deep.

Zel offers a little sigh at my side, whispering, "There's nothing girlish about that man."

A wave of smug emotion rolls over me, letting me know he heard and appreciated her words. As Zel launches into a conversation with Asha about her deadly fan, I drop my arm from around the girl. Stepping to Greymore, I pat his shoulder and say, "At least you can charm the young ones."

Before I can move away, he stops me with a hand on my back. "Not just the young ones." His thumb trips lightly up my spine as his emotions roll over me, colliding with my own. He leans closer, whispering, "Asha likes me, too."

I jerk away from his well-earned arrogance and say, "We'll start here," with an embarrassingly unsteady voice.

Dagger flicking between my fingers, I point to the massive building we just exited. A mix between a thatched hall and a tent, the building's roof is covered in rushes, but the walls are a stiff canvas staked to the ground. At the doors, the canvas is tied back, revealing the long rows of tables. "This is the common area and community hall. This is where you'll come for meals, meetings, and mingling."

"Who cooks?" Xandra asks, always thinking with her stomach.

"The cooks," I answer with a smile. "In Avalei, all resources are pooled together and jobs are chosen. If there is a need unfulfilled, the community leaders meet and discuss a solution, which is then voted on. Majority rules. And women vote here, too."

"Very forward thinking," Reilynn says, her helmet tucked under one arm and a wistful turn to her wide lips.

"Yeah," I say. "For this time…" At the curious looks from those around me, I continue, "The other buildings here on the base level are a smithy, a weapon's hold, a storehouse for goods and supplies, a healer's hut…all structures used by and accessible to the community."

"But this," I lean back, my arms spreading wide, to stare at the trees rising over us, "this is the best part."

Above us, nestled in the trees, are houses and hammocks. Built in all shapes and sizes, the structures are interconnected with ropes, wooden bridges, and pulley systems. The bridges even extend into the third and fourth levels of the wall, a network winding in and out of the defense. The stark, grey chiseled rock melds with the worn wood and fraying ropes—order and whimsy combined.

"Everyone sleeps up there," I say. "We can string up our hammocks—"

"We saved your house!" Zel exclaims.

"What?" I give Torren a sharp look. "I told you to use it!"

"No one needed it," he claims, a determined gleam in his eye. "Besides, it's yours now for the reason it was yours before; no one wanted a house that high. Too difficult to cart up provisions."

I look over the bustling settlement of no less than five hundred, obviously more populated than in my youth. "I find that hard to believe."

"I imagine you do. Probably as hard as it is for me to believe you've been gone five years." He tempers his words with a smile, but I still feel their punch. Looking closer, I notice the streaks of grey in his hair, the pinch around his eyes.

Torren hasn't just been worrying about Avalei. He's been worrying over me.

"I'm sorry to have been gone so long and to have caused you stress." I apologize as sincerely as I can. I *am* sorry he worried, but I'm not sorry I left. I look to my crew, my adopted family—minus one half-orc—and offer a wistful smile. "Looks like we're sleeping in my old place." I point to a home at the highest level in the trees. Larger than most, the entire square structure is surrounded by a deck that connects to no less than three bridges, two pulleys, and a plethora of ropes.

"Can we see it now?" Asha asks, her soft tone doing nothing to hide her curiosity.

Not ready to face my crew's analysis of my former dwelling and unsure what embarrassing things I might find up there, I say, "Let's check out the rest of the wall first."

I lead the group, some eager, some reluctant, toward the wall. The ground is higher on this side, leaving us level with the second story of the fortification.

Stepping through a large archway, we enter the heart of the wall. Moving down the walkway that can easily accommodate three wagons, I point to the ladders lining the side and leading to four-foot square holes in the ceiling. "These all lead to the next level where there are more to the next and so on and so forth. They have trap doors that can be barred shut, but they're almost always open. If you want, we can go see the view from the top. We'll—"

"Mr. Tarklow," a deep, cultured voice interrupts us. "Is this the adventurer you were telling me about? Nix?"

"Chancellor Ivers." Torren turns to the man, his voice barely concealing his impatience, but I recognize that extra dose of formality in Torren's tone. It's the tone he used for me in my youth when I mercilessly demanded his attention for petty reasons while he had bigger problems on his mind. And, from the looks of it, this chancellor character is the demanding, pretentious type.

Dressed in a bedazzled tunic, fitted coat, and pantaloons better fit for court, the man should look ridiculous, but—with his dark, sweeping hair, strong jaw, and bright green eyes—he somehow makes the whole thing work.

And it works *extremely* well.

I hear Xandra sigh wistfully as Reilynn straightens to attention.

"Won't you introduce me?" the chancellor asks eagerly, throwing a dazzling smile my way.

With an indulgent smile, Torren gestures to me, his voice filled with fatherly pride. "This is Nix, the Defender of Avalei."

I flush at the title I once promoted—when I was a child with far too much interest in weapons and too little in farming. Strange that by leaving, I grew into the label I once naively claimed.

Ignoring my embarrassment, Torren continues, "And these are her companions, Reilynn, Asha, and Xandra."

Xandra offers a perfectly executed curtsy while Reilynn salutes sharply. Asha nods, but her hand rests lightly on her unique weapon. At least one of my crew still has her wits and memories.

My crew hasn't exactly had good experiences with chancellors in the past. They always want to work a deal, claiming to be saving money for the king, but those funds rarely make it back to the royal city.

Chancellor Ivers bows to each of us. Rising, he offers each member of my crew a disarming grin. I watch, amused, as even Asha is affected, her hand easing casually away from her weapon.

"How fortunate for me!" Ivers says. "My first royal assignment, and I happen upon the most prolific band of adventurers in the kingdom. Meeting not only Avalei's staunchest defender, but you three! Your deeds of heroism and support to the king are spoken of often in the royal city."

Xandra beams, Reilynn smirks, and Asha falls into a stance more relaxed than defensive.

Gesturing to the shadows, Torren says, "And this is...Greymore." He stumbles over the name, glancing at me, but I shrug. It's always been simply Greymore to us.

"Greymore?" Chancellor Ivers eyes the hooded man critically. "Isn't it Lord Greymore?"

Greymore inclines his head.

"Lord Greymore?" Xandra mouths.

"Shattered shields," Reilynn whispers in a stunned voice while Asha's lips curve in a knowing smile.

Chancellor Ivers offers him a sharp bow, which Greymore returns. Even dressed in a hood and leather armor, Greymore somehow makes the motion look exact...and natural. He really is a Lord.

Turning back to my crew, Ivers continues, "I believe it is almost time for the supper meal. It would be my honor if you would join me."

A smoldering smile enhances his request. "I could eat," Xandra says, sliding her arm through the chancellor's, ensuring his escort. Not to be outdone, Reilynn takes his other arm. Asha follows, Torren at her side.

I guess the tour is over.

As he moves to join them, I grab Greymore's forearm, letting the rest of the group leave us behind. "Lord?" I hiss. "Why didn't you tell me?"

"You didn't ask."

I release his arm to tap my fingers on the hilt of my scimitar. "I don't usually go around asking people if they're nobility."

"And I don't usually go around announcing it," Greymore responds with a smirk.

My hands still, and I glare at his shadowy visage for a time, trying to see all he hides—with little success. All I can sense from him is a sort of affectionate amusement.

"You know what?" I say, my eyes narrowing to slits. "I liked you better when you were mute."

I turn away, only to be assaulted by the *feel* of his smile, and—I must admit—it isn't an altogether unpleasant sensation.

CHAPTER EIGHT

Curled in my window seat, I finish shading in the hood on the sketched form. Greymore is nobility. I silently applaud my imagination. Maybe tonight I'll discover I'm really a princess. Princess Nix. It does have a nice ring to it. And Avalei… It was worth the months of dreaming to get there. If I could make anything in my fantasy world real, it would be Avalei.

Out of habit, I reach to check the time on my phone before remembering I'm grounded from it and everything else for two more days. It's been a long twelve days, but I honestly can't say I didn't deserve it.

The hardest part is the distance from Trent. Being in different grades, we don't have any classes together, and so lunch is really the only time we see each other.

Understandably, he's pretty put out by the whole arrangement, but in just two days, I'll be free again.

Suddenly, a pounding comes from the front door. I'm home alone, so I peek out the window. Seeing the familiar yet unexpected car out front, I rush down the stairs and throw open the door. "Jillian! Is everything okay?"

"It's fine, I'm fine," she assures me, but standing on the porch, nervously tossing her phone from one hand to the other, she doesn't look fine.

"Are you sure you're okay?" I ask as I step back, giving her room to enter.

"I'm really okay…I just," she pauses to take a bolstering breath, "Nix, I have something you've got to see." She pulls up something on her phone and stretches it out to me. As I reach for it, she changes her mind and pulls it back. "I was at the movies tonight with a big group of people…"

"Okay…?" I say, leaning against the wall at my back, sensing I'll need some extra support.

"Okay, well…about halfway through the movie I went to go to the bathroom, and I saw Trent with another girl." I open my mouth to argue, so she rushes on. "I wasn't sure it was him or if you were even still dating, so I asked Adam, and he told me you guys still were. But, Nix, he wasn't just with another girl, they were making out and—"

"No!" I say, cutting her off. "No, Trent was going to some family thing tonight. It wasn't him."

"Nix," Jillian huffs in exasperation, clenching her phone. "I *saw* him. I have no reason to lie. He's the liar, not me."

Numb, I mumble the first thought that crosses my mind. "Well, you never did like him."

Jillian throws her hands in the air. "I can't believe you. I wouldn't make this up. I wouldn't do that to you if I wasn't sure. I can't believe—" This time, she cuts herself off. "You know what, never mind. I knew that you wouldn't believe me. Somehow, I just knew you'd side with the cheater." She holds her phone out to me. "Just watch this."

With trembling hands, I take the phone, not wanting to see what's on there. If what she says is true, it's embarrassing. Embarrassing to be so wrong about someone. Tapping, I start the video as Jillian paces. It's almost too dark to make out the forms of two people locked together, but the camera moves closer, and I can see hair and a shape that could be Trent and not much more. "Jillian, this could be anyone."

She stops her movement to meet my eye with a look of pure disbelief. "Seriously, he's not even here and you're taking his word over mine?" She shakes her head in disgust. "Just keep watching."

I turn my attention back to the screen. The two people have pulled apart, but the image is bouncing and blurry. The only clear thing is the audio. I hear Jillian ripping whoever it is apart. Then he answers, and my knees give out, buckling under me.

I slide jerkily down the wall, listening as Trent laughs Jillian off. Then, his voice growing harder, he says to someone off camera. "Some kind of friend you are."

It's Adam's voice that responds. "I promised I wouldn't tell Claire, and I didn't."

The video stops, and I drop my forehead to my knees. "This can't be real," I mumble wishfully.

"Well, it is," Jillian says, her voice soft, but lacking warmth. She slides the phone from my limp grip. "At least now you know," she says and hesitantly steps away.

I want to call for her, but I don't think I have the right. As her footsteps retreat, my hands clench together, squeezing tighter and tighter. She opens the door but pauses on the threshold. "I'm sorry, Claire. I really am."

Then she's gone.

I don't cry. There's enough emotion for an overflow, but I've been a fool enough for today. It's all so mortifying. The betrayal hurts, yes, but the mortification is what presses on me, keeping me pinned in place. My mind scrambles, offering a wild assortment of reasons, excuses, and denials. I stay in the entry, my head buried in my hands, thinking until there's a knock on the door.

"Claire?" Trent's voice skyrockets me to my feet. For a split second, my flight reflex tells me to just run upstairs and bury myself in bed, but I tamp it down. I want to hear his version. I *need* to hear it.

After a couple of deep breaths, I open the door. Trent is leaning against the doorway, looking all stormy and broody and attractive. My weak heart skips a beat. "Can I come in?" he asks, a hint of desperation in his remarkable green eyes.

"No," I say, keeping the door between us.

Tense, Trent steps across the threshold. "Seriously? No?" he says with a tight, jeering smile.

Not up for games, I step past him to the stoop. Shutting the door behind me, I say, "I'd like to be ungrounded in two days, so breaking my parents' rule about not being alone with boys in the house is probably a bad idea."

Seeing I'm willing to talk, Trent gives me a smoldering grin and says, "I'm so ready for you to be free."

Strangely, his expression and words don't affect me. Instead, I find myself blaming him for not only tonight, but for the last two weeks. I cross my arms over my chest, pretending to not be a mass of hurt and confusion. "Why?" I demand. "Seems like it would be easier for you to date other girls with me grounded."

"Claire." He reaches a hand toward my face, fingers outstretched. When I step out of reach, he sighs. "You know my dad is looking to run for office this next year, right?"

I nod, wondering where he could possibly be going with this.

He runs a hand through his hair, messing up his typical perfect style. "Well, that girl I was with tonight…" At his hesitation, my hand fists over my heart, and he quickly continues, "Her dad is doing a ton to support my dad's campaign. Our families go way back, so I've known Serena forever. I guess she just went through this horrible breakup, and my parents asked me to take her out…as a friend." He eases toward me, eyes wide and contrite. "But Serena had different ideas, and when she started…well, I didn't want to hurt her feelings after everything she'd been through, and I've been missing you so much and…" Inching closer, he places his hands on my arms and rubs his thumbs over my skin as he ducks his head to meet my eyes. "She was just a stand-in, and I was stupid and weak."

Curling his fingers, he pulls me to him. I resist, keeping my eyes locked on his. He lets me search his gaze, willing me to see his honesty.

It all makes sense, except… "Why would you ask Adam to lie to me?"

"Adam." A hardness flashes in Trent's eyes, and his lip twists. "I asked Adam not to tell you I was going to the movies with her, because I knew you already felt really bad about being grounded and us being apart, and I didn't want you to worry, babe." Removing one hand from my arm, he gestures between us. "This is what I didn't want: you hurt and these misunderstandings between us."

"You made me look like an idiot, Trent. And you could have just told me," I say as he continues drawing circles on my arm with his thumbs, causing my resolve to falter.

"How, Claire?" He brushes a finger over my cheek. "You didn't have a phone, and I didn't know my parents had committed me to taking Serena out until right before the movie." With his other hand, he cups my face. "Next time, I'll drive over here and tell you my plans first."

"Next time? Next time you take another girl out?"

"No, Claire." Trent looks at me with absolute adoration, and my lungs seize up before stuttering back to life. "Next time I think something might come between us, I'll be here at your door, making sure it can't and won't."

He cups my face in his hands and moves even closer. So close I can't breathe, can't think, can't hold on to my anger.

"Forgive me. Please," he whispers.

Before I've even made a conscious decision, I feel my head nod.

His face breaks out in a blindly bright smile before he draws me to him and kisses me slowly.

When he pulls back, he peppers my cheek and nose with kisses, all while murmuring his thanks and making beautiful promises. I reel from his sweet attention, from being absolutely done with Trent to barreling straight into love.

By the time I'm ungrounded, I've embraced my decision to stay with Trent. With conditions. He doesn't realize it, but I put him on a sort of boyfriend probation. I watch him closer and not just because he's nice to look at, though that doesn't hurt.

School is a little intense the first few days. I can practically hear people's thoughts as they label me a doormat. But once the story of Serena and her throwing herself at Trent surfaces, people are a lot less judgmental—at least toward me. I feel kind of bad for Serena, the homewrecking villain in our little drama. I imagine she was going through some pretty emotional stuff at the time, and her stupid move didn't help her in the least. Luckily, she doesn't go to our school.

Jillian keeps her distance, but I can sense her disgust whenever she sees Trent and me together. Sadly, I accept that in keeping Trent, I truly lost her.

As far as Trent and Adam go, there's a lot of tension—at least initially.

Apparently, Adam knew Trent was going to a certain movie with Serena—a movie he suspiciously showed up to with a huge group of friends. Adam is unapologetic about the whole thing, and Trent doesn't seem to want to discuss it, so they just let it go.

Every day, the resentment fades until things are back to normal between the two friends.

But Trent does start spending more time at my house and less with Adam. He does chores and works his charm on my parents in what I assume is an attempt to never have me grounded again. He gets along fairly well with Dillon, especially when they watch football. He befriends each member of my family, all while showering me with crazy amounts of attention—a whisper in my ear. A secretive smile. A sneaky kiss in the hall. He's constantly looking at me or touching me. It seems there's always a point of contact between us, like he needs to reassure himself I'm there with a hand on my shoulder, hip, or back.

I find his devotion intoxicating.

Within just a few short weeks, the past is behind us. The idea of probation is kicked right out of my mind to make room for Trent, Trent, and more Trent.

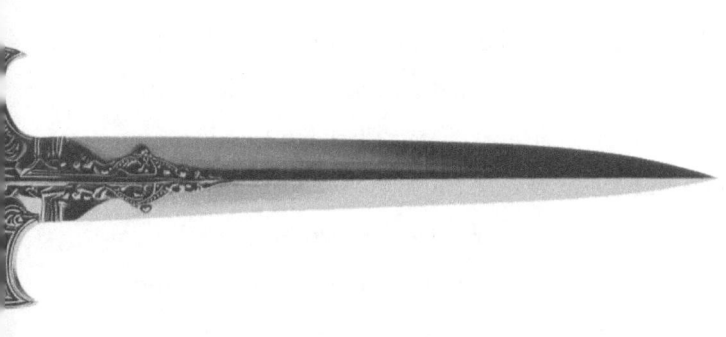

Chapter Nine

"It's Phillip," I say, reaching the top of another ladder. "Lord Phillip Greymore."

"No." Greymore offers me a hand, pulling me onto the fourth floor of the wall.

"Terrence," Asha supplies, handing her bow up before ascending the ladder with quick, precise steps. Greymore shakes his head, as I return her weapon.

"If we guessed it right, would you tell us?" I ask, beginning to doubt the success of our little game.

"Perhaps," Greymore answers, amusement coloring his response.

"If there isn't even a chance of winning, the game isn't fun," I complain. I spread my hands apart, palms up, in the universal gesture of surrender. "I'm done."

"So am I," Xandra says. "This climb is brutal." Belying her words, she springs from the ladder and strides down the hall to the next, and last, ladder. "I can't believe I had to leave my shield," she complains…again.

"I told you there was a wider opening further down," I say, catching up to her in the vast interior of the wall. Some of the holes connecting the levels are smaller than others, and we chose the more direct, narrow route for today's trip to the battlements. "You're just angry because Reilynn stayed back to chat with Ivers about all the glorious advancements in a knight's training."

"I *did* want to hear about the new weapons," she says with a sniff, flipping her loose mane behind her shoulder. "But I can see why the chancellor didn't want to come on this particular death climb, and I don't think our over-armored knight could have survived the trip a second time."

Glancing back, I catch Asha's eye and share a smile. I'm not sure how Ivers did it, but Xandra is obviously a little enamored with the chancellor. Poor tiny thing fell prey to all that tall, dark handsomeness. "I don't know what you see in the guy," I say. "He's a chancellor and wasn't it you who called them 'money-grubbing, sallow-faced secretaries'? That was *you*, right?"

"I was misinformed." She puts a little skip in her step, making it difficult for me to keep up. "Besides, Ivers is a rather fine specimen."

Refusing to agree, I tap a blade against the bracers at my wrist. "Shallow, aren't we?"

"As a stream." Xandra practically sings the words. Reaching the ladder, she hops up, skipping rungs the entire ten-foot climb. At the top, she peers down at me—thick hair nearly concealing her wicked smile—and says, "Unlike some people, I like men who don't cover themselves with a hood." Her eyes dart to Greymore as if surprised to find him following us. "Lord Greymore! There you are. I was just saying—"

The ominous scratch of my razor-sharp dagger against the wood of the ladder draws Xandra's attention. Balking at my not-so-subtle threat and malicious smirk, she says, "IguessBrutus" as if it's one word before disappearing.

"Good guess, don't you think?" I say, slipping the dagger back in place and winking at Asha before climbing up.

Reaching the top of the wall, I nod at the guard as he passes. There are always two active guards on the wall. During their watch, they walk a continuous circuit through the levels of the defense, always ready to raise the alarm.

I search around for Xandra before finally spotting her metal greaves peeking between two battlements as she leans to look out over Avalei.

Remembering youthful explorations, searches for magical elements, and mythical stories of power hidden within the valley, I come up beside my spunky friend and say, "This place is something else, isn't it?"

"I do like it here," she admits.

"A perfect refuge," Asha says in a hushed whisper, joining us.

We crowd between the stones, staring out over the massive valley below.

Avalei's settlement spreads across the shadow of the wall. Running the span of the defense, the bridges, homes, and community buildings are barely visible through the canopy of the trees. On the rising currents comes the buzz of activity below, of life.

Beyond the trees, fields and a large orchard are visible. A stream meanders through the fields before disappearing underground, the water blue and sparkling. At the far end of the valley, there are cog-sized boulders scattered about, encircling a small lake. And, rising over it all, are the sheer insurmountable cliffs of The Razor.

"I should invite the chancellor up here," Xandra says, gaze dreamy and distant. "Seems like a good place for a rendezvous."

"It is," I say the words before I consider the consequences.

Both girls turn slowly to look at me and—a battlement away—Greymore's hood tilts toward us. "How could you possibly know that?" Xandra asks, resting her chin in her hand. "Or, the better question: who?"

I pull a dagger. Embarrassed, I focus on flicking it up by the blade and catching it by the hilt. Blade. Hilt. Blade. Hilt. "Percy Penworth," I finally mumble.

"Percy P—" Xandra stops. "Wait. Is this the same guy who was attacked by the mosquito?" At my nod, she begins to laugh so hard I fear she might fall from the wall. "I wonder…," she gasps, "I wonder if kissing you was like being attacked by the mosquito…you both sucked!"

Now, I'm *hoping* she'll fall from the wall.

I continue flicking the dagger. Blade. Hilt. Blade. Hilt. Faster and faster as I say in an eerily calm voice, "I've heard there's a painless method for removing someone's voice box, Asha. Should we try it?"

Instantly, Xandra's laughter dies. "There is not."

"No," I say, leaning so close to her that the glint of my blade reflects in her eyes. "But I'm willing to try."

"Let us go to the tower," Asha says, cutting the tension caused by my knife.

I flip the blade back to my belt, a signal that I'm ready to drop the whole conversation. Xandra nods in agreement and, as one, we pull back and stride toward one of the three towers. Along the way, I point out the strategically placed murder-holes—openings in the floor used to fire on any attacker within the bottom levels of the wall.

Xandra pauses to stare down into one. "Think I could fit through that?"

"I think you could get stuck in it," I answer, dragging her away as Asha grins in amusement, and I sense Greymore's eyeroll. Of all my crew, Xandra is the only one who tries his patience…and mine.

We reach the nearest tower, an offside one. It's placed about thirty feet from the massive gate and the Dual Blades beyond. A huge arched opening creates a pass-through under the tower, making it feel like a tunnel. Another ladder waits in the corner to take us to the catwalk surrounding the structure.

"More climbing?" Xandra complains. "With all this upward movement, shouldn't we be in heaven by now?"

Following behind us, Greymore gruffly responds, "Hardly. Heaven's quiet."

As I choke back a snort and Asha's melodic laugh echoes through the space, Xandra faces Greymore, her hands on her hips. She cocks her head to the side. "You know. You're kind of like a puppy, always following us around. Is it Rover?"

Greymore refuses to acknowledge her guess, instead moving up the ladder.

"I believe I am through climbing." Asha resolutely spins away from the offending ladder. "I will check the fortifications at the gate."

"Don't open them," I warn.

"Why? And how do they open anyway?" Xandra is wholly curious.

Knowing if I don't explain it, she'll open it just to figure the whole mechanism out, I say, "Like a double door, they swing inward using a gear like the one below."

Crouching down to peer under the archway, I continue, "You can see the brace from here that keeps it securely closed. And you have to be on the inside to open or close them. But they're almost always closed. Keeps the snowcats out."

"Got it. Get to your climbing."

Curls bouncing, she flits away, calling over her shoulder, "I bet if you laid one on Greymore, he'd be more inclined to think of this as heaven."

Asha stops my hand inches from the dagger at my belt. "I was just going to give her a little haircut. She has plenty," I justify.

"She also has reason to suspect something between you and Greymore, but that does not mean she should mention it," Asha says, full of mature logic.

Hands gripping hilts, I ask in an overly controlled, tight voice, "What exactly is *suspect* about Greymore and me? You're with us all the time, so you know absolutely nothing is going on."

Asha flicks out her fan, spinning her deadly blades around. Smart, really. During this type of conversation, it's good to be armed. "It is the way you look at each oth—"

"You can't even see his face," I huff.

"And also, you must consider the emotional link," she continues, spinning her fan and ignoring my perfectly sound argument.

"An emotional link I have absolutely no control over!" I hiss. "It's not *my* fault the man speaks with his emotions!"

Fan concealing the bottom half of her face, Asha raises a brow in a look that would appear haughty on anyone less composed.

I grab the fan from her, snapping it shut. "Leave it," I say before thrusting the weapon into her waiting hand and storming up the ladder. I think I could happily throw each and every member of my crew off the tower today. All the innuendos about Greymore make me antsy.

I can't be involved with anyone here in my dreams because in *real life*, I have a boyfriend. What does it say about me that my subconscious created a love interest for my incredibly realistic dreamworld? Where's my loyalty? Admittedly, Greymore could be my mind's version of Trent, but something tells me he isn't. He's more introverted, more pensive, more….something. Just *more*.

At the top of the tower, I purposefully avoid Greymore, taking the catwalk to the side opposite the gate. On the stone below, Xandra twirls with her ball and chain. The two maces fly through the air as her hair streams around her, a girlish, yet deadly, movement.

I watch her for a time before turning my attention to the wall. My eyes track over the well-maintained stone battlements with pride.

Noticing a strange shadow, I lean forward, squinting. Six feet behind Xandra, the color of the wall looks right, but the shape is wrong. The outline almost looks like…a tail flicks in the shadows.

"Snowcat!" I scream, diving from the tower.

But it's too late.

The animal lunges at Xandra, its massive claws extended. Still spinning, Xandra's maces crash into the side of the cat, throwing it back against a battlement…but not before its six-inch claws rake across Xandra's stomach, piercing through her armor and into her flesh.

In utter shock, Xandra stumbles back, arm clutching her stomach.

I land on the stone floor, somersaulting forward in an effort to absorb the impact, but my right shoulder slams into the unforgiving ground. Regaining my feet, I move between the cat and my injured friend.

Pain shooting through my injured shoulder, I unsheathe my scimitars and face the beast, who is now blending into the battlements behind it.

Feeling cornered, it growls before rushing me. With a cry, I lunge toward it.

The cat springs into the air. I jump to meet it—arms extended and airborne.

Midflight, I hear an arrow whir over me and a bolt skim by. Side by side, they strike the beast—embedding themselves between the cat's eyes.

The hits from Greymore and Asha drive the animal backward. With an earthshaking thud, it drops to the ground, unmoving.

I skid to a stop inches away.

Heart beating erratically, I search the animal for life.

Seeing none, I sheathe my scimitars and look to Xandra. She struggles to rise before collapsing.

I rush to her fallen body, my mind screaming in denial. It all happened so fast. So unexpectedly. I wasn't on my guard. Didn't expect danger here. Not on my wall.

Dropping to my knees in front of her, I roll her to her back. I flip her tresses aside and search her eyes.

"Nix," she says, but her voice is weak, fading.

Fumbling with the straps of her damaged breastplate, I toss the useless armor aside. Ripping my jerkin from my shoulders, I press the garment to the lacerations spanning her stomach, but the blood continues to gather beneath her, the pool growing at an alarming rate.

Helpless, I meet her pained eyes. "Don't go, Xandra. Stay," I plead, shaking her as her eyes grow glassy and flutter closed.

* * * *

"I've done everything I can." Reilynn exits the healer's hut, blood on her hands. "I tried to remember everything she told me about herbs and medicines," the knight continues, "but it wasn't enough. The healer's doing what she can now, but I don't know." Her voice cracks in a rare show of emotion as Asha puts her arm around her, sharing her grief. "I just don't know," she whispers.

And no one does. No one knows how the snowcat got through the gates. No one knows why these animals are attacking.

No one knows a blasted thing!

...except that Xandra might not make it.

Blood pounding, I turn away.

Infuriated, powerless, and terrified, I tear through the settlement, storming into the community hall where Torren, Ivers, and Greymore are discussing the attack.

"Tell me you know something," I say, approaching their table.

"I'm sorry, Nix," Torren says. "All we know is we did maintenance on the gate a few days ago. The snowcat might have wandered in then or…"

"…or it was let in." I finish the thought he won't put into words. "And there's no way it could have jumped in?"

"Before, I would have said it was impossible, but seeing what they can do…" Torren shakes his head in quiet disbelief. "I just don't know." No one knew of the camouflaging ability of the snowcat—another terrible surprise in a day of too many.

"Could magic be involved?" I ask, wanting to explore every option.

Ivers scoffs. I shift my body to him slowly, a dagger drawn.

"Nix," Greymore warns. I know killing the king's man would be in bad form, but—right now—a little threat doesn't seem too far out of order.

"We know magic is scarce in the kingdom," Torren says in a low, calming tone. "So rare some think it extinct," he glances at Ivers, "but I'm not willing to discount any possibility just yet."

"And after the mosquitoes, massive bees, and giant roaches you fought off, I'm not willing to call this a fluke attack," I say, dropping to the bench beside Torren. Putting aside my need for some violence, I think of the people. Tapping a blade against the nicked tabletop, I lay out my list of demands. "We need to add to the guard. No one should be out on the wall alone. Any oddity should be reported.

And everyone needs to brush up on their training." None of these changes would have kept Xandra from injury, but right now, I need to act.

"I'll make the announcements tomorrow," Torren agrees.

Jaw tight, I say, "Overall, we just have to be extra vigilant. Always expecting an attack." I stare into the flames of the nearest torch, working to loosen my overstrung nerves.

"Perhaps…," Ivers pauses, eyeing the dagger I'm twisting through my fingers. "Perhaps we should consider an evacuation."

"What!" I slam my dagger into the soft wood, nerves pinging apart. The movement causes pain to shoot across my injured shoulder, but I ignore it, consumed by the horrifying image of an empty Avalei. Leaving the blade buried, I lean across the table, leveling my glare on Ivers. "We won't abandon Avalei, Chancellor. These are people's lives and livelihoods we're talking about." Standing, I yank the blade free. "I'm going on watch."

I stride through the settlement like a rampaging bull. Abandon Avalei! Like it's replaceable! Like it isn't worth the effort to protect!

Reaching the outskirts of the settlement, I duck under the branches of a massive tree. The boughs droop down to brush the ground and offer a sanctuary of sorts. I lean against the trunk and close my eyes, attempting to rein in my emotions. But they keep pulling at me, bucking against my restraint, and tearing me apart.

I'm losing Avalei.

Failing these people. My people. I thought I would just stroll in, and my crew and I would solve all their problems, but instead, I've put Xandra at risk. After already losing Betah, it's almost more than I can take.

Is this what my dream world has become? A place where I watch the people I care about the most suffer and disappear?

A body leans against the tree beside me, dousing me with feeling. I don't even have to open my eyes to see who it is. "Go away, Greymore."

"No."

"Seriously, I'm not in the mood. Go away."

But he doesn't leave. He simply stands at my side, unwilling to leave me to face my demons alone. Absently, I rub my injured shoulder and remember the flash of claws, the fall of crimson blood.

Finally, I break the silence. "I brought her here. We came to protect this place. How am I going to do that when I can't even protect her? When I don't even know where the danger is coming from? How can I fight what I can't see? What I can't prepare for?"

"Nix, we'll figure this out." His tone is low and soothing, his emotions peaceful and calm.

But right now, peace isn't what I want.

I want a fight.

I just need to find the enemy.

Chapter Ten

With a spinning kick, I take my opponent to the ground. "Yes!" I yell at the screen, my thumbs flying over the buttons on my controller.

We're spending a lazy Saturday morning at Trent's with some old-school gaming. "You're going down now," I say as I scoot forward on the leather cushion, almost sliding off the couch in my eagerness.

Next to me, Trent jumps to his feet, slamming the buttons on his controller with a frantic intensity. "Quit button mashing, Claire," he growls.

Caught up in the moment, I ignore the warning in his tone. "I know exactly what I'm doing, Trent."

"She's totally cooking you, man," Adam says from the couch opposite us, laughing. He's sprawled lazily across the love seat, his relaxed stance in direct opposition to Trent's clenched hands and bulging veins.

Knowing he'll charge, I focus on the hi-def screen as Trent's character comes at me. I dodge, jumping over him, spinning, and crashing an elbow into his back. The massive character falls, his health bar dangerously low.

"Fin…nish him. Fin…nish him," Adam chants.

On my feet, I smirk and—with a series of quick hand movements—input my character's critical attack. The frost tower slams into Trent's man, throwing him into the air and slamming him down as I'm declared the winner.

Tossing the controller aside, I fling my arms wide, spinning in a slow, victorious circle. "Thank you. Thank…" My words and beaming smile fade when Trent's eyes lock on mine.

Furious, he chucks the controller at the couch, where it bounces to the floor. "You cheated," he states, his tone flat.

I bite back the urge to apologize. Because Trent's basketball schedule has been crazy, this is our first Saturday together in weeks. I don't want to ruin it. But I also didn't cheat. I didn't do anything wrong at all.

I won.

Which, apparently, was wrong in and of itself.

I open my mouth to attempt to appease Trent when Adam interrupts. "—don't be a poor loser, dude. She warned us she used to play Street Fighter with her brother." Taking the controller from my sweaty hands, Adam sits back on the couch. His actions are non-threatening, but there's a hint of steel in his voice. "Let's you and me go a round or two before I have to leave."

"Fine," Trent says, scooping his controller from the floor and flopping onto the couch. "But no cheap moves."

"Those are the only kind I know," Adam jokes, breaking through the strain of the moment.

Trent laughs, a shallow, light sound as he shifts in his seat, completely ignoring me. "I'm gonna crush you."

As they choose their characters, I make a mumbled excuse about needing a drink and step to the stairs. Glancing back, I find Adam's eyes on me, concern and something I can't immediately identify in their depths. Whatever it is makes my stomach clench. Twitchy, I rush upstairs.

In the kitchen, I grasp the counter of the island. With my hands clenching the edge, I put a name to the emotion in Adam's gaze. It was pity. My head sags between my outstretched arms. Adam pities me. But why?

Sure, things aren't perfect in my life, but they are good. There is some lingering tension with my parents, but that's not totally unexpected. Trent is still super intense, but he's also amazingly sweet. Things are good, but...

...but there's a part of me that's always stressed. I hate it, this anxiety that bleeds into all the good. It's like I'm waiting, waiting for the next time I mess up, the next time my emotions take over, the next attack. And the events of my dream world aren't making things any easier. There, my anxiety multiplies, consuming something that used to be entertaining and leaving me touchy and irritated.

I wish the dreams would just stop. I just want to relax, to actually sleep, because nothing sounds better than true rest right now. My dreams are becoming too intense, too personal, and too overwhelming. Sometimes I think my heart is more invested in that fake world than the real one. And maybe it's something there or someone there keeping me from connecting with Trent the way I want to.

Maybe Adam's right, maybe pity really is what I deserve.

With a heavy sigh, I release the marble countertop. Rounding the extensive island, I open the fridge and grab a water bottle. Leaning against the sleek white cabinet behind me, I sip my drink. Absentmindedly, I look over the highly polished and expensive kitchen. White is everywhere: white tile, white cabinetry, white counters. All offset by brass hardware and accents. It's a reveal-worthy room, and—like every space in Trent's home—always looks perfect. Sterile and flashy.

Uncomfortable with my thoughts, I move to the stunning living room. Here, the floor-to-ceiling glass doors lead to the pool area. My gaze drifts from the tropical plants to the waterfall feature before landing on the jacuzzi. Now *that* sounds heavenly right now, a place to just relax and let all my stresses melt away—both real and imagined.

"Claire?"

Lost in depressing thoughts, I start. "Hello, Mrs. Evans," I say, hoping Trent's mom won't ask why I'm absentminded and jumpy.

"It's Moira, dear," she responds.

Dressed in slacks and a flowy white blouse, she's remarkably casual today—Saturday attire for a real estate mogul. From the little I've gathered, most of Trent's money and ambition come from her side of the family.

"Yes, Mrs...Moira." Try as I might, I can't seem to get used to calling her by her first name. I follow her into the spotless kitchen.

"How are you today, dear?" she asks, unloading a grocery bag from the nearest health food store.

"Good," I say, hating the platitude even as it falls from my lips. I twist my fingers together in front of me, missing my sketch pad and pencil, but I don't carry them with me all the time like I used to. "Can I help you?" I ask.

She waves me away, her beautiful diamond sparkling. "No, this is the only bag. But I would like to thank you."

"Me?" My curiosity drives me to lean her way.

"Yes, for keeping my Trent closer." With a smile, she stows her reusable bag away.

Having no earthly idea what she's talking about, I flounder, "Umm...closer?"

"Yes," she continues, unaware of my confusion. "Trent always talked about going to college out of state. California or back east somewhere." She waves her hand dismissively in the air. "But now he tells me he's applying to Arizona State to be closer to you. I've been praying he would stay close, and now he will. He may even keep living here."

She glows with joy as I struggle to match her excitement. I *should* be elated at the news, but I'm not. Because, first of all, this shouldn't be news to me. Should it? And second, it changes everything, ramping up my anxiety to all new levels.

I had plans for next year. Plans to play basketball again and try to repair my friendship with Jillian—if she doesn't move away. Plans to do all the stuff I did before a boyfriend took up so much of my time. Of course, I still hoped to be dating Trent, so this is good. Really good. I push my plans aside. Those are short-term, and Trent is long-term. He's fully committed, and I should be too. "He didn't tell me," I say.

"Oh! He was probably going to surprise you." Her face drops, and she clasps my hand. "I'm so sorry!" Patting the back of my hand, she says affectionately, "That's so sweet of him."

"Yeah," I say. "He's pretty great."

She beams at me, pride filling her eyes. "Yes, he is."

I smile into her eyes, hoping my face looks as alight and alive as hers when I think of her son.

"Hey, Mom." The subject of our conversation strides into the room, Adam at his heels. "Claire, there you are. Adam said you went to grab a drink, but I stocked your favorite in the fridge downstairs."

"I just wanted some water." I hold up my nearly empty bottle, searching his face for a hint of his previous anger.

When I whip Dillon at a game, it usually takes him a good half hour to get over it.

Unexpectedly, Trent slides an arm across my shoulder and drops a kiss on my temple.

Apparently, my boyfriend is better at keeping an emotional balance than my brother. Offering us a soft, knowing smile, Moira pats her son's cheek. Then she turns to Adam, asking, "How are you, dear?" I guess, to Moira, everyone is a dear.

"I'm great, Moira, thanks." Adam uses her first name, sounding completely natural and at home. I guess after years of friendship, he is.

"What have you three been up to?" Moira asks. Trent's hand twitches at my shoulder.

"Playing video games," Adam says, almost too casually. "But I'm heading out. My grandparents are coming over for dinner tomorrow, so Dad and I have to do our monthly cleaning."

"Sorry, man," Trent says. "If I wasn't hanging with Claire tonight, I'd come help."

Adam chuckles, smacking Trent's arm. "No, you wouldn't. You'd come over and complain about how I don't have any good food in the house."

"And you don't," Trent says as a matter of fact, slapping the back of Adam's head. Moira shakes her head in disapproval.

"You gotta learn to appreciate a little flavor in your life," Adam says, his eyes darting to mine for a split second, trying to communicate something. I just don't know what. Glancing at the clock, he says, "Wow, I really gotta go. See you guys later."

"It's good to see you," Moira says.

"Bye," I mumble, thrown off by his strange behavior.

"Later," Trent says before easing onto a barstool. One arm still around me, he pulls out his cell phone. "I'm going to order some sushi."

"Just for two," Moira says, gathering her purse and phone from the counter. "I already ate and have some work to catch up on."

"But you'll be here?" I clarify, determined to follow my parents' rule and not totally comfortable without that buffer.

"Sure. I'll be in my office if you need anything."

She leaves, and the house is silent aside from Trent's tapping on his phone. I swallow self-consciously. "Trent—"

"—I know you don't like sushi. But this is from a new place." Trent glances up, offering me a deep, dimpled smile. "I think you're going to love it."

"Oh, okay." Willing to overlook his earlier behavior, I snuggle closer to him. When he tucks me more firmly against his side, I breathe out a little sigh and begin to relax.

* * * *

I was right, the jacuzzi is heavenly. I rest my head on the cool marble as the jets pound into my back. With my eyes closed, I hear Trent approach and climb in.

"Did you like the sushi?" he asks once settled.

"As much as any," I quip, opening my eyes to offer him a teasing smile. He shakes his head as if my dislike of his favorite food is unfathomable.

I ease closer to him, finding his hand in the churning water. "It's nice to hang out with you all day." Overall, it *had* been nice. Really nice. Trent had confessed his future plans, talking about us and forever and how lucky he was, until I'm pretty sure stars and hearts were shooting from my eyes. It had put my head in the clouds, but also grounded me firmly in this world, in the here and now, in what was real. In Trent.

"Aside from your little prank, it was perfect," he says, his thumb running over the back of my hand.

"What prank?" I can't help but ask. He can't still be upset about me beating him.

"You embarrassed me, Claire," he says as his dark green gaze studies me, blaming.

I pull my hand from his. "Are you serious, right now?"

"Yes, Claire," he says as if I'm daft. "Adam will give me crap about it for weeks."

Thinking of how uncharacteristic that would be, I scowl. "I don't think—"

"Yeah, you didn't."

My mouth gapes open as steam rises around me. Suddenly, I want to be anywhere but here. Troubled, I shake my head and stand, but Trent grabs my wrist, his hold softening when I stop. "Don't go," he says, apologetic. "Just hear me out." I wait, willing to be convinced, to forget this whole thing ever happened.

Trent continues, "You just don't know how it is with guys, Claire. In front of my friends, it's different. But when it's just you and me…," he drops his voice until it's low and intimate and chill-inducing, "When it's you and me, you can do whatever you want." He pulls me toward him. I maneuver in his hold, ending up beside him rather than on his lap.

"Come on, Claire," he says, whispering the words in my ear before scattering kisses on my jaw as his hands seek to pull me closer. "After barely having you to myself for weeks and everything today, I need this."

Indecisive, I freeze. The game really isn't a big deal. Was his reaction extreme? Maybe. But Trent is intense, and his anger died so quickly. *And* he's been so great, so focused on us lately. I mean, the guy is willing to change all his plans for *me.*

While my mind whirs, Trent kisses his way to my lips. There he stops, finally sensing my lackluster response.

Pulling back, he takes my jaw in his hands. He studies my face for a long time, eyes tracking over my forehead and down my cheeks, across my lips and up to my eyes. "You have no idea how perfect you are," he says in a hushed, beseeching, melting voice. "I need you." Then he draws me to him, kissing me hard.

I give in, kissing him back with a wild desperation. Desperate to connect. To forget.

To fill my emptiness with his clarity, excitement, and confidence.

His hands start to wander, snapping me back to myself. "Claire," he murmurs, his hold tightening. Fully regaining my senses, I realize I'm practically sitting on his lap. I jerk backward. Water splashes around us, droplets sliding over my too-warm skin.

"No," I say in a voice that wavers. "I know where this is…" I gulp. "I'm just…I'm…" I ease away, unwilling and unprepared to take things further.

Trent leans back, drapes his arms over the sides of the jacuzzi, and offers me a long-suffering smile. "It's okay, babe." I twist my fingers around each other under the water, for some reason feeling as if I should reach out and comfort him. "I'm sorry. You know you're my first boyfriend and so…" I flounder again, hoping he'll interrupt and not make me actually say it. Instead, he offers me a slow, smoldering smile and lifts a brow, waiting for me to stumble on. "I've never…been with anyone, Trent."

"I figured," he says, and I can't tell if he's insulting my kissing skills or just stating a fact. "So, I'll be your first." *This,* he states as an irrefutable fact.

I stammer, I blush, and I panic. "No, Trent—"

"No?" he says in disbelief.

Calling on my conviction, I exhale. "I'm not going to be with anyone until I'm married."

Trent throws back his head and laughs. It's mocking and grating and seems to go on forever until he realizes I'm not laughing with him. "You're serious," he says, still fighting amusement.

I lean toward him, willing him to understand. "Trent, Jillian and I made a vow when we were younger. It was kind of a silly, little girl thing to do, but then I got older and started to understand things more and we both became more committed to it. It's also a faith thing; I believe God wants me to wait. I believe in saving myself for one person." Trent's eyes narrow more and more as I go on. "So even though Jill and I aren't really friends anymore, it's really my vow to me, to God, and to whoever I marry. So...," I square my shoulders. "I'm committed to you, Trent. I really am. But I just won't do that."

With a careful movement, Trent reaches for me, his fingers gliding up my arm before resting on my neck. "You know," he says, considering me. "I don't think you've ever been sexier." I start to pull against him, but he refuses to let go, holding me gently in place, his forehead practically touching mine. "And I'll still be your first and only. When you're ready, love. Okay?"

"Really?" I reach to touch his face, shocked. The man pretty much just admitted he plans on marrying me.

He smiles and skims his fingers over the back of my neck, undeterred. "Of course, babe," he says. I begin to relax, tension draining away under Trent's understanding and soft touch. "I can be patient," he murmurs, kissing me softly. "You'll be worth it."

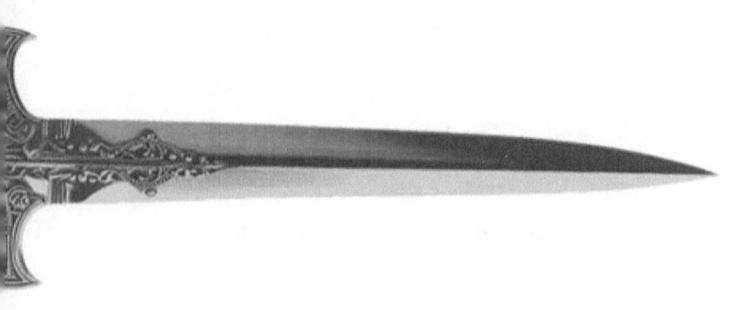

CHAPTER ELEVEN

"She's still not improving." Standing outside the healer's hut, I drop my voice to an undertone so Xandra won't hear my bleak words. "It's been over three weeks. She shouldn't still be confined to that bed." I clench the hilt of my scimitar, staring at the door as if it's the obstacle barring Xandra's recovery and my glare alone can disintegrate it.

Asha slides a lean hand to rest on my shoulder. The shoulder that *was* injured in my dive from the tower but has since healed completely. Unlike Xandra.

"She is not getting worse either," Asha soothes. "She just needs time."

Standing near the side of the thicketed hut, Reilynn takes a long drink from her water skin. Wiping her mouth with the back of her hand, she says, "It seems we have plenty of that." She glances around the settlement, eyes resting on projects we've completed and settlers we've served.

As our time in the warm climate has lengthened, Reilynn has slowly shed her layers. Rarely does she dress in full armor anymore, in fact—unless she's on guard at the wall—she wears only her hauberk for protection. Due to our service in the fields, her freckles are more visible than ever, and the ends of her spikey red hair are touched with gold.

The knight brushes a hand over the short hair at the back of her neck. "Torren says they're harvesting more oranges tomorrow, but I'm scheduled to lead training all day. Will you be able to help him, Asha?"

Giving my shoulder a final squeeze, Asha drops her hand. "Yes, I plan to implement a new, faster method." With her incredible inspiration, the elf has made herself indispensable to Avalei. In the past few weeks, she's altered methods, procedures, and systems, making Avalei even more efficient.

A small child skips past, shouting a greeting to each of us by calling out our names.

"Hello, Ember," Asha replies, and Reilynn waves.

They've become far too comfortable here. And something tells me we shouldn't be—probably the wounded member of our crew one wall away.

Where Asha and Reilynn have relaxed into life here, I resist.

Instead, I stay on edge, alert to any danger. Initially, I tried to relax, logically knowing it's idiocy to stress so much about a dream, but the urgency of this world and my role as a leader suck me in and keep my tension high.

The healer exits the hut, and I snap upright. "How does she look?"

She shakes her head, Xandra's lack of improvement as much a mystery to her as it is to anyone. "The same, Nix. She looks the same." I droop under the weight of her words. The woman's wrinkles pull as she offers me a sad smile and pats my hand with her age-spotted fingers. "She's awake now, but probably won't be for long."

"Thank you," I say, trapping the woman's hand in mine for a moment before moving to the door.

Inside the hut, Xandra is propped up, her eyes wan and dulled with pain. With her tiny fame, the cot dwarfs her body.

In fact, if it wasn't for her dark hair falling in knotted clumps around her, she would fade into the bedding. As I do every day, I swallow hard at seeing her so diminished.

Reilynn and Asha file in behind me. I sink to a stool beside the little warrior and, taking her hand in mine, ask, "How are you today?"

Through pale, cracked lips, she replies, "Ready to mingle with a megaspec..,"

"...swim with a cephador...," murmurs Asha.

"...antagonize an arachnid...," adds Reilynn.

"...and skin a snow cat." With a tight smile, I complete our daily greeting. The only part that ever changes is Xandra's. If only she were up to doing any one of those things or upright at all. With a weak tilt of her head, Xandra offers us an expectant look.

I cave first. "Alright, you got me this time. What is a megaspec?"

She laughs at her victory before cringing, her hand flying to her wounded side. As one, we rush to her, but she waves us back with the other hand. After a few deep breaths, the tension on her face eases.

Relaxing back against the pillows, she says, "Giant man-eating bat." Her voice dips, dwindling as exhaustion overtakes her. "Had a dream about one last night."

"Comforting," Reilynn murmurs drily as Xandra's eyes droop.

Asha tucks the blanket around Xandra and unsuccessfully attempts to tame her wild mane. "If you would like, I'll return later to wash your hair," she quietly offers.

"Sounds wonder...ful." Xandra smiles dreamily, drifting off, out of energy even faster than she was yesterday.

"Get better," I demand before walking away, every part of me screaming in frustrated helplessness.

✳ ✳ ✳ ✳

"Then Percy said I wouldn't be able to hit the target, so I told him I could shoot better than him. Then he told me to prove it, and so we went to the range and," Zel stops to take a gasping breath, "and I beat him!" she screeches. "I hit the target dead center, and his shot was inches away!"

Awaiting our reactions, Zel expectantly eyes my crew. We're scattered around my tree-top home, listening with various degrees of interest to the young girl. From the small corner table where she's sharpening my daggers, Reilynn looks up and says, "That's what the boy gets for underestimating you."

Eyes on the arrow she's fletching, Asha says, "You *have* improved vastly in the last month." Sitting cross-legged on her cot, the elf looks ethereal as soft candlelight shimmers over her loose, pale hair.

"Percy never did grow up," I call through the door from my seat on the balcony. My feet swing in the space beneath me, the ground four levels below.

Satisfied with our input, Zel goes back to her story, relaying every detail of her shot and Percy's reaction. Sighing, I lean against the rope railing, staring down into the darkness. The fibers of the rope scratch across my cheek as I stare at everything...and nothing.

The moon offers little light tonight. Candles and torches flicker through the settlement, guiding the remaining stragglers to their beds. One by one, the lights are put out. The night deepens, the oppressive thickness of the darkness overwhelming but for the chatter floating from my old home. I sit in the in between, too anxious to join in the conversation yet reluctant to be alone with my thoughts.

A barking hoot and melodic laugh draw my attention back to the girls inside the house. "Demonic daggers! You're serious!?" Reilynn says.

Zel's girlish giggle sounds before she responds, "That's what my dad told me."

"Nix," Reilynn says before dissolving into gut-busting laughter again. "Get in here," she pants between sniggers.

I ease from the deck and, placing my hands on either side of the doorway, lean into the room. "What's so funny," I say, growing a little nervous when I see even Asha's shoulders are shaking in mirth. Could they have found some old, secret diary?

"Your name," Zel says, pleased to be the center of such humor.

I frown. "My na—"

"Nix," she says, beaming. "N I C K S. My dad said your nickname came from all the times you cut yourself while training."

She waves her hand with a flourish. "Nicks."

Turning red, I curl my scarred fingers out of view. "It had nothing to do with that…" Then, deciding to embrace the truth, I stride into the room. "Or it might have had everything to do with it." I hold my hands out for everyone to see the marks. They are tiny, hardly noticeable unless you're looking for them.

Asha reaches for my hand, turning it over. She seems almost fascinated by the scars, but she is the type to think of scars as a beautiful story of their own.

"By my blade," Reilynn says, taking in the extensive network of minuscule scars.

"No," I say with a grin. "By *my* blade."

Another laugh bursts from her, and she turns away, shaking her head and wiping her eyes. She points to my daggers all laid out in a long, neat row. "Maybe I shouldn't be sharpening these."

"It's been years since I've slipped," I say, snatching my largest and favorite dagger to toss around. "Besides, sometimes you have to hurt to learn."

"True," a deep, familiar voice says at the door.

"Hello, Greymore," I say, hoping he didn't hear the whole of our conversation.

"Hey, Tomas?" Reilynn asks, still determined to discover his real name.

"No," he says before turning to Zel. "Your father is looking for you," he tells the young girl. Blushing, she says her goodbyes and hurries away.

Greymore watches her leave, making sure she makes it safely down to the lower level. Then, dashing my hopes, he catches my dagger in midair, tucks it into his belt, and takes my hand to study the scars.

Interest. That's the only word I have for the emotion coming from him. Deep, intense, acute interest.

I glance to Reilynn and Asha who are showing a pretty intense interest in their own tasks, pretending to ignore the man holding my hand in the center of the room.

Like everyone else, Greymore has settled right into Avalei. So much so, one would think it was his birthplace, not mine. After the first few weeks, I thought he might leave, but every time I ask him about his land and other responsibilities, he brushes me off. Apparently, he has a 'great steward', 'well-managed estate', and 'orders from the king'. None of which really explains why he stays, training, assisting, and defending my homeland.

I slide my hand from his. "Where have you been all day?"

"With Ivers," he says, his words a growl.

"Why hasn't he moved on yet?" I ask, careful to keep my voice from betraying my dislike since my companions and I have very different views of the chancellor. Reilynn is quick to defend the man as a 'loyal servant of the king' and 'keeper of a noble calling' when what she really means is 'a pretty face I'd like to keep looking at'.

"Securing the asset," Greymore responds with his usual vague wording.

"You mean he'll stay until Avalei is safe," I clarify. "Didn't he want to evacuate?"

"There hasn't—"

A piercing scream interrupts our argument. A scream from a person far too young to be that terrified.

Zel.

I dash to the door, snagging my lone dagger from Greymore's belt as I move past. A mysterious rushing sound echoes across the settlement as I sprint to the center of the rope bridge, peering into the inky darkness.

By the light of a torch, I make out the hunched form of Zel.

On the ground level, she's running in a crouch, scurrying toward the shelter of the smithy. Dark shapes lurch around her, shadows bumping into her and blocking her way. As the discordant sound of numerous flapping wings fills the air, she falls to the dirt, scrambling in a crab-like crawl away from the creatures circling her and back into the clearing.

I dart over the rope bridge, watching as they herd her to a more vulnerable position.

Once Zel's in open space, a shadow dives, grabbing her by the arms. In horror, I watch it lift her from the ground as the torchlight reveals its identity. A megaspec.

With a body the size of a human, wings twice as long, large rounded ears, a horn-like extension on the end of a thick snout, and protruding fangs, it must be the man-eating bat. And, somehow, Xandra knew they were coming.

A horde of deadly creatures.

And one has Zel.

"Reilynn! Catch!" I yell. The knight is already dropping, swinging from a rope toward the chaos below. Zel's thrashing and the pervasive darkness make firing a shot at the megaspec holding her too risky. With a parting glance at Asha and Greymore firing into the fray, I lurch forward.

Tracking the beast carrying Zel from light source to light source, I dart across bridges, twist around pulleys, and fling myself from rope to rope. They are still below me. The megaspec is rising slowly, Zel struggling frantically in its grip. Toward the far end of the settlement, where the wall meets the mountain, there's a break in the canopy of trees—the bat's escape route.

Zipping over a boarded bridge, I reach the wall far before the bat and his prize. There, I propel myself through the stone arch and into the defense's walkway. To have any hope of saving Zel, I'll have to reach the far side of the wall before the thieving megaspec.

I dash over the hard stone, whipping by settlers armed with bows. Through the windows, I spy growing flames. In an effort to frighten the beasts, the bonfires have been lit.

The screeching of the megaspecs increases, hammering into my head. As my feet pound down the walkway, the cacophony of sound spurs me on. Faster. Faster. Faster.

Through the window, I glimpse my target, claws latched onto Zel's arm. With two more beats of his wings, we're level. Eye to beady eye. I put on a burst of speed, angling for an arched opening mere strides away.

Then, with a giant pump of its wings, the creature lifts.

I spring from the wall, arms wind-milling, stretching to reach the fleeing creature.

By some miracle, my grasping fingers close around a scabby leg. My body swings, crashing into Zel as the megaspec falters. The claws of the foot I'm gripping release the girl, leaving Zel to dangle by one arm as we sink, losing altitude.

Zel screams in terror.

Fleeing the fire and rushing the opening, the remaining megaspecs swarm around us.

Frantic, I scan the ground, searching through the flapping wings for Reilynn. I spot a flash of her bright hair directly below us, body leaning out from the second level of the wall, eyes on Zel's flailing body above her. Held in place by our combined weight, our bat struggles. Unwilling to give up its prize, Zel's arm remains clenched in the megaspecs claws while my hand is wrapped around its other foot.

Drawing my newly sharpened dagger, I swing my arm back. "Now!" I scream the warning in the same instant I slash the megaspec's opposing leg, severing it.

The animal lurches as Zel falls with a scream. Tipping halfway out the window, Reilynn snatches at the linen of Zel's dress. The girl crashes roughly into the rock before being yanked to safety.

Free of her weight and reeling from the attack of my dagger, the megaspec quickly ascends. Spinning wildly into the swirling mass of leathery wings and brown bodies, I struggle to maintain my grip. The injured creature's movements fling blood across my face.

Unnerved, I wipe the warm stickiness away, searching for a clear view.

When I finally get one, I'm too far from the wall, trees, or bridges to jump. A hundred feet up and not a way down in sight. Unless…my eyes drift to the mass of megaspec bodies circling and swarming below.

With no better option in sight, I tighten sweaty fingers around my dagger and—with a gulping breath—let go of the bat.

Immediately, I clasp my free hand over the other. With both hands wrapped around the dagger's hilt, I strike out.

The blade catches on a leathery wing, tearing down the length of it and pulling a megaspec askew. There's a jerk as I hit the bone, then I'm freefalling to the next bat. And the next. I drop, ripping through wings to slow my ascent like a pirate cutting through sails.

The creatures swarm me, attacking my falling frame. They're so thick, I cease falling, instead bouncing from creature to creature as I struggle to avoid scratching claws and beating wings.

Halfway to the ground, I right myself by hooking another wing with my dagger. Slicing through the gristly skin, I hit the bone at the same instant a claw rakes across my arm. Trembling and jarred, my fingers lose hold of the dagger, and I fall free.

Weaponless, I flip in the air and land on my hands and knees directly in the center of a bat. Lurching forward, I instinctively grab a hold of the junction between its wings and neck.

My name sounds over the endless screeching, and my gaze finds Asha's across the melee. Seeing her with bow drawn, arrow pointing in my direction, I tighten my hold and pull my feet up under me.

The elf's arrow flies. Aim true, it slams into the bat's heart. The beats of its wings stagger, and we begin to fall, whirling down in an erratic flight.

Fading and out of control, the megaspec drifts...falling right toward a massive bonfire.

Seconds before impact, I shove off the bat's back, launching myself upward. Twisting in the air, I brace for landing. My feet hit first, but the impact knocks me off balance and I crash—seemingly every part of my body making rough contact with the ground—before coming to rest in a dusty sprawl.

Dazed, I lift my head long enough to watch the megaspec crash into the bonfire before collapsing in an exhausted heap.

I remain unmoving, cataloging hurts and watching the screeching hordes retreat until a different type of shadow blocks my view.

Greymore looks down at me and, for an instant, I see his eyes. They're brown. Brown and broody and tinged with panic. But then the vision clears, leaving the shadowed hood.

Teeming with adrenaline and survivor relief, I reach for the clasp of his hood and jerk him down beside me. His surprise bursts over me as I pull him closer. I can't see his face now, but that momentary glimpse urges me on.

"Greymore," I say. Tightening my hold, I tip my head up toward him as his hand drifts to my side and emotions pour from him: relief, adoration, anticipation, and...arrogance?

Yes, that's it. Arrogance. The impossible man is feeling positively, absolutely *smug*.

I pull him a bit closer. "Greymore, I," closer still, "need," close enough my lips practically brush his, "you...to find my dagger," I finish with a smirk.

Sensing the cocky man's surprise, I release him and flop back to the ground. I'm grateful to be alive and relieved Zel is safe. Grateful, relieved, and smug. So very smug.

CHAPTER TWELVE

I crunch down on a celery stick, imagining it's a Cheeto. But as healthy as my imagination may be, bitterness floods my mouth instead of cheesy goodness.

Frowning, I take another bite, staring out the window at the jacuzzi. The steam rising from the water reawakens a kaleidoscope of emotion.

Guilt.

Anxiety.

Want.

Fear.

Nothing positive and everything confusing, which is why I avoid the thing like the plague.

"Adam's coming over," Trent says, pulling a container of hummus from the fridge.

"Oh?" I pop the last bite of celery in my mouth and—grabbing the tray of veggies—follow Trent downstairs. "What are we going to do tonight?"

Depositing the humus on the table, he turns to take the plate from my hands. "He's bringing a new game." Grabbing two bottles of flavored water from the mini-fridge, he says, "Gotta get my action somewhere," and raises a challenging brow.

Lately, Trent has been pushing me to take things further. He's not physically demanding, but his words...his words are a different force entirely. Tired of fielding his stinging barbs, I drop onto the leather couch. "I thought you were okay with waiting until marr—"

"Until you were ready," Trent interjects.

"Which will be when I'm married," I argue.

"Maybe," Trent says with a knowing grin. This is another element of our argument. He's understanding of waiting and being my only one, but less understanding of waiting until marriage.

Unwilling to argue even more, I concede. "Either way, it's waiting until I'm ready and...well, I'm not," I say, my words uneven and awkward. "You just seem so...disappointed in what I offer." Leaning down, Trent fastens his arresting green eyes on mine.

"I like it all, Claire," he says as he drags a gentle finger over my cheek, sweeping my hair back.

His voice softens me, and I tilt forward, touching my lips to his. Hand moving to the back of my neck, he says, "I may tease, Claire, but I *am* being patient. Very patient," he whispers, urging me closer.

"Trent, your mom could come down any minute," I say, shifting away from him.

"So?" He grins before spreading fiery kisses across my jaw.

Trent's kisses are methodical—each brush of his lips and touch of his hands designed to slowly break down my defenses. He's practically perfected the art of making me forget everything except him…but only practically. And it's *my* practical, determined side that keeps coming between us.

There's guilt too, because it isn't just the vow and my faith holding me back, but the feeling that something is missing. Like the landscape I have yet to get right, our relationship is still lacking something. We're stuck, not getting any closer despite all the time spent together. I can't tell Trent though, because I'd seem so ungrateful. After all he does for me, all the gifts, all the time, and I'm going to complain about not feeling connected? No. I won't. Which leaves me to figure all this out on my own.

Why does everything have to be a battle? A battle between the part of me that considers leaving to search for something more and the part that's desperate to keep Trent in my life. A battle to push our relationship forward and grow together. Or a battle to honor my faith and keep some part of myself for me.

"Trent." As always, I pull away first and feel the familiar stab of guilt at the flash of disappointment in his gaze.

Frustrated, I curl against him, wanting to just be held.

He eases away, taking my shoulders in his hands and looking down at me. I fasten my gaze on his shirt, not wanting him to see my doubts. "Claire…love," he says in a slightly condescending way. "We—"

"—Hello, hello!" Adam calls from the top of the stairs.

Not one for PDA's, I lean back, but Trent is slow to move away. "Down here," he answers as some strange emotion flits across his features. Before I can interpret it, he jerks me close, smirks into my wide eyes, and aggressively kisses me.

"Hey—oh, sorry," Adam stammers. "I'll just—"

Trent brusquely sets me from him, leaving me reeling from the harsh embrace and quick release. Trembling fingers pressed against my lips, I watch him turn to Adam with a self-satisfied smirk and ask, "Did you bring the game?"

"Umm, yeah." Adam waves the game in the air, his eyes avoiding mine as I smooth my disheveled hair.

Leaping from the couch, Trent snatches the disc from his hand. "Awesome, let's get this party started."

"Right…" Adam says, shaking off the awkward moment. "Are you still trying to pass this healthy stuff off as party food?" Frowning, he takes a carrot from the veggie tray.

Powering up the gaming system, Trent throws out some comment about Adam's eating habits over his shoulder.

As they fall into their usual smack-talking routine, I remain off kilter—thrown by Trent's possessive move and the spark of…something I saw in Adam's eyes.

Needing a distraction, I pick up my phone, browsing through my apps. "What're you looking at?" Adam asks as a load screen comes up.

"Just some music," I say, still unable to meet his gaze.

"Yeah?" Trent cuts in, eyes on the game. "Maybe you should play *I Can't Get No Satisfaction* for us." Amused at the blatant innuendo, he chuckles darkly.

My face burning, I stare down at the screen. Tears prick at the back of my eyes, and I blink them back in horror, biting the inside of my lip.

I will not cry. I will not cry.

I reign in my emotions, focusing on the images on my screen. Tucking my feet under me, I hunker into the side of the couch and wish I could disappear. Instead, I settle for letting the world fade as I flick through inspiration pics. Twenty minutes later, still feeling the sting of embarrassment and seeing Trent is completely distracted with yelling at the screen, I disappear upstairs.

I pace around the pool before dropping into a deck chair. If Trent's just kidding, why does it bother me this much? And knowing it bothers me, why does he keep doing it?

I stare vacantly into the water, gathering my scattered thoughts. With a frustrated exhale, I let go of my confusion. At some point, everything will be clear. Until then, I'll just continue getting by.

I reenter the house to find Adam scrounging in the fridge.

Closing the door, he turns to me with a victorious smile, a Dr. Pepper in hand.

"I stowed this away last weekend," he admits. Twisting the cap, he takes a long swig, and I swear my mouth waters. Seeing my expression, he grins, his eyes gleaming. "Want some?"

I glance at the empty stairs before lunging forward. "Heck, yeah."

I hold myself to a small sip, but when I try to hand it back, Adam shakes his head. "That was an insult to the glory that is caffeinated soda."

With a laugh, I willingly take a longer drink, downing a quarter of it. "Better?" I demand.

"Much." With a light chuckle, he takes it back and polishes it off.

Tossing the bottle in the recycling bin under the sink, he says, "So…drawn anything interesting lately?"

Across the island, I slide onto a barstool, pursing my lips. "Sadly, no."

Adam's smile drops, his eyes darkening in intensity. "Why?"

"Trent," I answer without thinking. Adam's brown eyes spark as I rush to explain. "I've been working on a landscape for him and just can't get it right. Other than that, I've just been sketching."

"What do you want to do with your art?" he asks, resting an elbow on the counter.

With a faraway smile, I say, "I'd love to design fantasy stuff. Book covers, movie covers, game covers. So, my work would be recognizable, just not my name."

Adam looks thoughtfully out the window. "I can see it, Nix. Your stuff is really good."

"Thanks," I mumbled, pleased at his endorsement.

Still with his faraway look, Adam taps his fingers on the marble. "My mom was an artist. That's where I learned origami. She saw I couldn't draw, but still wanted me to have some type of artistic talent. I was actually pretty terrible at it, but then she passed and, well, no motivation like that, huh?"

"I imagine there's not," I say quietly, not wanting to lose the sincerity of the moment. "You *are* pretty talented," I add, thinking of the iris on my bulletin board at home. "But that's not what you want to do forevermore, right? A cop, isn't it?"

Adam focuses on me, his eyes brightened by anticipation, seemingly happy I remembered this about him. "Yeah," he says. "I always wanted to be a policeman—like my dad. For a while, Trent almost convinced me otherwise, but I know that as much fun as college with him would be, it isn't for me. I'd just be wasting my money and time."

I nod, remembering the day Adam told Trent he decided to forego college and work for a year before attending the academy. Trent had been furious. I didn't really understand Adam's choice either...until now.

"Well, I think it's smart," I say. "Why waste all that time and effort on something you don't really want or need?"

"Exactly," Adam replies in an undertone, again seeming to say more than actual words. I study him, trying to—

"Hey, where'd you guys go?" Trent tromps up the stairs. "And what are you talking about?"

"Art," Adam says.

"That reminds me," Trent says, coming to stand behind me. "Are you ever going to paint me that landscape?" He drags his fingers up and down my spine, acting as if he hasn't been ignoring me for the last hour.

Shivering in response to his touch, I say, "I've tried." Oh, how hard I've tried.

Placing a kiss on my temple, Trent says, "It doesn't have to be perfect, you know."

"Yeah, I know," I say. "But it has to be right."

✳ ✳ ✳ ✳

Curled in my window seat, I sketch a rough landscape in hopes of finding inspiration. This time, I'm trying a different route and sketching The Razor at sunset. My hands keep wanting to add the settlement, fields, and people of Avalei, but—so far—it's purely landscape.

"Hey, Claire-bear," Dillon says, walking past my room.

"Dilly!" I call out.

His head juts back into view. "Don't call me that."

"I won't." I point my pencil at him. "If you stop calling me Claire-bear."

He lifts his hands in surrender, entering the room. "What are you drawing, Clllllaiiiirrrre." He draws my name out sarcastically.

"Landscape," I say, tilting the sheet for him to see.

"Boring," he says, dropping to the edge of my bed.

Agreeing with his assessment, I toss the book and pencil aside. "How was the movie?"

"Good." His leg bounces. "Adam came."

"He said he was planning on it." Trent had decided to skip, saying he was tired after the basketball game and wanted to watch Netflix, but he didn't seem all that tired once the lights were down. I spent three hours avoiding wandering hands and reminding him that his mom could walk in at any minute.

He thought it was hilarious.

Fiddling with a loose thread on my bedspread, Dillon drops his eyes and asks, "How are you doing, Claire?"

His sincerity takes me by surprise. Not that he's uncaring, he's just…a brother. "I'm fine," I answer, eyeing him.

"You seem different," he says, his gaze lifting to mine before dropping again.

I shrug, unwilling to let him see just how much his words affect me. "Things change."

"Yeah, I guess they do," he says, slapping the bed and rising with an uneasy smile. "Well, good night."

"Dillon?" I stop his exit. Having no one else to ask, I say, "Would you ever break up with someone without a good reason?"

Glancing at the door as if afraid someone might catch him in a serious conversation, Dillon moves to the window seat. I tuck my feet further in to give him room. Sitting, he asks, "Does this have anything to do with Trent?"

"Obviously," I say, rolling my eyes in self-mockery.

"Well," Dillon starts. "I don't think you should break up just because things aren't great. Now, I'm no expert…" His lips curve in a crooked smile because he kind of does think of himself as an expert, just not of the serious stuff. He continues, "From what I understand, all relationships go through phases. Maybe a good phase is just around the corner. Now if you have a reason...?" His fists tighten protectively, only half-joking.

I shake my head. "Trent's awesome. He's just pushing for more...physically."

"No, no, no, no." Dillon plugs his ears, closes his eyes, and jumps upright. "I'm going to pretend like I didn't hear that."

"Dillon," I say in exasperation, pulling his hands away. "You're such a dork." I shake my head. "Just forget about it."

"Thank you," he says dramatically and makes his way toward the door. At the threshold, his steps falter, and he turns back.

"Guys are idiots, Claire. Remember that. And sometimes we just forget that there's more than the....," he coughs, "physical stuff. But if you want to break up with the guy, do it." His expression grows hard. "And you should never feel forced. Ever. Into anything. Okay?"

"Okay, Dilly," I say softly, needing to lighten the moment.

With a nod, he slaps the doorframe and scurries away.

* * * *

Traveling for an away basketball game, Trent is gone the next day at lunch.

Instead of sitting alone at our table, I shove down a taco, chug a soda, and head to the library.

There, I browse books, studying the covers. Focused on the nuances of one particular design, I don't look where I'm going and bump into someone.

"I'm sorry," I say, glancing up. "Oh, hi, Gabriella."

Trent's stunning ex-girlfriend freezes, shocked I'm addressing her. But why wouldn't I? Dating the same guy doesn't mean I have to be mean by default. Of course, Trent doesn't have anything positive to say about her, but I assume that's on par for exes.

"Nix." Her tone is a whisper. From what I remember, Gabriella was always quiet. But her looks make her stand out. Today, she's wearing her cheerleader uniform, showcasing her fit frame and long, tan legs. With her dark hair and unique, green eyes, it's no wonder she dated Trent; they're probably the two most beautiful people in the school.

Her figure is better than mine. Her cosmetic skills are obviously better. Her...

Stop.

I end the mental flow of jealous comparisons, suddenly aware of all the reasons addressing her was a bad idea.

Gabriella shuffles her feet nervously before blurting, "How are you?"

Her question surprises me. Not just because she asked it rather than run away, but that she asked in such a deeply sincere tone. "I'm fine," I answer automatically, tucking the book under my arm. "And you?"

She studies my eyes, searching for the truth of my words before answering, "I'm okay." The awkwardness of our conversation settles, and she hefts the books in her arms, saying, "I'd better go."

She opens her mouth as if to say something more, snaps it shut, and turns away.

Giving in to a crazy, impulsive whim, I ask, "What happened. With you and Trent?"

Gabriella turns back to me slowly, her eyes darting from side to side, like a cornered animal. "Nothing, it just didn't work out. I have to go."

Spinning, she flees. Dropping her books on a nearby table, she leaves the library, not even pausing to take the time to check anything out.

Her extreme reaction bothers me all afternoon.

What did she think I was going to do?

When the bell rings, I take my time returning to my locker, my feet and thoughts dragging.

Distracted, I almost crash into someone standing next to my locker. Looking up, I'm beyond shocked to find Gabriella there, apparently waiting for me.

"Nix," she says, fingers tapping on the spines of the books in her arms. It's like the last three hours didn't happen, and we're back in the library all over again.

"Gabriella, what's up?" I force nonchalance into my tone. She doesn't answer as I input my combo and open my locker. The hallway starts to clear around us, the remaining stragglers heading home, and still, she says nothing.

Not wanting to send her running again, I take an inordinate amount of time placing my books in my bag and organizing my stuff.

Finally, disturbed by her nervous presence at my side, I shut the door and sling my bag over my shoulder. Gabriella's hands are clenching her books, and she's looking out the window, gaze distant.

I follow her gaze to the nearly empty parking lot outside and spin a pencil through my fingers before breaking the silence. "I—"

"You deserve to know," she blurts, gaze darting to mine before returning to the deserted lot. "Why we broke up."

Highly curious, I still the pencil, clasping it in my unsteady hands. "Yeah?" I ask in a soft voice. "Why did you?"

Her weight shifts from one white tennis shoe to the other. "He cheated."

Images of Trent cheating on me flash through my mind. My grip flexes, cracking the pencil in my hand. "I see," I say, thinking she's done, but she doesn't leave, just trains her eyes on the scuffed tile of the hall. Eager now to end this whole conversation, I say, "Thanks for telling me...I know it was weird for me to ask, and well—"

"I gave him everything," she whispers, her voice quiet, but her words piercing. "Everything. But he always wanted more, took more. Took whatever he wanted."

Reeling with the insinuation of her words, I ask, "What do you mean—"

"Just be careful, Nix. Okay?" With that, she gives me a heartbreaking smile before turning away.

"Gabriella?" I try to call her back, but she just shakes her head and rushes down the empty hall.

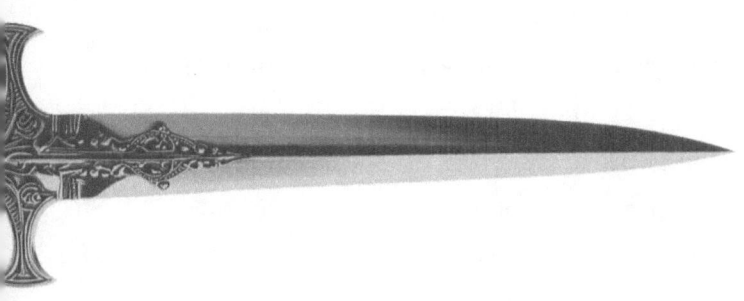

CHAPTER THIRTEEN

Half-listening to the voices swirling around the common area, I trace the flat of a dagger over the raised red scar on my forearm. The megaspecs haven't returned, but they left a mark, and it isn't just physical.

The whole of Avalei is changed.

Smiles don't reach eyes, shoulders are rounded, and spirits are low. All because of the unexpected and unprecedented night attack.

After two weeks, minor wounds have healed, but the fear is pervasive, driving strong hearts to falter and crushing our fragile peace.

Feeling eyes on me, I scan the occupants of the long table. Everyone in the room has their focus on the aging sea captain sitting at the far end, everyone except Greymore.

His dark hood is turned in my direction. However, he must be holding back because the waves of his emotions are faint—apprehension with a hint of yearning. But aren't we all yearning? Longing for explanations, healing, security, even? I avert my gaze, focusing on our visitor.

A man weathered by the ocean and time, Captain Perry basks in the hospitality and attention of Avalei's people. "With the southern invaders, the kingdom is stretched thin. Unrest is everywhere," the captain says and pops an orange segment in his mouth, closing his eyes at the burst of sweetness. Holding the remainder of the fruit in the air, he says, "I'm sure the nobility will be grateful to receive our shipment. Fresh fruit is quite the morale booster."

Torren offers a shallow smile and says, "I'm grateful you came and docked here. With the rumors swirling around, our last trade ship refused to dock, forcing us to transport our wares to a dock three days down the coast."

"Don't put much stock in rumors," Captain Perry says, wiping juice from his thick beard.

"But what if they're true?" Ivers asks. The chancellor dabs the corner of his mouth with a small cloth hanky before adding, "What if Avalei is cursed?"

I throw a biting glare at the chancellor before sharing a concerned look with Torren. Rumors are easy to overlook; curses aren't.

I want to assure the captain, tell him the rumors are just kingdom gossip. And while I wouldn't go so far as to say Avalei is cursed, we do have a problem. One I was hoping the captain would share with the king. Until the crown realizes the extent of our troubles, we won't be receiving any aid. It's a fine line to walk. By simplifying our problems, we risk being denied assistance, but by exposing the severity of the threat, we risk being written off as a lost cause.

Unaware of my apprehension, Captain Perry laughs, yellow teeth showing through the white of his beard. "Nonsense! A few random animal strikes do not a curse make."

I wish I could believe it was random, but it is so much more. The attacks feel personal and planned. Leaning on my elbows, I face the captain. "Did you know snowcats can blend into their surroundings or megaspecs can communicate with each other through sound waves?"

The man pauses, an orange segment at his lips. "They can?"

Spinning my dagger by the side of its hilt on the tabletop, I decide to go all in. "I witnessed a cat blend into the fortress wall, and a fortnight ago, a group of megaspecs led a somewhat organized attack, targeting specific people. Then, when we fought back, the bats turned to target the most threatening individuals. None of that is normal. The attack, the abilities."

As the man shifts in his seat, I realize I may have gone too far. If he gets too spooked, he'll leave without the shipment. Avalei needs the funds, but I won't downplay the threat, denying these attacks are growing in intensity and frequency.

"Nix of Avalei," a smug voice says from his spot at the head of the table, and my head droops, knowing I just gave the chancellor the right words. The right words to use against me.

Ivers continues, "I'm glad you finally see what I've been trying to tell you for weeks. Avalei isn't safe. The unnatural and unknown can't be fought. And with the king unable to send assistance, evacuation…temporarily…is our best chance."

I flick the end of my dagger, keeping it in motion as I confine my anger. Contained, it sits low in my gut, burning.

Until now, I've managed to stay polite to the chancellor by jokingly rebuffing or actively avoiding the man, but I'm tired of constantly undoing the harm he causes with his very vocal doubts. Adamantly promoting the need for evacuation, Ivers feeds on the fears of the settlers, compelling them to forget everything worth fighting for.

Refusing to turn to the man and fully acknowledge him, I respond, "There is no *our*, Ivers."

Clamping a hand over the rotating knife, I stop the blade and pocket it before adding, "Avalei isn't your decision to make."

I can practically hear the chancellor puffing up, preparing to throw his rank in my face. Clearing his throat, he says, "I am a representative of the king. As such—"

"Let us show you to your sleeping quarters." Rising, I address the captain, keeping my back to Ivers who inhales sharply at my cut.

The seaman's eyes dart between us. "Of course," he says.

There's a scuffle as everyone rises. Asha appears in the crowd, taking the captain's arm. A knowing look passes between us. If anyone can smooth things over and ensure a successful exchange tomorrow, it's her.

I edge to a smaller side exit cut into the canvas, but I am stopped by a surprisingly strong hand clamping around my upper arm. "I will not be ignored, Nix of Avalei," Ivers hisses in my ear.

From the corner of my eye, I see Greymore purposefully turn in our direction.

Ivers' hold tightens and, in an instant, I have the point of my dagger pressed against the back of his hand. "I would reconsider the placement of that hand, Chancellor," I say, my eyes locked on his.

Rather than release me, his hand constricts, fingers digging into and wrenching the muscles. "And I would reconsider threatening the king's man, Nix." He practically spits my name.

We stand at an impasse, the chancellor's unrelenting hold numbing my arm as the point of my dagger bites into his skin.

A drop of blood appears, blooming on the tip of my blade. Ivers' eyes darken into something frighteningly feral, and he hisses, "You're going to get these people killed."

His words feed my biggest fear, dousing my fire. The point of my dagger eases back. "This wasn't my choice, it was Avalei's—the majority voted to stay."

Ivers jerks me closer, his minty breath washing over me. "At *your* behest. And who's to vote against Nix, the *Defender of Avalei?*" his voice mocks, his words picking at my conviction.

"That's enough, Chancellor," Greymore says with lordly authority. "You've had your say."

I stow my dagger, and Ivers releases me. Feeling floods through my arm, but I resist the urge to rub his touch away. Keeping his eyes on me, Ivers backs to the exit, saying, "I only ask you to reconsider. To think of the people above the land."

Ducking through the canvas door, he disappears. Listlessly, I stare at the vacated space, his words echoing through my mind.

Greymore's hand bumps against mine, startling me. I curl my fingers away from the accidental touch, but he slides his palm against mine, grabbing hold and letting me know it was no accident.

I look up in surprise as he moves, pulling me from the building.

Titters and whispers follow us as he hauls me none too gently through the settlement and to the tree on the outskirts. The sheltered tree I think of as ours, though I'll never admit it. The second we step under its boughs, he drops my hand and begins...pacing.

The staid, ever-collected man *paces*, his steps sharp with emotion. It's oddly fascinating to witness.

"Greymore, are you—"

"Ivers is wrong. And an idiot," he interrupts.

My jaw drops. I never could get a read on Greymore's opinion of Ivers or of evacuation. He always seemed determined to remain impartial, but…there it is.

"I agree," I say, flexing my aching arm.

"But do you really?" He pauses in his pacing to face me. "When he was talking to you, it felt like he was getting to you, like you were really considering his words. You were doubting. Wondering if it was worth it. You felt—"

"Wait, what do you mean 'You felt'?" I ask, shocked. All of this time, I thought it was just me feeling *his* emotion. That, in a weird way, it was just how he communicated. *Not* that it was a two-way connection. I peer under his hood, trying to bring his features into focus. "Do you *feel* my emotions, too?"

"Of course, I do, Nix!" He throws his hands into the air in frustration, the movement arresting. "That's why we're so connected. Why I—" he cuts himself off and goes still.

"Why you're what, Greymore?" I say in an undertone. I've never seen him so…raw.

He inches toward me, a curious blend of doubt and hope spilling from him as he whispers, "My name isn't Greymore, it's…"

I hold my breath, waiting. Knowing his name suddenly seems so important, so pivotal.

Shaking his head, he lets out a husky sigh. Then he straightens, his body falling into the lordly, restrained lines I know so well.

I exhale my disappointment, absently rubbing at the marks on my arm.

Noticing the motion, Greymore pulls up my sleeve. The area is already showing signs of finger-shaped bruising. Greymore brushes his hand over it as a wave of protectiveness almost knocks me backward.

Needing to lighten the moment, I stagger dramatically. "Whoa, emotional overhaul. Next time, give a girl a warning."

"Tip of the iceberg," Greymore says.

His words are loaded with meaning, but his voice stays light.

I attempt to rein in my reaction, reminding myself he can feel my response.

Emotions jumbled by this new realization, I move to stare across the valley. The lake glimmers in the distance as children race each other home from the field and the smell of orange blossoms fills the air. Greymore moves to stand beside me. "Do not evacuate Avalei," he says, each word deliberate and controlled.

"What aren't you telling me?" I ask.

"I've seen this before," he admits. "A settlement giving in to fear. Resources going to waste. People abandoning the very thing that gives them life." He looks out over the beautiful valley, highlighted by the final rays of the setting sun. I stare at the land before me, trying to imagine it overgrown, left to animals who will never care for or appreciate the beauty of it. The image horrifies me.

Again, I rub my hand over my aching arm. Greymore is right. Giving in to doubt will only cause more pain. Discounting the value of this land will damage our very souls. By leaving and losing Avalei, we'll also lose a part of us.

"They rarely come back," Greymore says in a low tone. "They think they can and will, but they rarely do. Once a person abandons it all, it's almost impossible to find the strength and the will to win it back."

I reach for his hand, needing the reassurance. "Well, I guess I'd better do my job and defend Avalei."

He squeezes my fingers. "You are."

* * * *

"The bolts fit into the block and form a row, so he can slide them directly into the crossbow and fire one bolt right after another."

"Really?" Xandra's eyes actually brighten at Reilynn's description of Greymore's upgraded weapon.

"Ten at a time," Reilynn says, tipping forward, her stool wobbling precariously. "Blazing bolts, it's awesome. You'll have to ask him to show it to you."

Recalling her invalid status, Xandra's face drops, and she twists a strand of hair around her finger. "Yeah, I guess I will when he comes for his daily dose of my awesomeness."

Reilynn, Asha, and I exchange glances, knowing Xandra would much rather see the weapon in action and unable to guarantee she will. Lately, she's been able to stay awake for longer periods of time, but her wound is so sensitive that any type of movement hurts. The few times we've attempted to move her outside, she's promptly blacked out from the intense pain. I bump Reilynn, and she moves aside for my turn at the stool. "Your chancellor is leaving."

Xandra frowns. "He isn't mine. The greedy money-grubbing man hasn't visited me once."

I smile at her spunk. "Well, I'm relieved. He was a pot stirrer."

"A what?" Xandra says.

"Troublemaker," I clarify, rocking back and forth on the rickety stool. "Anyway, he's leaving with the captain, heading to the next port to torture another settlement with his good looks and bad personality."

"What do you think his report to the king revealed about Avalei?" Asha asks, her finger running over the fletching of an arrow in her quiver.

"That we're a lost cause, I'm sure." Three sets of eyes dart to mine. "What?" I say. "I don't agree with him, but I'm pretty sure that's what he'll say after our wee little argument." Asha's eyebrow tips up at my vast understatement, and Reilynn chortles.

"What did you do?" Xandra asks, somewhat horrified but mostly excited.

"I barely drew blood, while he..." I draw up the sleeve of my tunic, exposing the finger-shaped bruises encircling my arm.

Xandra reaches for her mace—which she insists on having at her bedside. I ease it from her grip, saying, "But now he's leaving." Carefully, I prop the weapon against the cot and admit, "He believes the worst is yet to come."

"And you?" Asha asks, her voice soft.

I sigh, tipping forward on the stool and tapping a dagger against my boot. "That's the one thing we *do* agree on." I keep my eyes lowered, studying the scuffed leather, a little scared to see their reaction to my next words. "Before the captain leaves, I want to make sure you three know you can leave at any time. Xandra, we can give you a draught—"

"—no." Xandra's harshly spoken denial draws my eyes to hers. "I will not leave Avalei. I won't leave *you*, Nix."

"I can't believe you even offered!" Reilynn's face is as red as her hair. "Sinning saints, Nix. Of course, I'm staying with you."

I look to Asha. With her fist pressed to her heart, she says, "I am at your service. Always."

Swallowing my emotions, I slap my hands to my knees and stand. "Well, now that that's settled, let's go load a boat and get rid of Ivers."

* * * *

My wagon bumps from the massive iron ramp to the sandy dune. Carrying the last of the captain's shipment, we follow the other wagons across the sand. As a precaution, we've spread the caravan out with Torren and Captain Perry riding in the first wagon, Reilynn the second, Greymore the third, and Asha the fourth.

I'm bringing up the rear, sitting next to my old pal Percy as he drives the team. The road through the dunes is practically invisible, but he easily guides the team using memory and landmarks. If we're lucky, veering from the path means buried axles. Unlucky? A wagon swallowed whole by the shifting sands.

Everyone is eager to get the shipment loaded, especially the captain, who has been extra twitchy since Ivers departed several hours ago to wait aboard the ship. Captain Perry is probably worried the chancellor will stage a mutiny, and I don't blame him.

"Are you sure it's not to the other side of that rock?" I ask to annoy Percy.

"Nix, I've driven this route a million times. I know exactly what I'm doing," Percy says, not bothering to mask the long-suffering of his tone.

"Kinda like when you told me you had kissed a million girls and knew *exactly* what you were doing? By the way, you didn't." His hands clench the lines, and I bump his arm, teasing. "Don't be mad, Percy. If the gossip is true, you've improved."

Percy huffs. "I—" The back of the wagon hits something, bouncing us forward.

"What was that?" I ask.

Pulling up on the lines, Percy glances back at the wheel and says, "We were close to the softer sand, see the tracks? But there aren't any rocks there, so what did we hit?"

I stare at the dunes, mountains of sand blurring into each other. The wagons ahead don't seem to be having a problem. "Well—" Percy picks up the traces, but at another movement in the sand, I stop his hand. Pulling a dagger, I step onto the seat, crowding Percy with my wide stance.

From my new vantage point, I stare down at the dunes. A breeze blows past, pelting grains of sand against the wagon. The horses shift, stamping their hooves.

"Come on, Nix," Percy says, growing anxious.

I'm about to tell him to move on when I spot it again: a mound of sand lifting and dropping in a curling wave. Under the undulating surface, there's a flash of scaly blue. The wave isn't curling, it's *slithering*. I jump to the bed of the wagon directly behind Percy, bracing my feet on the sides.

"Get us to that dock!" I demand, securing four throwing daggers in each hand. At my tone, Percy doesn't ask questions. Hollering, he snaps the lines.

The horses lunge forward, the wagon jerking along behind as a massive serpent explodes from the sand, missing the load by inches. The creature's thirty-foot-long, scaled body arches through the air, sailing over the firm ground of the path. Hurling daggers, I hit the serpent and it screeches—a high-pitched hissing sound—before disappearing into the dunes.

As the wagon jolts down the unseen road, I count ripples in the sand. At the least, there are three serpents. A manageable amount for my crew—if we can get them into the open.

Our spooked horses easily alert the other wagons. Coming up behind them, I gesture to a point in the trail, yelling, "Get to the end of the deep sand. We'll draw them out there!" Harnesses clanging and wagons bucking, our horses gallop across the sand, but the serpents gain on our little caravan.

Sand churning behind us, I struggle to line up a good shot. The roiling sand comes within feet of the wagon, and I give up hopes of a clear target. Pelting the serpent with knives, I attempt to discourage its attack. From the other wagons, Asha fires arrows at a monster, and Greymore peppers one with bolts.

Thankfully, the serpents slow their pursuit, then taper off and turn away.

As we reach the end of the dunes and their deeper sand, our wagon rolls to a frenzied stop beside the others. I dive from the bed, joining Asha, Reilynn, and Greymore at the edge of the dunes. For a second, the only sound is the gusting breath of the horses as we all turn to the abandoned dunes, watching.

The serpents are moving away until, suddenly, one turns and the others quickly follow, rushing back toward us at unprecedented speeds.

"Get the shipment to the dock!" I holler to the drivers. The others react instantly, slapping lines and urging their teams, but Percy and Torren hesitate. Reaching for his bow, Percy shakes his head at me.

"Percy, we can't lose the shipment!" I snap in frustration, looking from him to Torren. They meet my eyes, acknowledging the stark truth of my statement. Without the income from these wagons, Avalei won't survive the winter.

Seeing their acceptance, I add, "If they get past us, use the giant crossbow, do what you have to…just make sure that cargo gets on that ship!"

Percy reluctantly bobs his head before joining the other wagons in their charge to the dock.

Torren pauses long enough to toss me an axe with an overlong blade. "Good luck," he yells, urging the horses forward. "We know our part!"

Turning from him, I face the mounds of sand slithering toward us. "And we know ours," I mutter, hefting the weapon in my hands. Where my dual scimitars are shorter, this axe is a longer, better head-cutting-off tool.

Asha, Reilynn, and Greymore stand spaced apart, weapons at the ready. Spread out over the barrier between dunes and packed sand, we wait for the serpents to rise. "Our daggers and arrows aren't causing much damage!" I bounce on the balls of my feet. "Use your blades."

My instructions are unnecessary. Greymore already has his chain and blade unfurled. Asha's fan is snapped open, new, longer blades locked in place. And Reilynn is wielding her broadsword in one hand, her spear ready in the other.

The earth rumbles, and the serpents simultaneously burst from the ground. Sand pouring like water from blueish green scales, the massive snakes slither to the shallower sand in front of us.

I step to meet the closest one as the creature rises, looming. Its yellow eyes find me, and I freeze. My mind moves forward, swinging the axe, ending the fight, but my body is stuck, completely immobilized. A muffled scream catches in my throat as I struggle to move, fighting against the horrifying truth: I'm paralyzed.

Trapped in place by the serpent's gaze, terror courses through my blood. Sweat builds on my brow. My muscles quiver but remain immovable. I'm frozen with my arms raised overhead, clutching the now-useless axe.

My eyes dart to the side. Reilynn has been caught by the stare of the second serpent, a frozen knight rushing toward battle.

Beyond her, Asha is still as well. With her war fan extended, she looks like an exquisitely detailed statue.

Keeping me in its line of sight, my serpent closes the gap between us. It coils around me once, scaly body sliding within striking distance.

Heart pounding in my chest, I hear a whip-like crack. Dragging my eyes from the scales inching closer, I watch Greymore snap his chain and blade at the serpent paralyzing Reilynn. The weapon slices through the greater part of the creature's neck before catching on skin and scales. With the chain embedded in its neck, the serpent falls, jerking the weapon from Greymore's grip.

Released, Reilynn stumbles forward before turning to attack the serpent encircling Asha. Greymore struggles to free his weapon, but it's embedded too deeply.

All the while, my serpent inches closer, its body sliding across the sand as the coils tighten, forming an ever-diminishing circle around me.

Its head hovers above me, and I swear the atrocity smiles down on my helplessness.

I sense Greymore's approach as the serpent rears back, its shadow falling over me. Hissing in triumph, the serpent's jaw unhinges. Terror courses through me, squeezing my heart, seizing my lungs, and assaulting my mind.

Then, two hands reach around me. Crossing, they grab the hilts of my scimitars and—as the serpent strikes—they free my weapons and swing them in a crossing, deadly arch, slicing the attacking serpent in two.

Gore rains down as I fall forward, free. The axe crashes to the ground, its weight carrying me down. I land across the writhing body of the serpent and scramble away, kicking out and scooting backward. Twisting, I roll to my knees only to come face to face with the massive head. I lurch to my feet.

Crashing into something, I whip around, dagger drawn.

"Easy there."

At Greymore's wry tone, I lower my weapon and attempt to slow my erratic breathing. Scanning the area, I find all three serpents dead.

"Stupid sand suckers!" Reilynn exclaims, hacking at the body of one while Asha studies another.

Adrenaline draining from me, I slump forward, resting my hands on my knees. I'm not really injured, but still feel wounded from the attack and my helpless fear.

Taking a minute to process the whole terrible thing, I begin to come back to myself. Recognizing I'm no longer under attack, I relax enough to notice the squishy, sticky substance coating my whole body. It covers my legs, arms, and torso, but the worst is my head.

Doused in gore, my hair sticks to my scalp, itching my skin. "Nasty," I grumble, flicking snake bits from my tunic. "This was no clean kill."

"My apologies," Greymore says as he steps behind me, moving closer than a body should to a walking cesspool. Crossing his arms in front of me, he returns my scimitars in one smooth motion. Then—instead of moving away like a sane person—he drops his hands to my hips. "Thanks," he breathes into my ear before pulling a grime-soaked strand of hair from my cheek. "Now, Nix…," his voice drops, and my heartbeat jumps, racing twice as fast as it was minutes before. "I need you," he pauses, allowing the emotional electricity to flow freely between us before whispering, "…to find my chain and blade."

CHAPTER FOURTEEN

I t's going to be a rough night.

If Trent's earlier rant wasn't enough to warn me, the fact that he asked me to go buy him a Diet Coke is. Trent only drinks the stuff on special occasions...or terrible ones.

Offering in hand, I trot up the steps to the porch. Before I can reach the door, it flips open, and the drink is snatched out of my hand.

"It's about time, I've been out of the shower forever," Trent says and twists the lid.

Taking a long swig, he turns from the door, expecting me to follow. "I'm telling you, Claire. You should be glad you missed the game."

He stalks through the house and to the kitchen. Dutifully, I trail behind him, dropping his car keys on the counter.

Aside from my grounding, this is the first basketball game I've missed. I couldn't get out of Dillon's birthday dinner, something to do with us being related. I was sorry for missing the game at first, but—after hearing about it for the last hour—I'm not disappointed at all.

Trent chugs the last of his drink, slamming the empty bottle on the counter. "I hate that school! And those refs—giving me a technical. A T, Claire!" Cursing, he slaps the bottle from the counter.

My eyes bulge as it pings off the cabinet before spinning to the floor. I've seen Trent upset before, but this unrestrained temper is new.

Growling, Trent pulls his hands through his hair. It's damp, and he hasn't styled it—a look I usually like—but tonight it looks a little *too* wild. Linking his hands behind his head, he looks at the ceiling and blows out a harsh breath. "I just want to forget about the whole thing."

That makes two of us.

He tips his head down, meeting my eyes for the first time since I got back. Unsure how to react, I keep my face blank and wait for him to take the lead.

"Come here, babe." With a sudden move, he tugs me into his embrace. I tense, crushed against his chest. "Claire," he mumbles as his arms encircle me like iron bands and he buries his hands in my hair, securing me against him.

Slowly, I link my hands behind his back. His hold tightens to the point I can barely breathe. It's as if he's trying to press every one of his undesirable emotions into me, and it's pretty effective. Beneath my ear, his heartbeat slows, his stress fading while my tension grows.

Finally, his hold loosens, and I ease back.

Taking a desperately needed deep breath, I smile tentatively. "Feel better?"

He leans forward, his hand gripping my neck. "You could make everything better." He presses a quick, hard kiss to my lips. Then, abruptly, he releases me.

I rock back on my heels.

I *could*? What does that mean? I could, but I don't?

Trent smiles at my bemused expression. "Let's watch a movie," he says, winking at me.

"Sure," I agree, more because it seems like the right thing to say than what I really want to do. "Is..is your mom here?" I tentatively ask.

"She'll be back soon, my little nun," he bitterly responds.

My head down, I follow him to the stairs, but Trent pauses at the top. Running his tongue over his teeth and clicking, he curls his face in disgust. "First, I've got to go brush that nasty aspartame taste out of my mouth. Meet me down there," he says, dropping a kiss to my cheek.

I nod, descending in a daze. I don't like this on-edge, moody Trent. I don't know how to handle him...

But Adam does.

Whipping out my phone, I text him.

Trent's 2nite?

I tap the phone against my thigh, waiting for his reply. *Please, please, please.* I silently chant.

Wouldn't recommend it…bad game.

Reading his response, I sink to the couch.

Too late.

Good luck.

I shake my head, smiling despite myself at the devil emoji he attaches.

"What's so funny?"

I jump, phone bobbling in my hand. Securing it, I clutch the device to my chest. "Trent, you scared me."

"What is it?" he persists, nodding to the phone.

"Just a text from Adam," I say, wondering why I feel the need to add *just* to that sentence.

His eyes never leaving mine, Trent drops to the couch next to me and snatches the phone from my hand. I don't know whether to be offended at his rudeness or worried about his temper. "Let's see what my best friend and my girlfriend have to chat about." He stares at the screen, his dark brows pulling closer and closer together as he reads. His hand tightens around the phone, my case creaking. "You think this is funny?"

"Trent," I say, voice soothing. "You have to admit you were really mad."

He meets my gaze, and I flinch away. "No, Claire. That was upset." He types something and sends it before I can read his response. He turns to me. "Now? Now, I'm mad."

"I'm sorry," I say, dropping my hand to his knee. He glares at my fingers, and I slowly pull them away and awkwardly tuck them in my lap.

My phone still in hand, he scrolls back through the history, lips pursed, nostrils practically flaring.

I don't know what he could possibly see there that would justify his increasing anger. I rarely text Adam and, nine times out of ten, it's one of us asking the other if Trent is with them or clarifying our plans. Once, he sent me a fantasy movie cover saying it reminded him of me, but there's nothing remotely questionable. Absolutely nothing.

Jaw rigid, Trent finishes and flings the phone to the floor. Luckily, it's carpeted. "Making fun of me is one thing," he says. "But flirting with my best friend is another."

I sputter. "Flirting? Adam? No." I shake my head violently. "It's not like that."

"Really?" He inches toward me on the couch, every movement deliberate. "Maybe if I were Adam, you'd be putting out by now."

I'm so offended, I forget to be afraid. Shooting to my feet, I say, "I'm going home."

Trent laughs, but it's a dark, mirthless sound. "We both know it's true, Claire. All that talk of vows and your self-righteous purity?... A lie."

Stunned, I stare at his smirking face. He arches his eyebrow, challenging me.

Baiting me.

Using me as an outlet for his anger.

Scooping my phone up, I hold it in my trembling hands and attempt to persuade him. "Trent, there is nothing in here to justify your anger." In response, Trent's eyes narrow, the green brightening with a toxic intensity as his gaze becomes a hazard warning. Knowing nothing good will come from staying, I say, "I'm leaving," and turn to go.

"Claire…" Trent's voice rumbles, threatening. "Don't you leave."

My stomach churning with emotion, I start up the stairs, saying in a small voice, "I don't want to stay, and I don't have to."

"Yes, you do!" In a flash, Trent is off the couch.

Grabbing my wrist, he jerks me to a stop two steps up. Using his body, he presses me against the wall, hissing, "You've strung me along for months and months, Claire. I've done everything for you, but somehow, it's not enough."

His volume increases, hot breath slapping across my cheeks. "How high maintenance can you possibly be? What do I have to do, Claire? What!?"

His hands clench my shoulders, searching my face, his pupils dilating to the point that all I can see is black. Looking into those fathomless pits, I realize how blind I've been. All the times I felt fear around Trent, I assumed it was a complex, projected emotion.

But now, staring into his unveiled eyes, I see it isn't a fear of *losing* him or of *disappointing* him…it's simply a fear *of* him.

I wince at the pressure on my shoulders. "Trent. You're hurting me."

"You've been hurting me for months, babe," he says, angling on the step until our bodies are flush. "Guess we're even."

"Tren—"

His mouth falls on mine. Unyielding and unrelenting. Working my hands between us, I shove him back. He stumbles to the base of the stairs.

"Trent, just stop. Stop."

He looks up at me, lips curling in a twisted version of a smile.

Run, run, run. My panicked mind screams.

"Trent? Claire?" A voice chops through my fear. Moira.

"We're down here, Mom," Trent says, his voice even and relaxed.

"Okay!" Her voice drifts from the kitchen. "I'll be upstairs if you need anything."

Taking courage from her presence, I turn back to Trent. "I am leaving."

"Claire," his voice warns and pleads as the fire in his eyes dims. "Don't go."

Backward, I inch up the stairs. Keeping my eyes locked on Trent's, I will him to stay in place. He lets me move away, his gaze a curious mix of longing and loathing. Out of reach, I whisper, "We're through," and turn to dash up the remaining steps.

As I pass his mom in the kitchen, I say, "Goodnight, Moira," and, clinging to my dignity with both hands, I stride from the house and down the street.

As the cool night air sinks in, I start to crumble. I shake my head, pushing away the emotions threatening to overwhelm me. I have a long walk ahead of me.

"Claire!" Adam's car pulls up next to me on the sidewalk. "Where are you going?"

"Home," I say, unable to meet his eye.

"Well, let me give you a ride." Leaning across the seat, he pops his passenger door open.

Thinking of Trent's accusations, I say, "That's a really, really bad idea, Adam."

"What happened?" Adam asks in a soft undertone.

"We fought." I glance back at the house, wanting to get further away from it. "I know he's upset, but he said some things…"

And did some things, I think. But I can't form the words.

I turn away, but Adam jumps from his car and follows. With a huff, I stop and meet his eye. "Why are you here?"

He looks me over, his eyes carefully assessing. "I got your text…the one that obviously wasn't from you."

"Then I guess you know what happened," I step away, "and why giving me a ride is a bad idea."

"Well, no matter what, you shouldn't have to walk home," he says. "Especially when it's this late." He steps up beside me, texting someone on his phone.

"Adam," I shake my head. "Just go."

"Fine," he says, surprising me by giving in. He backsteps toward his car and Trent's massive home. "I'll see you later, Nix. Oh, and I texted Dillon," he says as an afterthought. "He should be here in about ten minutes." Then, turning, he jogs away, leaving me with no room or will to argue.

* * * *

For the next two days, I become an expert at avoiding Trent. Knowing his schedule like I do, it's far too easy. Dodging his calls is a little harder, leaving his texts unanswered difficult, and ignoring his constant visits to the house practically impossible. However, Dillon really seems to enjoy his unofficial job as the Claire-club bouncer, repeatedly denying Trent entrance.

The day before Valentine's, I decide I'm ready to face him. I need to either make our break-up official or forgive him. That night, I was sure, determined when I told him it was over, but now I'm not so sure. Emotions were high. I could have been misreading his intentions on the stairs, just like he misread the communication between Adam and me. To be totally honest, I wouldn't have liked it if he were texting and inviting another girl to come over and hang out with us either. And he didn't actually hurt me, he just scared me.

Knowing Trent's ability to charm, I probably should go into the conversation more decided, but I just don't know. What to do. How I feel. What I want. All I *do* know is confusion. And loneliness.

Without Trent, I recognize I'm a little isolated from everyone. Everyone. Even God.

I try to pray, needing guidance, but words don't come. Maybe it's because I've gotten out of the habit. Maybe it's because my faith feels like a barrier in my relationship with Trent. Maybe all my convictions were imagined. Whatever the reason, I can't find the words. I can't find the divine help, overwhelming peace, or powerful convictions I've discovered in the past.

All I find is silence.

Trusting I'll find the answer in the moment, I decide to call Trent after his practice ends.

Biding time, I sit down to sketch. Unwilling to start another landscape that's sure to fail, I go for some whimsical indulgence. Picking up a piece of charcoal, I begin a self-portrait of me peering from a stone archway on the wall of Avalei.

Time passes as I move my hand over the page, one half of my mind engaged while the other is far, far away. When I finish and pull back, I'm struck by the expression I've drawn on my face.

It's haunting.

My shorter hair blows around my shoulders, eyes staring with fear and longing into the distance. Giving in to what's already there, I add a small tear to my cheek.

"Claire?" My mother's light voice sounds from the hall. She's been incredibly sympathetic about my problems with that 'nice boy' Trent.

I didn't tell her much about our argument, just that there was one. Her only advice was that a little distance would probably be a good thing, and even if he was 'the one', there was no reason to get too serious, too fast.

"Yes?" I say, rubbing my charcoal-covered fingers together.

"Trent's here."

My fingers freeze, and I gulp. "Where's Dillon?" I ask, wondering how Trent slipped past his guard.

"I think he got tired of being on duty," mom jokes with a gleam in her eye, "and you can't keep hiding from the boy. I'll send him to the backyard. You can have some privacy there."

I nod, accepting her logic. "Okay. I'll be down in a bit."

Rushing to the bathroom, I scrub my nervous hands. When I drop the hand towel for the third time, I throw my hands in the air, leave it on the floor, and head downstairs. The sliding glass door is open a crack, and I slip through soundlessly.

Trent is on the deck, standing with his hands in his pockets, staring out over our yard. At my approach, he turns. "Claire." His voice is soft, reminiscent of our beginnings. I meet his bright green eyes as a slow smile spreads across his face.

At his expression, I suck in a sharp breath, afraid to even blink. It's him, the Trent I fell head over heels for. The attentive, adoring guy who makes me feel amazing and special. If I blink, he might disappear, revealing the harsh, demanding man I saw two days ago.

Keeping his eyes trained on me, he says, "I've forgotten how stunning you are."

His words give me the courage to join him on the edge of the deck. I drop to sit, dangling my feet over the side and gesture for him to join me. Scanning the yard, Trent perches near me on the steps. Our seating arrangement puts him at eye level—an unusual thing with Trent being so much taller than me.

Clasping his hands in front of him, he stares out at the yard. "I want you to be happy with me, Claire."

"Trent, it—"

He holds up his hand. "Please, let me finish? I have been thinking a lot about what I need to say. Okay?" He waits for my agreement, something he hasn't done in weeks.

At my slow nod, he leans to rest his arm across his knees, locks eyes with me, and says, "I want you to be happy, and I realize I haven't given you that. I've been pushing you for more than you want to give. It's created a tension between us, and that tension snapped last week. I don't ever want that to happen again." He covers my hand with his. "I know I get a little...intense, and I took it out on you. I know I scared you. It scared me too, how much you make me feel, and sometimes it just feels like all that emotion has nowhere to go, you know?"

"Yeah," I whisper. It makes sense, but a little voice inside is raging, screaming at me to not give in to his charm.

"We don't have to rush anything, Claire," he continues. "I plan on being with you for a very, very long time. You're it for me, and I'm it for you. So, it doesn't matter if you're not ready now. I'll be here when you are. I just want you. Whatever you're willing and ready to give."

His eyes drop, and he studies my hand as his thumb traces circles over the back of it. I wait for more, needing something more.

"I missed you," he whispers. "I was miserable without you." He offers me a wry smile. "I had to hang out with Adam." He shakes his head with self-loathing. "I know there's nothing there. I mean, you and Adam? Yeah, right. That was just me being stupid and jealous." His eyes lift to mine, deep and sincere. "Next time, we'll just talk things through, and we'll learn how to work through things together. And we'll be that couple that everyone wishes they were. So, please, Claire." He turns my hand and threads his fingers in mine. "Come back to me. I won't take you for granted anymore. And I'm ready to woo you if I have to." He gives me a smoldering smile. "Every day." His expression becomes heartfelt, resolute. "Always and forever because...I love you."

My breath catches at the three little words that feel so very, very big in this moment. So suffocating and overwhelming. "Trent..." I exhale his name. But I don't have any other words, I'm absolutely speechless.

He leans forward, easing closer inch by inch. He doesn't rush, giving me time to pull away, but suddenly I don't want to pull away. Because why should I say no? He's given me every reassurance I need. And if I do say no, what will I be left with? Regret? Loneliness? That terrible isolation?

I want to feel that belonging. I want to feel like I did when we first began, like our relationship was a gift, a blessing. When his lips gently touch mine, I find the memories there. Memories of sweet little gestures and fluttering butterflies and giddy expectations.

Stunned and unsteady, I pull back. "I'm sorry I invited Adam—"

Trent gives my hand a light shake, his eyes bright. "Babe, it's over…Just tell me we aren't."

"You're sure you can wait?" I whisper as I study him, his vulnerability only adding to his amazingly good looks.

Sensing I'm caving, he pulls me to my feet, holding me gently. "You're worth it, Claire."

"Then I guess I should tell you yes…" I pull back to stare into his elated eyes. "And I love you, too."

With a whoop, he spins me around. I can't help but giggle as he returns me to my feet. With a quick peck, he rushes to the door. "Where are you going?" I ask.

"It's Valentine's tomorrow. I have a big, romantic date to plan, don't I?" he says with a wink.

"Yes, I guess you do," I say as he backs out the door. My lips curve in a smile. He's back. My Trent is back. And he loves me.

In a daze, I make my way back to my bedroom. Shutting the door, I flop against it with a hearty sigh. Reviewing all of Trent's words, I let go of all my concerns and embrace his commitment.

He's it for me. I'm it for him. This will be great. This *is* great. My hope and happiness bloom, stretching a smile across my face, but then my gaze catches on the portrait.

My euphoria slips, and again I feel that prodding unease. Drawn, I step closer to the artwork, searching for something to explain my emotions.

Inches from the canvas, I examine the unsettling likeness.

I rub my brow, feeling the same concern that pinches hers, but it's as if she sees something in the distance I can only guess at.

An enemy she's prepared to face.

As the sky darkens outside, I continue to stare at the portrait, trying unsuccessfully to find some joy in the likeness.

Instead, I'm left wondering what she's fighting, when the pain appeared behind her eyes, and why she feels so trapped when love is supposed to set you free.

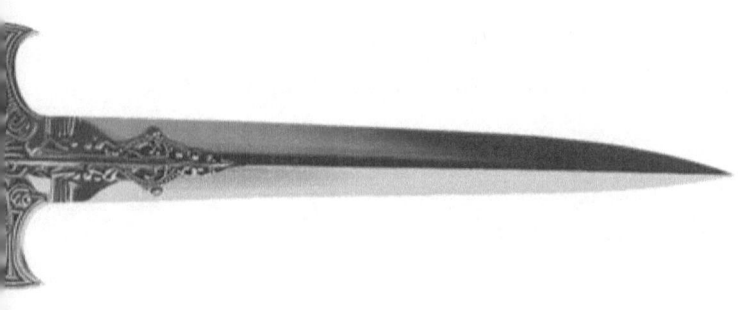

CHAPTER FIFTEEN

"I miss Betah."

Xandra's softly spoken words surprise me. Propped up in her bed, the tiny fighter smiles crookedly, reminiscing. "Can you imagine what she would have done to those serpents?"

Shifting on the bedside stool, I shudder to imagine the combination of Betah, serpents, and explosives.

"By the time Betah and her axes were finished with them, we would have all looked like Nix," Reilynn says from her guard-like position near the doorway. "Soaked in slimy snake." Her tone dips with remembrance as she stares at the scimitars curving from my hips. "That was awesome."

I give her a dirty look and rub at something behind my ear. No matter how many dips in the lake, I can't seem to rid myself of the nasty and pervasive snake remnants. "Disgusting is the word you're looking for, Reilynn," I say as I scratch at my sticky skin. "Not awesome. Disgusting."

With reinforced vigilance, Asha stands at the window peering out, hand resting elegantly against the thatched wall. "She is referring to how Greymore killed the serpent, not the aftereffect. Dispatching the serpent by reaching around and crossing your blades, all while avoiding eye contact, was *awe-inspiring*."

Xandra actually giggles, clutching her side at the pain of the motion.

Desperate to help, I reach for her, but she waves me back, panting, "I'm sure...it..." With a huge effort, she transforms her grimace into a sly smile. "...it...was both—an awesome heroic action and an awesome gore bath."

My desperation to help her diminishes.

Pleased, the weak warrior's muscles relax, but her brow stays knit. Her expression is no longer strained but confused. "Why didn't Greymore use his weapon?" she asks. "Why not unfurl that beautiful chain and blade?" She sighs dreamily at the thought of the weapon, eyelashes fluttering in a move that's only partly sarcastic.

"It was lodged in the serpent that had paralyzed me," Reilynn explains, voice alive with the glory of battle. "That blade almost sliced the sand sucker all the way through, but it was pretty nasty by the time Greymore freed it."

"But not as nasty as Nix, I'm sure." Xandra grins at my death glare as Reilynn—distraught at the thought of a damaged weapon—pulls her sword from the scabbard, checking to be sure the blade is still in impeccable working order.

I watch Reilynn's intent perusal. She tips the sword this way and that, unaware we're all staring in amusement.

Turning before she sees me, I catch Xandra attempting to hide a yawn. Body limp, the frail fighter hides her growing weakness, saying, "Well, ladies, I'm finding all of this talk of heroic deeds and swoon-worthy weapons exhausting."

It's easier for Xandra to deny her infirmity. If she keeps pretending it's not there, she doesn't have to accept it may never go away.

On the other hand, I'm fully aware of the horrible extent and strange persistence of her injury...and that constant awareness is wearing on my faith.

Looking at Xandra's semi-content face, I'm convinced denial is the better option.

My eyes drift to the floor, unwilling to let the crew see my growing hopelessness. If Xandra isn't improving by now, it may be time for us to accept the inevitable and stop trying to heal her pain and focus on making it bearable.

I kick my toe against the dirt floor of the healer's hut, conflicted—unwilling to give up, but needing to be reasonable. I've sat in the stool too many days, waiting too many hours, hoped for too many miracles.

"Nix." At Xandra's entreaty, I realize a silence has fallen over the room. Banking my emotions, I look up. She's leaning forward on one elbow, curls tumbling over the bed, dark eyes filled with the fire of war. "I'm not done fighting yet, Nix. And I will beat this," she clenches my hand in a surprisingly strong grip, "I promise."

Unable to speak, I merely nod my head.

"Now, go."

Reluctantly, I stand and follow Asha and Reilynn toward the door. "Tomorrow," I say as Asha and Reilynn murmur their goodbyes.

Xandra waves her arm, frustrated at our slow departure. "Away with you all and your exhausting, overly entertaining stories. Don't come back until tomorrow, you renegades."

As we duck out the doorway, she sinks down, practically disappearing into her bedding.

We walk in silence until we reach the center of the settlement. There, Asha stops, asking, "When will we meet to discuss the attack?"

"They met last night when you were with Xandra," I say. I point to the top of the wall. "You probably noticed they doubled the guards. And no one is to leave the safety of the valley and the wall without consent and an escort of some kind."

Wearing more armor today than she has been, Reilynn stamps her spear into the dust, frustrated. "No one could explain the paralysis. Our best guess is that our eye contact with the beast caused it. Because the serpents never looked away from our bodies again, we guess that they have to keep a visual to uphold the paralysis, but we can't be sure. It may remain until they're killed."

I toss my larger dagger back and forth between my hands, as antsy as Reilynn is frustrated. "No one had ever heard of the serpents being able to cause paralysis before. It's another enhanced ability and—like all of the other animals and their attacks—the behavior was suspicious, too."

Asha stares at the network of rope bridges above us, watching Zel scamper across a bridge with an armful of linens. I continue my report, "Sea serpents have been known to occasionally come on land, but never have they been known to hide themselves in the sand, stay in groups, or go such a distance from the shore."

Reilynn adjusts her breastplate and locks her knees close together in what I fondly think of as her reporting stance, saying, "We all agreed they seemed to be targeting the wagons and crops. Their attack originally focused on them, and they didn't even show themselves to the chancellor or the ship's crew, who took the same route prior to us."

"Yeah, like every other attack, we can all agree on the strangeness, but not the reason," I say, finishing our synopsis of the meeting.

Absently, I watch Zel drop from the fourth level using a pulley, riding a basket down with her laundry piled high beside her. Going down hand over hand is a tedious process. Riding the basket back up is much more fun…especially if you get help.

Basket rides are a favorite pastime in Avalei. One person rides and one grasps the end of the rope and runs as fast as they can, lifting the pulley basket. The stronger and quicker the runner is, the zippier the ride. I smile, thinking of a time Percy tipped from the basket, unprepared for the force of my pull.

Putting my dagger away, I step from my friends, needing a little distance from our shared worries. "I'm going to go help Zel with laundry…and maybe bathe again."

"Stinking Sinkholes, Nix," scoffs Reilynn. "It's all in your head, you smell fine."

"And Greymore did not appear to be bothered by your scent," Asha inputs unhelpfully.

I flush, recalling the closeness of his lordship when I was decorated in innards. "Greymore was high on adrenaline, so his opinion counts for nothing," I say, veiling my embarrassment.

"Certainly, more than nothing," Greymore says, appearing at my side.

"Certainly not," I say, mocking his uppity tone. I haven't been too happy with the man since he refused to let me rinse off in the ocean, saying it was too dangerous, and tried to convince me I looked good with my hair slicked down. Interestingly enough, snake guts *do* make a very effective pomade. But the absolute worst part of the whole serpent shower was Greymore's enjoyment of it—an overriding glee that drifted for hours through our emotional breezeway.

And the jerk didn't even try to temper it.

Ignoring my well-practiced death glare, Greymore nods a hello to Reilynn and asks Asha if she would take his watch on the wall, saying, "I'd like to talk to Nix."

"She wouldn't like to talk to you," I mumble under my breath.

"Of course," Asha says, arching a perfectly shaped eyebrow in my direction before adding, "Christian?"

Greymore shakes his head.

"Gavin?" Reilynn guesses, tapping her nails against the hilt of her sword. When Greymore's answer isn't affirmative, she groans, "Leaping Lords, we're never going to guess it."

"I know, I've got it." I smirk. "It's Lucifer, right? Can I just call you Lucy for short?"

"If I'm Lucy, you're Cessy," Greymore says, his tone too level and serious for my liking.

"Cessy," Reilynn snorts. "Like a pool...I like it—"

Flicking a throwing knife from my sleeve, I slash the plume from the top of her helmet and casually turn back to Greymore. "Satan?"

Reilynn slowly removes her helmet, brushing a trembling finger over the shorn bristles. Asha slides a comforting arm around her shoulder, leading her away from my blood circle.

Greymore laughs.

I'm instantly nervous.

"What is it?" I practically snap, feeling overly sensitive. At the all too familiar feel of his amusement, I realize I'm holding the knife between us, threatening him with the tiny blade clenched in my fingers. I take a deep breath and stow the weapon.

Linking my arm through his, I force a false smile. "How can I help you, dear?"

"Endearments again; that's promising," he says and begins leading me through the settlement. His steps are slow, like we're promenading. Which, with all the looks and greetings we receive, we might as well be. I wait for him to tell me the reason he searched me out, but—in typical Greymore fashion—he isn't very forthcoming.

Finally, I give up and pull him to our tree. With the valley at my back, I say, "Do I have to ask, or will you just tell me?" I can see the white of his teeth flash and assume he's smirking.

Lately, Greymore has become a little less mysterious...at least visually. The shadow seems to dance around his face, revealing bits and pieces here and there. Not enough for any type of recognition, but enough to deduce he's not going to be painful to look at...if I ever truly see him.

"Well, since you did just ask, I guess I'll tell you," he says, answering my demand with sarcasm.

I flick a throwing knife from my belt and tap it against the clasp of his hood, saying, "I don't think I like you very much right now."

He curls his fingers over mine, easing the blade back. I slide my hand away, pretending his touch doesn't make me shiver. He slowly releases me, dragging his fingers over the back of my hand, saying, "There are rumors that might explain why someone would want to drive the people from Avalei...and The Razor."

Knowing exactly what he's referring to, I spin the hilt in my hand, bemused. "I never took you for the fairy-tale type."

"Nix, it's a motive."

"Did you hear the whole story? It's—"

Glancing over my shoulder, Greymore tenses.

As he steps forward, loading his crossbow, I spin around.

Across the valley, near the lake, there's an odd movement. From our low position, all I can make out is a waving in the grass. "What is it?"

Greymore shakes his head, unknowingly. "It's moving toward the stream."

"Zel," I say, running before the word leaves my mouth.

Following a well-worn path, I rush toward the girl and the bank where she usually does laundry. No one is shrieking and no alarms have been raised, but my intuition is screaming, urging me to move faster.

Feet skimming the grass, I drive my arms and legs forward as the wind brushes by, dancing around my panic. I near the stream. Straining my ears, I hear only splashing and the murmur of voices. Searching with frantic eyes, I spot the strange movement again. Something large and dark is on the opposite side of the stream, moving with an odd gait—halting but quick.

It draws closer to the oblivious settlers.

"Fall back!" I yell, sprinting onto the bank. A dozen settlers snap to attention.

Zel is the first to my side, and I push her behind me. As the settlers group at my back, a different sound comes from over the steady gurgle of the stream. A clicking noise.

Zel's hand latches around my left arm. "What is—"

Her question is answered as something with far too many eyes and far too many legs leaps from the thick grass and lands on the opposite bank. "Stay behind!" I scream as I pull my largest dagger free and embed it between the arachnid's many eyes. It releases an ear-shattering shriek before dropping dead, legs curling upward.

Behind me, the women circle up, many armed with weapons—all our preparation and training paying off. I unsheathe my scimitars and—as a group—we retreat, stretched into an oval shape, inching back toward the open ground of the settlement.

At my side, Zel jerks at every real and imagined sound in the grass. "Steady," I murmur as the sound of a scuffle comes from our side.

Reilynn burst from the grass and we all start. "Dangit, Reilynn!" I slap the flat of my blade against her metal greave. "I almost put this blade in you."

Unhearing, she glances behind her, sword drawn and covered in slime. "Crushed Crawlers, I hate spiders," she sputters, swinging her sword at a sound on our left.

"Where are Greymore and Asha?" I ask as we continue inching backward.

The pace is torturously slow, the tension pulsing around the group.

"In the trees," Reilynn answers, slicing her sword to the side as a creature appears to our right, cutting the legs out from under it. I finish it quickly, cutting off the head. Zel gags.

Finally reaching the clearing of the settlement, our group scatters to get better positions and weapons.

"Zel, get to the healer's hut," I demand, knowing the safest place for her is in the center of town and out of the way. Without a single word, she darts away.

"If worse comes to worse, Xandra will protect her," Reilynn says, eyes on the meadow and the unnaturally moving grass.

"And she can protect Xandra. But it won't come to that," I vow, bouncing on the balls of my feet, waiting for the next spider to pounce.

Hearing the twang of an arrow followed by a thump and shriek as it finds its mark, I glance up, spotting Asha on one side of the settlement and Greymore on the other. "How many?" I yell.

"Forty-nine," Asha answers. Eyes narrowed, she lets another arrow fly.

As the clicking closes in, I swing my scimitars, electrified. The arachnids spring from the grass into the opening, beady eyes searching, fangs snapping.

Lunging forward, I slice through one, but the majority are kept at bay as Asha, Greymore, and other archers systematically take them out. The settlers rally behind Reilynn and me, creating a wall of defense, but the bulk of the creatures are unable to get within snapping distance. Any time they attempt to leap toward us, a well-placed shot from above drives them back, leaving them squealing in frustration.

Suddenly, the animals stop attacking.

But they don't retreat. Instead, they bunch together, as if regrouping.

Their creepy eyes dart to the trees, finding Asha in her sniper nest. As one, they jump forward, rushing up the trees and over our rope systems toward the elf.

With a startled cry, I dart into their path, striking one as it springs over the top of me. My scimitar slices through its underside, and I somersault forward, avoiding another gore bath.

Above me, Asha jumps from her lookout and springs across the rope bridge as no less than five spiders close in on her. A spider jumps, shooting webbing at her, but on her nimble feet, she's a difficult target. Determined, the arachnids stay locked on her, ignoring the volley of arrows coming from the settlers. Falling a level, Asha spins, shooting the nearest spider and knocking it to the ground, where the settlers attack it with gusto.

From below, I attempt to follow Asha's flight, ineffectively striking the arachnids with my throwing knives, hoping to draw their aggression. Asha makes a wide leap, somersaulting to land in the middle of the long rope bridge near my dwelling. A spider lands on the opposite side, giving her the perfect shot.

But she doesn't take it, instead coming up empty-handed when she reaches for her quiver. She's out of arrows.

Greymore and the others must be running low as well because the attacks from their side are tapering off.

Flipping her fan open, Asha throws it like a boomerang, dispatching the creature with its spinning blades. Another one down. Three to go.

The largest remaining arachnid springs to take its comrade's place. As it rushes Asha, she pivots away, retreating. The disturbingly agile spider scrambles after the elf.

Out of daggers and throwing knives, I clasp a scimitar in two hands. As the creature closes in on Asha, fangs nipping at the ruffle of her cloak, I chuck the weapon. It sails end over end, striking the creature's side hard enough to force it from the bridge and pin it to a nearby tree.

I track the remaining two animals giving chase. They're still a level down from Asha and across the rope bridge. If we can just knock them down, the settlers can finish them off with their short-range weapons.

Soaring across the bridge, Asha keeps an eye on the creatures behind her as she attempts to reach my house and the weapons stored inside. She's almost made it when an arachnid appears on my roof.

Three. There are three left.

I scream as the creature drops, practically landing on the elf. With inhuman speed, Asha dodges and spins away, but the creature shoots webbing, catching her by the ankle. Before my horrified cry can end, the creature has Asha prone on the deck and is wrapping her in webbing.

"Reilynn!" I screech. Springing into a nearby basket, I toss the pulley's rope her way. Instantly understanding my unspoken need, she takes off running, hitting the end of the rope at a dead sprint.

With my feet balanced on the top of the basket, I shoot skyward, one hand gripping my lone scimitar, the other clasping the rope. As I approach Asha, I fling myself away from the basket. Sailing through the air, I crash into the side of the arachnid, knocking it from the deck. It screeches as it falls, but I don't pause to watch it land as I take out an approaching arachnid with my remaining weapon and reach for the webbing wrapped around my friend.

Jerking the sticky substance aside, I uncover Asha's face. When her calm, steady gaze meets mine, I say, "Be right back."

Rushing to my home, I grab a knife from the table and spin back to Asha just as a spider reaches the bridge. Against every instinct, I let it stalk toward the elf while I cower in the doorway, waiting for it to get closer.

Just before it reaches Asha, I attack with a battle cry, bracing my hands on either side of the bridge and kicking it with all my might. The arachnid falls.

I hurry to cut the web from Asha and pull her to her feet. She teeters slightly before pushing me. "Go," she whispers.

It's then that I see the creatures retreating. We need to know how they got in. Giving the elf a once-over, I spring over the railing. Catching ropes, I swing down through the levels of the settlement, my hands burning.

Ignoring the shouts of victory, I sprint through the settlement and into the meadow. Following the clicking noises, I tear across the stream. In my haste, water splashes over my leather boots and sprinkles across the shore.

As I sprint, my legs and lungs begin to sting. Strangely, so do my hands. Ignoring the burn, I reach the orchard. There, I weave around orange trees, following the sounds of the arachnids' retreat.

Closing in on the giant spiders, I near the lake. The clicking stops as the pain in my hands flares, making it hard to focus. Pushing past the agony, I listen, hearing a solitary splash. Tracking the sound, I leap from boulder to boulder, skidding to a halt at a high vantage point.

I scan the area for a sign of the arachnids, but there's nothing. Nothing but huge boulders, clear water, and a pain that just won't stop. The arachnids have disappeared, but— as the throbbing in my hands becomes excruciating—I cease to care.

Dropping from the rock, I stumble to the lakeshore and plunge my hands into the cool water. It doesn't ease the pain. Though they look whole, my hands feel as if they are disintegrating, being eaten away by a pulsing fire.

Through the pain, I feel Greymore's arrival. He's anxious, probably sensing my hurt. When he sees me at the water's edge, his anxiety doesn't ebb. If anything, it multiplies.

"What is it?" I ask, my heart hammering as my hands twist, clenching in pain.

"It's Asha," he says, glancing knowingly at my hands in the water. "The webbing is poisoned."

CHAPTER SIXTEEN

"Why hurdles?" Trent asks, twisting the key in the lock. Swinging his front door open wide, he gestures me inside.

"Coach needed someone, and I've always done them," I say as I spring forward to duck under Trent's arm.

I'm practically giddy after the first day of track practice and don't bother to temper my enthusiasm. I've been looking forward to this season for months, a sport Trent and I can do together and an outlet for my nervous energy. I've always been energetic, but lately my gut twitches and churns if I'm not moving and *doing*.

"I know I probably won't place," I admit with a half-smile as I drop my homework-weighed bag on the island and slide onto a barstool. "I'm not very good at hurdles with my stubby legs and all. The 100 and relay are my best events," I shrug, "but I like hurdles."

Puzzled, Trent rolls his shoulder causing his bag to slide down his arm before he catches it in one graceful, careless move. "Why compete in something you can't win?" he asks, dropping his bag next to mine and tossing his keys into a nearby tray.

His attitude makes me cold, reminding me of Trent's overly competitive nature…and the last time he lost big. That night is a dark thought I consistently avoid. Like always, I redirect my thoughts to the positive, seeing no benefit in focusing on the bad. Things with Trent have been great since we got back together, rebooting our relationship with a perfect Valentine's date.

For the occasion, Trent made dinner reservations at a high-end, swanky restaurant. An hour before he picked me up, a beautiful dress and a bouquet of irises arrived for me.

The skirt of the black dress was covered in a deep purple sheer overlay that sparkled and flared out, reaching my knees. The dark satin top had sleeves draping over my shoulders and a front that crisscrossed in a flattering cut that wasn't too low. The diamond necklace I found at the bottom of the box was stunning in a simple yet elegant way. The whole outfit was a dream, the exact look I would have picked for myself if I had money to burn. The fact that Trent picked it all out made the whole thing even more swoony.

After our amazing dinner, we went back to Trent's house to a pool surrounded by firelight. There were at least a hundred candles spread across the deck and floating on the water's surface. We spent the rest of the night in the pool, gliding carefully through the enchanting water, laughing when one of us accidentally put out a candle.

All the while, Trent didn't push for anything physical. He was a gentleman in every sense of the word—charming, suave, kind.

And it didn't end that night.

He's been amazing every minute since, but...

...I feel like I'm waiting. It's like I'm living in my fantasy world and surrounded by danger. I'm constantly aware, ready, and prepared for an attack. Things may be quiet. Things may be great. But I don't trust they'll stay that way.

The simple fact is, I don't trust my boyfriend.

But we're getting there.

Again, I redirect my thoughts, pulling myself back to the positive of the here and now to answer Trent's question about why I do hurdles. "For fun?" Unzipping my bag, I pull out my math book and scrounge around for a pencil. Being back in the action and not just watching it, I'm going to have to spend more of my time at Trent's doing homework. But since my boyfriend is ridiculously smart, it's a win-win for me.

As I begin my work, Trent moves to the fridge, searching through the shelves, tension marking his shoulders.

I pretend not to notice his edginess as I tap the eraser on my paper, my frantic energy returning. Why can't I just trust him? I spin the pencil between my fingers, staring at the sun glistening on the water of the pool. What kind of girlfriend am I to always be suspicious? What kind of person is so unforgiving?

Redirect yourself, girl. Forcing my thoughts back to the positive, I decide I just need time. The trust will come in time.

"Claire." Trent catches my free hand, causing me to jump and lose control of the pencil spinning through my fingers. It clatters to the marble as I meet Trent's probing gaze. Leaning across the island, he studies me with concern and a glimmer of frustration. "You okay?"

"Fine," I say, more than a little embarrassed at my overreaction. "Just spacing."

He traces a finger over the back of my hand. "Well, I was just saying that I really don't think you should do it."

"Shouldn't do what?" I say, my mind jumping to a million things I shouldn't be doing. Questioning my boyfriend. Holding on to one single second of the past. Being so stingy with my affection.

"Do hurdles," he says, his hand tightening over mine.

For a second, I'm relieved…but only for a second. Then, I'm on edge all over again, debating against pushing the issue or giving in. I hook my foot around the barstool, saying, "I don't see the problem with doing them, Trent."

Pivoting around the counter, Trent takes the seat next to mine. Easing his grip, he flips my hand so it's lying palm up in his. "Babe, just listen." He runs his finger across my palm. "You're awesome at the 100 and at the relay. You could also be great at the 200." I puff up a little at his praise. I am fast. "But," he says, still skimming his finger over my palm, "you aren't great at hurdles. Just think how much better you could be at your other events if you took the time you spent practicing for hurdles and devoted it to increasing your speed and start." His eyes meet mine, alight with competitive drive. "You could make it to State."

State. A whole lot of misaligned stars would have to fall into place for me to make it. On the other hand, Trent's position is practically guaranteed—he's amazing at the high jump and the long jump. "I'm not really counting on State this year," I say, ever the realist.

"If you made it, we could go together." Trent grins, melting my resolve.

Going to State with him *would* be awesome. "I'll think about it," I say, returning his smile.

"That's all I ask, love." He drops a kiss on my cheek and releases my hand. "I just don't want something you only *like* to prevent you from winning something you love. It would be horrible to crash and burn at hurdles, then fail at every other event you actually had a chance in." Laughing at the perceived idiocy, he shakes his head and spins from the bar.

I mumble some kind of assent, pretending to return my focus to the math problem in front of me. But the numbers on the paper aren't the problem my mind chooses to focus on. Instead, it's the methodical, logical way Trent laid out his argument—the way he made it so obvious my emotions and wants were illogical, silly, childish…

...and wrong.

Redirect.

Again, I force my thoughts back to the positive.

✳ ✳ ✳ ✳

I'm still thinking about our conversation and whether I'll stick with hurdles when Adam welcomes himself inside.

I haven't seen much of Adam these past few weeks. Trent's accusation made things awkward, so by unspoken agreement, Adam and I have been more distanced. He seems to show up at Trent's house less and less. We still have lunch together and hang out in group settings, but it's rarely just us three anymore. I miss it.

"Hey, Nix." Adam finds me sketching at the bar. "Where's Trent?"

"He's in the office printing something out," I answer, a part of me hoping he'll hurry to find Trent and a part of me hoping he'll linger. With my head down, I keep my hand moving, drawing pointless, ineffective lines.

Not hearing him leave, I glance up to find him studying me.

"What are you drawing?" he asks, his tone probing, and I sense the real meaning behind his spoken words. What he really wants to know is how I'm doing.

The trouble is, I don't have an answer.

"Iris," I mumble, not answering his true question or meeting his eyes. Adam has a way of seeing things I don't want him to see. Of making me painfully aware of the things I'm determined to avoid.

I continue filling in the lines of my favorite flower, my picture looking more childlike and pathetic with every stroke.

"Can I see?" he asks.

I answer by stopping and lifting my pencil.

Tentatively, he pulls my pad from under my raised hand and across the counter. Shifting my focus, I stare at the pencil, flicking it through my fingers. I keep my eyes on the movement, listening as he flips pages.

He won't find much in there. Drawing after drawing of flowers, a few of Trent, and a couple of landscapes. Nothing fantastic...or inspiring.

"May I?" he asks, holding up a blank sheet in the book. Realizing he's asking if he can rip out the page, I nod. He tears the paper, then slides the book back under the pencil spinning through my restless fingers.

Forcing myself to still, I tuck the pencil behind my ear as Adam grabs some kitchen scissors and cuts the paper down. Then he begins folding, his large hands quick and impressive. I divide my attention between watching him work and flipping through my sketchbook, trying to find some redeeming features in the art.

"Why don't you draw fantasy stuff anymore?" Adam asks, again with that voice that says so much more.

I shrug, chancing a glance at him, but he's focused on his origami. "I stopped for a while, focusing on other stuff and now..." I drift off, unable to explain the pain in my fantasies. My dream world used to be a refuge, a place I loved to visit in my drawings. Now it's painful...a place I ignore unless I'm asleep. But it was once an inspiration, an inspiration I've set aside.

"You should pick it up again," Adam says, his words more encouraging than even he knows. "Those drawings were great." He waves toward my pad. "Don't get me wrong, those are awesome, too. You're obviously talented, but the other ones…well, they were something special." He snorts, a soft sound of self-mockery. "But I don't really know anything, it's just my preference, I guess."

"Mine too," I say, practically whispering.

"So? Draw them," he says, offering me a small smile.

I tap the cover of my pad. "Yeah, maybe I will."

Maybe if I again embrace my dreams instead of ignoring them, I'll shape my imaginings, finding some peace in that world.

"Some inspiration," Adam says, sliding the folded paper to me with an almost sheepish expression. I pick it up, my smile spreading as I realize he's made a paper sword.

"Thanks, Adam," I say, meeting and holding his gaze for the first time since his arrival.

Looking almost guilty, Adam glances away. "Well, I'm going to go find Trent."

"Okay," I say in an undertone, twisting the tiny sword in my fingers. With its odd weight and material, the blade should feel strange in my hands, but it's just the opposite. It feels right, like protection and power and belonging. Like all the things I'm missing.

* * * *

That night, I stand in front of my canvas. It's late, and I should be sleeping.

Instead, I'm thinking of hurdles and fantasy worlds. I grip the charcoal in my hands, almost afraid to begin. Images of Avalei pass through my mind, a world so full of vivid detail, I don't know where to start.

Should I draw Xandra dancing in front of a snowcat? Reilynn laughing with Zel in a cozy treehouse? Asha practicing archery with the settlers? Greymore slaying a serpent? Nix the Defender plummeting through a swarm of bats?

That world has become so extreme, so out there, and yet so personal. Putting it on paper is claiming it, owning my imaginings and making them a part of me. Closing my eyes, I let the images come. My mind creates a vision I haven't dreamt, but one I want to experience.

I open my eyes and break the white field of canvas with a bold, dark stroke…and another. A quiet knock sounds at the door. Intent on my work, I don't immediately answer, and my door creaks open.

"Claire?" My mom peeks through the crack between the door and the frame. "It's late. Are you getting to bed soon?"

I spin on my swiveled chair. "I tried," I admit with a small smile.

Hearing my soft confession, she steps fully into the room. "I didn't get a chance to ask you about track. How did it go?"

"It was fine."

I drop the charcoal and rub at the smudge on my finger. "But I'm thinking of dropping hurdles this year."

Her expression grows quizzical. "But I thought you loved them."

"I do," I say. "I'm just not very good at them."

Tipping her head, my mom looks at me, really looks. Then, with a sigh, she squats down onto the corner of my bed. "Claire, you've always been a pleaser."

"As my parent, isn't that one of the things you love most about me?" I tease, twisting in my seat to face her more fully. "I'm pretty sure that's what you said."

Her returning smile is pinched. "This past year, I've seen you do a lot of…uncharacteristic things. And I wonder if you're doing them because you really want to…or because you're pleasing someone else."

"Trent, you mean," I say, surprised that my voice is so hard. She's not exactly wrong.

She holds her hands up. "I don't know, sweetie," she says, her tone vibrating with honesty. "What I do know is that a little distance can give you space to find yourself. To find what it is that makes *you* happy."

"Mom, I am happy," I say, but the statement doesn't exactly ring true.

With a sad shake of her head, my mom leans forward and places a hand on my knee. "Maybe you are, but you aren't fulfilled."

I open my mouth to argue, but Mom's knowing look causes me to reconsider. She continues, "I won't tell you to 'do what makes you happy' because momentary happiness doesn't always lead to lasting joy. And God wants us to find the lasting joy. So do the things that make you feel fulfilled. Do the things that *inspire* you to feel happiness, to share happiness, to feel closer to heaven. Whether you're the best at it or the worst. Find fulfillment. Like me and yoga…" A small, surprised laugh leaks from me, and my mom grins.

My mom's lack of balance, but determination to do daily yoga is a running joke in our family. "Yes," she says. "I know just how bad I am at it." She shakes a finger at me. "I see you and Dillon giggling about it…constantly. And you aren't wrong, but it makes me *feel* fulfilled…and it's good for me."

Taking my hand, she brushes at the marks on my finger, thoughtlessly grooming as only a mother can. "Just do what's best for you, Claire. Best for your future happiness." Giving up on removing the charcoal, she rises.

"Thanks, Mom," I say, my thoughts distant.

"Is this going to be of a fantasy world?" she asks, gesturing to the rather barren canvas.

"Yes," I answer with a small amount of chagrin—my mom usually appreciates more traditional work.

But, surprising me, she leans forward and drops a kiss on my forehead. "Good," she says. "That's some of your best stuff."

"Oh," I falter. "Well, um…thanks."

"Goodnight, my Claire-Bear." With a last, wistful smile, she exits the room. I stare at the door, her encouragement coursing through me, strengthening me, reminding me that

God does want my lasting joy and will help me find it in big and small ways.

Before I can change my mind, I grab my phone from the nightstand and call Trent. I won't take the cowardly way out and text him.

Besides, he'll probably call to try to change my mind anyway.

"Hey, babe," he answers, sounding wide awake. I'm not surprised, Trent thrives on small doses of sleep.

"Hi, love," I respond, clutching the phone a little too tightly. "I just wanted to tell you…"

With a deep inhale, I spout my decision in one long breath. "I've been thinking, and I've decided to do hurdles. You were right about everything you said, but I really enjoy them. More than any other event, and I'll regret not doing them."

"Did you seriously consider this, Claire?" he asks. Sounding incredibly put out, he adds, "It's not like you to be impulsive, and you *are* calling me after midnight."

"I'm sure, Trent," I say, unwilling to argue about something that's ultimately all my choice.

"Okay." His response is curt, annoyed.

"Well, I just wanted to let you know," I say, deflated. I'm not sure what I was hoping for, maybe a little support or even an accepting you-do-you type of thing. Instead, it's just disappointment.

The silence stretches, and I finally say, "I'd better go get some sleep. I'll see you in the morning?"

"Sure," he says, dismissive. "See you then." He hangs up before I can return his goodbye. I stare at the phone, my finger hovering over his name, desperate to call him back and not go to sleep feeling this...weirdness between us.

Instead, I purposefully walk to the nightstand, plug the phone in, and return to my art desk.

Picking up the charcoal, I get back to work.

It's hours before I finish, and I'm exhausted but exhilarated.

Easing away from the canvas, a wide smile covers my face at the image of Xandra, Reilynn, Asha, Betah, Greymore, and Nix the Defender. We're all standing atop the wall of Avalei, smiling, laughing, and celebrating a victory.

But that isn't the best part. The best part is each and every one of us looks absolutely, completely fulfilled.

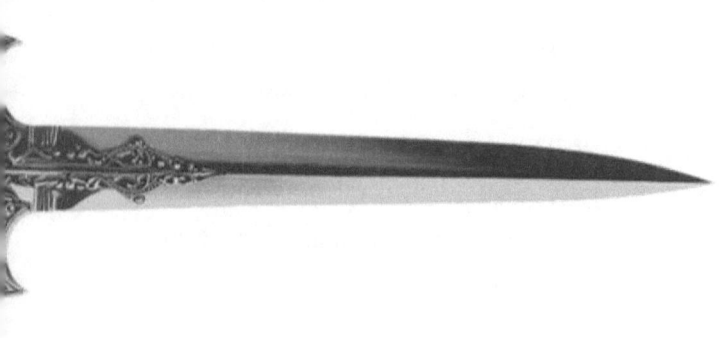

CHAPTER SEVENTEEN

Xandra is killing me...and herself.

I'm not sure who will be the first to go, but either I'll die trying to convince her to stop fretting over Asha or she'll die from overprotectiveness.

"The healer says she'll pull through," I cajole as, for what seems like the hundredth time, I guide Xandra none-too-gently away from Asha's bedside and back to her own. "Her elf heritage saved her."

Xandra grunts, dropping ungracefully to the cot, her face contorted with pain. "Those elves are hard to kill," she mutters.

Then, jerking upright, she says, "We should try some tarrow root." With a hand on both of her shoulders, I push her back down.

"You gave that to her an hour ago," I say. "See? You're getting delusional. Not to mention the physical damage." Pulling up her tunic, I inspect the bandages circling her torso in the sputtering torchlight.

In the beginning, frantic hours of Asha's illness, Xandra had been incredibly strong, her worry over the elf overpowering her own pain. I had almost forgotten her injuries, but as the hours wore on, Xandra's sympathetic adrenaline wore off, and she could no longer hide her pain. Her wounds had reopened, another blow after so many. To keep her from hovering at Asha's bedside, Reilynn forcibly escorted Xandra to bed…and forcibly kept her there until she slept.

Now it's nearing dawn. Xandra's been awake for an hour, tromping all over my frayed nerves. Of course, her wounds are still weeping, and the warrior isn't helping matters. Keeping my face passive, I pull the covers over her battered body, saying, "Now, go back to bed. I'll put Reilynn on watch if I have to."

"Stupid knight," Xandra mutters. *"I'm bigger than you. You have to do what I want."* She does a surprisingly accurate impression of Reilynn's voice. "Meeh, meeh, meeh."

I shake my head as she continues to grumble, her voice tapering off as she falls asleep. Little does she know, I wouldn't dare go wake the knight now, not when she's finally sleeping after a night of little to no rest. But none of us could sleep until we knew Asha would make it. The spider's web didn't immediately affect Asha. Like my hands, it was slower—a toxin sinking through the skin and damaging the nerves. As I chased the creatures, Asha was able to cut herself free and descend from the upper living spaces before succumbing to the poison.

When she dropped to the forest floor in convulsions, everyone was shocked...and helpless. Luckily, Xandra had an herb that we were able to force down her throat to protect her brain from damage. Two long hours later, the full-body tremors stopped, and the healer declared she'd live. It had been horrendous—a nightmare.

During that time, I also lost all use of my hands. They shook uncontrollably and burned like electric fire. It was agony, especially knowing the vile poison affecting only a small part of my body was attacking all of my friend's.

I study my hands, front and back. Less than a day after my poisoning and there isn't a lingering sign of the ordeal, not even a twinge of pain when I close my fists. I step to the elf's bed, hoping her recovery will be as complete. Finally stabilized, Asha's face looks peaceful, the picture of serenity at first glance.

However, looking closer, I can see her skin isn't the beautiful translucence of health, but the grayish pallor of near-death. Dropping to the stool I just forced Xandra from, I bury my hands in my hair, digging my fingers painfully into my scalp. I have to stop this.

Somehow, those spiders got in and disappeared back out of our fortress. Now that Asha's immediate health is stable, I need to find out where.

I eye the door that seems so very, very far away. Vision blurring, I rub at my irritated eyes. I'm exhausted. So exhausted. Even if I could make it to the door, I wouldn't make it to the meadow. My body groans at the thought, muscles screaming and nerves wasted.

Slumping forward, I rest my arm on the side of Asha's bed. My lids droop, shuttering my bloodshot, gritty eyes. My body resists the call to sleep, but my mind drifts, thoughts becoming disjointed.

Can't go yet. Wait for Reilynn.

Rest, I'll just rest.

* * * *

"Nix." A hand gently jostles my shoulder. I grunt at the pressure, blinking in confusion.

"Nix," Reilynn says again. "I've got this. You'll rest better in your bed." I stretch my arms, my muscles protesting the movement and my awkward sleeping arrangement. Light shines through the window.

I snap upright. "What time is it?" I demand.

"Almost afternoon." Reilynn looks sheepish—my knight never sleeps this late. But, then again, none of us has ever come so close to death. It seems this is a place for setting new, unhealthy standards.

I ease my aching body from the stool. "You'll take watch here?" Reilynn nods, still too emotionally drained for conversation. "Great," I say, sorting through the haphazard heap of weapons and armor I left near the door. Starting with my thick, leather greaves, I begin to rearm myself.

"Burnished Blades, Nix. Why are you suiting up?" Reilynn asks, her dark eyes flashing with worry…and interest. If she's dead on her feet, she'll battle on her knees. It's the knight in her, the part that can't be taught, but just *is*.

Strapping my bracers to my arms, I readjust the throwing knives in their looped holds. "Those spiders didn't come in or over the wall," I say. "They came from somewhere on The Razor side." I slide my last dagger into my belt. "And I'm going to find out where."

Reilynn looks between our companions and the door, torn. "Please stay," I say. "I want you here if anything goes wrong."

Turning to Asha's too-still form, she nods sharply then demands, "Take Greymore."

I roll my eyes. My crew used to think I was independent.

Reilynn stands, coming to tower over me. "There's no shame in needing support, Nix." She leans down, her jaw so tight she can barely form words. "Let him be yours."

Knowing better than to argue with her current mood, I say, "I won't go alone." Sheathing my scimitars, I turn away. "We'll be back by dark," I promise, ducking from the hut.

Needing some supplies, I turn toward the community building, practically jumping from my skin as Greymore steps from the side of the hut.

"Twenty-four hours," he says, falling into step beside me.

"Twenty-four hours for what?" I ask, shaken by his sudden appearance and Reilynn's words. I can't lean too heavily on Greymore.

He's a temporary member of our group, and you don't rely on temporary.

"Twenty-four hours before beginning your search for the unknown entrance to Avalei," he says, holding out a water skin and three strips of salted meat.

I eye him a moment before taking his much-needed offering. Changing direction, I glance over my shoulder at the hut. "Were you eavesdropping, my lord?" I provoke him, uncomfortable with how comfortable he's become.

"Don't *my lord* me, Nix," he all but growls.

"Fine, Cronar." I smirk, taking a huge bite of the meat. "But if you *weren't* doing something as unlordly as eavesdropping, how did you know my plans?"

"Nix, Nix, Nix," he says, his voice dropping with each successive word. Without breaking stride, he leans closer to me. "I know you." I choke on my food, and he tilts away, saying, "Besides, it's what *I* would do. We were only waiting for you."

I pound on my chest and clear my throat. "We?" I ask as we near the end of the forested settlement.

Seeing us, Torren pushes himself from the tree he's leaning against. "We," he says, giving me a gentle one-armed hug, his expression soft with affection. "I couldn't pass up the chance to find the entrance you somehow missed on all of your youthful adventures."

"If I had found it, things would be different," I murmur, staring over the valley. "Xandra would be well. Asha wouldn't be struggling for her life. Avalei would be safe."

A heaviness falls over the group. Before the two men can offer any unwanted platitudes, I say, "I'm sorry," and, forcing levity, I add, "I guess I was just saving the discovery...for today!"

With that said, I lead the way through the meadow. All signs of the battle are gone except a few scorch marks randomly dotting the area. I study the blackened earth as we pass.

Noticing my scrutiny, Torren explains, "We didn't know what was poisonous and what wasn't, so we burned every part of the arachnids."

"Of course," I say, remembering the overpowering smell, like burnt rubber. A breeze pushes a pile of ash in front of us, kicking up the scent, a sensory reminder of aching hands and an elf clinging to life.

"We did save some of the webbing," Torren continues, "to study and use later. We also started making some larger, stronger bows. As soon as Asha is better, we'll have her begin training with those. Zel recommended looking into a stronger, sharper ore for the arrows, and Percy..."

I listen to Torren's report on the settlers with one ear. He's always been a planner who plans aloud. Greymore offers occasional insights, and I voice my support, but it's mostly Torren's words keeping us company as we trek through the valley, cross the small stream, cut through the orchards, and stop at the lake.

I climb to the top of the rock I stood at a day ago, again searching. "They disappeared from right around here," I say.

Torren and Greymore spread out, searching the surrounding area.

I scan the small lake. Massive boulders line the water, leaving tiny stretches of beach between. To my right, the boulders offer a small access point between the water and The Razor. The cliffs of the mountain range rise sharply above the lake, throwing a shadow over the clear water for the greater part of the day.

Closing my eyes, I think over the sounds of that night. My memory is dampened by the trauma, but slowly it comes back: the clicking of the arachnid's legs—softer through the dirt, sharper on the rock—and then, the splashing of water. Smiling, I open my eyes, slide from the rock, and begin to remove my armor.

"Nix?" From a nearby stone, Greymore makes my name a question.

Tossing the armor and boots aside, I grin over my shoulder. "I'm going for a swim." Before he can protest, I dive from the rock.

The water is like most everything else in Avalei…perfect—just bracing enough to be refreshing, but not cold enough to drive me away. The lake is so pure that I can see around fifteen feet down. With the amazing clarity, I start systematically searching, moving between the boulders dotting the shore nearest the vast mountain.

Hearing a splash behind me, I'm not surprised when Greymore swims to my side. "What are we looking for?" he asks, treading water.

Glancing at his head bobbing next to me, I choke. Greymore's hood is still on…and plastered to his head. Honestly, I'm not sure if the sight is hysterical or impressive. A little of both, I guess.

Covering my reaction to the drowned rat/superhero beside me, I gesture to the shore and boulders before us, water dripping from my arm. "The arachnids jumped into the lake, so we're looking for some kind of access point on this side of the shore. If I'm right, it will lead to a tunnel and into The Razor."

"Spiders hate water," Greymore says, clearly doubting my reasoning, but I'm not the one wearing a cape in the middle of a lake.

Pushing a soaked strand of hair from my forehead, I argue, "But they can survive it." I begin to feel along the shore. "I'm almost positive the other entrance is here, hidden between or under the rocks. If it were anywhere else, it would have been discovered long ago."

"All right." Without further argument, Greymore joins me, swimming along the west bank of the lake.

Our progress draws Torren's attention. After hearing my suspicions, he paces the shore above us, looking for an opening from above because 'full immersion on any day other than bath day is a sin'.

We search for an hour, and I begin to doubt my memory. "Maybe I heard wrong," I say to the two, my arms crossed over a rock on shore, fingers hastily tapping on the warm stone. "The arachnids might have swum across the lake or not even entered the lake at all. I could be remembering everything wrong and wasting time. Maybe we should—"

"Trust yourself, Nix," Greymore says, still wearing that ridiculous hood that shadows his face like a strange oval censor strip. I nod at his reassurance and look at a point over his shoulder, frustrated at my obnoxious inability to actually *see* him.

My focus narrows in on the massive rock I originally stood on…the one I assume the spiders bailed off of that night. It isn't on the shoreline running parallel to the Razor, but along the bank curving away from the mountain into the valley. But what if the path doesn't run straight into the mountainside? What if it tunnels down before curving to meet the mountain?

Eyes squinting, I stare at the gray stone jutting out into the water.

"Nix?" Greymore asks, feeling the churning of my mind through our link.

Without responding, I lunge forward, ignoring the exasperated emotion Greymore sends my way. Swimming with sharp, swift strokes, I reach the rock and dive under.

In the shadow of the boulder, my visibility disappears. I stretch my fingers out, feeling my way along the wet stone. Running out of air, I surface, suck in a harsh gasp, and dive again.

One hand bumps against Greymore diving beside me while the other hits rock unexpectedly fast, jamming a finger back.

Shaking the pain away, I kick to the side and reach again to find…nothing. Greymore and I surface at the same time, speaking over the top of each other.

"It's there."

"You found it."

Treading water, my lips curve and I catch the flash of Greymore's smile—an instant of perfect, grinning clarity. It's enough to guarantee Greymore unshadowed is clearly the stuff of dreams.

"It's under there?!" Torren exclaims, breaking through my gushy thoughts.

"Yes, my friend," I say, not looking away from a once again concealed Greymore. "Get the soap, Torren. It's time for your monthly swim."

* * * *

Gasping, I surface into darkness. I suck in air again and again, forcing the black spots to retreat from my vision. The swim through the curving tunnel had been a little longer and more dangerous than expected.

An arm encircles me in the darkness, hauling me onto a rough surface.

"It'll just take a minute," Greymore says as I gather my legs under me.

Sparks come from nearby, and I groan as a torch sparks to life in Greymore's hands.

"Guess you lost that bet, Nix," Torren says, pulling himself from the water. The man is a surprisingly agile swimmer considering his aversion to the water.

In the dark, I smile with relief. I may have expressed some doubts concerning Greymore's strange flammable-when-wet concoction. Who would have thought he'd so easily get it to light? Not me. But who really wants to be stuck without light in a dark tunnel? Again, not me. So, if I had to choose, this was a great bet to lose.

Moving forward, my foot bumps against the steep incline of the rock. I slow down, stepping gingerly in the dark. Greymore reaches for my elbow, helping me up to a flatter, yet jagged surface.

"A favor," he says, handing me a sputtering torch. "You owe me a favor."

"I think you're confused about this whole betting thing," I respond. "Unless otherwise stated, I owe you money, not a favor." Raising my torch, I observe the area around us. With a torch of his own, Torren walks away from us, studying what looks to be a tunnel.

"Doesn't the victor choose his prize?" Greymore retorts, far too eager to have me in his debt.

"No," I say. "But if it's a favor you want…"

Grinning wickedly, I spring forward, throw his hood back, and drop a resounding kiss on his cheek. The darkness hides his expression, but not his sharp, unsteady inhale. "Debt paid," I exclaim.

"No," Greymore says, stopping my retreat by clamping his arm around my waist.

He leans closer as the shadows dance around us. He doesn't say anything else, leaving communication to our link.

Our emotions spin together, declaring and affirming what we won't.

"You know what this means, right?" Torren says, and I spring away, practically falling back down the ramp-like rise.

"Yes, no. What?" I stammer.

"These," Torren says, pointing his torch at the wall and running a hand over the jagged indentations. With an overly exaggerated, calm movement, I step to examine the tunnel.

Carved out of rock, it's about four feet wide and eight feet tall. A breeze flows down the passageway, chilling my soaked skin, but it's the gouges Torren is studying in the wall that make my blood run cold.

In disbelief, I take the light from Torren and hold it closer, touching the markings. They look familiar, a spacing I've seen far too often—a mark that's etched onto Xandra's very skin.

"Snowcats," I whisper. "This was dug by snowcats."

The implications fall from my statement, resting over us with a suffocating weight.

Snowcats will dig through rock for shelter, for food, but they wouldn't dig a perfectly human-sized tunnel without reason. Without being compelled. Just like sea serpents wouldn't strike a wagon party at random, giant spiders wouldn't raid without reason, megaspecs wouldn't terrorize a settlement, and mosquitoes wouldn't attack in broad daylight.

This is all unnatural behavior. And on top of all that, there's the beasts' unheard-of abilities. It all points to one thing, one truth I've been hoping to disprove: a higher intelligence is behind all of this.

"It means the legends are true." Torren's voice is hushed with excitement. His conclusion is more positive than mine. While I'm hung up on what kind of person or group we'll find behind the attacks, Torren's jumped straight to motive. Why would anyone want to scare people away from Avalei? Because Avalei has something valuable, something they want to keep hidden.

"So, it was *you* who told Greymore about the altanium," I scold, placing a hand on my hip, but the effect is lost in the darkness of the space. "You told *me* it was all a myth."

"Yes," Torren admits, holding his torch between us. He meets my gaze, the flame reflected in his dark, honest eyes. "I told you it was all a myth because I didn't think a young girl with your unquenchable thirst for adventure needed a legend to chase."

"But now you believe it?" I ask, still unwilling to believe in the legend of altanium—something that's never been seen.

"Yes," Torren says, his tone heavy. "If we believe in the miraculous goodness of this world, we also have to accept the pervasive evil."

"But altanium is inherently good," I argue, remembering the myths, the stories I used to cling to of The Razor and the magic buried within.

"In the right hands," Torren says caustically, staring down the tunnel and into the darkness beyond our small circle of light. I follow his gaze, wondering what we'll find at the end.

"Whether the altanium is real or not, the person behind all of this most definitely is, and there's nothing right about their hands—as covered in blood as they are," I say, nails digging into the handle of the torch as I think of the pain and fear coating Avalei. "Let's see if we can flush this coward out." Vengeance pushing me forward, I step into the darkness, ready to finally meet the real enemy.

Greymore and Torren fall in line behind me, their footfalls a supportive reassurance in the unnerving, clawed-out space. My sphere of light reaches in front of us, displaying foot after foot of carved rock. The passageway curves toward the mountain, leading us to the underside of The Razor.

We walk for a time, our footfalls echoing strangely in the space as we go deeper and deeper into the mountain. My vengeful energy fades into a calm determination. I will find and stop whoever is doing this—it's as simple and complicated as that.

"Tell me about altanium," Greymore says, breaking the silence. Speaking of complicated...

Stopping, I turn to him and say, "Wow, I wouldn't have bet on you being the one to break the silence, Lord Greymore." Smiling, I reach for my water skin.

"In your case, I wouldn't recommend betting at all," he replies. "Unless you *like* being in my debt?" I snort a little water up my nose.

Torren gives me a rough slap on the back. "Why don't you just tell him what you know about altanium," he says. "If

I know you, you know more than me and definitely more than you're letting on."

Greymore shoots me an all-too-familiar smug emotional current. Bested too many times today, I cave, "Alright, alright. *Apparently…,*" I start, shooting Torren a significant glance, "…altanium is an incredibly valuable metal, but unicorn rare. Its scarcity gives it worth. An item made from it would be worth more than I will ever see in a lifetime…or your summer manor, my lord." A wave of exasperated emotion hits me, but it's tinged with humor and an appreciation Greymore can't hide.

Grinning, I turn back to the tunnel, keeping my eyes on the flickering light before us. The floor is uneven, so every step is a challenge. "Anyway," I continue. "Legend has it that it can be found in the heart of The Razor—which is the direction we are heading. Of course, something like that would be hundreds of feet below the peaks, in an animal-made tunnel, miles inside a mountain where chances of collapse are high and survival low. Where an evil psychopath hides in his lair, waiting for unsuspecting visitors…that's where the altanium hides."

When I don't add anything else, Torren huffs, "She's forgetting the most important part. Altanium is also believed to hold great power. Or rather, it possesses the *ability* to hold great power. Those with magic can use an orb created from the metal to store their power. The more altanium you have, the more magic you can store. Leaving even those with a tiny spark of magic the ability to do amazing things—"

"—or deadly things," I add. "Luckily for us, magic beings are as rare as altanium. Myths."

"Most myths have a basis of truth," Greymore says.

"Most everything a person believes has a basis of truth; it's the lies surrounding the truth that are the problem," I say, sidestepping a large pile of snowcat dung.

"Well, Nix," Torren says, sounding slightly winded. "Even *you* have to admit that magic is likely at play here. How else would someone control the animals and strengthen them? It's undeniable."

"I'm not denying it," I mumble. "I'm just not admitting it." Because admitting it means admitting I'm about to fight a powerful and magical unknown entity. It's terrifying, and I don't have room for terror.

Greymore sends a current of emotion my way, offering a potent dose of courage as Torren grumbles at my response, but sensing my mood, my mentor doesn't push.

We sink back into silence, our pace increasing as the passage of time becomes more and more pressing. In a few short hours, we'll have to turn back.

Suddenly, the flickering light changes, drifting upward, rising to fill a greater space. I step into the massive cavern. Inching forward, my eyes straining to see past the vast darkness.

In the center, there's light. A small amount, but in this void, that's all it takes. Creeping over the slippery ground, I step into the circle of light. It's about six feet in diameter. Following the beam, I look skyward to an opening in the cave about fifty feet up. The tall, sheer walls are reminiscent of the valley of Avalei—unscalable and breathtaking.

I peer past the light to the cliff face surrounding it. Stalactites hang from the ceiling. Scattered between the cave's unique formations are dark, teardrop shapes.

One shifts.

"Megaspec," I whisper, quickly moving from the light. I bump into Greymore. His hand latches on my upper arm as I slide my feet backward, pulling him with me. We slip on the floor, and I only now realize it's covered in guano. Stupid bats.

"Nix," Greymore whispers, his breath touching the area just behind my ear. I fight to hold steady as he points over my shoulder toward the opposite side from where we entered. "The tunnel continues there. Do we keep going?"

A little breathless from the imminent threat of man-eating bats and Greymore's continued proximity, I nod and begin inching toward the opening.

Greymore keeps his hand on my arm as Torren follows us both, the bat waste covering the sound of our passage. We reach the tunnel without incident and release a collective breath.

"If I could take them one by one…" Torren's voice drifts off, violent thoughts flashing through his mind. I'm guessing he's not too happy about the megaspecs attempting to make a meal of Zel. I can't blame him, even I'd like another shot at them, and I took out quite a grouping with my creative freefall.

Greymore leans back into the cavern, hood tracking slowly from side to side, mumbling lightly. I yank him back, clasping the fabric of his hood in my hands. "Do not even consider it," I hiss.

"What?" he says in a voice that doesn't have a trace of innocence, only arrogance.

"I see you counting them, figuring out if you can take them or not." I shake him. "No, Greymore. Just no, no, no."

"He isn't a dog," Torren says, pulling my hand from the hood, leaving the fabric rumpled.

Greymore jerks the hood straight. "No harm, Torren. I don't mind being Nix's pet."

"You aren't—" I cut off my retort, sensing Greymore's quiet amusement.

Shooting a knowing glare at both the insufferable men, I lift my torch and start down the newest tunnel, keeping a leery pace. This tunnel is wider. The sides are still snowcat-made, but the space can fit three of us walking side by side.

After what feels like hours but is less than one, another opening comes into view.

As we reach the edge, my mouth drops open, not at the size of the massive cavern before us, but at the glow emanating from the ground. The floor seems to be made up of a solid metal that reflects light like a prism, throwing rainbows around the space. The color isn't clear, but more of a translucent gold. And, on closer inspection, it looks as if the rainbows are there, trapped inside the awe-inspiring metal.

I comb the cavern for danger, for threats, and find nothing but stunning beauty. "It's real," I say, my voice hushed as I accept another myth come to life. "Altanium is real."

* * * *

As the sun sets behind me, I wring water from my long braid. Thankfully, our journey back through the tunnel had been quick and uneventful. Still twisting water from my hair, I study the rock ledge hiding the tunnel entrance. "I'd like to collapse this whole thing right now."

Torren sighs, repeating his argument. "I can see the reason you're eager to close the entrance. But—like I've been saying—if we close it, we lose the chance of finding who made it. Also, I don't think you're really considering the benefits of mining the altanium and what it could do for Avalei."

"It makes us a target," I snap.

The altanium, while beautiful, puts me more on edge than anything else. It's the motive we've been looking for—a huge, dangerous motive.

"We shouldn't bury what is beautiful and rightfully our own out of fear, Nix," Torren says, gathering the few supplies he left on the shore.

"We're protecting it and ourselves," I argue, scooping up the gauntlet and greaves I left on the lakeside rock earlier in the day. A day that seemed like a lifetime ago. Calming my voice, I say, "We should probably get back or Reilynn will worry."

Nodding their agreement, Greymore and Torren fall in line as I set a jogging pace back toward the settlement. With their longer legs, the two men easily keep pace.

"I'll call for a council meeting tonight," Torren says, coming to the same realization I have—that our argument is at a standstill and ultimately the decision isn't ours alone, but all of Avalei's.

"We should hold the vote then, too," I say, nervous about our indecision leaving a clear breach in Avalei's defenses. We reach the stream, and I vault over a narrow point, my wet boots squishing as I land on the opposite bank. "I think we should also increase the guards and change the watch to cover the lake," I say.

"Don't you think we have enough protection?" Torren gestures to the wall as it comes into view, guards dotting the top.

Torren's lax attitude bothers me, leaving me to wonder if his desire to claim the altanium has clouded his judgment. "Greymore, thoughts?" I ask, needing another opinion and hoping it's closer to mine.

Our pace slows to a walk as he answers, "I'd hate to see something so amazing buried out of fear, but I'd also hate to see an obvious weakness lead to Avalei's destruction. Vulnerability is a fine line—too vulnerable and you're overrun, too closed off and you're burying potential."

My step falters—not only because of the quantity and depth of his words—but because they strike a chord in me, expressing a fear I've never put into words.

The fear of vulnerability taking my power away.

I study his shadowy form, waiting to see if he'll say more. His shoulders rise and fall in a shrug before he adds, "It won't be an easy choice."

He leaves the rest of his sentence unspoken…it won't be any easy choice, but the consequences of making the wrong one could prove disastrous.

Deep in thought, we enter the settlement. I catch Reilynn's eye as she spots me from the doorway of the healer's hut. Her shoulders drop, her relief obvious. This constant state of high alert is wearing on us all.

Before I can ask her how Asha and Xandra are doing, Percy comes charging forward. "Nix!" he shouts, looking befuddled. "There's some…one here. She's asking for you."

"Some…one," I say, mimicking Percy's strange phrasing. Why would he stumble over that word? Unless…

I grab his arm. He grimaces at my tight, excited grip.

"Is her name Betah?" I demand.

A whoop comes from the direction of the healer's hut as Reilynn hears my question and—with a flash of bobbing red hair and gleaming metal—rushes toward the wall.

Percy nods, and I beam as he falls back, stumbling from my abrupt release.

I chase after Reilynn, damp boots pounding across the settlement, through the wall, and to the lowered drawbridge. Reilynn and I reach the archway and spy the half-orc at the same time. Betah looks exactly the same. Looming over the spears and blades pointed at her, she wears her signature axes, vibrant purple hair in a half bob, and a long-suffering smirk.

"Stand down!" I laugh as I rush through the guards, pushing weapons aside. "Betah!" I clutch her massive greenish hand, giving it a solid shake. She clasps my arm in return before pulling me in for a hug. I sputter in surprise as I'm engulfed in a tight squeeze, crammed against her unforgiving armor.

I barely get a chance to breathe and step away before Reilynn latches onto her. I had almost forgotten how massive the half-orc is, but watching her toss my knight around, I'm quickly reminded.

"The elf?" she asks, setting a disoriented Reilynn on her feet.

"She was poisoned by an arachnid web," I say.

"Arach—"

At the deathly pallor on Betah's face, I cut in sharply, "—but she's recovering. She should be fine."

"And the gnat?" Betah asks, referring to Xandra.

"She was injured by a snowcat months ago," Reilynn says, her voice small and devoid of hope.

"The wound just won't heal," I admit as a somberness falls between Reilynn and me, but it doesn't touch Betah.

"Did you treat the wound with bog root?" Betah asks. Reilynn and I look at each other and shrug.

Betah rolls her eyes as if she can't believe we survived this long without her...and I honestly can't believe it either. "You must remove toxin transferred by snowcat claws or wound never heals." She points to her side. "Wound never heals inside."

"You don't happen to have—" Reilynn starts.

Flipping her pack from her shoulder, Betah searches inside, pulling a nasty-smelling squashed plant from the mess of items. "Bog root!" she cries. In two strides, she's up the drawbridge, calling over her shoulder, "Betah will save our little gnat!"

She passes the openly gaping guards, seemingly unaware of her effect on them.

She's a tower of unwavering resolve, this half-orc friend of mine, and I'm inspired by her confidence. A weight lifts from my shoulders, a suffocating fear disintegrating in the face of Betah's self-assurance.

Revived, I take a soul-cleansing breath and smile as my conviction returns.

With my crew complete, I can save Avalei.

CHAPTER EIGHTEEN

The pre-spring sun shines on the freshly mown lawn, and I've just discovered a way to shave a few seconds off my start.

A perfect day at track.

The hurdles line the artificial rubber of the course, their height seeming to mock me, but it's a challenge I'm excited to face.

Trent hasn't said anything about my decision since our phone call, but if he happens to jog by while I'm at hurdles, his jaw will clench and his pace increase.

Some days I take perverse satisfaction in my little show of independence, and some days the look in his eye reminds me of the fear I felt on that night.

Today, I'm feeling ornery, so satisfaction it is.

As Coach Meyers goes over form, particularly my bad form, I wave at Trent passing by. With a sharp shake of his head, he barely acknowledges me.

"Did you hear me, Nickelsen?" Coach barks. With her long legs and short, compact body, she was built for running hurdles. Unlike me.

"Yes, Coach. I need to jump earlier and stretch my non-existent legs out more by curling my body so I can make the reach," I repeat her instruction.

"Right," she says, seeming upset to not have a reason to make me run laps. "Now, why don't you just jump a couple, and we'll see if you can get the motion down."

"Sure!" I hop up from my seat on the grass, noting the pole vaulters practicing on the field nearby.

Adam is over there finishing his practice for the day. My wayward foot moves in his direction before I can catch myself. I want to show him my new sketchbook full of fantasy world drawings, but he comes to Trent's so rarely that I haven't had the chance. I should probably just pull the art out some day during lunch. Even if Trent doesn't care for it, at least Adam will.

Gathering my thoughts, I turn my focus to the hurdles. After a couple of smooth jumps and further correction from Coach Meyers, I set up for a full-on practice run.

Rolling my shoulders and springing up and down, I wait for Coach's head nod—my signal to start. At the sign, I sprint forward, charging at the hurdles. There's something so challenging about this event, and it isn't just about speed for me. I feel accomplished any time I finish without bumping one bar.

As I sail over the first one, I realize this isn't going to be one of those times. My landing is off, it throws my steps off and brings me too close to the second hurdle. I attempt to correct myself and somehow make it over, but there's no way to clear the third.

My shin slams into the bar, flipping the hard plastic and twisting it around my leg. The hurdle and my body tangle together, and I tumble toward the ground.

I throw my arms out, attempting to stop the inevitable disaster. But as I hit the track, my skin drags across the rough surface, breaking and peeling on impact. I skid to an abrupt stop.

The blasted sun winks down as the pain hits, and I flop onto my back. Cataloging my hurts, I stay in that position, staring upward. The road rash stings as blood beads on the deeper scrapes. Despite the embarrassment, I can't withhold a small whimper.

"Nix?" Adam's face blocks the light. "You, okay?"

"Uh hummm," I eloquently respond.

"Nickelsen, you're supposed to clear the hurdle, not dance with it," Coach Meyers says. Far less compassionate, she comes to stand beside Adam. "What do you have to say?" she asks, pulling the hurdle from where it's wrapped around my legs to set it upright.

"Ouch?" I cough out the word, pushing the pain aside and offering a droll smile.

Adam hides a grin behind his fist.

Coach shakes her head, ever serious. "You should probably call it. Go to the trainer's room and get bandaged up." Already walking away, she looks to Adam over her shoulder. "You can see her there?"

"Sure," Adam says, crouching down to help. My hands and arms are a scratched mess, so he puts a hand on my back and eases me into a sitting position. The instant I'm upright, he drops his arm.

I curl forward, biting my lip as I brush bits of gravel from my knee. Somehow, only one knee is scraped up, and my hip burns. But with Adam looking on, I'm not willing to peek at *that* injury just now.

"I'm okay," I say, composed enough to meet Adam's eyes. "I can make it to the trainer on my own. But thanks." Adam doesn't leave, probably waiting for me to prove I'm fine.

Adrenaline still pings through my system, but nothing seems too injured. With a strained smile, I lean forward and start to rise, my weight on my uninjured hip and knee. I make it to my feet, but once I step forward and put pressure on my left leg, a sharp pain shoots from my ankle.

I stumble, throwing my weight back to the right and almost going down. Adam's hand at my side steadies me. "Yeah, you look perfectly fine," he says in a voice filled with sarcasm and hints of frustration.

"It's my stupid ankle," I groan as the reality of the injury I didn't notice at first hits. A few scrapes I can deal with, but—as I again try to put some weight on my ankle and cringe at the pain—I realize this is more than that. It's probably not broken, but injured enough to break the remainder of my season.

Adam hovers beside me, hands reaching out, then pulling back. My poor attempt at another step seems to stop whatever internal battle he fights.

With a sure, assertive movement, he steps to my side, takes my arm, and drops it over his shoulder. Then he curls his arm around my back, tightening his hold on my waist.

It isn't a comfortable position.

Adam's too tall for me to really rest my weight on his shoulder and there's a visible tension in the hand resting on my hip. "Where's Trent?" he mutters as we take a hobbling, awkward step forward.

"Running...a...closing circuit...around the school," I say, my words punctuated by tiny hops.

The bouncing movement jars my ankle, and I consider resting in the grass until Trent can get back from his run and carry me. But knowing he'll be disappointed and not wanting to face him just yet, I keep hopping.

A member of my relay team jogs past, her eyes asking if I'm okay. I offer her a tight smile. I'll survive, but I probably won't be racing again this year.

I blink at the sudden onslaught of tears. I ruined the relay for them, I ruined my great season running the 100-yard dash, and I ruined any chance of going to State with Trent. All because I was too stubborn to give up hurdles.

Adam doesn't mention my rapid blinking, probably assuming I'm in horrible pain.

After a dozen pathetic hobbles, he asks, "How bad is it?"

"Enough to end my season," I admit.

He nods, understanding I'm more upset about that than the pain shooting through my ankle.

We enter the building, and I release Adam to lean against the wall. His arm stays around my back, steadying me. "Just…a minute," I say, my tone tight with controlled pain. "I just—"

With a mumbled exclamation, Adam twists, swinging his free arm behind my knees and sweeping me into his arms. I gasp in pain and shock at being lifted so naturally and effortlessly. "Thanks, Adam," I whisper. I must still be reeling from the fall because my voice is really breathy. It's embarrassing. This whole thing is embarrassing. I should have listened to Trent.

Stupid. Stupid. Stupid.

I force my back straight, holding myself distant from Adam with my arm, ignoring the impulse to curl into him and hide from my stupidity.

We pass through a couple of doors on our way to the trainer. It's an awkward approach, with me attempting to unlatch them before Adam kicks them wide. Using this method, we burst into the training room.

It's empty, but I'm sure one of the trainers will be back soon. I wait for Adam to set me down, assuming he'll leave me and be on his way.

I assume wrong.

Adam carries me all the way to the table, setting me gently on the seat. Unlike before, when he releases me, he seems reluctant. As he straightens and inches away, he peers down at me, assessing.

"Thanks, Adam," I say, pushing back the urge to lighten the moment with a quip about the benefits of healthy eating keeping me light…or gym time keeping him buff. Or some other nonsensical garbage.

Instead, I let the significance of the moment sit heavy in the air, a weight that feels familiar, comfortable. Like a thick blanket on a cold night. "You're welcome, Nix," he says, the tone of his voice and look in his eyes intriguing.

Disturbed by my thoughts, I flick my gaze away.

Adam steps back as the medic enters. "What do we have here, Nix?" she asks.

"She fell doing hurdles," Adam says, still making no move to leave.

"That's a kind description." I grunt as I shift sideways on the table, lifting my legs up and onto the stainless-steel surface. "It was actually really pathetic. Like a runway camel crashing through a roadblock."

Adam chuckles despite himself, and the medic grins. "That bad, huh?" She lifts my arms, examining the road rash. "It'll sting to clean this, but should heal quickly. Is that all?"

I grimace. "No, my ankle."

Her eyes drift to my feet and instantly spot the swelling ankle.

Mouth twisting in an expression that's both sympathetic and troubled, she says, "Got it."

Turning from friendly to all business, she gets to work. Adam stays, distracting me from the sting of cleaning my road rash and the disappointment of a severely sprained ankle with track horror stories.

In a stolen swivel chair, he leans back against the wall, hands laced behind his head. "Her triple jump became an octo jump. I swear she couldn't stop. She just kept skipping over the sand."

"So, what stopped her?" I ask as the medic smirks at the visual.

"I did." Adam shrugs. "Who knows when she would have stopped otherwise."

Grinning, I say, "You know, I never thought of you as the knight in shining armor type…"

"Believe me, I know," he says, his voice all intriguing again.

Avoiding the beautiful heaviness of before, I say, "Well, you saved me today." I tilt my head, dramatically batting my eyelashes.

Ignoring my sarcasm, he says, "Always." Before I can respond or even decide *how* to respond, Trent strides into the room.

"Claire, I heard you were here." Grabbing my hand, he squeezes it, not seeming to notice my grunt of pain as he puts pressure on a scrape.

"Careful, man," Adam says.

Trent's eyes dart to his for a split second. "What happened?" he asks, turning back to me, his eyes full of emotion.

"I fell…" I hesitate, hating the reason for my fall—a reality Trent practically predicted and I ignored.

Springing from his chair, Adam claps his hand on Trent's shoulder. "I'm taking off now. I'll talk to you later. Thanks, Trina. Take care of that ankle, Nix."

I mumble my goodbye as Trent stays focused on me, his eyes narrowing with sudden suspicion. "Just how *did* you fall?" he asks.

"The hurdles," I admit, feeling once again small and guilty for my selfish decision.

His jaw tightens, his eyes darkening. "I knew it."

"Yes," I say as Adam disappears down the hall. "Yes, you did."

Finished wrapping my foot, Trina rises and says, "I'm done!" with false brightness. With a final tap to my uninjured knee, she turns to Trent and, flushing at his brooding good looks, says, "I'll leave her in your hands."

"Thanks, Trina," he says, flashing his winning smile—the one that doesn't even reach his eyes yet is still disarming.

"Alright…I'll just…," Trina stammers. "I'll just go. Take care." Pleased to have Trent not only know, but say her name, Trina leaves with a skip in her step, not seeming to notice the lack of warmth in his expression. Has he ever looked at me in that cold, clinical, and controlled way without me being aware of it?

Am I so distracted by his looks, I've become as oblivious as Trina?

Trent's eyes follow the trainer from the room, and when he turns back to me, his gaze is enigmatic. I hold my hands up—a move that's entirely placating and a little self-loathing. "I know. I know. I should have listened to you. I let the relay team down and myself down, too. But maybe this is for the best." He steps toward me, one questioning eyebrow raised, and I rush on, "...now there's no chance I'll miss watching your events at State while I'm running one of mine."

Again, I redirect, focusing on the positive. "I'll be sure to be there, cheering you on," I say and reach for his arm, still unable to read the expression on his face. "Watching you win...?"

A smirk breaks through his façade.

He scoots me off the table, guides me to my good ankle, and encircles me in his arms. It should feel comforting, but it doesn't. Nothing like...*Redirect! Redirect!* My mind screeches.

I snap off my wayward thought, unwilling to complete it. Trent is mine, and he's here caring for me, being a great boyfriend, the amazing boyfriend of the past month.

Bracing my forearms on his chest, I look up at him and allow myself to fall into his charm. He studies my face, systematically tucking my hair behind my ears. "You're probably right about State...especially the winning part." His lips curve in a cocky half-smile. "And I like the idea of having you in the stands. I also like hearing I'm right. Can you say that part one more time?"

I shake my head, but humor him. "You were right, Trent."

His hands lock on the sides of my face. "See, Claire? I'm a pretty smart guy. You should listen to me more."

"Trent, I never m—"

"—No, babe." He pulls me against me, cutting off my defense. "It's done. Next year—without hurdles to stop you—I'll be cheering *you* on at State." He drops a kiss on my hair, sweet and attentive.

Reeling from his declaration, I barely react.

I'm regretting my fall. I'm regretting letting everyone down. But am I regretting choosing to do something I enjoyed, to do something just for me? Should I have done hurdles? Should I try them again? After today, I wonder. But even if I did have an answer right now, I don't trust myself to have the right one.

"Maybe you can add in the 200 like we talked about. You'd place there. Yes, your senior year will be your year, and this year will be mine. It'll be perfect." His arms tighten around me. "Nothin' in our way."

No, nothing.

Nothing but a sprained ankle, a plethora of pesky doubts, and a world of conflicting emotions.

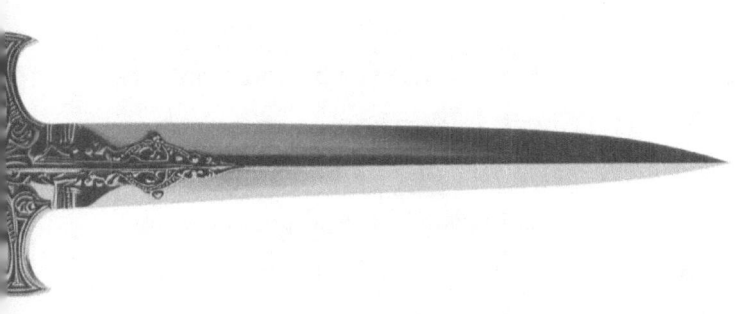

Chapter Nineteen

"**B**listering bog root!"

Reilynn's shout drifts from the forest floor to my position on the top of the wall. I peer between the battlements at the fight below. Reilynn is down, and Xandra circles her, prancing exultantly.

The settlers have created a wide circle around the knight and the tiny warrior, forming a makeshift sparring arena. Xandra raises her wooden pole in the air, soaking in the cheers of the crowd and basking in a rare takedown.

Unable to hide her joy at fighting a healthy Xandra, Reilynn gains her feet and retrieves her staff. With a crooked smile, she points the long pole at Xandra and taunts her into a rematch. Despite my concerns, I lean against the sun-warmed stone, smiling at the sight.

Outside the crowd, Asha hovers next to Betah, watching the fight with a critical eye. It's hard to tell who coddles who more—her or Xandra. Either way, they both seem completely healed. After taking the bog root or 'foul swamp sludge', Xandra's improvement was rapid. And ten days after her poisoning, Asha is back in ethereal fighting form.

I turn my attention to Betah. She's deeply focused on the fight, pointing out weaknesses and cheering impressive attacks. Her massive hands clench the pole in her hand, conveying an itch to fight. But finding someone willing to spar an overeager half-orc is no simple thing. If the wide berth the settlers are giving her is an indicator, Betah's chances of a match are unlikely at best.

"Everyone's back," Greymore says, joining me. Crossing his arms over his chest, he rests his back against the battlement and leans sideways to track the duel below.

"Yeah, they're all in fighting form," I say, glancing over my shoulder to be sure Percy is watching the ocean side of the wall. "But there's nothing to fight…at least not yet." From our side of the wall, I look across the valley, toward the lake. The rock hiding the easily accessible entrance to the cave is barely visible, jutting out over the lake. "Nothing to fight, but plenty to guard."

"Do you still disagree with the vote?" Greymore asks, watching the sparring but reading my thoughts.

Sighing, I rest my elbows on the rough stone and squint into the late afternoon light. "I understand it. Altanium could add so much to this place. And leaving it buried in the heart of the mountain for some other fool to happen upon isn't the best option." I flick a dagger from the bracer on my wrist and toss it from hand to hand. "It will be interesting to learn the king's opinion. Until the messenger returns, I agree it's best to leave it alone, but guarded." Clenching the hilt in my fingers, I offer a twisted smirk and add, "I *do* agree, but I *don't* like it. Having that entry point makes all of Avalei harder to protect...and more threatened."

"Power is a funny thing," Greymore says. "People either threaten *with* it or become threatened *by* it." He looks to the towering peaks of The Razor, offering me a clear shot of his unique profile—a thick hood and an unremarkable nose.

I tap the flat of the blade against the rock battlement and say, "Well, altanium is power—a person could make a virtual fortune selling it, or worse, acquire a wealth of magical strength. It would be a horrible miracle if the person behind all of this wanted it for its magical purposes." Knowing Greymore can already sense my emotions, I don't bother disguising them and let my voice drop with feeling. "That's what scares me, Greymore...and it's the most likely reason for this whole thing."

Greymore doesn't respond verbally, simply letting his emotions speak—determination, concern, and even a little fear.

I sympathize with them all, especially with the fear. The altanium ensured it. I stow my throwing knife, lay my hands flat on the rock, and force a calm I don't feel. Reviewing what I know, I say, "Because the creatures seemed to plan attacks and have strange abilities, I'm assuming whoever is doing this has some magic and wants the altanium to store more. I wonder if they'll give up on Avalei and find another way to transport the altanium out of The Razor."

"There wasn't another exit," Greymore reminds me—we had searched the altanium cavern thoroughly for one without success.

"But the snowcats could dig another one, could be digging it as we speak." I gaze at the mountain, wishing its secrets were mine.

"I doubt it," Greymore says, watching Reilynn crow over a victorious takedown. I wait for him to expound. As expected, he doesn't. "Greymore," I growl.

"Logistics, Nix," he says, sounding far too lordly. "Avalei is closest to the coast, the tunnel is already dug, and even if he's using it for magic, the altanium needs to be transported to a secure space."

"So, you're thinking they'll—"

"Attack," Greymore finishes, his voice thick with irony as a loud buzzing fills the air. At a motion behind me, Greymore throws his body over mine, flattening us to the ground. The loud drone of wings breezes over us.

Flat on my back, I see some mosquitoes zipping past while others gather overhead. Hawk-sized, they swarm.

One lands on Greymore's back, its fuzzy leg skimming my cheek. The freakish creature begins to extend its blood-sucking proboscis, and my eyes bulge as the massive needle lowers toward Greymore's back.

Without thinking, I reach up and grab the appendage. Wrenching sideways, I snap the proboscis in half. The creature emits an ear-piercing screech and flies away.

Greymore rolls across the stone walkway, pulling me with him. Kicking, he sends another mosquito into the side of the battlement. I gain my feet for a split-second, but again they swarm, and again Greymore takes me unceremoniously to the ground.

The wind knocked out of me, I gasp, struggling to refill my depleted lungs. Clumsily, I gather my knees beneath me as Greymore lashes out with a crossbow bolt, stabbing four mosquitoes and clearing the area.

Gulping, I free a dagger from my hip and take his offered hand. We stumble toward the tower, stabbing and swinging at the dive-bombing mosquitoes. Greymore distances himself, wordlessly giving space for us to draw our larger weapons. Scimitar's flying, I clear a path.

Glancing at the settlement, I see the expected flurry of movement. At another attack from the mosquitoes, the plan was to light the fires and get to the wall. Hopefully, there, the settlers will be protected and the flying mosquitoes will be easy prey. In a fierce line, Xandra, Asha, Betah, and Reilynn provide cover for the retreat, blades arcing and arrows flying.

Behind me, Greymore is using his chain and blade, the snap and whistle of the weapon singing a deadly song as it connects with any mosquito stupid enough to fly in range.

Reaching the tower before Greymore, I snatch a bow and quiver of arrows from a hook on the wall. A humming sound closes in, warning me that some stragglers slipped past the chain and blade. Hands steady, I notch an arrow and twist to the archway just as three mosquitoes soar through the opening. Before they can adjust to the shadowy light, I fire three arrows, planting them straight into their heads.

Greymore rushes through the door as the last mosquito falls, landing with a splat at his feet. "For me?" he says.

"I know you wanted pink, but I could only find it in brown," I quip, attaching the quiver to my wide belt.

Storing his chain and blade, Greymore loads his bolt using his new ten-shot clip, saying, "I've had worse gifts."

"Yeah?" I ask as we both fire off shots, dropping two more wayward creatures. "What?"

"My title," he says, offering me a smile I can actually see before dropping through the opening to the floor below.

Adrenaline, humor, and the energy of battle flowing, I rush down the ladder after him. On the fourth floor, I rush to light the fires, heating the tar as Greymore closes the better portion of the windows—slamming the metal shutters closed and bracing them with wooden beams.

"We've got this! Take up position on the third!" I shout at Percy as he drops from above. Wiping sweat from his brow, he hurries to the level below.

The noise of combat changes as the mosquitoes are either killed or retreat. Then, the intensity rises feverishly—a cacophony of distressed warnings and terrified screams.

I rush to the nearest open window. From the dunes, serpents rise. Frantically, the settlers close the second-story windows as the beasts slither closer. Lifting their heads from the sand, the serpent's massive bodies rise to eye level and paralyze one person after another.

We were wrong. They don't have to keep eye contact— only make it.

Finding an opening, a serpent slithers up the wall, seemingly unbothered by the fortifications. As its tail disappears through the window, a scream cuts off sharply. The sudden silence is too much. How long before the creatures stop paralyzing and start attacking? I need to be down there. Now.

As my eyes track the wall for a way down, I spy Xandra through the bars of the lowered portcullis. On the outside, a snake rises and freezes her in place. The iron gate between it and its prey, the beast begins snapping at the gate, banging against the heavy metal.

My panic shifts to a whole new, debilitating level.

"Nix." Greymore appears at my side, a rope tied around his waist. My eyes follow the frayed line of the taunt rope as it snakes under the corbels to where it is tied off farther down the wall.

Instead of terrifying me, the rope clears my mind, freeing me from my fear. Snatching a blazing torch from inside the wall, I step to the ledge of a corbel. Once on the jutting stone outcrop, I sling my free arm around Greymore's shoulder.

"Ready," I say as Greymore braces me against his side. Tightening his grip on the rope, Greymore steps off the ledge. Like a pendulum, we swing sideways down toward the attack on the first level.

At the lowest point of our swing—inches from the ground—I toss the fire to the wood defenses of the first floor. The flammable wood lights, fire racing across the wall. With a fleeting glance upward, I see Percy on the third floor doing the same, dropping torches down to light the wall's defenses.

As we swing upward, I gather myself. Before we reach the third level, I bail, tiptoes landing on a second-story opening. I windmill backwards, stretching to brace my hands on the stone, but the arch is too wide. The fire I just lit spreads beneath me as my fingertips skid across the rough stone.

About to lose my battle with gravity, I'm suddenly shoved forward by a force from behind. Off balance, I fall to my knees. Expecting a snake, I spin with my scimitars drawn, eyes closed.

A hand latches on my forearms, stopping my attack. "Don't kill me for saving you," Greymore says, a devious smile in his words. A snake, true…but not the kind I expected. No, this is the kind of snake that looks like a gentleman but will throw you through a window in a fight.

I turn away, keeping my eyes solidly on the ground. "Remember, don't make eye contact."

The pinging release of Greymore's crossbow sounds at my side. "I never do."

Smiling, I slice at the body of a serpent, flinging my body forward and striking out. Vision useless, I focus on the sounds. The screaming further down the hall, the satisfying thwack of a weapon meeting scales, the banging of the portcullis, the almost constant snap of a firing crossbow.

"Greymore!" I hold a scimitar out, offering him the blade. "This will be quicker."

"No," he says, pointing my outstretched arm to the walkway before us. "That will."

Trusting his assurance, I peek up, leveling my head at the scene before us. With remarkable grace for someone so large, Betah is darting, spinning, and rolling between paralyzed settlers and slithering snakes. Noticing the threat, they all turn toward her, trying to catch her eye.

She turns to the one nearest her, looks it in the eye, and...smiles. Then, she calmly hacks its head off with one battle axe, turning to dispose of the serpent attacking at her rear with the other.

"But...how?" I ask, momentarily stunned.

"Practice," Greymore drily says.

I slap his arm. "I wasn't talking about her weapon mastery, you—" The banging stops. "Xandra," I whisper in horror. A path clears before us, and I can see her surrounded by the remains of one snake but still frozen in front of the portcullis. The portcullis which is now hanging at an awkward angle. Knocked from its track, it creates a gaping weak point.

Betah is too far down the hall, and I don't see Asha or Reilynn anywhere. Desperate, I sprint forward, nimbly dodging serpent bodies and settlers shaking off paralysis.

As expected, a serpent begins to squeeze between the damaged portcullis and the wall, its head a bloody mass from banging against the gate. The yellow greedy eyes are locked on Xandra—the perfect little bite-sized snake snack.

I scream to try to get the beast's attention. Blood drips over its milky eye—an eye that stays trained on Xandra, determined. Raising to strike, the serpent's jaw unhinges.

I spring forward, a heartbeat closer.

And another.

Dropping to my knees and raising my weapon overhead, I hit the gore surrounding Xandra and—sliding between her and the serpent—feel the satisfying slice of my scimitar through scaled hide.

Spinning, I skid to a stop, bumping against the wall.

The serpent's head lies at Xandra's feet. Xandra, who is alive…and covered in innards.

Blinking in shock, she looks at me. For once, her curls are flat, pasted to her face and armor-like a clingy gore coat. Her dark eyes narrow. "You. Did. That. On. Purpose," she dictates in a dangerous voice.

"Saved you? Why, yes. Yes, I did," I say, refusing to show a hint of humor or regret.

"Gnat, you stink," Betah says, appearing at my side with Greymore. Xandra shoots her a withering stare, but if a serpent's glare doesn't make the half-orc pause, I doubt a nymph's will.

"Where are Asha and Reilynn?" I ask. Around us, settlers move restlessly as the battle lulls, and they begin searching for missing loved ones. I glance down the dark hall, looking for the rest of my crew. The level is mostly shuttered off, impairing visibility.

"Diabolical devils!" The curse echoes from above us.

Xandra smirks. "Found them." Snatching up her huge shield, she rushes to the nearest ladder.

"To arms!" Betah says, hurrying to the third floor without bothering to check that she's obeyed. But—after watching her wedge her axe in an opening and swing herself feet first onto the third level—no one hesitates to follow.

I rush to shutter the remaining windows before joining the fray. The third floor is overrun with arachnids. While the snakes attacked from the front and the mosquitoes from above, the spiders came from the back. The benefit of being confined within the wall is that it seems much harder for them to use their poisonous webbing. Or maybe only a few were cursed with it.

Still, the nasty things are endless, crawling and spilling over each other and into the wall like a newly hatched egg sack. We retreat to the fourth floor, attempting to pour tar on them. But, for every one we kill, ten more appear.

By the time we decide to abandon the fourth floor— hoping to shut them off there and attack from above—my arms are numb from swinging, and I've lost count of the number of arachnids I've killed.

But I'm the only one.

"Seventy-six," Xandra says, swinging her ball and chain into another spider as we retreat.

In front of her, Reilynn gloats. "Ninety-four, little one."

Tossing her axe, Betah embeds it into a spider's head. Striding forward to retrieve it, she backhands another into the wall. "Nine and one hundred…and eleven serpents."

"Blazing blades," Reilynn huffs, impressed while Xandra pretends not to be. Seeing the last settler safely up to the top of the wall, I slam the trap door shut, severing several spider legs in the process. Sliding the lock in place, I step back to reevaluate.

We've used our fire and we've used our tar. We could gather in the tower, but since they can climb and we're running out of arrows and bolts, that's probably not our best method of attack. As I debate, the settlers and my crew continue the fight, throwing things and shooting arrows down through the murder holes. "Nix?" Torren comes to stand beside me.

"Do you have any ideas?" I ask, too desperate to be prideful.

"The Dual Blades," he says, meaning we leave the wall, shutting the animals inside and us out.

"And sacrifice Avalei?" I question, shocked he'd give up so easily. But—then again—this hasn't been easy. It's been months of fighting followed by horrific hours of battle. We've lost three people to the mosquitoes—bled dry. Five to the serpents—swallowed whole. And two to the arachnids— death by poison.

"We have to save the people, Nix." I watch the settlers lining up between the battlements, driving the arachnids from their relentless attack up the sides of the wall. We can only hold for so long.

"You know the gates don't close from the outside, Torren," I whisper, hardly believing I'm even considering this option. "To lock them, someone has to stay inside."

"So?" Torren says—not in an uncaring tone, but in a confident one. He believes I can figure this out. So, what am I going to do? How *am* I going to fix this? Wishing I had a better answer, I say, "So, we fight until we can't anymore."

Torren reaches a hand out, attempting to smile, but it's as if the muscles in his face don't have the heart for the deception. We both know we're losing. "Let me have one of those fancy swords," he says. I hand over a scimitar and watch as he blends into the group, shoring up the weaker areas.

We fight as the sun sets and the light grows dim. My mind and arms grow numb with the stress of battle.

Finally, there's a weakened cheer. With exhaustion, the settlers drop to the ground.

The arachnids are retreating.

Knowing I won't get up if I sit down, I walk down the center of the wall, scimitar dragging behind me, taking stock. The most serious, concerning injuries seem to be those who came in contact with the webbing, but Xandra is ministering to them with a new concoction that seems to be working.

As I reach the end of the line of settlers, I turn to study the battle-worn group with pride. We made it. We held our defense.

My knees waver, ready to give in to my relief, when a snarling sound nearby braces me with a jolt of adrenaline.

Twenty yards away, the gate to The Razor thumps once. Twice. Like my pounding heart, the massive wood doors push against the brace. Behind them, what seems to be a large group of snowcats snarls and growls. Eyes dart, looking to me, to the weary soldier next to them, to my crew—willing someone to tell them the sound is a figment of their imagination, not another nightmare come true.

"What fresh hell is this?" Reilynn bellows.

There's an audible gasp as everyone turns to the knight. Reilynn's cursing vocabulary is always creative, but she never swears for real. Never. I lift an eyebrow in question.

"What?" she says, looking about her. "If there ever was a time—" a familiar screeching fills the air, "—it would be now."

A group of megaspecs dive toward the settlers, drawing fire and attention, but it's the one moving toward the gate that chills me. Larger than average, this bat flies with a purpose, and the second his claws inch toward the massive wood beam, I know what that purpose is.

With a feral yell, I race toward the creature. I throw my scimitar, clipping the beast's wing.

The weapon embeds itself in the gate. From my limited supply, I throw my remaining knives. It slows the beast, but it is relentless in its mission.

I reach the gate in the same instant the talons close around the beam. Spinning, I kick out, driving the creature to the side. It crashes into a battlement before turning to me, shrieking.

The snarling and growling from the opposite side increases as numerous deadly snowcats attack the gate from the opposite side, mere feet away.

Standing in the middle of the wall, I'm weaponless, my scimitar buried high in the wood gate between me and the megaspec. The gate bulges, pulsing toward me. I hold my ground—trusting the brace will hold—and wait for the bat to attack.

The creature spreads its wings and rises from the wall, preparing to strike. Like a well-aimed arrow, the bat dives. I launch myself at the gate and, using my momentum, run up it, reaching for my weapon. As my hands close around the hilt, I wrench the blade free of the wood, push off the gate, and—backflipping—strike out.

The blade slices across the underside of the megaspec. I land awkwardly, rolling across the walkway. Keening, the bat stumbles and crashes over the side of the wall, dropping out of sight.

My victory is short-lived as two more megaspecs appear and grasp the beam.

Forcing my exhausted body upright, I rush forward. A heavily armored form joins me. With her helmet lost, Reilynn swings her broadsword overhead, screaming a battle cry. Reilynn manages to kill the creatures with a single stroke, but the beam drops free from one brace, lying sideways across the stone.

Frantic, we scramble to lift it back in place.

Another bat knocks Reilynn sideways, raking its claws across her forehead.

I throw my back against the gate, knowing I can't hold it, but desperate to do something. For an instant, everything slows, and I take in the battle before me—Greymore and Asha firing from the tower, Xandra blocking an attack on Zel, Torren yelling at the settlers, and Betah securing the opposite gate.

I failed them all.

The snowcats ram the gate.

Thrown skyward, I smash into a battlement. My head explodes with pain and blackness. Blinking the two away, I attempt to rise, but stumble to my side and drop.

My body becomes distant, foreign—willing to give in to the peace of surrender. Exhaustion overtakes fear, overtakes everything.

In a stupor, I watch a snowcat stalk toward my prone form. I'm helpless. Helpless as Greymore scoops me up, and Reilynn hacks a way clear for our retreat. Helpless as a mass of snowcats rushes onto the wall. Helpless as Percy is thrown from the wall, flung aside by the massive paw of a cat. Helpless as my crew and Torren place the settlers behind them, forming a wall between them and the beasts—a wall that inches backward, unable to hold. Helpless as Betah throws a bomb into the fray, destroying a part of the wall, but buying some time and space. Helpless as we escape to the Dual Blades. As we retreat.

Helpless as Torren tosses my scimitar back to me, tells me to take care of his family, shoves Betah aside, and closes the gate. Helpless as I scream for him, for all we've lost. Helpless as the darkness closes in around me.

Helpless as we abandon everything that is Avalei.

Chapter Twenty

Y ou were a little off your game today, man," Trent says to Adam. The two are lounging next to the pool, likely burning in the fierce spring sun shining through the glass windows.

Sitting at the pool's edge in shorts and a tee, I swing my foot through the cool water.

My ankle is almost healed, but the water trickling over my skin is still soothing.

"Way off," Adam says, taking a long swig of soda. "I didn't even come near my PR." He holds the bottle in the air, brandishing it like a weapon. "But I have my comfort drink now, so I just might survive."

"That's probably what messed with your game in the first place," Trent says.

I'm relieved Trent doesn't mention my terrible performance. With my ankle taped and wrapped, I had gotten the go-ahead to run today. Luckily, Trent chalks my horrible times to being out for a week. But it had nothing to do with my ankle and everything to do with Avalei.

Fantasy world trauma has put me in an irrepressible funk. Trent called me out on it multiple times today, wanting to know why I'm not acting like myself. But how would I explain it? I'm feeling off because I lost a father figure last night…in my dreams. I'm depressed because my land was overrun…in my dreams. I'm upset because I almost died…in my dreams. I'm scared to sleep because I don't know what will happen…in my dreams.

All morning, I was not functioning normally, much less *feeling* normal. After the meet, I had taken a nice, long shower where I attempted to process everything from my dream. I relived every brutal moment. Then, I compartmentalized it all, storing it next to weird dreams and disturbing movies in my brain. Now, I *think* I might be able to act somewhat normally.

Draining his bottle of water, Trent chucks the container Adam's way.

Dodging, Adam laughs and leans back in his chair, arms over his head, sunglasses in place. "You're just jealous I look as good as you do without eating tasteless crap all the time."

Trent looks at him from under his glasses while I try to hide a smile. "I think you're delusional," he laughs. "Let's ask Claire if you look good." Suddenly, I find the water *very* interesting. Because when I had finally gotten myself centered in reality again and a ride from Dillon, I arrived to find both guys shirtless and poolside. At the time, it was like a little thank-you gift from karma. *You're a nice girl and have been having a tough time…here, check out some hot guys.*

Guys. Plural. I'm ashamed to admit I liked the sight of both of them. But I'd have to be blind not to notice, and my mind might be a bit muddled, but my eyes are working just fine.

"So, Claire. Who looks best?" Trent puts me on the spot.

It doesn't tax much of my scrambled brain power to know the right answer here. But how to deliver it without betraying I did some appreciative comparisons the second I stepped poolside? I dip my hand in the water, saying, "I'm a completely biased third party in this, Trent, but…" with a damp finger, I trace his name onto the rough tile on the pool's edge, "…there you have it."

Trent leans forward, reads his name, and offers me a sultry wink. "That's right, babe."

"Rigged." Adam doesn't move from his spot, merely flops his hand over his eyes in a show of disinterest.

I pull a foot out of the water and rest my head on my knee. The late afternoon sun makes me drowsy, and I close my eyes to soak it in—it's going to be an interesting dream night tonight, might as well get some rest where I can.

"Trent?" Mr. Evans calls through the screen door. "Can I talk to you?"

"Sure, Dad," Trent says with a subtle roll of his eyes.

He never lets his parents see any outward sign of disrespect, but he certainly acts like they are a hardship. I guess it's fair since we're as much a hardship to them as they are to us. Trent scoots past me, brushing a hand over my hair. My lips twitch in a fleeting smile as I twist my head to look at the pool, dragging my fingers through the water.

"I never took you for a cheat, Nix," Adam says in an undertone.

"A cheat?" I ask, letting him bait me.

"Yeah," he tips his glasses down, peering at me over the top and giving me a wide smile. "We both know I'm way better looking."

Unable to help it, I laugh and flick water at his audacious smirk. "And humbler," I add.

"No," Adam motions to the door. "No one is as humble as Trent."

Again, I can't hold back a giggle. Smiling at our shared joke, Adam holds my gaze. He really is good-looking—one of those guys who gets cuter over time as you learn to appreciate the soft humor in the lines on his face, the goodness in the curve of his mouth, and the quiet confidence that lights up his eyes.

Trent is hands down the more stunning, classically sculpted guy. But it doesn't overwhelm me like it used to...I guess I've just become accustomed to his particular brand of perfection.

Noticing I'm staring at Adam—and have been for far too long—I jerk my gaze back to the water. My hands drift over the top of the crystal-clear surface. Feeling his stare, I turn and flick water at Adam. "Stop giving me the evil eye." Cupping my hand, I toss a stream of water his way…and miss. "I don't cheat."

"No," Adam says, dropping back and closing his eyes. "You wouldn't."

I narrow my eyes at the possible double meaning to his statement. Adam has been doing this more and more lately. Saying something but meaning more. And he's more restrained, like he always has something to say but isn't sure he should say it. What is he holding back? I suspect he's questioning Trent and I's relationship and wants me to question it as well. The truth is, I still do question, wondering if I could be happier with someone else, but the loyal, unequivocally taken part of me hates those doubts.

Hands close around my shoulders, startling me by shoving me toward the pool. I link a hand around Trent's wrist as he pulls me back, laughing. "I wouldn't push you in, babe," he claims.

"Not now that I have a hold of you," I say as I turn to beam up at him and grip his arm.

He pulls me to my feet and—having nowhere to go—my hands drop to his bare sides. "We could both go in," he teases.

I inch closer to him and further from the water. "You do that, and I'll have to go home and shower again. And I'll take my time getting ready. Our whole night…ruined." I click my tongue.

He leans toward the side, debating before letting me go with a smile. I sit back, dropping my feet in the water as Trent eases down onto the lounge chair, saying to Adam, "The trouble with having a smart woman, huh?" Adam mumbles some garbled response before his phone's chime brings him completely out of his doze. Looking at the screen, his grumbling resumes.

He responds to the text, setting the phone aside only to have it ding again. "Is that your prom date?" Trent asks.

"Yes, unfortunately, she thinks me asking her to prom means a lot more than one night. I'm pretty sure when I said 'Hey, we should go to prom?' Diana heard, 'Hey, will you have my babies?' She was cool before, and now..."

He shudders. "I mean, she practically cried when she saw me talking with Gabriella the other day."

At Gabriella's name, Trent's face—which was smirking—morphs into a tight line. "Gabriella? She's a filthy..." Glancing at my expectant expression, he schools his features. "She's a liar. A dirty liar."

"Sorry," Adam says. "I know you don't like to talk about her, being an ex and all that."

"She was just mad I broke up with her, and..." He drops his voice, grumbling something I'm pretty sure I don't want to hear under his breath. "I just hate that girl."

"Well, anyway," Adam says, apparently used to Trent's harsh reaction to his ex. "This girl acted like I cheated on her. Even if we *were* dating, I can talk to someone else. Yet, somehow, she made me feel guilty."

"Wait, did you say Diana?" I ask as my face splits into a wide, wide grin.

"Crap," Adam says at the look on my face. "You know…" He stops, a look of dawning horror coming over his face. "She dated Dillon, didn't she?"

Forgetting Gabriella, Trent smiles. He's remembering Diana and Dillon's history now, too. I bob my head a little too eagerly. "I'm surprised Dillon didn't warn you. She wanted to exchange promise rings on their first date. A promise ring!" I lean forward on my arms, absorbed in the story. "Dillon didn't even know what it was, but the sound was enough to have him bolting. Seriously, he left her at the restaurant. But the next day, she showed up at the house and apologized to *him* for freaking him out. Somehow, she even got a second date out of him, but—you know Dillon—he managed to avoid the third." I tip my head and purse my lips thoughtfully, fighting a grin. "You might want to ask him how. Maybe a repellent of some kind?"

At this point, Trent is laughing hysterically, and Adam is looking at his ever-dinging phone like it's a viper about to strike. "You're serious," he says, studying my face, begging me to be lying.

"Call Dillon," I say, chuckling at his expression.

Phone clutched in one hand, Adam grabs his stuff. "I have to go."

"Good luck!" Trent jeers as Adam waves dismissively, phone already pressed to his ear. Still beaming, Trent turns to me. The sight leaves me breathless, and I reconsider my earlier traitorous thoughts. He's stunning, and his looks still blow me away.

His eyes darken as he reads the appreciation in my gaze. "I'm glad you scared Adam away, Claire," he says, his voice doing funny things to my insides. It's like I'm lining up to run hurdles, not knowing if I'm going to sail over them or fall on my face.

"I've been thinking about prom," he continues.

"Yes, I'll go with you," I tease, my voice a little too soft and breathy for my liking.

"Of course, you will," he smiles softly, "but I've been thinking more about the night as a whole. I want to make it amazing. A night you won't ever forget—your junior prom." The way he says *your junior prom* makes those three words seem significant, so much more significant than a dance.

I pull my legs from the water and stretch them out on the deck, taking time to gain my bearings.

Trent leans forward, resting on his knees, totally intent. "Tell me more about when you made this vow of yours."

Afraid of where this conversation is leading, I look at my brightly painted nails. Orange with white flowers on them. I curl my toes, watching a drop of water run down the side of my foot, joining the puddle on the deck. Eager to make Trent understand how important this is to me, I carefully consider my words before starting.

Taking a deep breath, I say, "It was years ago, and Jillian and I were watching some Lifetime movie—one of those really dramatic ones about some girl having a baby as a teenager and having to raise it on her own. Or something equally traumatizing to young girls."

I glance to see Trent's hypnotic green eyes on me, interested, so I continue, "Anyway, Jillian was going on and on about how stupid the whole movie was and the girl for sleeping with the first guy she even remotely liked. She was really on one." I pause, remembering Jillian, her hair piled high on her head as she swung her arms around, talking with her hands, and punctuating meaningful words with a stomp of her foot.

"You miss her," Trent says, seeming surprised.

"Yes," I practically whisper. "A lot."

Trent opens his arms, and I rise from the deck to sit on the chair beside him. Pulling me with him, he leans back. It's a tight fit, so I drape my arm over his bare stomach to balance myself.

Dragging his fingers through my hair, Trent says, "I'm sorry, Claire. I'm sorry she shut you out."

Feeling closer and more understood than ever before, I burrow into his side. "Thanks." I enjoy the feel of his hands in my hair as I relax against him and continue my story in a soft voice. "As for the vow, I agreed with everything she said. I think we even wrote it out, but who knows what happened to it." I scrunch my forehead, trying to remember. "It was something like—I, Claire Nickelsen, vow I will not sleep with the first, or second, or even third guy I date, but will wait until I am not wholly controlled by hormones that will make me stupid and impulsive, being an adult and of sound mind, before I give myself away. To this I vow. Signed, Claire Nickelsen." I huff, amused at Jillian's flair for the dramatic.

"Wow," Trent says, his tone truthfully awed. "That's...something."

I poke his side.

He grabs my hand, slowly threading his fingers through mine. "So, am I the fourth guy?" he asks, looking for a loophole.

"Nope, if you count my two-week relationship with Tony my freshman year, you're the second. So, no, not even close." More relaxed than I have been in a long time, I close my eyes. Trent smells of chlorine and sunscreen and cologne. Not sure how he managed that combination, but it's nice.

Trent falls silent, running his fingers through my hair with one hand and tracing my fingers with the other. When he breaks the quiet, his voice is serious, a whispered confession. "I like this vow."

Shocked, I sit up, resting my forearm on his chest. "What?"

"I don't love the wording, but the meaning is perfect. You didn't want to be hasty. You didn't want to give yourself to the first guy who came along. And you didn't want to lose your virginity on an impulse." He leans upright to kiss my nose. "I like it." I bite my lip. The vow was about all of that, but I had personally vowed more. Vowed to wait until marriage, although Jillian wasn't willing to be quite that specific in our written words.

But I had wanted that…wanted to only ever give that part of myself to one person. I believed God wanted me to wait. I still believe it.

"Claire, I hope you know, with me, it won't be stupid. I'm not just some guy. I'm not a hormonal impulse." He takes my face in his hands, staring into my eyes. "I'm your boyfriend and more than that, we're in love. There's nothing more perfect than that, nothing more to wait for."

"Marriage," I whisper, reminding him my personal convictions go beyond a youthful vow.

He doesn't pull away or seem concerned in the slightest.

"Claire, I will marry you. So, whether this happens now or later, it will happen. I just don't see a point in waiting. Until you're eighteen and suddenly wise? Or until we're engaged and tired of waiting? Until we're married and our wedding night is a mess of inexperience?"

I flounder for a response.

Guiding me gently toward him, he kisses me in that slow, burning way of his, breaking down my walls. "Claire," he pulls back, breathless. "You are mature. You know what you want."

Him, my mind fills in the blank. You want him.

He kisses the corner of my lip. "You don't want to wait any more than I do." My body hums in agreement. "And I will make it amazing," he promises, running a thumb over my bottom lip.

I pinch my mouth closed, holding in the agreement hovering on my lips. When I don't respond, Trent traces a finger over the curve of my jaw. "Please, my love." He follows the path of his finger with kisses. "Show me you're committed to our forever. Promise me yourself," he whispers in my ear. "Vow to me your prom night, and I promise you won't regret it." He kisses his way back to my lips. "I love you, Claire."

"Trent," I say, conflicted. He silences me with an insistent kiss, but he's not demanding. He's never demanded anything more than I've been willing to give…at least not for weeks. Not once he knew how important it was to me. He's been patient as we've dated for months. And if I choose, I *can* be with him forever.

I fall into his kiss, realizing I trust him more than myself. While I'm flighty, he's sure. A rock. A guarantee. He deserves greater commitment from me, not doubts and thoughts of other people. He's given all of himself, and he deserves all of me.

"Maybe. Maybe we could." Without a conscious decision, the words fall out of my mouth, a concession I can't take back.

"Yes?" Trent says, delightfully surprised.

"I'll *think* about it," I clarify, panicked that I've acquiesced as much as I have. What about my vow? What about my faith? Do I set it aside? Or is it time to reevaluate those beliefs?

"That's all I ask." Exuberant, Trent kisses me between smiles, making promises and spouting beautiful endearments.

I fight a growing sense of unease. Making him this happy can't be wrong…it just can't.

But all night long, I feel sick to my stomach, and my churning thoughts don't help. I'm miserable, and sleeping only makes it worse, not because I dream of my fantasy world…

…but because I don't.

No dreams. No Greymore. No crew.

No Avalei.

CHAPTER TWENTY-ONE

S lumped, I drag a spoon through my bowl of soggy cereal.

"I thought you'd be excited for today," my mom says, loading her bowl in the dishwasher.

I raise my chin slowly. For the life of me, I can't remember what I'm supposed to be excited about today. My days are blending together, my nights even more so.

I haven't dreamed of my fantasy world in almost two weeks. Did I die in my dreams? And if so, what does that mean? Without my dreams, I feel...less. Like half of who I am has been torn from me, leaving the weaker, miserable parts alone to cope with the emptiness.

I just want to feel alive again...like me again. So many times, I've wanted my dream world gone. But now that it is,

I realize dream world was an outlet—a place to release all my fears and insecurities…and then confront them with an army of support.

Now I'm stuck in reality, but I can't force my mind to be fully present. I would lose all track of time if not for Trent's constant references to prom. His daily reminders have become a countdown reminding me of a commitment I can make or a vow I can keep.

"Claire?" My mom's hand covers mine, stopping the swirling motion of my spoon and bringing me back to the present. "What is it?" she asks, her dark eyes searching.

I shake my head, snapping myself out of a raving pity-party. *Redirect. Redirect.* Dropping the spoon, I say, "Nothing, Mom. I just haven't been sleeping well." A nice cover. Honest, but…not.

Cocking her head, she studies me with far too much knowing. But instead of calling me on my obvious avoidance, she releases my hand. Giving my fingers one last pat, she begins to clear the counter. "Well, maybe you'll want to try for a nap after we're finished with our shopping."

Shopping? I give a mental finger snap.

That's right, we're going prom dress shopping today. Abandoning the idea of breakfast, I dump my cereal down the disposal.

"Guess we'll see how long it takes to find the perfect dress," I say, forcing a smile. After all, my mom is taking me shopping *and* paying. The least I can do is pretend to be excited. "I'll be ready in twenty," I say, taking the stairs two at a time, injecting a fake little burst of energy into the movement.

Hours later, I'm crowded in a dressing room with my mom and a dozen beautiful dresses—none of which appeal to me. "I like this rose one," my mom says, lifting the corner of the full skirt.

"It is pretty," I admit. "But too long and you said you can't hem that overskirt."

"You're right, it's too bad you didn't get your father's long legs." Releasing the material, Mom drops to the bench with a huff of defeat. "I think we've tried everything here."

"I'm blaming the stubby legs on you," I say, bumping her knee. "But I have an idea." I pull my phone from my back pocket and text Trent.

"Right," my mom says, rubbing her temples. "A cell phone and a boyfriend…the solution to all our problems."

With a lopsided grin, I appreciate her snark. My phone dings as Trent responds, and my smile turns smug. Upon reading his message, I say, "The phone and boyfriend have saved us this time. Remember that dress Trent bought me for Valentine's Day?"

Mom's eyes brighten. "That gorgeous black one with purple overlay? Of course, I do."

I shake the phone at her. "I found out where Trent bought it from. It's just down the road."

I cock a brow, waiting.

Reenergized, she snatches her purse. "Let's go." We make it to the boutique in record time, even finding front-and-center parking. The shop looks ritzy—a bad financial decision waiting to happen. Mom and I hesitate on the sidewalk outside.

"Mom," I say, putting my hand on her arm. "I'll stick to the budget."

"It's not you I'm worried about," she says, examining the elaborate gown in the display window, "it's me."

I laugh. "Okay, *we'll*. We'll stick—"

"Claire!" Trent rounds the side of the building, his mom at his side.

"Trent," I say, clearly surprised.

He smiles, putting his perfect teeth and show-stopping dimples on display. "We were in the area getting my tux fitted when you texted." Sliding an arm around me, he pulls me against his side. "My mom says she can get you a discount. She gets dresses for events here often enough."

"That's right, dear," Moira says, dropping a kiss to my cheek before turning to greet my mother.

Trent drops his head, brushing his lips against my ear, as he whispers, "I'd love to help you pick your dress for our big night." His words drip with innuendo. I shiver with anticipation and anxiety. I haven't committed to anything, just the possibility, but Trent is convinced I'll relent.

We enter the store—three eager shoppers and one overwhelmed teenage girl.

Moira leads us to her favorite salesperson, Trudy. Wearing stylish glasses and perfectly cropped hair, Trudy gives me the once-over with critical, but kind eyes before asking my favorite colors, styles, and textures. When I admit my affinity for purple, Trent opens his mouth to object, but reconsiders. I guess he figures if there's a chance he'll get what he wants, I can get the color dress I want.

A small concession.

Searching, Trent even finds a purple gown in our price range. Trudy locates a few more. But it doesn't end there...

Moira and my mother dart around like sophisticated kids in a high-end candy shoppe, pulling gowns in a variety of colors and styles. Seeing the growing pile of dresses, I shelve my napping plans.

Totally involved, Trent joins them, offering suggestions and browsing through the racks.

"That boy is sure devoted to you," my mom says as she helps me out of a dress that is again too long for my short legs.

"Yes," I say, fingering the material of a lace-topped gown. "Very."

"I think it's sweet." My mom pulls the gown from my hands to drop it over my head. I shimmy to get it in place. After dozens of dresses, we're getting the quick-change down to a science. "You would never catch your father in a place like this," Mom laments.

I can't help but smile at the visual. "No, you wouldn't," I say. The dress falls into place as she slides the zipper closed.

The flowing material swirls around my ankles, and I catch a glimpse of myself in the mirror. Clasping my hands together, I emit a tiny squeak of excitement. I may be a bit conflicted about this dance, but a perfect dress is a perfect dress. With the cinched-in waist and beautiful lace top, the gown fits like it was designed for me. And it's my favorite color…purple. Not a bright, flashy purple, but a deep, mature hue.

"I love it," I whisper.

"It's perfect," my mom says, her voice thick with emotion. "You look beautiful." Then, like a warrior springing into battle, she circles me, speed talking. "Let's not let Trent see it yet." Her fingers hesitate on the zipper. "But Moira should. You stay here…I'll grab her." An overexcited whirlwind, she exits the changing room.

Peeking in, Trudy offers her approval before taking an armful of the dresses from the room.

Alone, I admire the dress in the mirror, relieved at the strength of my emotions. I'm feeling again—excitement, awe, confidence.

As my mom and Moira approach, their animated whispers carry to me. "She is just the best thing ever to happen to Trent," Moira says, gushing. I blush at the high, undeserving praise.

"Well, if she had to have a boyfriend, I'm glad she chose him," my mom says, humor filling her voice.

"I don't think this is just a passing high-school relationship," Moira says, almost defensively.

"No, they have been dating seriously for quite some time," my mom agrees, too thrilled to argue. "Claire was never really serious about anyone before him."

"I can easily imagine us here after Claire graduates next year, shopping for *something in white*," Moira says in a sing-song voice. I freeze, leaning against the white swinging door, waiting for my mom's response. Waiting for her to tell her it's too soon. That it's all too fast. To tell her no, not for years and years.

Instead, she answers, "You might be right, Moira. I'm not sure if I'll ever be ready for it, but I believe you're right."

My emotions flip, making me nauseous. I clutch my chest, struggling to breathe.

My heart hurts, beating viciously in my chest. My lungs struggle to pull in air, gasping. My stomach aches, clenching in knots, twisting, turning. My head pounds, thoughts pummeling through my brain.

It's a full-on assault—pure, potent panic attacking my system.

Talk of marriage shouldn't throw me onto this ledge, but it has, leaving me teetering and terrified. Because when Trent mentions the future, it's romantic and hypothetical, but hearing our mothers discuss it grounds it in reality and possibility and inevitable fact.

Suddenly, it feels like all my life decisions are out of my hands, and I'm just along for the ride, hanging on for dear life.

* * * *

I lay in bed that night, actively forcing my thoughts far, far away from Trent and marriage. Instead, I envision a happy ending for Avalei. If I can't dream one, I'll make one.

It's slightly therapeutic, but—after hours of intense imagining—I still don't feel the tiniest bit drowsy.

Creeping down the stairs, I raid the freezer, finding my mom's stash of rocky road ice cream. Not my favorite, but it seems fitting. Since only half a carton remains, I decide to eat straight from the container.

Trent would be horrified.

I smirk, but my lips fall, curving downward as I imagine us married. There probably won't be any late-night ice cream binging. Or afternoon ice cream runs. Or ice cream period.

My heartbeat picks up, panic returning. I shovel in a huge scoop of chocolate, desperate to find some comfort.

"Claire!"

Someone pinches my sides, and I jump in the air, choking on a nut. I swing my spoon at my brother, my eyes watering as Dillon grins.

"Are you okay?" he asks, smart enough to not release the laugh building behind his eyes.

"Fine," I sputter between coughs. "But you won't be."

"Now, now, sister dear." He takes a seat next to me. "I did try to get your attention, but when you ignored me, I figured scaring you was my due."

"Jerk," I mumble, moving to the sink for a glass of water.

Taking my spoon and ice cream, Dillon helps himself. "So, what's up?"

"You're stealing my food, that's what."

"No, seriously." He takes a large scoop, talking around his mouthful of ice cream. "It's late at night, you're eating 'the devil's food'—your boyfriend's phrase, not mine—and I'm here. This is where we have a heart-to-heart, I give you some amazing older-brother advice, and we don't do this again for another year...or ever."

I eye him over the rim of my cup, surprised at what I find in his gaze. "You're serious."

"My yearly offer." He spreads his arms wide, dripping ice cream on the counter.

Grabbing the rag from the sink, I wipe it up. "I'm not sure taking advice from a mess like you is a good idea."

"That's who you want to take advice from, not the people with perfect lives, but the ones who have lived through the chaos and come out on top." He lifts the spoon in the air to accentuate his point, again making a mess on the counter.

"And if they're still in the chaos phase?" I tease, cleaning the mess.

He shrugs. "You get empathy."

I take a breath, needing someone to talk to.

Dillon's here and willing, so why not?

"Alright, here it is," I say. "Everyone thinks I'm going to marry Trent. That next year, I'll send him off to college across town and be miserable having to live every single day without him. That I'll suffer through my school year, distracting myself with sports and art. Then my horrible year will be over, and I can be with Trent forevermore."

"And the problem is?" Dillon says, scraping the bottom of the carton. Frustrated, I snatch the carton from his hands and shove it in the garbage.

"The problem is, I'm not sure I'll be miserable. I'm actually looking forward to it!"

Dillon taps the spoon against his lips. "Maybe you're more like me than I thought."

Disgusted, I throw my hands in the air and stride toward the stairs.

Dillon rushes after me. "Claire-bear," he says, stopping me with a light hand on my shoulder. Slowly, he turns me around. "There is nothing wrong with wanting some independence," he says in a soothing, serious voice. "You are with Trent a lot, and I'm not surprised you need space. This is normal. And once you get it next year, you'll probably be ready for the bigger commitment. It's human nature."

"But what if it feels like too much, too fast right now?" I ask, my tone quiet, my confession hushed.

Dillon smiles, squeezing my shoulder. "Relationships are life's roller coasters?"

I squint at him. "I don't think that's how that saying goes..."

"But I'm close, right?" Dillon presses, grinning.

"Pretty close," I say, my words falling flat because my relationship feels less like a roller coaster ride and more like a swim in shark-infested waters. Right or wrong, I'm thankful for my brother's advice, even if it is unusual. And rare.

I study him for a minute before asking, "How did you know I needed someone to talk to?"

"Chocolate fix?" he tries, but I can tell he's putting me off.

"I don't think so. Try again," I say.

"Omniscience?" he says questioningly.

I cross my arms, drumming my fingers on my elbow.

He rolls his eyes. "If you must know, Adam said something that made me think I should, you know...check on you."

"Said what?" I ask, leaning forward in anticipation.

Dillon throws his hand in the air. "Something about you and Trent getting serious and you feeling pressured. Which," he waves his hand at the kitchen, referencing our conversation there, "I guess you are."

"I see," I murmur, unsure how to feel about Adam checking up on me.

"You know, if it is too much and you do feel pressure, you can always break up with him. That is allowed," Dillon jokes.

But is it? Somehow, breaking up doesn't feel like an option for me. When we were apart during my grounding and again after the night on the stairs, I was miserable. Lonely.

And Trent clearly doesn't want to break up. At all.

Suddenly exhausted, I thank Dillon and give him a quick, tight hug. Pulling away, I offer him a sardonic smile. "Same time next year?"

"Sooner if we must," he says, matching my expression.

Saying goodnight, I make my way to my room, determined to be more like Dillon—carefree, optimistic, and happy with all the good I've been given. Because pressure isn't always bad, right? Like a diamond, maybe that's all I need to get my life in order. Pressure.

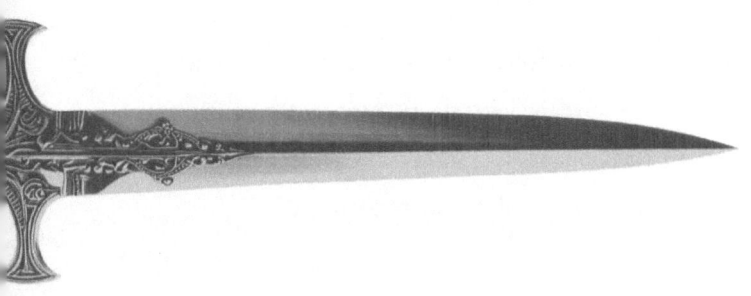

CHAPTER TWENTY-TWO

Sensing a change, my eyes open slowly, cautiously. Blinking to focus, I discover a white canvas fluttering overhead. I turn to the side, my head screaming at the movement, pain pinging around my brain before settling at the base of my skull. Despite the ache, I have a momentary sense of elation.

Dream world.

I'm back in my fantasy.

With deliberately slow movements, I roll to my side and push myself upright. A waterskin waits beside the furs I'm lying on. I gulp down the contents, my headache easing almost instantly.

Feeling better, I turn my attention to my surroundings. I'm in a makeshift shelter, a small tent made from staked canvas. The structure is barely large enough to fit my bedding, and I can only sit fully upright in the very center. The shadows of leaves are reflected on the canvas as the sun blazes down from the center of the sky. Nearby, voices can be heard passing my dwelling. I catch snatches of conversation.

"…king's messenger…"

"…no aid…"

"…weeks without a change…"

On my hands and knees, I inch from the crude tent.

I exit into the center of a clearing filled with tents like mine—a temporary settlement. As I straighten to a standing position, an awed hush falls over the clearing. I study the displaced of Avalei.

Haunted eyes and hopeless visages stare back at me. Their pain thumps into me, rolling my stomach as I feel the loss of our city and our people all over again.

"Living legends!" A voice exclaims before I'm lifted off my feet, swung in a circle by my favorite knight. The last time I saw her, she was covered in blood, fending off a line of advancing snowcats.

"Reilynn." Clasping her arm, I hold her away from me to examine the gash across her forehead.

The extent of her healing is my first clue as to just how long I've been out. I touch the mostly healed scarred skin. "Looks good on you."

"Nix!" A small form plows into me from the side, sending me staggering. "I can't believe it. I honestly didn't think you'd live to again experience the pleasure of my company!"

"Xandra," I gasp. "It's good to see you, too." I quickly peruse the rest of my crew as they enter the clearing, beaming. The settlers might be beaten, but my friends are alight, blazing with confidence.

Patiently waiting her turn, Asha steps forward, giving me a light but meaningful embrace. "I knew you would survive, my friend."

"Thank you," I whisper, blinking back tears as Betah gives me a side-hug, compressing my shoulders with one bulging hand.

"Nix, good you're back," the half-orc says, shaking me like a ragdoll in her excitement. "Now we fight."

"Maybe. I'm still a little disoriented. Where are we?" I glance around at the unfamiliar trees. "What is happening with Avalei?" I search the forest. "And where's Greymore?"

My companions glance at one another, each giving the other significant, encouraging looks. It's Xandra who breaks first, groaning dramatically. "Fine, I'll be the one to catch you up on everything, but let's get you some food to swallow with the bad news."

"So, after a horrid trek through The Razor, we're now camped a half day down the coast from Avalei. Greymore left, taking a message to the king, and the last spy you sent saw evidence of a human presence in Avalei." I summarize Xandra's report.

Tossing my empty bowl to the ground, I mumble, "Why didn't the king send men before it came to this?"

"He couldn't," Reilynn defends our monarch. "Rumor is he's almost driven all of the invaders from the land. If he sends troops, he'll weaken strongholds he can't afford to lose, not when victory is so close." I lean forward, rocking the stump I'm using as a seat.

"But he can afford to lose Avalei?" I reach for a dagger to fiddle with before remembering I'm unarmed, my weapons lost in battle. All I have left is a scimitar. A scimitar I can't bring myself to wield. I flinch at the memory of Torren tossing it at my feet and baring the gate, snowcats at his back.

"Avalei already lost," Betah says in her typical blunt way.

"But we can regain it," I argue, unwilling to admit defeat, to let the altanium fall into the wrong hands.

"We can," Asha reassures. "But we will be fighting alone."

"What have the people voted to do?" I ask. Again, my crew avoids my gaze. "Xandra?" I push.

"They won't fight." She absentmindedly curls a strand of ebony hair around her finger. "They're looking to move on, to claim citizenship somewhere new. Most say that their livelihood is already gone. That Avalei is done."

A cold shock rocks me, and I tip in my seat.

I knew they were disheartened, but this? "Done?" I breathe. "Done?" I repeat in a daze.

Asha crouches in front of me, drawing my attention.

"They need a leader, Nix. They await you because only you can awaken their forgotten sense of hope."

"I...I don't..." I fumble, standing unsteadily, rocked by the responsibility of such a role. Asking my overly-willing squad to fight is one thing, convincing settlers to risk their lives is another. Torren's charge to take care of his family and the likely consequences of an attempt to regain Avalei flit through my mind. An image of Zel, gaze dead and unseeing—a casualty of our ambition—churns my stomach. The impact of this decision would mean more lives.

We've already lost Torren, Percy, and so many others, and the chances of our victory are small, so small. But without the settlers, they are practically non-existent.

I want to save Avalei. I *need* to save it. But I don't think I can ask these settlers or my crew to sacrifice themselves.

I don't think I can encourage a battle we're unlikely to win.

"I need some space," I stammer. "Some time. I need to think...to consider." With worried eyes, my crew watches me lurch away.

I hurry to the surrounding woods, hoping to find solace there.

I was always a part of Avalei, but never the heart. And I'm not sure I have the strength, the fortitude, or even the right to take on that role.

* * * *

The setting sun finds me far removed from the despondent settlers. And even further removed from an answer.

If losing and regaining this fantasy has taught me anything, it's that there's something special here, something worth fighting for.

I'm back for a reason.

I just don't know what that reason is. To accept and cope with this loss or to lead a fatal charge? What if everyone dies? It may not be real, but to lose everyone....unthinkable.

Avalei. Responsibility for the people and the place weighs on me. It's a weight I've denied, shared, and crumpled under. Now, it rests fully on my shoulders, a devastating force.

How can I expect the people to fight, to risk their lives after already losing so much? But how can I let Avalei go, leaving altanium unprotected?

I rub my dry lips together, tuning into the sound of the stream I've been hearing since I left camp.

Pushing aside the undergrowth, I drop to the ground and drink my fill. I sit back, staring at the sky as the stars come out and darkness descends. The inky night cloaks me, amplifying my bleak mood.

After a time, I notice the sound of a waterfall carrying through the still air. Rising, I follow the stream until I find it. The fall isn't large, spilling from a ledge about six feet high.

Finding a groomed trail, I navigate to the top of the shelf and discover an eerily still pool. The surrounding vegetation looks manicured with trimmed shrubs on the outer circle and impeccably spaced white, glowing flowers nearer the water. Rocks are also spaced in a ring around the perfectly circular pool. This is a well-loved, well-honored place—a holy place.

Without knowing why, I drop to my knees at the side of the pool. Something draws me to the beauty, the serenity. With reverence, I watch the moon's reflection move across the pool. Slowly and steadily it rises, never hesitating, never questioning its role.

Bracing my hands on the rocks, I lean forward, staring at my reflection in the pool. It isn't an exact replica. The girl I see is sure, determined. The girl in the pond is ready to take risks and sacrifice if necessary. My reflection is everything I want to be, but I'm not.

Disturbed by the sight, I move away from the pool's edge, still unwilling to choose.

A twig snaps behind me, the sound followed by a wave of feeling.

"Hello, my lord," I call as Greymore appears.

He steps from the brush, hood firmly in place, but emotions dancing wildly. "Hello, Nix, my lady—Defender of Avalei."

My heart jumps when he calls me his lady, but crashes as he finishes the greeting. "It seems I failed at that," I murmur.

"You and I both know that's a premature statement, Nix. Avalei is still there, needing to be protected, to be remembered." He stops an arm's length from me, looking me up and down.

"Did the king send help?" I ask, but his emotions have already answered for him.

"He couldn't. But he believes the settlers, you, and your crew are enough to fight this battle…well, you and one wandering lord." He clears his throat. "I do, however, have news. Chancellor Ivers has disappeared. He never returned to the king and his heritage…well, it's likely he's our magic user."

I nod as all the pieces fall into place, making terrible, perfect sense. Ivers had magic in his blood. Somehow, he discovered the altanium, but he needed Avalei to access it, mine it, and ship it. He thought it would be easy to frighten the people away, making his takeover simple. Instead, the people of Avalei wouldn't abandon the place, so he upped the intensity of his attacks, forcing them to leave.

"And still the king sends no one?" I pace until a stark realization freezes me in place. "It's because he thinks we're a lost cause," I whisper. "That we aren't worth it.'

"He knows you're worth it, Nix," Greymore says, his voice vibrating with deep conviction. "He does. He also knows this isn't his fight—it's yours."

"And yours?" I ask, wondering why he returned to fight, to most likely die for a land that isn't his own.

"Your fight is mine, Nix. And mine is yours." In the darkness, I make out his eyes, clear as day and shining with honesty. "I'd like to think you had accepted that by now," he murmurs.

Emotion clogging my throat, I force my words past a lump of feeling. "I'd rather have you live than fight and die by my side."

"You better not be planning on leading these people into battle with so little hope," he snaps, stalking to the edge of the pond, frustrated. I blink at the vehemence of his words. He sighs, seizing control of his emotions, shutting himself away from me. "The choice is yours, Nix. Whatever you decide, I'm here to support you."

"Thank you," I say, at once appreciating his support and hating his refusal to tell me the right choice, to take this responsibility from me. "I suppose we should head back."

"What did you see in the water?" he asks in a soft voice.

"Nothing," I say, confused at the question. "Just my reflection."

"Interesting," he says, moving away from me toward the trail.

"Greymore," I reach for his arm. "What should I have seen?"

"It varies depending on the person and their needs. This is the Pool of Fortitude—the reflection shows you what you'll need to succeed."

"But I just saw myself," I argue, tempted to look again.

"Well, then...," Greymore moves away, speaking over his shoulder, "I guess that means everything you need is inside you. Find a way to bring it to the surface, Nix."

I follow Greymore, allowing his words to loop through my mind as we hike back toward the camp.

He doesn't say anything else, not even when I press for his opinion.

Pretty quickly, I realize my answer is the one that scares me the most. Honestly, I've known my choice all along. I've just been afraid to embrace it. My internal battle is just responsibility avoidance, which isn't going to help me do what I really need to do.

Now, I need to let the fears go. I need to become the reflection I saw, a girl who doesn't question her heart, her instinct, her strengths. I can be that person…I *am* that person.

With every step, my conviction grows, consuming my doubts, my fears, my weaknesses.

It's late when we reach camp, but—thrumming with newfound certainty—I don't waste any time in calling for a meeting. A few clipped demands and ten minutes later, everyone is gathered in front of my tent.

"People of Avalei," I project my voice, reaching for those lingering around the fringes of the group, the citizens with the most crushed of hopes. "Lord Greymore has returned, confirming our king's inability to send troops." At this, groans echo through the clearing. I speak over the top of them. "But that doesn't mean Avalei is to be left to evil, to be sacrificed. The king is fighting his battles, and we must fight ours."

I meet the scared faces before me. "I know this is a sacrifice. You won't be forced to make it, but I can tell you this—Avalei is worth it. Worth giving my best for…worth pledging my sword to. And with your power, we can overcome this evil. With our combined strength, hope, conviction, and loyalty, we can become strong, strong enough to purge the land."

"Hear, hear," someone shouts, and I smile at the voice.

"You may choose to call another city home, but know this: if we do not stand together, city after city will fall. If we do not recover the altanium and keep it from being misused, the entire kingdom is at risk. What we've faced is a mere speck of the power that a magical being can wield. With altanium, they will be unstoppable." I pause to let my words sink in.

"We can either hide, living in fear of the destruction," I gesture to the flimsy tents surrounding us, "or we can be a force working to keep it at bay. As for me, I won't go down cowering. I will continue, as I always have, fighting with my crew. Fighting with all I have and for all I have until I'm either howling in defeat or screaming in victory. But either way, I will fight! Even against the odds. Even when loss is all but guaranteed, I can fight. With the Great Creator on my side, I *will* fight."

"As will I," Greymore strides forward, firelight washing over him. "Now, who will join us!"

"Sweet Soldiers!" Reilynn shouts her agreement as Betah releases a terrifying war cry.

"Down with the magic!" Xandra exclaims, brandishing her shield while Asha touches her hand to her chest in a silent show of support.

Settlers step forward, joining my loyal friends, until, one by one, every survivor has committed to our fight. Enthusiastic shouts and calls for revenge fill the night air.

Hand pressed to my heart, I watch hope and passion flood back into the people of Avalei.

Tonight was a battle of the spirit. A major victory won. And tomorrow, we *will* win again.

CHAPTER TWENTY-THREE

P rom night.
   Primped and poised, coiffed and confident, I descend the stairs in my perfect gown. With a loose updo, new jewelry, and photo-ready make-up, I feel prepared for the dance.

"You're stunning," Mom says, snapping pictures like a paparazzi pro.

"Very nice," my dad says, blinking suspiciously.

I smile at their antics, my confidence elevated even further by the pride in their eyes. As I reach the bottom of the stairs, I give a runway spin, excitement building.

The doorbell rings, and Dad rushes to answer it while Mom documents every second. Flowers in hand, Trent steps across the threshold and meets my eye. Wearing an impeccably tailored tux, complete with a deep purple bowtie, he looks like air-brushed perfection. In an instant, my composure, my confidence, and my poise all fade, sputtering out like a doused fire. Thoughts of Trent's hopes for the night ground my soaring mood. As he looks at me with total adoration and eager expectation, my biggest fear becomes disappointing him.

All day I've kept my thoughts carefully ordered—focused only on dinner and the dance, but one glance at Trent and my mind fixates on the rest of the night.

On what I'm willing to give.

To lose.

"Claire," he says, his voice deeper and darker than usual. "You look perfect," he holds the corsage up, condensation dripping from the plastic container, "except for one thing."

"Of course," I say, managing a smile and remembering my decision to follow my gut and my heart and pray they're in agreement. "And you'll need your boutonniere." Clinging to my evaporating excitement, I grab the lone rose from where my mom left it on the counter.

Stepping to Trent, I'm overwhelmed by the smell of his cologne. He isn't wearing too much, but somehow, it's still suffocating.

My vision blurs as he smiles down on me, his free hand resting on my waist. Fingers fumbling, I attempt to pin the flower to Trent's tux.

"Let me." Mom saves me, pinning the rose in place with one easy movement.

Chagrined, I take a small step back, holding out my hand for my wrist corsage. I keep my eyes down, focused on the elegant arrangement of violet roses. I wanted an iris, but Trent assured me roses were classic…a universal beauty like me.

Right now, I don't feel like a universal beauty…more like a universal disaster.

As Trent slides the corsage into place—dragging a fingertip over the inside of my wrist—I fight warring desires, wanting to both flinch from and lose myself in his intimate touch. Instead, I slowly pull my hand from his and step to his side, posing for the camera.

Remembering it's my choice, that I'll always have a choice, rekindles a portion of my composure. Somehow, I make it through the countless pictures. I think I even manage to smile convincingly.

As eager as I am to get away, the minute Trent leads me out the door, I have a strong desire to rush back inside.

Not noticing my discomfort, Trent tucks my arm in his and gives me a slow, burning, intimate smile. My brain short-circuits, currents of attraction crossing with waves of dread. How can I want to be with him, yet not want to be with him?

Trent helps me into the back of the waiting limo. Once we're settled, he bangs on the ceiling with a superior smirk. The car starts moving, and I settle back into my seat. Next to me on the plush leather, Trent leans closer. "I love this dress." He runs his hand over the flowing fabric, brushing my leg. "I should have trusted you on the color purple long ago." He tilts his head, smelling my perfume. "You are exquisite."

I laugh—a tight, panicked sound. "And you're as hot as I knew you would be."

Smooth line, Nix.

Trent inches back, meeting my eyes. "And how hot is that?" he asks, his hand drifting to the edge of my lacey top, teasing the sensitive skin of my neck.

"Very," I practically squeak.

Trent stops his hand, never once moving to questionable territory. "You're too nervous, Claire," he says, encircling me with one arm and taking my hand in the other. "Relax, babe." His touch turns comforting as he squeezes my hand and tucks me against his side.

My anxiety cools. He hasn't mentioned anything about the vow. Maybe he realizes I love him, but I'm not ready. Clearly, he's noticed how anxious I am. Maybe this will all be okay. Maybe, maybe, maybe.

After driving a few blocks in comfortable silence, Trent dips his head, lips brushing against my ear, and whispers, "I love you, babe. And I'm excited to share this night with you."

Maybe…not.

* * * *

I clench my skirt in damp palms, likely ruining the material. It doesn't matter. I'm not sure I'll ever want to wear it again. Not when it will remind me of the anxiety of this night.

Standing at the edge of the dance floor, Trent leers at me, totally oblivious to my growing panic. "A couple more dances and we're out of here, babe," he whispers in my ear. "I'm tired of sharing you with everyone else."

I offer some kind of response, but have no clue what comes out. Trent smiles, pleased at the ridiculous words spewing from my mouth. I probably complimented his great foresight, an attribute I'm actually cursing right now. From the few comments he's made, it seems Trent has a prepaid room, a key in his pocket, and a plan.

Foresight is overrated.

But if I had a bit more of it, I probably wouldn't be in this mess—building up expectations I'm not able or ready to live up to.

Pulling me to the dance floor, Trent whispers, "Just a little bit longer." Numb, I nod. My feet move on their own, following Trent's lead.

The song ends. I find a drink in my hand and Trent looking at me with a raised brow. "Not thirsty?" he asks, surprised.

I am thirsty. Parched really. As I bring the glass to my lips, an image of a drug-laced drink crosses my mind. What is wrong with me? Frustrated with my growing paranoia, I down the entire glass.

"Hey, Claire!" Confused, I turn to the somewhat familiar voice. No one here except Trent and my brother call me Claire, and this voice was high-pitched and decidedly girly. A bubbly blonde bounces into view...followed by a less-than-eager Adam. For the first time since Trent mentioned a hotel, I feel like smiling.

"Diana," I say, recognizing Adam's date. "How are you?"

"Great, just great. This whole night has been great." She bounces on her toes, her bright orange dress swaying around her knees. "How about you?"

"I'm…great," I say, unable to help myself.

Adam covers his laugh with a cough while Trent reaches for my arm. "Babe, I love this song. Let's—"

"—Oh, me too!" Diana exclaims, grabbing Trent's hand. He looks at her, shocked like he's royalty being accosted by a peasant. "We should dance!" she practically squeals. "You can't come to prom and dance every dance with your girlfriend." She turns to beam at Adam. "We should switch! Adam, dance with Claire." Without releasing my boyfriend, she pushes his best friend toward me. "Trent, you're with me." She yanks on his arm.

Trent plants his feet, sending me a clear "help me!" look. I smirk back at him, wondering how he'll manage to free himself. In the end, his overly polished manners win out, and he allows Diana to tug him to the dance floor.

"Nix." Adam holds an arm out for me, a nervous, yet winsome smile in place.

I take his arm, tipping toward him. "I don't know how or why, but you planned that, didn't you?"

"I will neither confirm nor deny," he says. We reach the edge of the floor, far from Trent and Diana. Adam slides one arm around me, taking my hand with the other.

I lift a manicured brow. "Old-school, huh?"

"I prefer classic," Adam says, his voice a soft hum. His voice may be relaxed, but the constant repositioning of his fingers on my waist tells me he's anything but.

"What is it, Adam? You seem nervous. Problems with your date?" I tease.

"No, Diana and I came to an understanding last week. We're just friends." He smiles her way. "She's actually a pretty cool girl...once you get past the crazy, impulsive stuff."

Impressed, I lean back against his hold, studying his face. "How did you manage that?"

Adam smirks in his non-cocky, endearing way. "I have my methods. I will tell you it took many, many words. More words than I thought I had in me."

"Good for you." I ease forward, back into the circle of his arms. At the same time, he steps closer. I gulp at the sudden proximity. We aren't even that close—a pretty standard dancing distance—but it feels close, intimate.

I try to inch back, but Adam locks his arm, holding me in place. He smells good, a faint trace of scent that makes you want to move closer so you can identify every enigmatic element.

I give myself a mental slap. *Stop sniffing him.*

Forcing a light tone, I say, "You never really answered my question."

Adam clears his throat, his fingers tightening over mine. "My problem isn't with my date...it's with yours."

It takes a second for his words to click, bringing a sick premonition. "What's your problem with Trent?" I force myself to ask, knowing I won't like his answer.

"He's my best friend, Nix. Do you think he wouldn't brag about his plans for tonight?" He confirms my suspicion before continuing, "Who do you think stopped by the hotel with him earlier? Who do you think drove him here to drop off his car, hearing all about it?" With each word, his voice gets harsher, almost unrecognizable.

Buried in shame, I struggle to respond. "I…I'm…" I shake my head. There aren't words for this embarrassment. Tears prick my eyes, and I blink them back.

"Nix," Adam's voice switches, turning gentle. "It isn't my place to judge you, but it seems…" His chest rises as he takes a hitched breath. "…I think you don't want to do this and…you don't have to."

Scraping together the fragments of my dignity, I lift my chin. "And if I want to?"

"Do you?" he asks, searching my eyes.

"I don't know," I whisper.

"Does Trent know that?" he asks, and I nod, then shake my head, unsure. Adam huffs. "If you don't make the decision yourself, he'll make it for you."

"Maybe he should," I mumble.

"What?" Adam questions in total disbelief.

"Maybe he should," I repeat. Suddenly, the stress of the night, the humiliation of our conversation, and Adam's mortifying, insightful advice makes me snap. "Maybe I don't know what I want anymore, okay? And it's nice to be with someone who does." Adam's hand tightens on mine, and he pulls me closer.

"Nix—"

"Just quit, Adam." Knowing it's wrong, I can't seem to stop myself from venting on him, from letting my anger block my fears. "This isn't your problem. Trent shouldn't have even mentioned it to you." I keep my tone low, hissing my words through a clenched jaw. "It's embarrassing! And I don't know where you get off thinking it's your business." My emotions boil dangerously close to the surface. How dare he sit there with his life so perfectly in control and think he can understand mine? "It doesn't matter what I want. Don't you get that? It hasn't mattered for a long, long time." Knowing I'm precariously close to losing complete control, I cut off months worth of frustration.

"Nix…" Adam doesn't seem at all offended by my outburst. If anything, he looks relieved. Stopping our movement, he waits for my eyes to lock on his. "It should matter. You matter."

Seeing Trent watching us through narrowed eyes, I sway, forcing our dance to resume. Adam moves across from me, our steps disjointed and tense. "Just forget you ever knew about this," I say, my fire diminishing. "It's my problem, my choice…and my body. Understand?"

"Yes," Adam says, rushing his words as the song winds down. "I do understand, but I don't think you do. Or Trent."

The music stops, and he releases me, stepping backward. "If you ever need me...you have my number."

I stare at Adam, torn between anger and gratitude. "Claire!" Diana springs between us. "Your boyfriend is a great dancer. Just great!"

"Babe," Trent finally reaches us and slides an arm around me, curving his fingers over my hip. "Everything good?"

"Fine," I say, my voice too bright, strung with emotion.

Adam's gaze burns into me—questioning, offering. I look away, avoiding his eyes.

"Great," Trent says, unknowingly echoing Diana's favorite word and missing my overt distress. "I'm about done."

I withhold a disheartened sigh, keeping my focus on the floor as Trent makes excuses to a solemn Adam and ecstatic Diana. Turning his attention to me, he slides his hand into mine. "Are you ready to go?" he asks, pulling me away before I can answer.

But my answer would have only validated all of Adam's arguments and, in the end, not changed a thing...not one single thing. So, though I'm not ready at all, I go.

The drive to the hotel is surreal. I can't believe this is happening, that it has come to this moment, and I'm still frozen in indecision. I thought that with this moment would come clarity, but it's the opposite.

I'm in a haze as I follow Trent to the check-in counter and then up the stairs to our room. I stand in the entry of number 217 as Trent locks the door at my back.

The sound of the deadbolt sliding into place seems abnormally loud—an ominous sound echoing through my system, striking my core. Everything is too bright, too vibrantly real.

My chest constricts as my lungs crawl up into my throat, wedging against a massive ball of anxiety. Breath hitching in painful little gasps, I wring the purse in my hands, mangling the small clutch. Flight or fight activated, my eyes dart around the room.

It is a higher-quality room, but it's still a hotel. The layout isn't unique—a narrow entry hall with a bathroom to the right, windows spanning the wall in front of me, and directly to the left, the bed.

My labored breathing becomes louder, too loud to miss.

Kicking off his shoes, Trent grabs the remote and gets comfortable on the bed. "Come on, babe," he says as he turns the TV on. "Relax."

Thankful for his casual tone, I perch on the bed next to him. He curls his arm around me, pulling me against his side. To my relief, we flip through channels for a while as I attempt to relax. I kick off my uncomfortable heels and rest my head on Trent's chest, my terror receding, replaced by a manageable anxiety. There's a part of me excited about Trent's hand moving constantly over my back, arms, and shoulders with a light touch, but there's also a nervous part, questioning what will follow.

Eventually, his hand drifts to my face, tracing my jaw, eyebrows, and lips. Then he tips my chin and begins kissing me. It starts with a gentle press of his lips, but quickly builds to a fiery intensity. I feel myself falling, giving in to the storm of emotion when Trent's hand moves to my zipper.

I jerk away, holding my hand out, needing a barrier between us. "Trent, I…I just don't think I can. Tonight has been amazing. *You* are amazing, but I'm just not ready."

The passion in his eyes dwindles, replaced by determination. "Listen, Claire. It is your first time. No matter what, you will be nervous. And that's all this is, babe. Nerves. Next time, they won't be in the way, but this time we just have to deal with them."

He reaches for me, but I scoot away. "I don't want to just deal, Trent. I want to feel sure about this," I say, pleading with him to understand.

Instead, his deep green eyes narrow accusingly. "I'm all in with this relationship, but it doesn't seem like you are." He scoots back on the bed, shifting further away from me. "You say you love me, but you don't show it. I trust you, but you don't trust me."

"Trent—" Wishing there wasn't so much truth to his words, I reach a hand to him.

He shoves it away. "No, Claire. Don't play with me. I've had enough of your games. You said you would consider tonight, but you were just stringing me along. I don't even think you considered it. You never even thought about what this could do for our relationship, how much your willingness would prove to me. You have to know this type of thing is a deal breaker, Claire."

His intense gaze pierces me as he waits for my response.

I swallow harshly as my mind blanks. My feelings are so jumbled I can't sort them, much less respond.

Trent's eyes darken, the intensity breathtaking. Then he nods as if he's made a decision and says, "This is it, Claire. Either keep your word to me and show me you love me, or we're through."

The finality of his words sucker punches me. Emotions build behind my eyes, tears forming.

I reel at the ultimatum, one that feels deserved. I did lead him on. I don't trust him like I should. I don't show I'm committed. I am not giving him what he needs.

"I don't want to lose you," I whisper, a tear breaking free to slide down my cheek.

"Then prove it," Trent says, challenging me.

Cornered, guilty, and desperate, I find myself nodding before I even realize I've made a choice. "Okay," I say, wiping the tears from my eyes and accepting the fate I've brought on myself. Then, with more conviction, I repeat, "Okay."

Trent doesn't make a move, just stares at me, daring me with his silence to act.

With jerky movements, I rise from the bed and grab my purse from the nightstand. Trent watches my every move, his nonreaction suffocating.

Heart pounding, I say, "I'm just going to…going to go..to…just…a minute." I stumble to the bathroom, practically slamming the door behind me. Safe, I flip on the fan to cover the sound of my breathing, toss my purse to the counter, and stare into the mirror.

Excuses, justifications, truths, and fears flit through my eyes. I study the dark orbs, searching for an explanation—a reason for my dread.

You're being stupid, Claire. There is no reason to be so afraid. You're attracted to Trent, you love Trent. This is just an expression of that love. You will get married. You did save yourself for your husband. You will have honored your vow. You can do this, Claire. You love him. You can prove it. You need to prove it. You can do this.

I bow my head, pressing my forehead to the cool glass and closing my eyes. *You can do this.*

I repeat the words in my mind, trying to seal them in, to shore up my foundering resolve. But the words twist, changing and rearranging inside my mind. *You don't have to.*

The tenacious phrase sounds again and again, showing me the way out, changing my decision. There *is* a simple escape here—honesty. To myself and to Trent.

Can I back out on this? On an agreement I was pressured to make? Again, the answer is simple. Scary, but simple.

But can I really do this? Am I brave enough for the fallout?

Am I the scared girl, too afraid to fight for what she knows is right, or am I the reflection I saw in the pool last night?

I stare into the mirror, recalling my fantasy world. Images of Betah, Asha, Reilynn, and Xandra flash through my mind. With a burst of clarity, I understand it all. My dream crew is a symbol, a representation of all the people and parts of myself I need to succeed.

I see Betah. Betah, who represents my individuality. All of the crazy and unique things that make me Nix. Things I shouldn't give up.

I see Asha. Asha, who represents my hope for the future. My planning for better and better days ahead.

I see Reilynn. Reilynn, who represents my convictions, my morality. Her strength is mine.

I see Xandra. Xandra, who represents friends and family along the way. People who love me as I am, yet encourage me to become a better version of myself.

I see Avalei. Avalei is divine. Avalei is the potential that I can reach with God's help. It's who I am now and the promise of the glory I can find if I rely on God.

And I see Nix the Defender. The Nix who makes the right choice even when it's the hard choice. The Nix I drew that night, who looks past the struggle and doesn't just live in it. The Nix I saw reflected on a moonlit pool.

I can recreate the image I saw there. I can take control, here, in this moment. I can channel the fortitude I find in my dreams. I can show the same courage. I can cling to that endless hope.

I can be my own defender.

I drop to my knees on the cold bathroom floor and offer a pleading prayer. With shaking hands, I rise and pull my phone from my purse. Knowing Trent won't be happy when I back out, I text the only person I can think of for a ride.

Tucking the phone away, I give my reflection a lingering look.

There, I find a determined spark of hope and a growing glow of faith. Where I once saw less, now I see more. There I see someone who will own her own choices and her own self.

With a hefty exhale, I exit the bathroom.

Trent is perched on the edge of the bed, his bowtie undone and dangling around his neck. He's dimmed the lights in the room, creating an atmosphere I'm not willing to embrace. "Ready?" he asks, standing and stalking forward.

"No," I say, the word with full conviction.

"No?" He keeps advancing.

"No, I'm not ready, Trent." I hold my purse between us, a flimsy, ineffective shield. "I thought I could do this for you, but I can't do this...for me."

"Claire, I have been patient." Voice rumbling, he stops inches from me and grips my shoulders. "I deserve this. You owe me. For months, I have spoiled you. I have waited. Buying you lunches, showering you with gifts, not to mention all of the money I dished out tonight." His fingers curl, nails digging into my shoulders. "You owe me."

For a split second, guilt makes me waver.

You don't have to.

I jerk from his hold. "You don't buy people, Trent. I'm grateful for all you've done, but I do *not* owe you."

"Yes, you *do*." Trent's muscles coil, his expression turning savage.

Feeling as if I'm seeing a man unmasked, I remember the look in his eyes, the look from that night so long ago. The look that warned me to run before it was too late. The look I ignored. I won't ignore it this time.

Spinning, I flip the top lock of the door aside.

Grabbing my hand, Trent flips me around and shoves me back against the door. His body presses flush against mine, pinning me in place. "You are mine, Claire."

All at once, the realization of what is about to happen to me floods my system. *He isn't going to take no for an answer.*

Like a coating of ice, the thought freezes me in place. I can't win. Not this battle. Not this fight. Not against him. Because Trent doesn't lose.

The strength I once admired traps me, and I close my eyes for a split second in denial and defeat.

"…I won't go down cowering."

Words from my dream world—my words—drift to me, reawakening my spirit.

"I will continue, as I always have, fighting with my crew. Fighting with all I have and for all I have until I'm either howling in defeat or screaming in victory. But either way, I will fight! Even against the odds. Even when loss is all but guaranteed, I can fight. With the Great Creator on my side, I will fight."

My eyes snap open.

Taking my stillness for acceptance, Trent's hold has slackened. His lips are on my neck, his hands roving over my back. With one fluid motion, I reach between us and shove him violently backward. Trent crashes to the floor as I flick the last deadbolt back, throw the door open, and bolt forward, screaming for help.

With an animalistic roar, Trent lunges over the threshold, catching my ankle. I fall, my body splayed across the hall. Trent twists my ankle in his grip, and I yelp as pain shoots up my leg.

Outrage powering me, I kick out with my uninjured leg, my heel crashing into Trent's eye. He releases me with a howl, and our room door slams shut, a barrier between us.

Run, run, run.

I taste freedom, but know this is far from over. The stairs are in the middle of the hotel, and our room was all the way at the end. Seeing as how my cries and Trent's bellowing didn't draw anyone out, I'm assuming there's no one willing to help. I stumble to my feet, my ankle throbbing as I use the wall to brace myself and stagger down the hall.

Shock settles in, and everything seems to move in slow motion, the hall growing longer.

Run, run, find help.

I look for a camera, a person, a weapon—some form of salvation—only to hear the door fly open behind me.

With a cry, I redouble my efforts to reach the stairs. Trent's stomping tread closes in as I reach the stairway. He's calling my name, his voice harsh, yet cajoling.

Run, run, run to a camera.

Midway down the stairs my ankle gives way, and I tumble to the ground level. Splayed awkwardly, I finally spy a camera in the large entryway.

Drawn by the noise of my fall, the hotel's front desk worker appears in the archway. "Call 911," I groan, and she rushes away.

At the top of the stairs, Trent calls my name. Again, his voice holds contradictions—anger and pity. Affection and loathing.

Pushing past the pain, I rise. I'm not looking for safety anymore, but an undeniable witness. *Camera, camera, camera.* The panicked mantra in my brain has shifted, replaced by a strange calm.

Because, somewhere between the time he told me I owed him and the time he assaulted me, I've decided I don't just want to get away from this psycho…I want to *put* him away. And to do that, I need him in that camera's frame.

In perfect view, I rest against the wall. There's still terror, but it isn't overpowering…my conviction is.

Seconds later, Trent is on me. "Don't leave, Claire," his voice pleads, but his eyes demand. "Just come back to the room. We can talk this out. We can figure this out."

"I said no," I emphasize, shaking my head for the camera. "Multiple times."

"You're confused," he says, anger building. "You don't mean this."

"But I do, Trent. Because finally, finally I can see just what you aren't…and what you are."

"We belong together," he practically hisses.

"No, we don't. I will not and do not belong to you and never, ever will again."

His control snaps. "You think that will stop me?" He grabs my face, crushing my cheeks into my jaw. "It didn't with Gabriella, and it won't with you." He smiles down at me manically, even crazier than I guessed. But as terrifying as it is, this is what I wanted: to expose the real Trent.

Channeling some of dreamworld Nix's reckless bravery, I bait him, saying, "Can't get any action without force?"

Shocked, his hand drops from my face before clenching at his side.

Feeling every inch a fantasy warrior, I tip my chin up, daring him, bracing myself for the speed of his strike. "You're a fake, Trent. A pretty face with no soul and no substance." His muscles constrict, veins bulging. "And you will never ever have me."

A cry sounds from the direction of the front desk as his arm swings. I dodge, simultaneously bringing my knee up with all my strength.

With a pain-filled roar, Trent drops.

I move out of his reach, but keep my eyes locked on his writhing form, poised and ready for his next attack.

"Stay down." A voice demands, coming from the hotel entrance.

It's a voice I know, but the rich cadence of Adam's voice is gone, replaced by deadly menace. As I lean against the wall, he stalks to Trent, fists clenched. "If you move even one inch closer to her, you'll regret it."

Trent mumbles something that sounds like, "Can't take me."

Adam chuckles darkly. "I don't have to. It looks like Nix already did."

Flashing lights and screeching sirens punctuate his statement. Police rush the lobby, and my bravery flees.

Shaking uncontrollably, I watch as Trent is carted away.

Drowning in all the what-ifs, I sink to the floor, barely registering Adam's form beside me, the cops questioning me, the curious onlookers. I'm shivering, covered in residual adrenaline. I'm an abused girlfriend. A cautionary tale. A statistic.

A victim.

But there's something else I've become, a phrase that winds through and around the trauma of this last hour, begging to be acknowledged. As my shock recedes and I resurface, my mind grabs hold of that phrase. That phrase that validates my fight, my pain, and my choice. I cling to that beautiful, liberating phrase, repeating it to myself until I begin to accept it.

I'm free. I'm free.

I am free.

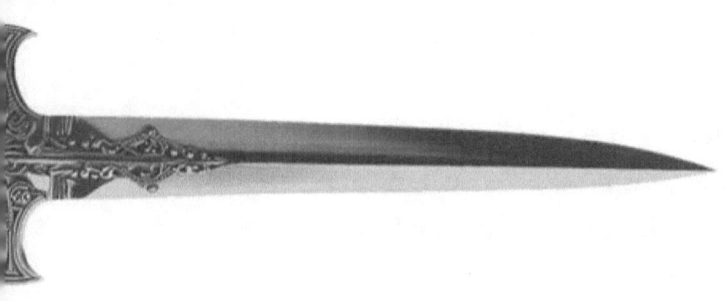

CHAPTER TWENTY-FOUR

"She's taking too long," I say, flipping a new dagger through my fingers.

Greymore may have come back from the king without reinforcements, but that doesn't mean he returned empty-handed.

Running a hand over the hand-stamped metal of her new shield, Xandra scoffs, "She probably stopped to visit with a few of her serpent friends along the way. You know, sneaking isn't Betah's style."

Beside her, Reilynn stamps her feet in restless anticipation. From the safety of a nearby rocky outcrop, I peer across the dunes to the wall of Avalei. "She was just supposed to spread the chemical," I gripe. "We have no idea how many serpents there are out there."

Xandra snorts. "Right…just a nice little stroll with explosive water."

Asha points her bow toward the dunes. "I see her, she is—" The elf's face contorts in dismay, and she drops to her knees as an explosion rocks the earth. Something slimy rains from the sky.

I throw my hands over my head, avoiding the goop. "Is that…?"

"It *was* a serpent," Greymore says, clearly entertained.

"Betah threw an explosive down the beast's throat," Asha admits, cringing.

"Outrageous Orcs," Reilynn murmurs, tightening her grip on her broadsword as I shoot to my feet.

"That was not the plan!" I yell, but I'm not sure at whom. Betah is still too far away to hear. I glance from the group crouched beside me to the settlers waiting for the signal at the bottom of the hill.

"Guess we might as well start," I mumble, turning to Asha. "Take the shot." With a nod, the elf dips her notched arrow in the torch Greymore holds and fires.

The missile flies high, dropping when it reaches the center of the dunes.

For a second nothing happens, then the sand bursts into flame, spreading to create two jagged lines across the dunes. Running parallel to one another, these lines create a fire-protected path from our hiding place to the defense. I can't help but smirk. "That should keep most of those serpents at bay. Now for phase two."

Betah strides toward the wall, taking out a serpent barring her path with a quick swing of her battle axe. Seeing her advance, I call the settlers to us. We move from our cover, skirting the rocks and dropping onto the dunes.

We rush across the sand in one large group. Greymore and Asha lead the way, the settlers fall behind them, and Xandra, Reilynn, and I bring up the rear. Weapons drawn, we're ready to take down any serpent brave enough to test the fiery barrier or unlucky enough to be locked in our path.

We're halfway across the dunes when the tell-tale buzzing sounds. We hear the mosquitoes long before we see them, but can do little but wait for their arrival. "This better work," I mumble to Xandra.

"It will...I think," she says, holding her shield a little higher.

"You think!?" I exclaim as the pests close in. Many are driven off course by the fire, but the greater part dive ever closer.

"Vile vampires," Reilynn mutters, weapon raised overhead.

With the serpents closing in and the mosquitoes looming overhead, we pause at the center of the dunes. We hold a collective breath, waiting. Praying.

A mosquito dive bombs directly toward me, its creepy eyes fastened on mine. Doubting our plan, I adjust my grip on my old scimitar, preparing for the attack. Just shy of striking range, the overlarge insect veers away, repelled by my scent. "It worked!" I say, beaming at Xandra.

"Yeah, of course it did." She plays it cool, her confidence returning tenfold. "That's what bathing in citronella and lavender will do for you. Good for the complexion, too. Why, we are all positively glowing."

"Could be that we're surrounded by fire," I quip.

"Tremor to the right!" Reilynn yells, springing forward and burying her sword in the moving sand.

The hidden serpent stills, dead. With a smug grin, Reilynn smacks Xandra's arm. "See, my plan worked too…we can kill the snakes before they rise and paralyze…and I rhymed."

"Yes, you're both very smart," I praise sarcastically. "Now take cover."

We surge toward the massive black rocks dotting the dunes, but we're either too late or Betah is overeager. A deafening boom sounds from the wall. The explosion knocks me back, the shock wave thumping into my chest. A projectile rock sails over my head, missing my skull by inches.

"Betah!" I scream, lying flat.

Struggling to regain my equilibrium, I check the group over. Somehow, the settlers had all reached cover, and everyone else was lucky enough to avoid the flying debris.

As the dust settles, I spy Betah—a dark silhouette striding through the massive two-story hole in Avalei's wall. I swallow my emotional response.

It was necessary.

We needed a way inside, and the fortification was too strong otherwise.

As one flowing force, we shake off the explosion and rush the opening. Crossing the remainder of the dunes, we dispose of a handful of serpents, attacking them before they can rise from the earth. A few attempt to pass our line of fire, but the chemical has soaked deep, and they turn back, hissing wildly.

Serpents and mosquitoes conquered. Next?

As if summoned, a clicking sounds from the opposite side of the wall. The arachnids. Our repellent probably won't faze them, but we have something deadlier planned for these little devils.

Planting his flaming torch in the sand, Greymore kneels behind it, lifts his crossbow, and rapid fires. Catching fire as they sail through the flame, his bolts fly toward the spiders. When the flaming bolts find their mark, the creatures hesitate, creating a massive pile up of squirming legs in the newly formed opening of the wall. With the last bolt in his clip, Greymore aims low.

Saturated in Betah's chemical, the ground under the arachnids erupts in flame. Scorched, the spiders retreat—at least, the survivors do.

With a war cry, the settlers flood the opening, stepping over charred arachnids. Climbing up the rubble, they battle a few stragglers to regain the wall.

We have our defense back.

I follow the settlers to the solid portion of the wall. "We need to close this hole. Those not doing that, fan out and clear the wall."

"What about you?" Zel appears at my side. I didn't want the girl to come, but she wasn't about to miss out on the chance to avenge her father's death, and I wasn't about to stop her.

"You know the plan. We're moving to clear the settlement, then on to the tunnel." She opens her mouth, but I cut her off before she can ask. "Stay here, Zel. Clear the wall and fight from its safety."

"Fine," she says, mulishly spinning a sword in her palm before scrambling up the ladder to the next level.

With a long-suffering sigh, I step to the large doorway. From the safety of the defense, I eye the settlement. A few arachnids hide in the trees. We could probably flush them out, but the real problem is the bats. The megaspecs have moved their roost to our settlement. The closer I look, the more of them I see.

"We'll have to burn it," I tell Xandra, Asha, Greymore, and Reilynn as they gather behind me. Uncharacteristically serious, Xandra nods in agreement while Asha places a supportive hand on my shoulder.

"Or blow it," Betah says, appearing out of nowhere.

"Flipping flames," Reilynn says. "No more explosives, woman!"

Betah shrugs, tossing a lit fuse to the side. An arachnid explodes nearby. "Maybe more later?" she says, hopeful.

Praying for forgiveness, I take Greymore's torch and touch it to the nearest pile of wood, and the nearest tree, and the nearest house while Betah throws her flammable substance over as much as she can, urging the fire's growth. Before long, the whole settlement is in flames, the smoke driving the arachnids away, back to the tunnel in the lake. We kill as many retreating creatures as we can, knowing if we don't, we'll most likely have to fight them again later. As the flames rise, the megaspecs abandon their roosts. The settlers on the wall shoot down any that fly within range. The smoke settles in the valley, thickening the air, stinging our eyes.

I lose sight of everyone but Greymore. "The settlers know to hold the wall. We need to get to the clearing!" I yell, choking on the fumes. A shadow drops from the sky. "Watch—"

Angered by the smoke, the megaspec attacks with a vengeance.

Greymore drops and rolls, swinging his arm out to bring his loaded crossbow up, but the beast pins his weaponized arm down as a second one latches onto his legs. Bucking, Greymore yells at the megaspecs—a horrifying sound that is part terrorized scream, part battle cry.

Matching his exclamation, I lunge forward, tackling the megaspec holding his arms.

The creature and I roll yards away, landing with the bat on top.

It screeches in my face, its breath smelling of rotten meat and fresh blood. Cocking my arm back, I punch it. The force throws the creature's head back and tosses it from my body. I surge to my feet, my scimitar instantly in hand.

Another heartbeat and the megaspec is dead.

I spin to help Greymore, but he's standing over the second beast's body, a bloody crossbow bolt in his hand.

I point a shaky scimitar his way, moving toward him. "You…" One stride. "better…" Another step. "not…" I stop in front of him, still holding the quivering blade out in front of me. "…die." His emotions flood me, or maybe the emotions are all mine.

Either way, they're potent, packed with meaning and promise.

"Why, Nix?" he says, his voice soft amidst the chaos surrounding us.

"Because…" I tap the scimitar against the clasp of his hood, my words spilling free. "…your fight is mine and mine is yours."

I catch a flash of his smile before he knocks my scimitar aside and yanks me to him.

Then he's kissing me.

I don't waste time, kissing him right back, matching his intensity. It's raw and impulsive and perfect.

Better than any real world kiss.

"You guys done?" A voice asks to my right as Reilynn emerges from the smoke, nonchalantly striking a megaspec from the air with her massive sword.

I glance at the dead bats littering the ground around us. We didn't kill this many, which means…

"We're getting tired of holding these guys off. I mean, I'm all for angsty, heat of battle kisses, but…" Xandra chucks her shield over our heads, braining an approaching bat.

Retrieving her shield, she continues, "…we *do* have a job to do."

Blushing, I attempt to casually retrieve my scimitar from the ground. When did I drop the thing? "We're done," I say, stabbing a megaspec at my back without looking.

"For now," Greymore murmurs as Asha and Betah appear. They grin at me, smiles so wide I'm afraid their lips will split.

"Be serious, ladies," I say as we group into a circle to combat the bat's attacks.

"Oh, that looked plenty serious," Xandra says, elbowing me a few times. I redden again, a flush I hope the smoky air hides.

"Blinking Bats," Reilynn says, back to the business of war. "How are we going to finish these guys?"

A human-shaped shadow comes into view—a young human-shaped shadow. "What are you doing, Zel?" I demand, lunging forward to cut down the megaspec on her tail.

"Bringing this," she says, holding up a flute. Then, without explanation, she puts the instrument to her lip and blows.

The awful, high-pitched sound she makes leaves everyone clasping their ears. To say Zel is a horrible musician would be a kindness.

"What are you doing? Keening for the death of music?" Xandra asks, rubbing her ears.

"No," Zel says, bringing the flute back to her lips.

Xandra lunges for the flute, but I stay her hand, pointing to the megaspecs.

As Zel plays her terrible song, they screech in pain, thrashing their heads back and forth. It's a horrible racket, but it's working. The bats abandon the clearing, flying over the wall where archers—now in position on the top—bring most of them down. The remaining megaspecs take off toward The Razor.

"Guess we'll get them in the cave," I say, taking the flute from Zel. "Finish blocking the hole in the wall and try to draw any remaining animals out. But first, make sure the gates are closed up top. We haven't run into any snowcats, and with any luck we won't." The teenager frowns, and I soften my tone. "You did amazingly well, Zel. That's why I'm trusting you to see to things here while we go for Chancellor Ivers and the altanium." I clap a hand on her shoulder, eager to finish this. "Good luck."

I turn and jog away. It's time for another swim.

* * * *

"I can't believe we haven't run into any megaspecs or spiders in here," Xandra complains, her torch light bouncing off the walls of the tunnel.

"Well, if your racket didn't draw them out, then nothing will," Reilynn says, still upset at Xandra for breaking our cover with her loud screams in the first chamber. In her defense, the tiny rat *was* aggressive. And it's not like Chancellor Ivers doesn't know we're coming, but I'm not going to argue that point with the knight.

"Hey, I might draw them in," Xandra says. "But I don't go around punching them…like Nix." All eyes turn to me.

I puff out my chest. "I'm actually very proud of that hit, knocked the poor, dead animal out cold."

"Flying Fists of Fury," Reilynn says. "That's awesome. Good option to keep in mind." She closes her fists, her fluted armor bending with the movement.

"Better option than leaving the bomb-happy orc behind. Do you honestly think that was the best choice?" Xandra asks for the millionth time.

Xandra complains, but we both know Betah is the only one with the knowledge to effectively collapse the entrance to the tunnel if we don't return…and the guts to do it. "Had to. And she'll only set the charge if absolutely necessary," I say, hoping Xandra will drop it this time.

She doesn't. "Had to? Absolutely necessary? Betah thought it was necessary to make a snake swallow an explosive."

"She didn't think that was necessary. She thought it was fun," Reilynn argues. "And you're just sensitive because of the whole snake gut thing from before."

"You would be too…"

I block out their argument, leaning toward Asha and Greymore. "Remember how quiet it was when she was on her deathbed…good times."

Asha looks appropriately shocked, but Greymore laughs. Not a little chuckle, but a full-on deep, resounding show of amusement.

"Wait." Xandra plows past me, grabbing his arm. "Did you just laugh? Sweet swords, you really are in love."

"Shh," I say, pulling on her arm.

"No!" she exclaims, and I clamp a hand over her mouth, dragging her tiny body backwards.

"I recognize this turn in the tunnel." I drop my hand. "We're almost there. Now shut your mouth and draw your weapon." I release her, and she flits forward, desperate to be the first on the scene.

The rest of us follow more slowly, nerves firing, adrenaline screaming.

Peeking over the edge, Xandra inches back to us, slightly stupefied. "I don't see Ivers. But there's a fortune of altanium. Gorgeous altanium," she says. "Oh,…and six snowcats."

"Dang and Blast, I hoped there wouldn't be any," I say, checking the pouch at my hip. "Still, six isn't bad."

"One is bad enough," Xandra whispers, her skin a little pale.

She touches her stomach and the scars there. They may not hurt now, but time hasn't dulled her memory of the pain.

"We'll take them," I reassure her, my dagger spinning freely. "Everyone will pick a cat. We'll use the element of surprise. After the initial attack, we spring out and take whatever ones are still standing."

Asha clears her throat, and we all turn to her expectantly, waiting for her superior plan. "Greymore and I will take the two in the back, Reilynn and Nix, the two closest cats. Then, as one, we will exit and focus on one beast at a time until all are disposed of."

I tap her bow with the flat of my dagger. "Yeah, that."

We move into position. As soon as Greymore and Asha get an open shot, they take it. But, within the next few seconds, our plan falls apart.

The long-range shots are perfect, but these cats are bigger or more armored or *something* because Asha and Greymore's remarkable head shots don't bring them down.

The two continue firing at their beasts as Reilynn and I step up. My dagger pierces the snowcat's skull but doesn't slow it down. Reilynn's snow cat grabs her spear, smashing it in its jaws before tossing the broken pieces aside.

When Asha and Greymore finally bring their snowcats down, we jump into the cavern as a synchronized group. As we land, a camouflaged snowcat materializes in the rock behind us.

We scatter, becoming separated.

The cat with my dagger sticking out of its forehead advances on me, backing me against the wall. "Vengeful little bugger," I hiss as I take stock of my squad.

Overwhelmed by the beasts, each fights their own losing battle. Desperate, I pull a little gift from Betah from my pouch and toss it into the fray, shouting for cover. The bomb explodes, a loud pop, more sound than anything. The cats ease back, giving us just enough time to regroup.

We retreat to a sharp curve in the wall, narrowing our vulnerable areas by half. "We have to be methodical about this." I throw a couple more noise bombs, driving the cats to one side.

"Me first!" Xandra says, stepping up with her mace and chains. She swings the weapon twice, making contact once. After her, Greymore steps forward, striking the cat multiple times with his chain and blade. Then Asha and her deadly fan, me with my scimitar, and Reilynn with her broadsword.

Between our turns, we fire off arrows, bolts, and bombs, keeping the attack alive. We kill nine cats before they retreat.

"Pretty numerous six," Reilynn mutters.

"I said I *saw* six cats. I never guaranteed there wouldn't be more. Besides, aren't you supposed to expect the unexpected or something?" Xandra snaps.

"I expect very little when it comes to you," Reilynn fires back.

"Girls!" I yell as Xandra knocks Reilynn over with her shield.

A loud clapping fills the cavern, echoing through the silence. "Good show, ladies…and a lord," Ivers says as he glides into view on the back of the largest and most deadly looking snowcat I've ever seen. The creature is entirely black with vivid yellow eyes. "I really hoped the cats would kill you off," he says, clicking his tongue. "It's a shame to waste magic, but when I have so much to spare," he gestures to the altanium glowing from the ground, lighting up the room, "it isn't a huge loss." Never one for small talk, Greymore fires his crossbow. The bolt pings off the chancellor, striking some invisible barrier.

"No, no, my lord," Ivers says, wagging a finger. "Let me show you how this is done." He pulls a glowing orb from his belt and tosses it at us.

We spring apart as the sphere crashes toward the center of our group. Shattering on impact, the magical component instantly evaporates, becoming a bluish smoke. The gas doesn't look dangerous or even smell, but then it brushes against Greymore. The second it comes in contact, the smoke soaks into him. Greymore falls to the ground, muscles seizing in pain. "Greymore." I move toward him as Ivers laughs maniacally.

Greymore holds out his arm, waving me back as he moans in agony. "Don't... touch me," he gasps.

Another ball comes hurtling our way.

We dive away, but a current—an evil breeze—blows the smoke toward Xandra. She drops with a scream.

Enraged, Reilynn rushes toward Ivers, but he changes things up, throwing two. She dodges the first, but the second hits her square in the chest.

Asha is next, the bluish smoke dancing over her ankle when Ivers throws a line of orbs her way.

They're all down. Every single member of my squad, except Betah. Betah, who we left behind to seal us in this tomb.

"Just you and me, little defender!" Ivers cajoles as my friends writhe in pain.

I wrack my tortured brain for options. Sensing weakness, the snowcats circle, closing in.

Realizing I have little chance of winning and nothing left to lose, I whisper, "Avalei, I'm sorry," before darting forward in a headlong sprint toward the gloating chancellor.

Surprised, Ivers fires three globes my way. I dodge the first two before snatching the third from the air. With a quick flick of the wrist, I send it hurling at the massive snow cat's feet. The smoke rises in a wisp, disappearing into the beast's midnight coat.

As the cat drops, I jump to the top of his head. Springing off its neck, I kick out with both feet, driving Ivers from the top of the yowling beast before he can react.

I land on my feet as the chancellor falls to his back, his one remaining globe cushioned in his hands.

Snatching the orb from his grasp, I hold it over him. "Save them or I will end you."

"There is no saving them," he wheezes. The remaining snowcats ease away, blending into the shadows, scared off by the pained whimpers of their dying alpha. We may be safe from the cats, but the magic continues to attack my friends.

Their muffled, tortured cries call to me.

Desperate, I squeeze the globe.

The altanium sphere gives slightly under the pressure, responding to me. A current of energy flows over me.

"No," Iver's eyes widen. "Impossible!" Kicking a leg, he takes my balance. Trying to protect the globe, I stumble back.

I land on my side, my arm outstretched, the orb resting in my fingers.

A force crashes into me, throwing me to my stomach.

The globe rolls away, bouncing across the cavern floor as Ivers buries a knee in my back and shoves my face to the ground. The unmined altanium beneath me shimmers—a magic I can't access.

A leather strap encircles my neck. Ivers twists the ends together, tightening them until I'm gasping for breath.

Pulling my hair, he jerks my head up. "Look at them, little defender," he hisses. "I want them to be the last thing you see before you die, knowing you couldn't save them. Couldn't save Avalei."

My gaze flickers between my friends as tears pool in my eyes and spots fill my vision. Greymore is curled away from me, far too still. Xandra is thrashing against the ground, her dark hair flipping wildly. Reilynn's jaw is locked, her neck bulging in an effort to contain her pain.

And Asha, never without hope, is reaching a faltering hand toward her quiver.

I tilt my head back even further, needing a tiny bit more air, another minute of consciousness. "You failed, Nix," Ivers hisses as Asha reaches for her bow. "Avalei is dead."

I stretch my arm out, waiting.

Using her last reserve of strength, the elf strings, draws, and fires an arrow.

My reaching hand closes around the airborne shaft. Thrusting my arm over my shoulder, I plunge the arrow into Ivers' chest.

He falls, releasing the strap.

Gasping, I flip to find the chancellor clutching the shaft of the arrow—the arrow embedded in his chest.

Unraveling the strap from my throat, I stand. "Avalei isn't dead, Ivers. You are."

The chancellor's eyes close as the pool of blood surrounding him expands rapidly. I turn away, leaving him to die alone. Throwing the leather aside, I move to collect the globe and rush to Greymore.

Placing the globe in his hands, I wait. Nothing happens. I look back to Ivers. His chest is unmoving. He's gone, but his deadly magic isn't.

The orb has to work. The magic *can* save them. Its response to me earlier scared Ivers, which means I can somehow control this power.

Bursting with emotion, I touch the globe in Greymore's hands. The same current of energy as before moves from the sphere to me before crashing into Greymore.

With a groan, he eases upright. The second I see he's recovering, I move to Xandra, then Reilynn, then Asha.

As my last friend is saved, I fall back onto my heels, holding the now dim globe in my hand.

Asha smiles serenely at me.

I offer her an emotional grin. "You saved me," I whisper, amazed we're alive, amazed Avalei is finally safe, amazed I caught that arrow.

"No, Nix," she says. "You saved us." She points to the globe in my hands. "You saved us all."

CHAPTER TWENTY-FIVE

"**S**ave me," I mouth to my brother.

It's the day after prom, after the worst night of my life, and my parents are suffocating me.

I can't say I blame them.

I totally get it.

I *was* relieved when Mom crawled into bed with me this morning, hugging me as if I were a five-year-old recovering from a nightmare. And I *was* grateful when Dad sent away the officer who came to ask more questions and take another statement, telling her to return tomorrow. I was also happy to sit crushed between them as we watched my favorite movie and ate ice cream for breakfast. I was even thrilled to binge-watch mindless television and eat delivery pizza for lunch, my parents checking my appetite by offering slice after slice after slice. But now they're pulling out photo albums and threatening to turn on home videos. It's like they need to remind me I'm safe, blessed. A fact I'm painfully aware of...now more than ever. The problem is, after living with a suffocating boyfriend for months, what I need is space.

Dillon has hovered in the background all day—ready to jump when I need something, but willing to tease me like only a brother can. At my silent entreaty, he clears his throat. "Claire, I'm running to grab a Dr. Pepper. You want to come with?"

My parents turn identical glares on him as I stand cautiously, mindful of my sprained ankle, and say, "Sure, let me just grab a hat and some shoes."

"Claire, I'm not sure..." My dad hesitates to admit he wants to lock me away from the world.

"Honey, you should stay." Mom doesn't bother to hide her desire to protect me, to keep me under her watchful eye forever.

I stand before them as they sit on the couch, looking more terrified than concerned. We can't keep dancing around this, pretending I'm fine and they're acting normal. Tucking a hair behind my ear, I say, "I won't lie and tell you I'm perfectly okay." I point to my cheeks, bruised from Trent's crushing hold. My mom flinches, and my dad's gaze hardens. I continue, "I won't deny it, I won't pretend I'm the same. But I can't hide. Because if I hide today, I'm afraid I'll keep hiding." I swallow back my emotions, refusing to give them control. I let myself feel and hurt and cry all night, and I probably will again—a lot, but I will not let this pain consume me. With an unsteady voice, I continue, "A horrible thing happened to me, but I refuse to be ashamed of it, to be controlled by it... and I don't want you guys to be either. I have a lot of things to face. How much I justified Trent. How much I fooled myself into thinking I was happy." I choke a bit on my pain and have to wave Mom back into her seat. "But I've also had some pretty awesome revelations. I've learned some pretty amazing things about myself and God's willingness to help me. I want a chance to process that and to face and embrace this freedom," I say, my tone soft, almost pleading. "Okay?"

"Oh, Claire-bear." My mom opens her arms, and I move into her embrace. My dad's arms encircle us both, sandwiching me. "I'm sorry I didn't see how controlling he was," my mom practically sobs. "How he was hurting you. I should have seen, should have warned you to stay away from that boy." I smile through my tears, knowing that Trent will forever be nameless to my parents, referred to only as 'that boy'.

"He fooled everyone, Mom," I say, my voice muffled. Her arms squeeze me, tight with guilt. Hopefully, she'll forgive herself in time. I return her hug. "I love you guys."

"We love you, too," my dad says, patting my back as Mom smooths my hair. "So very much and we're so, so proud of you." We sit for a minute, soaking in each other's comfort and sharing our pain.

Finally, I pull back, wiping tears from my eyes.

"Sooo, about that D.P.?" Dillon asks, interrupting the moment.

I give him a watery smile. "Yeah, I'm coming." I turn to my parents. "Right?"

"Okay," my mom says, her voice thick with emotion.

Dad pulls a twenty from his wallet, offering me the money. "Grab me one too…and whatever else you want," he says with a wink.

Emotional, I nod. This kind of coddling isn't so bad. In fact, it might be just what I need.

That and time.

* * * *

Dillon cranks up the air conditioning before reclining in his seat. Sunglasses in place, he stares out over the park. A few people brave the heat, kids running through shaded playground equipment, a man throwing the ball for his retriever.

"I think I'd like a dog," I mumble, chewing on my straw as I track the ball bouncing across the brittle grass.

"Now would be the time to ask," Dillon says with a conspiratorial, devious smile. "Mom and Dad would give you just about anything right now."

"Extortionist," I mumble, feeling horrible for even thinking of playing their misplaced guilt against them.

Dillon shrugs. "I would get you one."

I study him, seeing all he means but isn't saying. "Dillon, this wasn't your fault."

"Oh?" he says, his voice thick with self-loathing. "I'm the one who told you guys were just like that. That you shouldn't worry about Trent's temper. That his pressuring you was normal. That you should enjoy being in a roller coaster relationship…"

Crumpling a napkin, he chucks it at the dash. "Yeah, not my fault at all." Processing his words, I tuck the napkin into a bag of empty wrappers and consider my response.

Holding my hand to the gust of cold air, I shift in my seat. "Your advice wasn't necessarily wrong, Dillon. I mean, you have a bit of a temper, you like a little action and aren't above romancing someone to get it, and you *do* enjoy crazy relationships. But I would still tell any girl who asked to give you a chance, to not let those things stop them from being with a really great guy. The difference is, Dillon, you're a decent human being. Trent…isn't. Trent is not a decent human being," I say slowly, trying to get my heart to absorb the truth, because there's a naïve, wistful part of me still looking to justify his actions. I dip my hand through the air stream, feeling the cold gust between my fingers. "He was good. So subtle. I didn't even realize just how much he manipulated me…and everyone else. He always got what he wanted…and when he didn't, he just lost it." I huff, shutting out images of Trent's cold eyes, his hand raised to strike me. "You want to know the saddest thing?"

Not sure he's ready for my confession, but determined to be a willing listener, Dillon reluctantly bobs his head, asking, "What?"

"I wasn't all that surprised when he snapped. My instinct tried to warn me time and again. But I didn't trust it. Didn't trust myself. Trent was perfect on paper, in person, in photos—yeah, don't even get me started on his looks..." I shake a finger at the injustice of it. "It's just *wrong* for a guy like that to be so ridiculously hot."

"Despite all his *perceived* perfection, no matter how much I tried to convince myself he was the one and I was lucky, it never felt true." I stare, unseeing, over the dashboard. "Honestly, Dillon. I can't blame anyone but myself for not trusting my instincts."

Regrets and missed opportunities cross my mind.

Moments when I should have walked away...and stayed away. Moments when I allowed him to make me feel small and insignificant without him by my side. Moments when Trent stripped away pieces of me, chipping at my confidence. Moments when I sacrificed something important just to keep him. Moments long before last night, when he hurt me, stealing parts of me that were never his to take.

Drawing me from a world of lamentation, Dillon lays a light hand on my shoulder and, with a self-depreciated smile, says, "So, next year—when we're having our yearly ice cream and advice night—I just need to tell you to trust your instincts?"

I laugh, appreciating his attempt to lighten the mood. Trust Dillon to make something complicated simple. I guess—in that way—he keeps me balanced. "That should work," I tease.

"Great," he says, putting the car in reverse. "We'd better head home before all the ice melts in Dad's drink."

I shake the cup. "There are still a few cubes."

We exit the park, Dillon tapping his fingers on the steering wheel. He opens his mouth to say something, then stops, shaking his head.

I pretend I don't notice, more than happy to avoid another awkward conversation.

But when he does it again, my curiosity gets the best of me. "What is it, Dillon?"

"Why did you call Adam?"

Realization floods me.

He's hurt I didn't turn to him first. "Adam knew all about the hotel...and I was embarrassed for anyone else to know. He actually tried to convince me not to go with Trent...when we were at the dance."

"So, you two...?" Dillon wags his eyebrows.

"The guy watched me make an idiot of myself over his best friend for months. I doubt there's anything but pity on his part," I admit, the truth of my statement hitting me hard.

"But on your part?" Dillon asks, suddenly pushy.

"I liked watching him threaten Trent," I say with a droll smile.

Dillon's hand clenches the steering wheel. "I've never been so jealous. You think I can take a shot at Trent later? Or two."

"No," I answer quickly. "Because you wouldn't stop at two."

"Fine," he grumbles. "But will you tell me again how he looked when you hit him in the junk, so I can pummel vicariously through you."

Grinning, I fill him in on the rearranging of Trent's groin, Adam's threats, and the cops carting Trent away. I embellish the story, filling the remainder of our ride home with the last few events of the night. I go into detail, but I don't mention anything that happened in the hotel room, unwilling to revisit that feeling of helplessness and unable to express the awakening of my convictions. As we pull into the driveway, I see an unfamiliar car parked at the curb. As I hobble to our porch, Gabriella exits the vehicle.

So much for avoiding awkward conversations.

She walks up the drive, looking perfect and put together. But I know now how very, very deceiving looks can be.

"Hey, Gabriella," I say, greeting her first.

Flushing, Dillon mumbles a hello before making some excuse about getting my dad his drink and disappearing inside. Gabriella has the ability to tongue-tie my brother...interesting.

"Can we sit?" the dark-haired beauty asks.

"Sure," I say, and—my porch being too small for a chair—I ease down onto the top step, propping my ankle in front of me.

"Did he do that?" she asks, pointing to my ankle.

"Yes," I say.

"Jerk," she grumbles the most massive understatement of the year.

I struggle to think of something to say as the sun beats down on us. It's actually kind of nice having her here, someone who understands. Someone who knows the horror of having a guy you'd do anything for turn that love against you.

I shift on the step to face her more fully. "Thanks for trying to warn me...I should have listened."

She waves her hands in frustration before dropping them to her lap. "No, Claire. I came to apologize—"

"You don't—"

"Yes, I do. Just let me get this out. I'm sorry for not reporting Trent. I'm sorry for leaving him free to do this to you. I knew the chances of getting a conviction were slim, but I should have tried. I should have done something...and I am doing something. Now."

She angles her body toward me, eager. "First, I'm starting therapy. I finally told my mom everything, and she's found an awesome therapist." Here, she hesitates. "Talking about it helps. I didn't think it would, but it has." She picks at the fringe of her jean shorts. "I want you to know I'm here if you want to, you know...talk."

"That sounds good," I say, considering not only talking with Gabriella but with a therapist.

For starters, it will probably give my parents peace of mind. Also, I need to learn to trust myself again, especially in relationships.

"Perfect," Gabriella says, her smile reaching her eyes. "I also wanted to tell you, I just got back from the police station. After I heard what happened to you, I knew I needed to give a statement and file charges." Her eyes light with victory. "I ran into Adam as I was leaving. He was there discussing Trent with his dad. I guess Trent's dad went into the station determined to defend Trent, convinced he was innocent. But after he saw the video, which luckily had audio, he flipped." My mouth gapes open, and she grabs my arm, shaking in her excitement. "He's going to make Trent an example. He wants to show that the system works, that even his own blood won't escape justice."

"You're serious?" I knew I had created a strong case against Trent, but I never thought his parents would turn on him.

Gabriella nods sharply, but I'm still rocked with disbelief. "They're throwing the book at him?"

"Because of you," Gabriella says, smiling. "That's why I really came. To thank you. Nix, you did what I couldn't do. What I was too scared to do." She grips my hand, her voice vibrating with feeling. "So, thank you. Thank you so, so much."

I open my mouth to tell her it wasn't me, that I just pretended to be someone stronger, someone I literally dream of being—Nix the Defender. But I remain silent, realizing I *am* her, that I've *become* her.

She isn't a dream. She's my stronger, braver, and better reality.

CHAPTER TWENTY-SIX

"I like this one," Jillian says, picking up a drawing of Xandra.

I've captured the expression the warrior gets when she's said something she's sure is funny—her eyes crinkled, her mouth twisted in an effort to hold back a smile. Jillian tilts her head thoughtfully. "You know, she kind of looks like me."

"She does," I agree, tempted to tell her she kind of *acts* like her, too.

"I'm taking this," she says and gently rolls the picture before putting it in her bag.

I stammer a half-hearted objection. "Whoa, whoa, whoa. First, you force me to come run the bleachers with you at this ungodly hour, and then you steal my pictures?"

"Yes," Jillian answers primly. "And you should be thanking me for getting you into shape for our two," she holds up her fingers, "count them. Two basketball camps this summer."

I pretend to be put out by my agreement, but I'm thrilled to be doing anything with Jillian again—even basketball torture.

She tried to push for a commitment to attend a couple tournaments, but I held her to our initial agreement. After all, I need time to work on my hurdling.

Rebuilding our relationship has been a slow process, starting with small talk and acknowledgements as we passed in the hall.

Our interactions were kind, but awkward because what do you say?

After Jillian attended the trial yesterday, I guess she decided nothing more needed to be said and reminded me to get ready for summer camps. I was actually *excited* to be asked to meet her at the school track at dawn. After a brutal thirty minutes of running up and down the bleachers and a cool-down jogging around the track, my excitement had waned.

But as I collapsed on the bleachers and sucked down a water bottle, Jillian found my art and my excitement was revived as she 'caught up' on all the sketches she had missed. Honestly, mostly everything she's found was drawn in the last two months.

After Trent.

Chin resting on my knees, I listen to Jillian's commentary on the sketches and stare out over the track field.

I close my eyes as the early morning breeze brushes over my bare legs.

After yesterday, I needed this early morning run to clear my head. Trent's trial had been successful—if those things can ever be called that—but even though he received the maximum sentence, it still seems like my punishment and Gabriella's are greater and more lasting than his. And having to testify? The absolute worst experience of my life, because not only did I have to relive that horrid night, but I had to do it while being pinned under Trent's hateful glare.

This path to healing is a slow one. In the days following the attack, I felt positive, full of relief. But there have been many, many days I have drowned in negativity. Those days, the fear of what could have been eats at me, and my self-loathing is tangible. Thankfully, my dreams help tune me into a mental toughness I often struggle to find in the real world. Overall, I feel changed. Different. Empowered, yet regretful.

Over the past two months, clarity has arrived bit by bit, realization by realization. The problems with Trent didn't lie solely in the person he was, but in the person he was making *me*. He didn't make me the best version of myself—he made me someone else entirely. With him, I lost my individuality, my confidence, my friends, my hope, my faith.

I stayed in our relationship not because I really wanted to, but because I felt I had nowhere else to go.

Now I'm free, but I feel stupid for being trapped in the first place. A sound pulls my attention to the base of the bleachers. "Stealing art?" Adam asks, pointing to Jillian as she slips another page into her bag.

"No," she says, looking anything but innocent.

"Pretty high-brow crime there. Jillian the art thief," Adams says, his smile soft in that gently teasing way I've missed.

"Well, I'm all class," Jillian says, gathering her stuff. "And now I'm going to go and celebrate a successful heist. And you two...," she pauses, looking back and forth between us. "You two just, yeah...Well, see you tomorrow morning at six, Nix!" Laughing at her inadvertent rhyme, she skips down the bleachers, waving over her shoulder when I holler my goodbye.

Looking both determined and unsure, Adam offers me a shallow smile. "So, Dillon said you were here—"

"Yeah," I say, "He keeps pretty close tabs on me since...well, you know." Self-consciously, I twist my fingers in the air before gathering up my sketches to clear a place for him to sit.

"I wanted to check on you," he says in a subdued voice before sitting next to me. "After yesterday, I just wanted to see how you were doing."

Propping his feet on the bench in front of us, he drops his elbows to his knees and nervously drags his hand through his hair. "You doing alright?" he asks without meeting my eyes.

"I'm holding up and just...feeling glad it's over."
Unhurried, I allow my eyes to track over him, cataloging his
features in a way I never allowed myself to before. I've
missed him. Aside from some short conversations in passing,
we haven't talked since that night. As I watch, he continues
raking his hand through his hair.

It's slightly mesmerizing watching him messing with the
dark strands. Snapping myself out of my trance, I finally say
what I've been wanting to say to him for months. "I'm
sorry."

Adam's eyes narrow as he finally meets my gaze. "For
what?"

Trying to shake off the awkwardness with a shrug, I say,
"I'm sorry that you lost your best friend, that it came to
that."

"Nix." Adam's voice is strained, holding back emotions.
His brown eyes fix on me, penetrating my defenses. "You
have to know, I'd choose you every time."

"I believe you," I say, refusing to read too much into his
statement. "That's because you're the knight in shining
armor type. Remember? One of the good ones."

"Right." Looking away, he scrubs a hand through his hair
again, this time leaving a section out of place.

I link my fingers together to keep from fixing it. Staring
at my clasped hands, I build the courage to bring up that
night. "How did you get there so fast?" I say, my voice soft.

Adam's hands still, and he takes a deep breath. "I was
already on my way. I had dropped Diana off and was

heading home when I just *felt* I had to go to you. About two minutes after I turned around, I got your text."

"I prayed you'd come," I admit.

"Then I guess God sent me," Adam says thoughtfully.

At his words, his admission of a faith so close to mine, another piece slips into place.

This is connection. The connection I had never been able to find with Trent.

Dropping his feet, Adam twists his body towards mine on the bench. When his gaze locks on me, it's filled with intimate concern. "I always went out of my way to smooth things over for Trent. Especially with you. Because…well, because I liked having you around. But I'm sorry I ever defended him… He was always a horrible boyfriend."

I snort-laugh. "The worst. But, you know, I really had myself convinced he was the best. Looking back, it's sad." Embarrassed by how obvious our problems were to Adam and the relationship as a whole, I turn my attention to the field below us, my eyes tracing the lane lines around the track.

Adam clears his throat. "I should have—"

"No!" I cut him off sharply.

Softening my voice, I continue, "I've heard too many *I should've's*, Adam. Too many people trying to take responsibility. But ultimately, Trent was my decision, my mistake. No one else's. Mine alone." Looking back to the track, I admit my biggest regret. "I hate what he did. What he took from me, but more than that, I hate what he made me."

Adam shifts closer, speaking softly. "What did you think he made you, Nix?"

I give a shaky sigh. "He made me a questioner. I question other people. I question their motives, but, mostly, I question myself." I pause, letting that truth sink in, letting my insecurities show. I can be strong with Adam, but I can also be weak. "He made me doubt everything," I admit, my voice almost inaudible.

"That's not what I see," Adam says, offering me a shallow smile. "I think he made you stronger, Nix. Sometimes the worst things do that. And I think you shouldn't doubt yourself or worry that you've lost something, because what I see is…more. You're the same person you always were, but there's more depth, more strength, more conviction."

I nod, letting his words seep into me, clinging to their power. "Thanks, Adam," I say softly before reaching to squeeze his hand.

Once my fingers connect with his, I can't bring myself to pull away.

Instead, I stare at my hand resting on his. "You know, I realize now that Trent made me an idiot, blinding me to everything. Not just who I am and all that stuff, but also how great you are. Do you know all my positive memories of Trent had one thing in common? You. You were there in every one." I laugh—a harsh, mirthless sound. "I mean, how blind does a girl have to be to not see that?"

I turn toward him, but avoid his eyes, staring at the collar of his shirt. "Thank you for being the best part of this last year…for being my shield, my sounding board, my friend. You are…" My voice tapers off when I risk a glance and see the expression of wonder, triumph, and longing on his face. "…the best," I finish with a whisper, returning his look.

"The best," he echoes. Eyes shining with a feeling I don't dare name, he grins at me before inching closer.

His smile tips as he says, "It goes good, better, best, right?"

"What?" I whisper, barely able to think, much less breathe.

He stops his forward movement, focusing on my eyes. "Remember at the pool, you said Trent was better looking. But now that you can see, you realize that I am not only better looking, I am the *best*," he explains with a smug smirk.

"That you are," I say, joking but…not. Relieved to not have to deny my attraction, I lace my fingers through his and say, "In fact, you are all three. Good, better, and best." I smile, loving how easy and natural it feels to be here with Adam.

He smiles back at me, his expression awed and slightly unsure.

"I've missed you," I admit, feeling both brave and foolish for laying it all out there. "I've missed you so much."

"I've been crazy about you from the start, Nix." Adam matches my confession, causing my already racing heart to skip a beat.

Wave after wave of emotion barrel into me as I look at Adam, seeing what's always been there, what could have always been. "I wish it had been you and me all along," I say, surprised when a tear spills from my eye, trailing down my cheek. Adam catches it at my jaw, gently wiping it away before pulling me into a tight hug.

Releasing me all too soon, he begins to ease away. With one hand on his neck and one on his shoulder, I stop his retreat...and slowly reel him back. Closer and closer, until our pulses are hammering and our lips are mere inches apart.

"You're sure?" he says, hands frozen at my sides. I know he's worried about my reaction to anything physical after Trent, but...

"I'm sure."

With a barely audible sound, he drags one hand across my cheek and into my hair, curls the other around my waist, and presses his lips to mine.

Our kiss is slow and tentative and restrained.

Adam is a mix of comfort and excitement, home and adventure, safety and risk.

He kisses me like he has a million times before, knowing exactly what to do to make me feel adored, valued, cherished.

It's a wonderful, heady, perfect mix of emotion...

And even better than my fantasy world kiss. This time, reality wins.

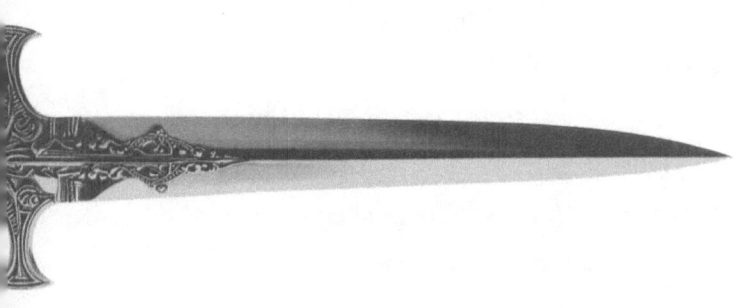

CHAPTER TWENTY-SEVEN

"At this rate, the settlement will be entirely rebuilt next week," Asha says, analyzing the work taking place in the valley. From our vantage point on the wall's tower, we can see most of the construction.

Xandra flits to the edge, peering over the stone barrier. "Ah, the benefit of wealth."

"I'd say the benefit of industry," Reilynn argues, adjusting the strap of her breastplate as she joins us.

"Pah," Xandra twists the chain of her mace around her finger. "Without the payment from the king for the altanium, they wouldn't have had the money to buy the materials to rebuild." I nod. Xandra is right about the money.

In fact, the king paid so well for the altanium, Avalei now has the richest people in the land. Not that the king got all the altanium. After discovering I have some form of magical ability, I kept some of the enhancing metal for myself. I haven't been able to connect to the power like I did that day, but someday I'll figure it out.

I turn my attention back to Xandra as she points to a group of men building a massive new community hall. "Those fellas don't look familiar. Oh, that's right, they're hired labor. Hmmm…" She taps her chin. "Again, a benefit of…wealth. I think I'm going to like being rich."

"Irritating imp," Reilynn mumbles.

"I throw gnat from wall?" Betah asks, reaching for the slight warrior.

Xandra springs sideways. "Stay back, orc."

Betah laughs at her reaction, a sound so untainted and unrestrained that Reilynn and I join in while Asha smiles indulgently and Xandra fights a grin.

"What's so funny?" Greymore asks, climbing from the ladder and joining us at the ledge.

"Nothing, Archer," Xandra says, back to guessing Greymore's name. I have to admit her guesses are becoming more reasonable.

But still wrong.

"No," I say, surprising everyone, Greymore included.

"He told you?!" Reilynn screeches. "After all my amazing guesses?"

"No." I wink at Greymore. "That just doesn't seem right. It *isn't* Archer is it?" I ask, my knife spinning between my fingers.

"No," he says, eyes on me.

"Well, there's a heated look," Xandra says, curling a strand of hair around her finger. "Makes me think I should find a man."

"Xandra," Reilynn scolds, bumping her with her hip. "Enough."

"Oh, but it isn't," she says, getting comfortable with her hip leaning against the wall, her focus on Greymore.

"I think we're needed below," Asha says, moving to the ladder, Reilynn at her heels.

Xandra relaxes further against the wall, yipping when Betah scoops her up by the back of her armor, holding her with one hand. "Is it Benjamin?" Xandra hollers before being unceremoniously stuffed down the opening.

"No!" I yell as Betah offers me a salute and disappears down the hole.

Greymore flashes a smirk my way. He's still shadowed, but it seems the longer I look, the easier he is to see. "So, you think you have it figured out?" he asks.

"I have my suspicions," I say, moving to look out over the valley.

"But you won't share?" he asks, shifting so we're standing shoulder to shoulder.

I shrug. "Hey, you started this game."

"I actually think that was Xandra."

I lift my shoulders again. "Yeah, but you kept it going."

Greymore chuckles low. "I suppose." Watching in silence, we observe the people below us for a while.

The settlement is being rebuilt much the same as it was before, the only major difference being the number of wire cables and steel sides reinforcing the structures.

Somehow, few trees were burned beyond rehabilitation, and the settlement's homes are still, for the most part, being built suspended above the ground.

Under us, the wall is completely repaired—the blasted hole so well patched that the signs of damage are nonexistent. And all of the defenses are back in place, better than before.

A banging sound emanates from the far side of the wall, and my chest tightens.

To honor Torren's sacrifice, the settlers have rebuilt the gate to the Dual Blades. The new one is made of thick steel engraved with images of Torren—his life, love, and sacrifice honored.

It's a beautiful tribute—one I can't look at without tearing up.

Determined to think of lesser sacrifices, I say, "We lost a lot, but we also gained a lot. I'll admit I was devastated by the fire and the need to blow the wall. I never thought I'd willingly tear down parts of Avalei, especially parts of its defense."

"Sometimes we have to tear things down to build them better...stronger," Greymore agrees.

"And she is stronger," I say, staring over the land with pride.

"What will you do next?" Greymore asks.

"I'm pretty sure we covered that sometime in the middle of a swarm of megaspecs," I answer, a wry smile on my face. "Fight...at your side."

"I wasn't sure if that was the heat of—"

"It was...and it wasn't."

"Good," he says, sliding his hand over my wrist and threading his fingers with mine. "Your crew will be joining us?"

"They're packed and ready to go."

"I suppose if we're traveling together, I should tell them my name."

"I suppose," I say, smiling as the shadows fade on his face.

Fascinated, I watch his familiar features come into focus—dark hair, crooked smile, brown eyes.

"Well...?" He pushes his hood back, making it undeniably obvious who's been with me, supporting me through this whole thing, fighting by my side.

"I always liked the name Adam," I whisper with a small, satisfied smile before kissing the face I know so well.

Easing away from him, I say, "Thanks for believing in me. For trusting me to make the right decisions and being there even when I made the wrong ones."

"Always," he says, kissing my hand like the lord he is.

With his hand in mine, I step to the wall and look out over Avalei.

My excitement builds as I anticipate a future on *my* terms. A future full of untold adventures, battles, and victories...

Whether dreaming or awake.

THE END

ACKNOWLEDGMENTS

Wow, we did it!

This book is the product of so many that the writing of these acknowledgments (and fearing I'll miss some pivotal person) scares me almost as much as the writing of this story did.

But it is done and here because of so many wonderful, supportive people.

First, to my young women. I love you all, your strength and struggles in discovering the power of your souls inspired this story.

To my godsent encourager and beta reader, Danel. You kept me authentic and realistic. Thank you for your part in this story.

To my wonderful mothers, Karlene and Wendy, who read this story and loved it for entirely different reasons. Thanks for helping me dig deeper and be better.

To my sister beta readers, Heather and Shalene, thanks for helping me find the purpose in the story.

To my wonderful children and husband, thank you for believing this story was worth the sacrifices.

To my readers, thank you for being patient with the process. This one has been a long time coming. I hope it was worth the wait.

And to my Savior, thank you for giving me the inspiration, the courage, and all the aid I needed to tell this story. May it lead others to their strength and your light.

Thank you all!

ABOUT THE AUTHOR

After living throughout the western U.S., Tenille now claims rural Northern Nevada as her home. If she's not reading or writing, she's enjoying a beautifully ordinary life with her amazing husband and four outstanding children. She loves the Lord and is grateful for the many opportunities she's discovered through serving Him. Her writing goals are to entertain, uplift, and strengthen.

Want to know more?
You can find her at www.tenilleberezay.com

ALSO BY THE AUTHOR

The Converters Series:

The Convergence-Book 1

Hiding unbelievable physical abilities, seventeen-year-old Desiree Morgan buries herself inside the realities of high school. But when Blake Thomas infiltrates her life, all of Desiree's secrets begin to unravel. With answers come more questions, and soon she is entangled in a world of secret societies, human experimentation, perilous power struggles, and ultimate sacrifice. To escape, Desiree can't be simply extraordinary...she must redefine the impossible.

The Keep-Book 2

After a pardon from the convergence, Desiree returns to the protection of home. But safety is an illusion, and her family is shattered by the violent retribution of a desperate enemy. On the run again, Desiree struggles to keep those she loves from a host of gathering threats--debilitating doubts, manipulative converters, dark technology, and a murdering madman. To save them all, Desiree will need more than her ability to convert, she'll need to redefine her strength.

The Conclave-Book 3

Having escaped the dangers of The Keep, Desiree is determined to free Blake. But when a government-enhanced converter goes rogue, the ensuing battle for power, control, and lives makes Blake's rescue a secondary mission. As Desiree struggles to overcome past demons and new, stifling expectations, she faces converters more powerful, dangerous, and desperate than ever. To protect those she loves, redeem the convergence, overtake The Keep, and honor her conclave, Desiree will have to redefine the future.

The Café-Book 0.5

Living an absolutely ordinary life, Sarah works her way through college by earning money as a waitress at Café Columbia. When an unlikely connection is formed with one of her regulars, Sarah's life becomes anything but normal. As her new relationship develops, Sarah finds the strength to embrace an extraordinary life and, when tragedy strikes, to redefine her love.

Reversed Retellings:

The 12 Fighting Princes-Book 1

Prince Humphrey enjoys fighting—fighting to outdo the soldiers in training, fighting to outsmart the king's strict rules, and fighting to outshine the first female captain of the guard. Humphrey enjoys it all, until...the curse. Being forced to fight is not particularly enjoyable, and being one of 12 princes forced to fight monster after monster, night after night, is absolutely terrible. Humphrey needs help—and surprisingly, it comes in the form of one determined captain.

The Tangled Tower-Book 2

Princess Flynn loves adventure—setting out on dangerous missions, exploring new lands, and battling formidable creatures. Flynn wants to do it all, until...the tower. Being stranded on a forbidden island with a mysterious magic, a disappearing tower, and a trapped mage is unnerving for even the bravest of adventurers. Flynn needs answers—almost as much as the mage needs freedom.

(Coming May 2026)

www.ingramcontent.com/pod-product-compliance
Lightning Source LLC
Chambersburg PA
CBHW030551260626
47157CB00006B/2265